Black Power:
The Superhero Anthology

EDITED by BALOGUN OJETADE

ISBN: 1542694582
ISBN-13: 978-1542694582

DEDICATION

I dedicate this anthology to Orrin Cromwell Evans, president of *All Negro Comics* and co-creator – along with his brother, George J. Evans – of *Lion Man* (1947), the first Black Superhero (and the superhero Stan Lee ~~stole~~ borrowed HEAVILY from in the creation of the Black Panther in 1966). Until lions have their own storytellers, stories will always glorify the hunter.

CONTENTS

FOREWORD

Two words thrown around in popular culture with little regard for substantive reasoning: Divas and Heroes. Merely reaching a high note doesn't make one a diva nor does reaching supersonic speed or altering time and space make one a hero. Just as we should understand there is so much more to diva-osity, there is a social complexity to what makes and who is deemed...a hero. Layered nuances of heroism are explored in this literary collection; layers of heroic definitions, heroic apprehensions, and consequences of heroic proportions. Complementing and complicating the layers is the infusion of soul; the clash of heroic sensibilities interwoven with perspectives from the oft-overlooked lens of the Black diaspora.

An inquiry of the word *Hero* in online search engines produces the typical representations promoted by mass media. To find an image that remotely resembled the heroic dreams and values of a people who, throughout their history, could have used someone to swoop down, puff a barreled chest, and allay fears of injustice and oppression. The image of that hero was sparse, if not absent altogether.

Our heroes were real. They shed blood, stood alone, and in most cases, suffered the ultimate sacrifice for the right and the righteous. We were fortunate to have them because the heroes of our creation, the ones whose lives, philosophies, actions, and interactions from the surreal to the outlandish, rarely saw the light of day; not in print, on shelves, and definitely not in the collective cultural consciousness.

Today is a different day! Today is a better day. A day of greater access, control, production, and distribution. We bring to a world stage the heroes who are the hopeful manifestations of our values and beliefs. Heroes defined by our perspectives and experiences. A heroic amalgamation of strengths, foibles, sinisterness, and folly without apologies, explanation, or need for outer-cultural approval. To date, many of the heroes given to us have existed as orphans in the world. Nomads who appeared to serve as extensions or add-on features in an alien world that looks like ours...but today is a different day.

As you experience this anthology, page by page, you will enter spaces of the creative, inventive, and intellectual. Within the words, the *cool, hip,* and *'round the way* elements adds flavor to the familiar *bam, pow,* and *whap.* In your mind's eye, you will hear dialects that conjure images...images without the need to be darkened by colored pencils just to make them palatable. Whether the action takes place on a different plane of existence, on one square city block, or in the infinite of space, you will know that you are there because the heroes we create...be us.

Guy A. Sims, Ed.D.
Revelation, the Brotherman Graphic Novel
Living Just A Little: A Novel
The Cold Hard Cases of Duke Denim series

HEROES AGAIN
Balogun Ojetade

ONE

Akin leaned back on the loveseat and kicked his boots up on the old oak coffee table before him.

The woman sitting beside him pressed her sock-covered feet against his thick thigh and thrust her legs into locked position.

Akin's legs flew off the table. His feet landed on the hardwood floor with a thud.

"Hey!" Akin protested.

The woman inspected the table. "You better not have scratched my table, Akin!"

"Afrikah, you trippin'," Akin said. "Ain't no scratches on that old table that weren't already there. Speakin' of scratch, though...on the real, there's some *serious* scratch to be made in exorcisms."

"I thought you were a Babalawo," Afrikah said. "Or a Yoruba priest, or whatever you call it."

"Best damn Babalawo you'll ever meet," Akin said. "And what you mean, 'whatever you call it'? How is your name 'Afrikah' and you don't know?"

"My mama named me 'Afrikah'," she said, pursing her lips. "You already know that, though. And I said 'Babalawo', so obviously I know a little something."

"What do you know?" Akin asked.

"I know Ricky Martin is a Babalawo, too," Afrika said. "And Forest Whitaker."

"Okay, I see you've been googling," Akin said. "Anyway, Christ Holiness Cathedral ain't got a monopoly on dealin' with demons, we do exorcisms, too. But the key is to make that loochi. Now, the way to get *paid* doing exorcisms is this: you find a big church, with a mostly white congregation and get them to invite you in."

"Why a white church?" Afrikah asked.

"'Cause white churches spend money on exorcisms," Akin answered. Black folks see a possessed congregation member, they run...or rebuke him in the name of the Lawd."

Afrikah laughed.

"You tell 'em you're a visiting pastor who's anointed with a special gift to sniff out and exorcise demons," Akin went on. "Tell 'em you want to have a special meetin' where you will share with them what the Lord has blessed you with. Wednesday nights are good; white folks spend big money on hump day...that's a well known fact."

Akin jumped up from the couch, clapping his hands. "Make sure to build up a little advance publicity a week or two ahead of time. Warn them about how demons slowly take hold of their victims, infecting them with their hunger...all demons got some kind of hunger – drugs; sex; gamblin'; even goin' to church. That gets 'em all turnt up, to where they can't help wonderin' if Aunt Becky or little Bobby Earl is possessed by Ol' King Peacock, hisself."

Afrikah peered at Akin side-eyed. "How much do you charge those folks for that 'special meeting', Akin?"

"Who said anything about money?" Akin said with a sly smile. "The demonstration is free. You just work your hoodoo and those demons will pop out of those white folks like D's in a training bra. That's when you pass the plate a couple times and stack them chips!"

"How are you going to exorcise any demons when you don't even believe in Hell?" Afrikah said, shaking her head.

"Who says demons come from Hell?" Akin replied. "The Book of Job, first chapter says: 'The sons of God came to present themselves before the Lord, and Satan was also among them.'"

Afrikah raised an eyebrow. "So, you're saying demons come from Heaven?"

"And Earth," Akin replied. "People manifest extraordinary abilities every day. They use those powers for good, bad and in between. Do enough bad with what you got and you're as much demon as any from the Christian Hell. What do you think of that, Afrikah?"

"I think a lentil burger and sweet potato fries would hit the spot right about now," Afrikah replied.

The bridge of Akin's nose wrinkled. "Ew. Vegan food depresses me."

"Whatever," Afrikah said, rolling her eyes. "Let's go to the waterfront. You can get that grilled fish you like and I can get what I like."

"Ok, let's go," Akin said. He reached in the front pocket of his jeans and pulled out a ring with a car key and a house key attached. He tossed it to Afrikah. "You drive."

***

Akin and Afrikah sat at the waterfront enjoying great food from the popular *Waterfront Eatery*. Afrikah claimed to love the food, but Akin suspected she really just wanted to go there all the time in hopes of getting discovered by some big time movie director or actor. Akin had to admit, Afrikah was one of the most beautiful women he had ever seen and her acting skills were top notch. They should be, he had paid nearly a hundred thousand dollars for her combined education at Columbia University – where she earned her MFA in Theatre – and at the Sidney Poitier School of Acting, where she received private instruction from the iconic master actor.

The money was well spent, however. Afrikah was one of the best grifters in the business, though she preferred to see her cons as simply acting, not criminal *acts*.

Afrikah was a good person, too. It was only she and his spiritual beliefs that kept Akin from going completely off the rails, spiraling downward into a life of total darkness. He wanted her; to make her his wifey, if not his wife. There were only three things stopping him: she was already married; she was married to his best friend; and although his best friend was locked up on a twenty-five year bid, with no chance of parole, his friend fully expected Afrikah to wait for him until he got out and had made Akin promise to keep suitors away until his return home.

Akin watched two speedboats race across the water, a common sport for the young, affluent Blipsters – *Black Hipsters* – who lived in the area.

A homeless man shambled past Akin and Afrikah. Akin held out his plate of fish and hash browns to the man. The man took it, grinning toothlessly as he issued thanks and well-wishes.

"What's with you tonight, man?" Afrikah said. "You never give anything to the homeless; and food you barely touched? What's up?"

"Filled with the Holy Spirit, I guess." Akin said with a shrug.

"Don't blaspheme, for Christ's sake," Afrikah said. "This is me, Akin, remember? Afrikah Baptiste, from Simpson Road, not one of your marks. And..."

The crash sounded like a bomb going off.

The boat lurched over the boardwalk. It took to the air, just barely grazing Akin, but slamming, full force, into Afrikah before crashing into an old oak tree.

Akin grunted as he struggled against the darkness trying to overtake him. He looked over at Afrikah. Her head lolled forward.

"Afrikah, you all right?" He groaned. "Baby? You all right?"

She moaned like someone refusing to be roused from sleep.

"Afrikah! Say something!" He cried.

Akin was answered with silence.

A heavyset man appeared at Afrikah's side. He looked to be around forty, with a thick beard but no mustache. His face was nearly as black as his beard and he breathed through his mouth. His beard was wet as if he had just been on the water.

Akin pulled himself to his knees. The darkness was fading. He touched Afrikah's neck. He felt a pulse. He breathed a sigh of relief.

"Don't try and move her yet," the bearded man cautioned. "Best wait on the ambulance."

"Call 911. Please," Akin begged.

"I already did," the man said.

"Are you the guy that hit us?" Akin asked.

"Hell no," the man replied. I was the Good Samaritan that pulled over to help y'all."

"Good Samaritan...you a church-going man?" Akin asked, instinctively.

"Yes, sir, I am," the man replied. "I've been a member of Christ Holiness Cathedral all my life."

"That big church in Fayetteville?" Akin said, shocked. "That's a white church, isn't it?"

"God sees no color, friend," the man said. "Nor should the man of God."

"Amen, brother!" Akin said. "Brother, I would like to visit your church sometime. What is your name?"

"My name's Timothy Robinson," the man said.

"Pleasure to meet you, Brother Timothy," Akin said shaking his hand. "I'm Reverend A.J. Pearl."

"Reverend?" Timothy gasped. "It's an honor!"

Akin felt Afrikah stir. She was conscious. Her eyes were still closed because, obviously, she was on board with his grift.

He turned his gaze skyward, placed one hand on Afrikah's forehead and one on her abdomen and prayed loudly. "Lord, resurrect and heal this woman – thy faithful servant, Lord. Restore her soul into her broken body... heal all her broken bones, torn tendons and damaged ligaments! Rebuild the flesh torn asunder in this terrible accident and take away her pain and suffering! In Thine Holy Name we pray...amen."

"Amen!" Timothy echoed.

Afrikah sat bolt upright. She raised her hands high and waved them. "I...I was headed toward a bright light and I heard your prayers, Reverend. I heard you calling me back and then a voice like still waters said 'It's not your time, my child. My servant is calling you back home.' I've been resurrected!"

She sprang to her feet and danced, doing the Whip and the Nene before Akin. "I've been healed, praise Jesus!"

Akin stood. He took her hand in his and raised them above her head, echoing, "Praise Jesus!"

Timothy's mouth hung open in awe. "I ain't never seen no man perform a miracle like that!" he gasped. "You...you brought her back from the dead, right before my eyes!"

"Only God can raise the dead," Akin said. "Give God the praise."

"Praise Jesus!" Timothy shouted at the night sky. "Praise his Holy Name!"

Akin placed his hands on Timothy's shoulders. "The Lord got a message for you, Brother Timothy."

"For me? Really?" Timothy said, startled.

Akin nodded. "He says he forgives you. He knows you caused that poor soul over there to crash his boat on purpose... 'cause of him sleepin' with your wife and all."

Timothy took a step backward from Akin. Sweat ran down his forehead, over his cheeks and then settled in his beard. "I... um..." he stuttered.

"Now, now, Timothy," Akin said. "The Lord knows it was a just killin'. He only requires one thing for you to appease him. A simple task, really."

"Name it," Timothy said. "I'll do anything!"

"He just wants you to introduce me to your pastor; that's all," Akin replied. "The Lord got a message for him, too."

"Praise Jesus!" Timothy said, waving a hand. "I'll get right on it!"

"You do that," Akin said with a wave of his hand, as if he was shooing Timothy away.

"How can I reach you, to let you know when the meeting is set?" Timothy asked.

"The Lord will let me know," Akin replied. "Now, go!"

Timothy trotted off, singing the Lord's praises.

Akin turned to Afrikah. "You okay?"

"A little sore," Afrikah said, tilting her head from side-to-side. "But I'll be like brand new in a few minutes."

"Good!" Akin said.

He nodded toward the visitors to the waterfront and to the destroyed speedboat and its unmoving driver. "We'd better get going before people start asking questions. My influence is starting to wear off."

"Akin?" Afrikah said as they walked away from the scene of the accident.

"Yes?" Akin answered.

Afrikah grabbed the waist of his jeans and lifted him a few inches off the ground as she continued to walk. "If you ever pull a stunt like that again without letting me know first, I am going to shove your nose up your navel. Are we clear?"

"As Crystal, baby," Akin croaked. "I didn't plan that. When I picked up on Timothy's thoughts, I rolled with it. I knew you'd be okay, though. You've been through worse."

Afrikah put him down. "Yeah, but it still hurts like a mother."

"Apologies," Akin said.

"So, do you miss it?" Afrikah said.

"Miss what?" Akin said, feigning ignorance.

"You know what?" Afrikah said.

"Look where being a hero landed Milton," Akin replied. "A brother who saves the world is still just a nigger to these folks."

Afrikah grabbed Akin's wrist, stopping him. "But if they knew the good we did that day, maybe they'd see us differently. Maybe Milton wouldn't be spending damned near the rest of his life behind bars."

Akin shook his head. "If 'ifs and buts' were candies and nuts, every day would be Christmas. We can *never* let the world know what we can do. Remember what they did to Ben Underwood? To Henrietta Lacks? They hate and fear the *weakest* of us. Those of us with power, with influence, with abilities they don't understand, or possess? We'd be murdered outright after they tore us apart to see what makes us tick."

"I guess you're right," Afrikah sighed.

"Damned skippy," Akin said. "Now, let's get home and get changed. Timothy is setting up the meeting right now. The pastor will be expecting us tonight.

TWO

Deacon Robinson – Timothy – scooted out of his Corvette. He stretched the cramped muscles of his long, sinewy legs before sauntering toward the church. He sported a suit of charcoal gray sharkskin over a pale blue Yves St. Laurent shirt and silver-gray silk tie – his "Deaconing suit," he called it.

The fresh, close cropped, faded cut of his hair and beard was equally precise.

The Bishop is dead, he mused. *Long live the old redneck.* Timothy smiled.   He felt it – destiny. The Reverend A.J. Pearl was coming and he was going to take the Bishop's place. Finally, there would be some soul in the pulpit! He felt it deep inside him with a sense of terrible excitement and exultation.

He did not know why he had these feelings, but something spoke to him in a voice that could not be denied, of a time now for great change at Christ Holiness Cathedral, time for his part to be played.

THREE

Angela Rafael was smart, attractive...and haunted.

She wasn't sure exactly when the latter characteristic surfaced, but it was shortly after she'd picked up an old bible at a yard sale and wine-tasting a couple of months ago, but really, something had been simmering in her gut, like an emergent disease, for quite some time before that.

She fled her own apartment, where the haunting began, and moved in with her fiancé to escape the spirits that assaulted her. That move, and a few days off from work, did the trick. For the past two nights, Angela had slept like a baby; no night terrors; no runs to *QT* at 2:00 am for coffee to avoid sleep.

This morning, the day rose uncharacteristically cool for a June morning in Atlanta. Angela awoke convinced that the strange dreams and presences that had been haunting her since that first terrifying episode ten days earlier had left her apartment by now, had given up waiting for her to return home and moved on, perhaps to find some other poor soul to terrorize.

Sorry, that's their problem, she thought.

Buoyant with renewal, she sang in the shower – Minnie Riperton's *Loving You* was her favorite shower song; she sang all the way to work – Prince's *She's Always in my Hair* was her favorite driving to work song – with the car stereo on full blast and was still humming cheerfully as she entered the front doors of *Donkey Bottoms Sportswear, Inc.* just before 7 am. She even managed a warm smile and friendly greeting for Chanel, the receptionist. Usually, Angela didn't give her the time of day.

"Oh, hi right back atcha, Ang'," Chanel said, smiling tentatively as she pulled her too-tight pink pencil dress down over her voluptuous curves.

Angela continued past Chanel into the large inner office where her desk, with its perpetual pile of unfinished paperwork, awaited.

Luna, the other production assistant – and Angela's best friend – ran to Angela and wrapped her thick arms around her. "O...M...G, you're back! Girl, I am so glad to see you! You-know-who has been giving me hell since you've been gone!"

Luna took a step back and gave Angela the once-over. "You okay now?"

"Yeah, Lu'," Angela replied. "I'm fine. Sorry my absence made extra work for you." She lowered her voice to a whisper. "He is such a bastard!"

"Nah, it's cool," Luna whispered. She indicated Mr. Grimes' office with a jerk of her chin; "I worked fifty hours and he refused to pay me overtime; even threatened to suspend me for working too many hours... for his trifling ass! Honestly Ang', I don't know how you deal with it day after day; I'd get sick too."

"He shouldn't have done that crap to you," Angela hissed. "It's his responsibility to deal with customers and suppliers, but he's gotten so used to dumping that job on me that I guess he figured he could unload it on you, too. And not pay you for the extra work? I've half a mind to go tell him so, right now!"

"Just let it go, sis," Luna said. "It's not worth it. It's all just part of the game."

Angela nodded, but something Luna said was bugging her. "Why?" she demanded.

"Why, what?" Luna asked.

"Why did you say 'let it go'?" Angela answered. "Is there something going on I should know about?"

Luna's gaze fell to her feet."It may be nothing, but..."

Angela craned her head toward Luna. "But?"

"I heard Grimes on the phone yesterday talking to Mr. Brookes," Luna replied.

"And?"

"And it sounded like he was getting chewed out for something, so I eavesdropped a little bit," Luna said with a shrug. "And I heard him mention your name a couple of times. I couldn't hear exactly what was being said, but I got the impression that the little bastard was trying to shift the blame onto you for whatever it was that pissed Mr. Brookes off."

Angela nodded. "Go on."

"Anyway," Luna continued. "I heard him say something about putting you on probation when you returned from sick leave."

"Probation!" The word exploded from her, much louder than she intended.

Chanel peered around the doorjamb. Angela lowered her voice to a whisper. "That ugly frog-faced little punk gets twice the salary I do and for what? Sitting on his goddamned hands? But he's got the huevos to put me on probation?!" Her Cuban accent got stronger. It always did when she was angry.

"Ang', it's a job," Luna said, putting her hand on Angela's shoulder. "You either want it or you don't. If you don't, go tell Grimes to kiss where the sun don't shine. But if you *do* want it, or need it, you just have to accept the fact that..."

"Yeah yeah, I know," Angela said, interrupting her. It's all just part of the game."

***

The news she was to be put on probation faded the brightness of the day. The entire morning, as she caught up on her memos and correspondence, Angela vacillated between anger and depression over the manager's treachery and lies. At 11AM, shortly before the temporary reprieve of lunch, the intercom on her desk buzzed.

"Ms. Rafael," Fred Grimes' high pitched, nasal voice piped through the metal box. "Please come to my office immediately."

The line clicked dead before she had a chance to reply. Her stomach twisted into knots. Her legs felt weak as they propelled her reluctantly across the room and through the heavy door into the production manager's office. The door wheezed shut behind her.

A scattering of reports were spread across the highly polished – and seldom used – surface of the oversized desk that dwarfed the small, middle-aged man behind it – Angela described him to others, with great disdain, as "petite." He was hunched over the reports, studying them – for her benefit no doubt – his plump little belly bulging hard against his too tight suit as he tapped his pen against the papers thoughtfully. In truth, he was simply making Angela wait what he felt was an appropriate period of time before acknowledging her presence; a trick she knew only too well.

"Sit down, Ms Rafael," he said without looking up. It was an order, not an act of hospitality, designed to get her down to a physical level where he could – at a moment of his choosing – rise to loom over her threateningly with all sixty three inches of his gnomish body.

After six years of working for the man, she was wise to all his tricks. Despite her quaking knees, she remained standing.

"What's up, Mr. Grimes?" She asked, trying to keep both the fear and the belligerence out of her voice.

He looked up, giving her a ferocious scowl. "Ms Rafael! I asked you to be seated. I suggest you comply!" Anger shook his face, bulged his already protuberant eyes. Angela wanted to laugh; she wanted to continue to defy him. But she needed the damned job. Since he was obviously looking for any excuse to jump on her, she grudgingly sat – sullen, silent, waiting for him to get on with his prepared line of bull.

"Our summer line of short-short overalls is not selling as well as we'd projected, Ms. Rafael," he said. "And do you know why?"

Yep, because they suck, Angela thought, compressing her lips. Aloud, she said nothing.

"Because they were late getting to our distributors, Ms Rafael, that's why," he huffed. "They got there too late to compete, and *that's* why they aren't selling. And do you know why they were late getting out, Ms Rafael? Do you?"

Angela grimaced, rolling her eyes toward the ceiling.

"Don't give me that look! Don't you give me that look!" Grimes shrieked, jumping out of his chair and banging a tiny fist on the desk so hard his pens jumped in their holder. His face was beet red and his trembling lips made his wispy little mustache twitch. "You know you dragged your heels on this project from the very start and continued to drag them all the way through production. That's why the damned things were late and that's why they haven't sold!"

"Mr. Grimes," Angela said calmly. "That's a load of crap and you know it."

The petite man sputtered in shock and outrage, waving his soft, professionally manicured little hand frantically in the air.

"First of all, the order was less than two weeks overdue," Angela continued, her voice growing stronger. "Well within our four-week margin, Mister Grimes, so 'late' was not the problem. As a matter of fact, even if they had been late, if the design had been worth a damn, our regular customers would have bought them up anyway. But frankly sir, the design...*your* design... sucked."

"Ms Rafael, you'd better watch your mouth!"

"Or what?" Angela rose to her feet in a fury. But something made her pause, fading her anger-contorted features into a softer look of puzzlement. Her hand dropped to her side. Something had subtly changed in the atmosphere of the office. The air had thickened to invisible syrup and felt charged with electric energy not unlike when a summer thunderstorm approaches. Some small being in the pit of her stomach cried out, scraping at the base of her spine. Innately she knew what was coming, but also knew there was not a thing she could do to prevent it.   The aura in the room said that reality had – once again – been displaced.

Mr. Grimes fell back into the chair behind his desk. A mask of terror was stretched across his face. She looked to her left, at the mirror on his wall and stared at someone who looked a lot like her, but with an eerie, mocking smile which bent the corners of her lips but left her eyes strangely cold and dead.

For an instant, her features seemed to melt and ripple, as if a wave had passed through them.

Angela blinked rapidly to clear the haze from her vision, but the image didn't fade; it continued to grow more vivid and complex. Her face was changing, melting and remolding before her eyes. First, it turned into a caricature of her: her chin receding further and further until it disappeared altogether; her wide, thick-lipped, pretty mouth stretched, exaggerating into a grotesquery; her big, pretty eyes enlarged until they seemed about to pop from her head.   Angela gasped, trying first to say something, then to turn her head away from the vision: She found she could do neither. Her nose grew shorter and shorter, flattening into nothing but two slightly ridged nasal apertures; her caramel complexion took on a greenish hue, gradually deepening into the color of Spanish moss, and her shapely body grew rounded and hunched.

"Ms. Rape-her-well, huh?" she hissed, her voice a hoarse rasp that slithered from deep inside her bulging throat. "That's what you call me, you and that lard-assed, rotten milk-toned idiot you work for...you thought I didn't know?"

"Oh, my God!" Mr. Grimes cried.

"No need to call me your God, you ignorant little mince," Angela wheezed. "Don't you know who I am? Here, let me give you a little hint."

Angela roared. Her face rapidly reformed itself again – her bulging eyes closed and then reopened slowly, exposing two fiery red, almond-shaped orbs, with vertical black slits for pupils. Her fat round head elongated and narrowed into the head of a lizard, her lipless reptilian mouth gaping open to expose two gleaming rows of needle-like teeth protruding from oily black gums. From deep in her throat, a narrow pink ribbon of a tongue uncoiled and flicked out an alarming length, nearly touching Mr. Grimes' face where he sat, paralyzed by terror.

Angela's eyes locked onto Mr. Grimes, fierce and unrelenting in their power. "And there were gathered before Solomon his hosts of jinn and they marched forward into battle."

Angela's mouth opened to an impossible width. She exploded forward, swallowing Mr. Grimes whole as he screamed.

FOUR

Murder hung in the air like a fog and clung to everything; a sticky miasma that made the flesh crawl and the heart pound. Something bad had happened at Christ Holiness Cathedral.

Akin crept into the church, with Afrikah at his flank.

Everyone in the church was dead except for Timothy and maybe the woman – who cloaked herself in the shadows of the Bishop's office – whose name Akin perceived was Angela. He wasn't sure about Angela, though, because she wasn't always completely herself. Sometimes she was Angela Rafael; other times, she was someone – or some*thing* – else entirely. But always, underneath it all, she was Angela.

The rest of the congregation was nothing more than skeletons, their flesh like tattered tarps, colorful shrouds for the dead.

A soft tap on the door and the creak of hinges announced Akin's arrival.

"Timothy?" Akin said.

"I'm here," Timothy replied. "I ate the organs of the congregation. I'm sorry, I shouldn't have."

"It's fine," Akin lied, dragging a crate filled with paperwork away from the wall to make an impromptu seat for himself. "But you and Angela can't deny what you are."

Angela lumbered out of the darkness. She had the appearance of a large, tailless crocodile, with features reminiscent of who Angela once was.

Afrikah raised her fists to her chin, assuming a boxer's stance. She shot a glance at Akin. He shook his head slowly. Afrikah lowered her hands, but they remained firmly balled into fists.

Angela looked down at the floor. "And what, exactly, are we?"

"You're a young man and young woman with some incredible gifts, Ang'."

"Don't call me that!" Angela snapped. "Only my friends call me that!" The floor creaked under her weight as she rocked back and forth on her heels.

"You can't afford to forget who you really are, Angela."

"Who I really am is why all of my co-workers and the good people of this church are dead. Who I really am is why I am going to come over there in a minute or two and tear you and your girlfriend apart."

"You're not a demon," Akin said. "You're not possessed by one. You're gifted. When they manifest, we may think we're going crazy, or that we are really aliens from the planet Zerburt-Five, or that we are possessed by Satan. I can help you learn who you really are. Or, you can kill us and never learn what you can *really* do."

"I vote we kill you," Angela said.

"But Angela, Reverend Pearl is destined to run this church," Timothy said. "Father revealed it to me."

"Do you know what Father revealed to me?" Angela said. "He revealed that your Reverend Pearl here is a goddamned liar. He was running a con. Going to make you think he was exorcising demons. Little did he know he'd

15

run into a couple of *real* ones."

"Satan isn't your father," Akin said. "I'm telling you, it's your..."

"Shut up!" Angela roared, cutting him off. She charged forward, her maw opening wide to expose her teeth, each the size and shape of an ice pick.

Afrikah whipped her leg in a wide arc, slamming her shin into Angela's gut.

Angela folded over Afrikah's leg. A whoosh of air erupted from her mouth.

The force of the kick sent Angela flying backward. Her back slammed into the Bishop's desk. The desk shattered into splinters. Angela landed on her haunches.

"Take a chill pill, Ang'," Afrikah said.

"No!" Timothy screamed. Oddly, the scream sounded musical, like the hard strumming of a harp.

Afrikah wailed in agony as scores of lesions appeared on her body.

Akin inhaled deeply. He sent fibers from his mind outward until he connected with Timothy's mind. Timothy's psyche folded in upon itself, whirling and shaking violently. Good, Akin thought. He's struggling. He can still be reached.

Akin sent instructions through the psychic filaments, commanding Timothy to shut his mouth.

The pain assaulting Afrikah subsided. Her flesh immediately began repairing itself.

Angela struggled to her feet.

Afrikah darted forward with blistering speed. She wrapped her arms around Angela's neck and squeezed.

Angela struggled to break free, but Afrikah was too strong.

"Akin..." Afrikah said, peering at him over her shoulder.

"Surrender," Akin said. "Surrender and I promise to help you."

"I...okay," Timothy sighed.

Akin felt the truth in his words.

Angela, however, wanted only to bring death; to silence the world forever and then pick the flesh from its bones.

Angela dug her claws into Afrikah's arms.

"Damn it!" Angela screamed. "Akin!"

"Angela," Akin sighed as he stared at the floor. "I'm sorry."

Afrikah tightened her hold on Angela's thick, reptilian neck, squeezing with all her might. She arched her back as she thrust her arms toward the ceiling.

Angela's head tore from her shoulders with a loud pop.

Afrikah tossed Angela's head into a corner. She snapped her head toward Akin. Tears spilled from the corners of her eyes. "Dammit, Akin," she said. "No more grifts!"

Akin nodded.

Afrikah stormed out of the church.

Akin turned his attention to Timothy, who stared, wide-eyed, at Angela's headless body. He did not move.

"Timothy, we have to go," Akin said. "The police will be here soon. Someone just reported a disturbance coming from the church."

Timothy blinked rapidly, bringing himself back into focus. "Where will we go?"

"We have a place," Akin replied. "A base of operations, if you will."

"And what happens if my mind doesn't get right?" Timothy asked. "If I don't get better."

Akin nodded toward Angela's severed head.

"Oh," Timothy croaked.

"Now, come on!" Akin said, turning on his heels.

Timothy followed him outside.

Afrikah pulled the car up beside them. "Are we ready?"

"Yes," Akin said, sliding into the front passenger seat. Timothy sat behind Afrikah.

"Where to?" Afrikah inquired.

"To the safehouse," Akin replied. "Time to resume the work."

"So, we're heroes, again?" Afrikah said, smiling.

Akin nodded.

"Praise the Lawd!" Afrikah exclaimed.

Akin just stared at her, shaking his head.

FALL OF THE CARETAKERS
Ronald T. Jones

The bus hurtled toward him.

Victor 'Ace' Jackson wrenched himself out of the huge projectile's path. The bus speared into a five-story apartment building, punching a massive hole through brick and glass. A ruptured tank hemorrhaged gas and a colossal fuel-fed eruption swallowed the bus, magnifying the hole's size. An incendiary carpet unfurled upward, racing to the top of the building.

Jackson whirled about to face the one who flung that bus. His Adjusted View Display (AVD) filtered out a swirling haze of previous damage to provide a vividly enhanced image of his nemesis.

Garbed in signature red and gold with a Black letter 'I' displayed on his broad chest, Invinci-Man stood in the middle of a gutted out street. He cut a majestic figure, as if carved out of cobalt. Built like Mr. Olympia, endowed with the strength to move mountains, the ability to soar beyond the heavens, the durability to shrug off any weapon short of a nuke, Invinci-Man once reigned as a shining exemplar of goodness and integrity. Once upon a time, billions called him a hero. That was then. This was now.

Jackson stared at his former friend, briefly torn between reasoning with him and continuing this contest. No. The time for reasoning was long past. Jackson solidified his resolve and prepared to meet whatever his opponent dished out.

Invinci-Man's costume appeared fresh and crisp, its wearer assuming an air of casual indifference as if he was strolling through the park on a sunny afternoon. Jackson, by contrast, seemed to have attracted every particle of debris to his Energy Field Supplemented Hyper Fortified All Environment Battle Suit, until its olive green surface was caked in gray ash.

Despite the suit's climate control, Jackson sweated bullets.

A burst of thermal energy rippled from Invinci-Man's eyes, striking Jackson in the chest. The Battle Suit's contact shield deflected 89 percent of the blast as Jackson tumbled backwards. A windstorm of a shock wave roiled equidistantly from point of impact.

A gasping Jackson plopped on his back. The center of his suit radiated a crimson patch of deadly intense heat. He felt like his chest had been caved in. A diagnostic readout crawled across the bottom of his AVD. His suit registered a nine percent power drain from that single hit. Jackson neuro-linked a command to his suit's core computer to compensate its powerplant's loss...and just in the nick of time. He leapt upright as Invinci-Man came at him. He linked a second command, phasing his shield from contact to absorbent mode and braced himself.

BAP! A combination of super speed and immeasurable strength barreled into Jackson, knocking him through the air at a velocity exceeding the force he received. One building, two buildings...after that he lost count of the buildings he penetrated before crashing on another empty street. A fifty-foot trench ending in a dredged up mound of smoldering black-top marked his hard landing.

Muscle stimulating fluids from his suit pumped into Jackson's body, accelerating his physical recovery. A dopamine compound cleared the fog from his brain.

Invinci-Man swooped from the sky, his fist reared back for a devastating follow-up.

Jackson raised his arm and his ordnance bracelet roared, releasing a spray of rockets. Each rocket was a tube of graphene, impregnated with a seething core of energy so dense it was as if the mass of Mount Everest was compressed into a space the size of an index finger. Jackson didn't take the time to aim. He couldn't. Fifteen out of 30 rockets pummeled Invinci-Man and the very fabric of existence seemed to come apart at the seams from the fury they unleashed.

Jackson witnessed his opponent being swallowed up in a boiling brew of unleashed energy.

Invinci-Man flailed to the ground some distance away, landing yards short of an SUV. The close proximity of Invinci-Man's impact swept the vehicle end over end as if swatted by the hand of an impetuous giant.

Jackson's AVD status indicator elevated off the scale. By engaging Absorbent Mode, his suit had borrowed the kinetic energy of Invinci-Man's blow, channeled it to its servos and stored it for potential use. This meant that for exactly two minutes and 35 seconds, Jackson would be as strong as the most powerful being on Earth. At least theoretically. Absorbent Mode was a new feature he hadn't tested. Now was as good a time as any. Jackson catapulted himself half a block, landing in front of Invinci-Man.

The super being looked groggy and was slow to rise.

Jackson delivered a roundhouse kick that sent Invinci-Man cart wheeling through a wrought iron gate fifty feet away. An astonished smile flashed across Jackson's face. It worked. He reveled briefly in his extra strength, ephemeral though it was. No time to waste. The clock was ticking and when this mighty strength was expended, he wouldn't be able to engage Absorbent Mode for up to eight hours.

He rammed into Invinci-Man with all the speed his suit could muster, inundating his foe with kicks, chops and punches.

Invinci-Man took the barrage for an initial few seconds, before defending himself. He lifted an elbow, blocking a punch and countering with a fist to Jackson's faceplate.

Jackson's head snapped back with bone rattling force. Briefly, he wondered how far it would have flown were it not shielded by field-augmented armor. He reeled on the defensive, straining the agility function of his suit as he tried to elude a flurry of strikes from Invinci-Man. A kick-boxing style blow from a super powered foot landed solidly in Jackson's gut, bending him over, but not knocking him down.

Invinci-Man switched to a short, sharp karate kick, but Jackson caught the other's leg and shoved, plowing his foe to the ground. He attempted to slide underneath Invinci-Man's guard, apply an arm lock, and for an instant he achieved a hold.

Invinci-Man shifted. It wasn't a brute motion. It was more of a soft, subtle, judo-style reflex, containing just enough exertion to free his arm and topple Jackson off balance.

Jackson pushed off the ground with one hand, flipping to his feet.

Invinci-Man stood, still appearing irritatingly unwinded. He regarded Jackson with keen, measuring eyes. "Your suit has always amazed me. I used to wonder what it would be like going up against it with you in it. My natural powers versus your mechanized prowess."

Invinci-Man's expression hinted at a smile. He so much resembled a young Sidney Portier, with a deep, resonating Barry White voice. A charismatic combination, one that used to wow the masses, especially the female element.

Jackson snarled a challenge. "Well, I hope I'm satisfying your curiosity. Allow me to satisfy it some more!" He charged. Jackson had one minute remaining of borrowed strength. He was determined to make the most of it. He delivered a forearm to Invinci-Man's rib, receiving a thunderous uppercut in turn.

Invinci-Man's close quarter skills were superb. Jackson never understood why, for all his prodigious powers, the super being trained so rigorously in martial arts...until Invinci-Man clashed with a villain of comparable strength years ago.

A warning alert warbled in Jackson's ear at the same instant a blip popped up on his AVD's threat sensor display. An incoming aerial bogie. But it wasn't a machine.

Jackson dove left, narrowly avoiding a vivid orange beam that drilled a bubbling hole into the spot he just vacated. His auto-targeter captured an image of the airborne aggressor: a tall, dark skinned woman, clad in silver breast plate armor, anatomically correct to the smallest detail. A matching kilt of glimmering lamellar flowed to mid thigh. She wore black ankle high sandals, attached to gray, spike studded shin guards. She wielded an intricately designed staff that appeared to be carved from hard wood. The world knew her as Candace, the Nile Goddess.

Jackson fired off an anti-personnel laser from his shoulder emitter.

Candace lifted her star staff faster than an eye blink, using it to catch the beam. The staff grew bright as it absorbed the laser, so bright it appeared a second sun had formed overhead. Instantly, the glare subsided and the staff reverted back to its cool earth tone.

Candace dove toward Jackson, her face a mask of ferocity. "Let me have at him!" She shouted to Invinci-Man.

Jackson soaked in her rage, and for a second, vestigial fear gripped him as he pictured how much of an avenging goddess she must have appeared to her ancient subjects. Assuming her claim to godhood was valid.

The Nile Goddess pointed her star staff, summoning a second stream of orange fire.

This time Jackson was not quick enough to elude its bite. The beam caught him in the side, wrapping him in a writhing hot blossom.

Candace reached into the mini-conflagration, grabbed Jackson's arm and hurled him effortlessly a full four blocks.

Jackson ricocheted off the corner of a building, ripping the roof off of a parked station wagon before slamming headfirst into a dumpster. The large metal container crumpled around him in a distorted hug.

A red tint shrouded his AVD. Diagnostic alerts shrilled with urgency until Jackson silenced the clamor. His suit's power level took a grave dip, forcing him to draw additional juice from his power plant. At this rate, it wouldn't be long before he had to tap into his reserves. He managed to pry his way out of the remains of the dumpster just as Candace arrived, looming over him like a hungry raptor, her star staff raised.

She brought her staff down in a swift, gleaming arc.

Jackson leapt clear. The staff struck the dumpster, incinerating what was left of it. Jackson slid behind the Goddess, neutralizing her staff arm while clamping a forearm to her throat.

Normally, Candace would have broken such a hold with contemptuous ease. Her strength was second to Invinci-Man's. While Jackson had 35 seconds left of Invinci-Man's strength, the physical advantage in this instance was decisively his. It was an advantage he utilized with zest as he increased pressure on the Nile Goddess's throat...squeezing...squeezing...

Candace strained to break free. She tried to wrench her other arm from Jackson's grip so as to gain room to direct her staff.

Jackson tightened his hold on both her arm and throat. The Goddess's struggle began to slacken.

Could he do this? He questioned himself. Could he kill her...like this...in cold blood? A former colleague?

A warning alert interrupted his musing. His scanner detected massive air displacement, an indicator of something or someone moving very, very fast. The threat was inbound on his five.

Jackson shoved the Goddess aside and turned in the direction of the source just as a streak of blue grazed him. The contact was peripheral but imbued with enough force to send Jackson spinning to the ground.

Marty Buckles, also known as the Blue Blur, the fastest man in the universe, stopped on a dime. He wore wind resistant head to toe blue spandex with blue-tinted wraparound sunglasses.

He threw a frat boy grin at the Nile Goddess. "Boy, I wish I could have recorded what I just saw. Ace nearly had you down for the count, lady!"

Candace straightened, rubbing her throat, murder burning a ruby light in her eyes. "If you don't shut your insufferable trap, *I'll* put *you* down!"

The speedster raised a lewd brow. "I think I'd like that." Then he was off.

"I'll bet you would," the Goddess murmured irately.

The Blue Blur bowled into Jackson at a speed that most certainly earned him his sobriquet, and held on tight. "How 'bout a quick ride, Ace?"

The Blur held Jackson for little over two seconds, which in distance translated to six long blocks. He let go and halted, but Jackson kept going, sailing across a park, through a playground until he collided with a tree, rupturing its trunk to splinters. Jackson lay curled on the grass, emergency bells and whistles again filling his helmet with a low key racket.

The Blue Blur was far from the strongest member of the Guardian Protectors. Still, even a rabbit, moving at supersonic speed, could cause considerable damage if it bumped into something.

Jackson stood shakily, orienting himself. He spotted the Blue Blur standing on the other end of the park wearing a cocky smirk. The next second the speedster was gone...in motion!

Jackson didn't think. He acted. He powered his foot repulsers. Tiny thrusters in the soles of his metal boots lifted him straight up. At the same time, he ejected a dark gray, marble-sized object from his lower torso harness.

The object fell in the Blue Blur's path and detonated. The impending blast threw the speedster back as if he'd bounced off a steel wall. Clods of dirt and grass, mixed with a bubbling froth of black smoke, bloomed from a ten-yard diameter crater gouged by the explosion.

The Blue Blur flopped limply on his back, the wind knocked out of him.

"Surprise, surprise," Jackson taunted. He switched his thrusts to flight mode and glided out of the park.

The mayor had evacuated the entire southern district of Valor City at Jackson's request. He needed to keep the battle within its bounds.

Something struck his right shoulder as he zipped over a wide avenue. Jackson spiraled out of control before regaining enough of his bearings to manage an off balance landing. He cast his gaze about until his threat sensor locked onto a red Ford Taurus 30 to 40 yards in the direction from which he came.

The car suddenly disassembled. Its parts shifted and shuffled in a dizzying array of motion that resolved into a man...at least from all appearances.

George Kennan, aka MachineWare, always had more of an affinity for gadgets than people. His psychic ability to manipulate machines made him a valuable asset to the Guardian Protectors. But as Kennan, little by little, converted himself into a gadget, that's when the corruption set in. It could be said that his humanity, and all the compassion and empathy it entailed, diminished with his imbibing of each new cybernetic component.

Ropes of super hardened overlapping metal coils, connected to metal plates, layered MachineWare's gaunt frame. Only his face remained bare of any markers denoting his bizarre transformation. He raised his right arm and it reconfigured into a Gatling gun. The gun's eight barrels rotated and a flaming chatter of titanium bullets ripped forth.

Jackson staggered backward as a sleet of hot metal pounded his suit. He pushed outward with his mind, extending the range of his shield to approximately seven feet in front of him. Waves of bullets deflected off the shield.

MachineWare raised his other arm. It lengthened and thickened in a clanking whir of adjustable parts, forming a long-barreled cannon. A black missile whisked out of the cannon's maw, plunging into the shield. A scorching shower of released energy gushed from the shattered missile, winking the shield out of existence, propelling Jackson into a brick-walled corner drug store.

MachineWare hurled five more missiles after the first, and the entire storefront, along with a good chunk of the building that housed it disappeared in a fiery, demolition collapse.

An ashen cloud belched from the flame-smothered ruin, encroaching on daylight like a horde of demon wraiths springing from the underworld.

MachineWare's armaments retracted into his body. He stood before this howling destruction he'd wrought, unaffected by the smoke and heat, unmoved by his action. His expression held a very machine-like dearth of emotion. "Pity, Victor Jackson. You should never have opposed us."

"Pity on you, George. You should never have gone rogue."

MachineWare whirled to find Jackson standing behind him.

Before the cyborg could react, Jackson triggered a beam from his ordnance bracelet.

A crackling web of electromagnetic energy surrounded MachineWare. The cyborg quaked violently, his previously impassive face twisted in a convulsion of agony. When the web vanished, MachineWare crumpled to the pavement in a short-circuited heap.

Jackson pumped enough EM into MachineWare to plunge all of Valor City into Stone Age darkness. It would require ten times that amount to fully and permanently disable him.

Jackson had neither the time nor the output to finish Kennan off.

A cold wind whipped around him. It was a winter-like gust in the middle of a humid summer day. Dark storm clouds boiled into sudden existence overhead. The odd weather was no natural occurrence. The wind grew more frigid, more active, becoming a raging twister.

Jackson powered his thrusts to get away, but the savage funnel snared him with irresistible force, driving him skyward.

In a wink, the twister vanished and Jackson found himself face to face with the tornado's conjurer, a flame-haired woman called Windrider.

Valerie Hewitt had been a climatologist in a past life. Ironic.

Windrider crossed her forearms. A tendril of lightning danced from the sky, poured into her body, surging out of her hands in a pulse of linear energy directed at the armored man.

Jackson extended his contact shield, blocking the pulse. He countered with a salvo of rockets.

Windrider waved an arm, scattering the rockets with a high speed blast of wind.

"Give it up, Jackson!" Windrider derided, her crimson mane waving in a self generating breeze like a flickering candle light. Her sky blue cloak vividly contrasted the yellow body suit that hugged her comely contours like a perfectly fitted glove. "You can't beat all of us. Hell, you can't beat *one* of us!"

"I'd say I've been holding my own pretty well so far," Jackson retorted.

The air temperature around him dipped drastically, frosting his armor. Within seconds he was encased in a block of ice.

"It's a cold, cold world, Jackson."

Windrider watched with psychotic glee as the man in armor plunged ground-ward from well over ten thousand feet.

Jackson didn't doubt that he would survive the fall, even encased in a ton of ice. He just preferred not to experience the impact.

He ignited his shoulder emitter. The light's coherence bored through a section of ice, providing a pocket of space for his emitter's turret to rotate. He also powered every thruster pimple on his armor, creating a sweltering buildup of heat. The ice dissolved to the point where Jackson could apply brute strength to break out. With servo-powered arms and legs, he hammered away at his confinement until he burst free in a sparkling cloud of ice crystals.

Jackson righted himself, and boosted his thrusters beyond their maximum limit, accelerating upward as if he had been launched from a rail gun. He fired over two dozen rockets at Windrider.

The weather-manipulator batted the projectiles aside with directed wind just as she had done the first time. The rockets twirled every which way, but Jackson linked on to one. He displaced the sole rocket's internal guidance with manual.

Windrider crossed her arms, summoning a second bolt of lightning.

Jackson stayed on his trajectory toward her, making no attempt at evasive maneuvering. He focused on the rocket, bringing it about, lining it up with its target.

Windrider must have sensed something. She glanced behind her just as lightning channeled through her body. She caught the most fleeting glimpse of the rocket and extended a hand toward it, redirecting the electrical energy pulse intended for Jackson.

Pulse and rocket met point blank.

A blinding, deafening eruption birthed from the collision. A flaming fist knocked Windrider out of the sky.

Jackson didn't know if she was dead or alive. He didn't try to find out. He ignored her and headed south, deeper into the district, where he needed to be. He checked his power levels and grimaced: 47 percent reading. Not good. His power plant was nearly depleted and his diagnostic screen painted a bleak picture of points of structural damage. Some of his primary functions were so busted he had to switch to auxiliary. He needed to keep this contest going until he was in a position to implement Phase Two.

A warning alert. Danger flew at him fast. Jackson pulled directional data from his AVD and banked to avoid what was coming...*too late!*

Invinci-Man slammed into him with a bone-crunching wallop, his massively muscled arms wrapping Jackson in a super powered bear hug.

Jackson squirmed to break the grip, but his borrowed strength had run out. He was helpless as a field mouse in the clutches of a hawk.

Gone was the look of casual indulgence on Invinci-Man's face. A cruel glimmer shined from his dark eyes.

Jackson felt exposed as a newborn in the light of the other's utterly ruthless gaze.

"We're done toying with you." Invinci-Man went into a sudden dive.

Jackson's gut lurched.

Within a millisecond of hitting the ground, Invinci-Man released his hold on the armored man with a shove and shot upward.

Jackson torpedoed into the top of a tractor-trailer truck. Both tractor and trailer were sheared in half on impact an instant before the collision's full force shredded them to scrap, producing a bruising shock wave that blew out every window in every building in the vicinity.

Jackson groaned. Half his body was embedded in concrete beneath the tractor/trailer's flaming wreckage. His climate control must have been shot, which explained the failure of his armor to provide insulation from the ferocious fire-generated heat. He needed to get up and out before he baked to death inside his armor. He tried to extricate himself, but the entire left side of his suit refused to respond to his neuro-linked nudge.

"NEED HELP?"

Jackson looked up to see the Nile Goddess plunging into the fire with star staff raised.

She brought the staff down in a blurring stroke, striking Jackson's paralyzed left shoulder. A crimson orb issued rapidly from the blow, followed by a powerful blast that tossed up an oil black mushroom cloud.

A hot breeze cleared away the worst of the smoke.

Jackson lay prone at the center of a deep, steaming depression. Parts of his armor hung in scorched, tattered strips, barely connected to its pliable, carbon-nanotube inner layer. In some places the armor became porous, oozing globs of inertial gel.

His AVD flickered in and out. Snowy static clouded the remainder of his displays. Of course he didn't need diagnostics to tell him that his suit was no longer functional. As for his body, he ached to high hell from that final round of abuse inflicted on him by Invinci-Man and Candace. The slightest motion ignited a firestorm of pain. But he weathered the suffering, rising slowly to his knees. He could rise no more. He pulled a string of release tabs along the upper section of his neck guard and removed his helmet, tossing it aside.

Jackson ran a hand down his face, wiping away perspiration. He lifted his head and saw that he was surrounded.

Invinci-Man, the Nile Goddess, Windrider, the Blue Blur, and Machine-Ware loomed above him from the ridge of the depression. Undoubtedly, they would have slaughtered him on the spot. All it took was one word from Invinci-Man.

Jackson stared at Invinci-Man, partly resigned, partly defiant, and waiting for the latter to give that word.

Instead, the leader of the Guardian Protectors hovered and descended into the pit, his expression softened by sympathy and memories of bygone fraternity.

Jackson remembered as well, and for a moment the two men shared fond memories in silence.

"What happened to you, Jeff?" Jackson asked with a tinge of anguish. "How did you, of all people, cross that line from a noble caretaker to being no better than the thugs, lowlifes, and murderers we used to battle?"

Invinci-Man tilted his head, his brow narrowing as if mulling over the question. "Call it enlightenment. One day an epiphany hit me. I realized that people don't need caretakers, they need prison guards. They need control, discipline, structure. And if they go astray they need swift, harsh punishment to correct their errors. Who else can provide these things other than those of us endowed with the capabilities, be it by accident, design or birth, to exert our will over this depraved planet?"

"How has the killing of innocents made this world any better than before you decided to run rough shod over it?"

"I don't worry about the innocent. What is that saying?" Invinci-Man caressed his broad chin in a show of thought. "Ah, yes...let God sort them out." He settled on his haunches, looking Jackson square in the eye, scrutinizing, searching. "Your self-righteous platitudes choke with hypocrisy. You hadn't always abided by the law in your crime fighting. For all the wonderful hi-tech toys that sprang out of that genius head of yours, you were still nothing but a vigilante."

Jackson dropped his eyes. "You're right. I was a vigilante, albeit a glorified one. I admit to operating outside the law when I had to accomplish an objective. But this...what you and the others are doing...I never embarked down that path."

"But you considered it! Didn't you, Victor?!" Invinci-Man leaned in close until his piercing, umber-eyed glare became the only object in Jackson's scaled down universe. "Be honest. You never thought once about using your suit to its fullest potential?"

Fullest potential. The question stung in ways Jackson couldn't disregard. He kept his eyes averted, unwilling...or unable to meet the other's gaze.

Invinci-Man stood, choosing not to press for an answer. His tone weighed heavy with regret. "You should have joined us, Victor. I hate that you forced me into this position. I would just love to plop you inside a maximum security lockbox somewhere far from civilization. But then I'd have to spend my every waking hour worrying that you might figure a way to escape. We can't be distracted by loose ends. Not while we're in the midst of whipping this world into shape. I can make this quick and painless for you. It's the least I can do for a friend."

Jackson eased his way to a standing position. Pain surged like electricity through his body. "Thanks for the offer, Jeff," he managed through gritted teeth. "But I have a second option."

Invinci-Man possessed multi-spectrum vision. Had he used the X Ray portion, he would have spotted a thumbnail size wafer lodged beneath Jackson's temple.

Jackson pressed a finger to his temple, activating an implant. That action sent up a transmission to a satellite orbiting in geo-sync directly above Valor City's South District.

Invinci-Man's brow crinkled in suspicion. Suspicion morphed into alarm. He made a move toward Jackson. "What are you…"

A haze of light suddenly filled the depression. Jackson squeezed his eyes shut. Even so, the searing brightness soaked through his eyelids, fully immersing him in a glaring void of white.

Seconds, moments, minutes may have passed. Jackson had no idea. It was like he slipped into a crease in time. Slowly, he opened his eyes. Invinci-Man was gone. Jackson searched the ridge. The others were also gone, seized by the light.

"And this was the least *I* could do for a friend." Jackson sank back to his knees as exhaustion took its toll.

***

Intelligence Chief Yohannes Brady approached the ambulance where a paramedic just completed wrapping Victor Jackson's ribs in bandages.

Jackson gently prodded the area above his injury and winced.

Brady expressed something close to paternal concern. "How are you, Ace?"

Jackson's lips parted minimally in a tired smile. "I could be better." He gave a thumbs up. "But I'm alive."

The intelligence chief looked around, taking in the bleak sight of a neighborhood resembling old footage he'd seen of Berlin in the aftermath of World War II.

The place had truly been a warzone. The difference in this case was that the combatants comprised one man, of extraordinary brilliance with technology to match, pitted against a squad of super-powered psychopaths.

Brady had to shake his head at the wonder of it all. "Your suit held out pretty well. Longer than I expected to be honest."

"It took some hellified punishment, didn't it?" Jackson boasted. On a serious note, he added: "I upgraded it. I needed it to last just long enough for me to gather them in one area."

"And spring your trap," Brady finished. "What exactly was that light beam from the sky? A weapon? Did it kill them?"

Jackson shook his head. "No, they're not dead...at least I'm pretty sure they're not. There exists multiple universes, multiple realities. I discovered a way to open a door to any one of them. The satellite I built created a portal."

Brady gave a look verging on merriment. "You sent Invinci-Man and his gang to another universe?"

"I'm not exactly comfortable with that outcome," Jackson qualified soberly. "I would've liked to have had time to vet universes before I used the portal. Now, I'm afraid I might have sent them to a populated realm where they'll be able to duplicate the terror they created here. But I needed to get them out of *this* universe with all due haste, before they caused further pain and suffering."

The intelligence chief nodded thoughtfully. "Humanity is going to be damn grateful to you for getting rid of them. And don't worry. Chances are you sent those bastards to a place without people. They could be stranded on a dead world."

Jackson considered the possibility. "Could be."

At that moment, a sleek, black SUV limo pulled up beside the ambulance. The driver, a long-legged, cocoa skinned beauty (whom Brady suspected might have served Jackson in other ways) emerged from the vehicle.

"Mr. Jackson, thank God you're all right," said the driver reaching for her employer's arm.

"Hello, Chastity...no, please, I don't need help. Thank you."

Chastity held back her assistance, but remained vigilantly close as Jackson moved gingerly toward the limo.

"And where are you off to?" Brady asked.

"Home," replied Jackson. "I'm going to hit the sack and sleep for a week...maybe two."

"Oh." Brady looked troubled and hesitant, but only for a second. He tried to mask his unease with affability. "Hey, uh, why don't you hang out with me for a little while. We can run to the local office, you provide a debrief, and afterward I'll treat you to your favorite restaurant."

Nothing in the intelligence chief's manner escaped Jackson's keen notice, which is why he enjoyed seeing the other trying to suppress a squirm as he refused the invitation. "Appreciate the invite, but I'll debrief later. And my favorite restaurant is not in this city. It's not in this country for that matter."

Chastity opened the limo door.

"Victor," Brady called out. "How does it feel being the only Guardian Protector?"

Jackson's expression dimmed with melancholy. "I'm no longer a Guardian Protector. They don't exist anymore."

He stepped into the limo and the driver closed the door.

***

An hour later, Jackson entered his ops center, located in the basement level of his mansion. Chastity Hunter, his driver and assistant, frowned her disapproval, insisting her employer get some much needed rest.

Jackson kindly declined her advice. Rest could wait for a few minutes. There was something he needed to check on. The side walls of his ops room were lined with book shelves that were neatly stocked with thousands of volumes. The facing wall was a gigantic terminal screen that doubled as a CCTV monitor. A brown, leather-bound swivel chair and a large maroon desk with a computer and keyboard sat in the center.

Jackson noticed the swivel chair was turned a hairbreadth of a degree to the left, evidence of an intrusion. His suspicion was confirmed.

There were other ways he could tell that he'd been breached. One of them he picked up from MachineWare, who long ago constructed micro-size video pickups the size of dust particles. Jackson had deposited a small handful of the micro-cams throughout the ops room, on the floor, the book shelves, the desk.

He pressed a key on the keyboard, bringing the wall screen to life. Then he input a code that pulled recorded visual data from the micro-cams and

34

transferred it to the screen. A view of the ops room from the perspective of the west facing book shelf came up.

Three figures in black skulked into the picture. One took a seat at the desk. The other two did a circuit around the room before taking guard positions on opposite sides of the door. Dressed in head to toe black combat gear and armed with short barreled assault weapons, Jackson had no doubt the intruders were Intelligence Branch Para-Military ops soldiers.

He fast-forwarded the scene. The soldier at his desk was typing on the keyboard. Jackson knew what the soldier was after. He was trying to crack Jackson's network, gain access to his files in order to steal his technology. It was the schematics to the armored suit that they wanted in particular. That was the prize.

Instead of feeling alarmed or violated, a certain amusement fell over Jackson. Brady's people thought they had executed a clean in and out operation, undetected. Of course, they did manage to bypass his security to get this deep into the mansion. Jackson would give them that. The Intelligence Branch didn't recruit slouches. Good as the organization was, however, it wasn't *that* good. The intruders still failed to hack into his files.

Jackson tapped another key, bringing up a schematic of his suit.

His network remained the most secure on the planet. If the full resources of the federal government couldn't break it, no one could.

He smiled. He actually liked Brady and had worked with the intelligence chief in the past. Strip away layers of subterfuge and a good person lay at the core of that which was Brady. Nevertheless, Jackson trusted the man about as far as he could toss the moon.

Jackson plopped in his chair, fixated on the schematic. His thoughts raced back to the question Invinci-Man asked him...the question he didn't want to answer. But Jackson knew the answer. The temptation to abuse the power of his suit dogged him like a bad habit since he built the thing. The urge still beckoned, a devil's enticing whisper appealing to the very worst aspect of himself, an aspect he could ill afford to let loose upon the world. He couldn't...would not follow the others down that dark path.

Oh well. There was only one way to overcome temptation: get rid of the source.

He could have turned over the suit's schematics to the government. No good. The military would have replicated it. One super advanced armored suit had been enough. A mass produced army of suit wearing killers amounted to an affliction the world could damn well do without.

His finger hovered over the delete button. He faltered for a few seconds before tapping the key. The schematic vanished from his screen. Years of research, development, creation... purged... gone.

Jackson's shoulders slumped. He was an ordinary citizen again. The world would have to tackle its own problems. Humanity didn't need superheroes. It didn't need caretakers.

He stared at a blank screen, staving off feelings of loss and emptiness. He would get over it in time.

He stood and walked out of the ops room. He never looked back.

ARE YOU EXPERIENCED?
Liberty Blair Charissage

In the grim night, the 40ft tall samurai wolf howled, its tentacles making a gurgling addition to the canine ululations.

"Ah, shut it! You whiner!" cried the gate patroller to the beast beside him. The gate patroller was a wiry, Japanese man in his union's military uniform. He sat in a box booth, a little away from the gate.

Quickly after ordering his comrade to shut up, the gate patroller spied three figures wandering out of the shadowy desert wasteland. They were covered by the darkness, so the patroller only made out their outlines. One was lanky and tall, while the other two were small as children.

The three came up to the gate of the town and the taller, adult figure walked to the box booth.

The patroller took out a piece of paper and a pen, and asked, "What is your business here in Bata Taun?"

"Uh, we're hoping to get out of the wastes, looking for a better life in the Canadian-Japanese Union territories," he replied in a musical, mellow voice.

"Hmmm," mumbled the patroller, writing down what he heard. "I shall have to ask you a few questions. I assume you are the caretaker of those children?" the patroller asked, pointing to the two smaller figures.

"Yes. I am."

"Very good. Name? Include any surname and your given name, please."

"Jim."

"Jim?"

"Jim."

"Your last name, sir?"

"Uhhh . . ."

"I see. Sir," said the patroller, marking an X on the last name place, "I'll assume you're male. Nationality?"

"Well, none, Sir; but previously, American."

"Uh-huh. Date of birth?"

"Uhhh...."

"I see. Sir, do you know your age?"

"No. 20-something."

"I'll put down 26. Size?"

"Uh, I would say 6 feet."

"I would say that too," the patroller agreed, scribbling it down.

"Weight?"

Jim appeared to look over himself in the darkness. "I would say 200 pounds."

"And none of that fat!" the patroller remarked, "Occupation?"

"Musician.

"Okay. Religion?"

"Well, Sir. I don't know."

"I'd recommend Buddhism rather than that new Windmill God. . ."

"I'm sorry," Jim cut in, "I would like to talk, but I would really rather like to get in."

"Oh, yes, ahem. Race?"

"Can't you tell?"

"Can't see anything in this night."

"African."

"What's that?"

"Black."

"Ah. Well...Hey, are you one of those griot guys?"

"Technically, I guess."

"Well, I believe that's everything. Oh, one more thing. Superpowers?"

"I'd rather . . ."

"It's mandatory."

Jim sighed deeply, "I have the ability to conjure up other realities into our existence."

"Oh? How?"

"If it doesn't need to be answered, I'd rather not say."

"Oh, right. Just curious. Okay, that's everything: give me the size, weight, sex, names and any other preliminaries about your kids. I'll assume they're the same as you in all others."

"Well, first thing, they're not Black, they're Caucasian."

"Hmm, what's that? From where in Asia?"

"White," corrected Jim.

"Ah."

"Their names are Mic and Red."

After the other preliminaries were done, the gate patroller said, "Welcome to Bata Taun. Anything you would like to state?"

Jim glanced up at the 40-foot tall samurai wolf with tentacles. The thing stomped back and forth on patrol on parrot feet.

"Yes," remarked Jim. "How do you make those beasts?"

"They prefer to be called warriors, sir. I heard from her," the gate patroller pointed to his giant comrade, "that her kind are grown in vats genetically modified with all the bloodthirstiness of Canadians combined with wolf, octopus, parrot, and superpower genes, then they're shipped off to the training ground to be trained as samurai and hone their superpower abilities, namely the laser-eye-mouth thing."

"Wow!" cried Jim. "Ever seen him do it?"

"No, and it's a *her*," said the patroller to Jim. "And a word of advice, Sir. Them inside can smell someone who's been out in the waste. I suggest you take a wash."

"Thank you."

The giant samurai let all three of them into the town of Bata Taun.

Two

Bata Taun, Canadian-Japanese Union territories, south side immigrant district. Four weeks later.

A woman in a hijab with a veil and many coverings knocked on Jim's door. The door opened. Red stared up at the ebony Black woman who was large and muscled. She knelt down to him and greeted, "Hello there, little one. Can you go get your father for me? I would like to speak with him."

Red nodded, saying, "Come on in."

The woman walked into the messy apartment. It was cramped and had not a lot of furniture in it, merely five wooden chairs in all of the living room. Half-eaten food and broken things littered the place. In a corner, Mic was reading a book given to him by Jim. It was written by the warrior-poet Philip Jose Farmer. Mic glanced up from it, nodded at the lady, and went back to reading the book.

Suddenly, the sound of a bottle smashing was heard from the other room. Then, Jim's muffled voice: "Red! How many times do I have to tell you! Don't come in here when I'm . . ."

"I'm sorry that I scared you. Look. A lady came to see you," came the calm, muffled words of Red.

"Alright. Alright. I'll see her."

Jim walked in. The woman looked over his frame: his skin was a mild-light colour of brown. It could be seen that he was very muscular, though he looked a little gaunt. His face was very handsome yet unshaven. Jim's hair was bizarrely cut. He wore white pants and a light, sleeveless, multi-colored coat with no shirt on. A candy bar was placed in one pocket of his many-hued coat.

He sat down, rearranging his chair.

"Hello," he greeted. "You, ah, are a proselytizer? If that's so, I have nothing against the fine religion of Islam, but I don't particularly . . ."

"I am not a proselytizer," said the woman. "Allow me to introduce myself – Maryam. If I may ask, what was going on in that room?"

Jim rearranged himself on his seat, blushing a little. "Sometimes, I get drunk and get into profound rages. I know, it's bad." He weirdly talked about it like it was normal, "I hate it. I always go to another room to be alone when it happens. I am never around these kids when I'm in that state."

Maryam straightened and looked at him, saying, "You must be in the late stages of one right now."

"Yes, but I'm sociable." This made it easy to understand why he was talking about his drinking so casually.

"Are you the father of those two?" She looked at Red who watched her and Jim, and Mic, who was still focusing on his book.

Jim mumbled, nodding, "Yeah, I'm their caretaker. Found them homeless and orphaned in the British refugee camps. Chose to take them in. I'm teaching them. I'm a musician."

"Yes. I think I've gone to one restaurant where you performed."

"Yes, I've done a few gigs now."

Maryam hunched over and stared more closely at Jim. "Jim, the reason I've come here is to offer a proposition to you. I understand that you have a superpower. I think you can put it to good use. I'm with a group, you see. We're having a meeting at Ray's bookstore soon. Would you like to come with me?"

Jim glanced up at Maryam, he didn't like the veil and the coverings which made all facial emotion impossible to see.

"Red? Mic? You have any plans?" asked Jim.

"No," replied Red.

"I can read my book anywhere, here or there," answered Mic.

"Good. We're going off to the bookstore."

***

Ray's bookstore was the only bookstore in town. Jim had found that out quickly. After the fallout, the paper and publishing industry had been hit hard, allowing for more independent people with a simple printing press to get by. Thus, this was how Jim was acquainted with the works of Philip Jose Farmer, the warrior-poet.

While Maryam knocked at the door, Jim looked at the tacky, tattered, and outdated architectural front of the bookstore, packed into the same building as many other shops. Jim, with his two kids beside him, wondered, "Why the hell am I here?"

The door was opened by a red-black, round faced man. He was in what must have been his best suit and tie, was clean shaven and had neatly trimmed short hair. He looked the opposite of Jim, who hadn't even changed his clothes when walking out the door.

The man stood aside and motioned the four in, saying, "Ah, Maryam, come in. And you must be Jim and his boys! Come in."

They entered the under-supplied store and walked behind the front desk and into a back room. There, in this back room, were two others around a tea table, drinking massive amounts of tea and coffee beside the piles of unshelved books.

One was a Korean man, handsome, kind-looking, and wearing a bouncer's striped shirt. He was sitting on a sofa.

The other stood behind the sofa, shaking her arms and hips in a little energetic dance. She was a young, tired looking, brown woman, who danced with a weird bounce with a seemingly unlimited amount of energy.

Maryam moved to a chair and seated herself, while the man from the door went to the table and poured her some coffee.

Maryam glanced at Jim and said, "Sit down, sit down, you're welcome here. Don't stand there looking embarrassed."

Jim sat down on another chair, while Red and Mic climbed onto the sofa.

"I believe introductions are in order. I'm Maryam, as you know. I work at the town hall as a clerk, that's how we found you. This is…"

The Korean man picked up the talk, explaining, "Hi. I'm Yi. I work as a bouncer for the bar down the street. I was brought here by my parents. The Canadian-Japanese Union needed workers here."

The constantly moving girl spoke up, "Hello! Hello! Hello! I am Ms Blank. I am not working right now and currently living at Maryam's place."

The man at the door then told his story, "I'm Ray Burroughs. I entered the U.S. military but was kicked out for heart problems. Started this bookshop here then."

"Oh, you were in the U.S. forces too?" spoke Jim, "I was in the Army…Airborne, but was invalidated by a broken ankle and injured back. I, uh, hiked it out in the fallout wastes deserts with those two for a while," Jim pointed at his kids, "I'm Jim, but you probably already know that."

Maryam sighed, then said, "Well, Jim, the reason we are all here is because we are trying to get a team up and running."

"You said something about superpowers?" asked Red.

"Yes, a superpowered team!" cried Maryam.

"So what are all your superpowers?" asked Mic, casually glancing up from his book.

Jim was about to tell Mic not to talk about superpowers so lightly, but was stopped in surprise and amazement when Maryam took off her veil, revealing that her jaw was without flesh and was only bare bone. Maryam spoke, but without moving the fleshless jaw-bone. "You want to know our superpowers. Well, I guess it's alright. First, I'm psychic. A telepath and…" From the folds of her robes, she drew out a handgun, aimed it at her hand,

and fired. The bullet bounced off her skin. "Have levels of invulnerability." She pointed with the gun to her fleshless jawbone. "I don't wear this veil for religious reasons."

Yi began to smile brightly and slowly started transforming into metal. His arms folded into his skin, until he was fully encased as a huge metal coil. The coil turned back into Yi. He laughed, "I can change into a giant, animated coil."

Ms. Blank stopped dancing and wiggling. She became very calm, focusing on Maryam's hand. The hand suddenly caught on fire and Maryam quickly blew it out. Being invulnerable, the hand was unscathed.

Ms. Black smiled, "I can conjure up fire but only when I'm calm. The thing is..." She started suddenly, violently, dancing again. "It soon becomes uncontrollable, so I have to always be in a state of high feeling or emotion."

"Ah, I see, that's why you're constantly jumping and moving around. Must be fun," said Jim.

"Fun!?" Ms Blank shouted, leaping in a single bound over Yi and the kids on the sofa and picking up Jim by the coat. She was in the highest pitches of fury and frenzy, "You think I enjoy this?! Always having to make a big deal out of everything! To have to leap with joy every time you get out of bed?! To have to be in the greatest of romantic passion about someone who you just have a little crush on?! To have a paper cut become one of the most unbearable tragedies?! Never to relax?!" Ms. Black stopped shaking in fury a tiny bit, "Peaceful." Her muscles rested a little, "Indifferent." She became less angry, "In perfect serenity." Her body suddenly caught on fire! Yet it burned out when she yelled, "That's something I can never have!!!"

Burroughs placed his hand on her shoulder, "Alright, Ms. Blank, calm down."

"Calm down?! Calm down?! That's the one thing I should never do!"

Burroughs sighed, "You know what I mean, don't take it out on Mr. Jim here."

Ms. Blank dropped Jim back on the chair.

Jim checked himself for burns and asked, "And your superpowers, Ray Burroughs?"

"Super strength."

"Super strength?"

"Super strength."

"That's it?"

"Yes, that's it."

"Really?"

"Really."

Red cut into the flow, stating, "That's kind of lame."

Burroughs smiled and shrugged, "It's lame, but practical."

JIm scanned the room, looking upon every one of the superpowered people one by one. He raised an eyebrow and asked, "And what are you guys exactly going to team up for?"

Yi laughed, "But Jim, you haven't told us your superpower yet."

Maryam, who had put back on her veil, held up her hand at Yi, explaining, "I think he would like to keep that to himself. I'll tell you about it afterwards. I found your file while going through the stacks and took an interest in you, Jim. To answer your question, Jim, come with me."

Maryam stood up and walked to the back of the room, to the back exit of the store. Jim, as well as everyone else, followed. She opened the door, "You may have heard about this," said Maryam.

Outside the door, rows upon rows of Canadian-Japanese Union soldiers marched through the street. On one edge of the street was Ray's bookstore, in the building complex, on the other was a gigantic factory. The battalions of the army cut striking figures between such buildings. They marched line after line, through the great gate of the city where Jim had entered out of the desert waste. The colossal samurai comprised of many creatures, wolf, parrot, squid, and Canadian looked over the troops, swaying her head as they marched along. She yawned when a supply wagon came by, drawn by mutated dog-horses.

"You know about the rumor of the American army marching across the wastes to challenge the western states, uniting the USA from coast to coast once more? It is not a rumor. The army is marching out today," explained Maryam.

Yi came in, remarking, "The stupid general thinks he can beat the entire invasion outside the town's walls!"

Ms. Blank called up, yelping, "So that's why we're creating a team."

Burroughs cut her off before the army heard her, adding, "To make sure the town of Bata Taun has a second line of defense."

Jim looked at them, then at Mic and Red. They had the same facial expression as Jim. Jim said, "You really think the invading America could actually defeat that beast?" pointing to the gigantic, hybrid samurai.

Maryam sighed, "Reports say that the attackers have a renegade samurai like that on their side. The battle is...uncertain."

Burroughs spoke, "Our superpowers will make us an army unto ourselves."

Maryam asked, "Will you join us Jim?"

Jim looked at all of them for a long time, then said, "You're idiots. We should be ashamed of ourselves. Our powers are the thing which made the world how it is. People like you are the cause for the fallout. Read the history. We can't use this power. It does nothing good. Nothing good. You can't use it for anything. I've seen people who've tried. It didn't turn out pretty. I'm sorry, but I can't be a part of this team. It won't amount to anything, or if it does, it'll only make things worse."

All of them were dumbfounded. They stood speechless. Ms Blank was lucky that her shock was strong, because if it hadn't been, she would have burst into flames.

Jim turned down to talk to his kids, "Come on Red, Mic, we're going home."

Red and Mic were sad looking but obeyed, moving out of the room to leave by the front. Jim was accosted by Yi, Burroughs, and Ms Blank to reconsider, to think about what he was saying, and, most of all, to stay.

Yet Jim simply moved on. He walked out of the backroom, through the small bookshelves and opened the door for the two kids. Maryam ran up to catch him and stopped right next to him.

"Jim!" she cried, "You are wrong. Yes, bad things have happened to and by people like us. But you have to be proud of what you are and how you can help the world with all of your abilities and being. At least think about joining us!"

Jim held the door, looked down, then back up at Maryam. "Maybe...I'll, I'll think about it." and left.

At the end of the day. At Jim's apartment.

Jim looked out of the door, out at the town's wall trying to see, to hear, to smell, to feel the great battle between two powerful forces out there. Mic came out and stood beside him, leaning against the doorway. Jim sighed, then after a couple of moments, asked, "Mic, what do you think I should do?"

"I don't know. You're the wisest of us," replied Mic. "All I know is that this place will get very mean if the army breaks through the walls and I also don't want to hide, but I want you to be happy, too, Dad."

Jim thought. He looked at his adopted son, then stood up, "I'm going out. Tell your brother." and he left.

Three

The battle did not end well for either side, but the Canadian-Japanese Union army lost. Quickly, by next dawn the American army was marching on to storm the town. There were no soldiers left to man the walls, only a tiny town militia. The militia thought it hopeless. They asked to surrender, but the messenger was met with no mercy; an answer to the plea, with that, the game was set. It was winner take all between the army of America and the town of Bata Taun. By the next day rows on rows of tents of the American camp lay on Bata Taun's doorstep. The siege began at dawn.

The militia stirred and mounted the walls. Under-manned as they were, they held at the sight of thousands of warriors, still held when all the warriors stopped mysteriously just out of gunshot. Yet, the militia fled when out of the horizon stomped a giant, 50ft tall, squid wolf-parrot samurai. The terrifying monster laughed at their screams and unsheathed a large katana which was American modified.

The monster swordsman swung the sword down upon the wall and with one great smash cleaved a section of it.

The army outside cheered and cried, running straight to the rubble. The first ones to climb the rubble were met by four masked figures, all in different costumes.

There was the Red Jaw (Maryam) who wore a black trench coat, shirt and trousers with a red scarf-bandanna around her lower face.

There was Emperor Coil (Yi) who was in costume, which was ripped to tatters when he transformed into a giant, 10ft steel coil.

There was the Flaming Calm Before the Storm (Ms Blank) who was in a Buddhist nun's garb with a faceless mask that had only slits for eyeholes.

Finally there was Mr. Strong (Ray Burroughs) who just looked like a giant Mexican wrestler.

The invading soldiers were confounded by the striking and flamboyant figures. They almost laughed, but they didn't have time before the heroes attacked.

The Flaming Calm Before the Storm scorched apart the first battalion with a pyrokinetic meditation; all who her eyes looked upon burst into hot fire.

Mr. Strong hurled large chunks of rubble down on the second row of the battalions.

Emperor Coil swung and snaked, smashing the third batch of the battalions.

The Red Jaw punched and spattered with psychic currents at the fourth wave of the battalions.

The attacking army was amazed. Never had anyone seen superpowered people use their powers this way, and more, they were holding off the troops from entering the city.

The hybrid samurai creature looked on the scene, annoyed. The wolf-squid howled from its parrot beak, "I killed a sister samurai the past night. I can unmake a bunch of superpowered ants!"

The monster flicked a claw-paw. A truck rolled near it, bearing a mighty, giant guitar.

The four superheroes looked in awe and terror. They hoped the Canadian-wolf-squid-parrot samurai wasn't what they thought it was.

The samurai took up the giant guitar, plucked a few strings and then it started. Out of the instrument an unearthly music twanged forth. The music shook the air, made the earth shake, yet more than the sky and the earth trembled: reality itself quivered in the cacophony of the samurai's reality quake. It was as the four heroes feared! The samurai was a reality shaker!

The heroes were shocked and unbalanced as the music tore and howled into their souls. The American legions redoubled in a charge and soon drove the superheroes into the town.

The streets were bare and deserted because of the attack, but not entirely, for in the middle of the road stood little Red and Mic.

Yi (Emperor Coil) was the first to spot them and shouted, "Hey! What are you two doing here?!"

Mic shouted back, "Our father told us to stay next to you guys, saying that it was the safest place in the town."

"Wise man," remarked Mr. Strong (Ray Burroughs), punching an American soldier into the sky.

Maryam (the Red Jaw) shot an eldritch blast of psychic energy to stop the reality quakes, but to no avail. She cried, "So is he going to come and help us or not?!"

Red cried out to reply, "Well, he..." Red was interrupted when a soldier broke through, tumbling over the Flaming Calm Before the Storm (Ms. Blank) and rushed toward the two boys.

The soldier's charge flung Red to the ground and Red flinched as the bayonet was lifted over him. Then suddenly, out of seemingly nowhere, there jumped down from a roof-top a figure – and Superman punched the American soldier to the ground.

It was Jim! He was dressed in a multicolored skirt and blouse, with a purple-colored cape. He was armed to the teeth with two rapiers, and a pistol on his belt, as well as two guitars on his back. He wore a mask shaped like a fox's head and had a fake tail running down behind his legs. Immediately he struck a pose and cried, "I am the Foxy Lady!"

Red, lying on the ground, muttered, "Really, man...you're, you're...Really going to do this?"

"Ah, shut up, Red! I'm having fun!" He rushed to the stairs of the walls.

"Hey wait! Where are you going!?" cried the Flaming Calm Before the Storm.

The Foxy Lady did not reply, he just ran and jumped to stand on the wall's top.

The reality quakes were bearing down hard, especially on the walls, yet through this the Foxy Lady picked out one guitar from behind his back. He suddenly blared out a tremendous counter shock-wave with one burst from the guitar. The immense shock wave made the army's horde stumble in the charge, and the squid-wolf-parrot samurai fell off its feet from the wave, crashing onto the truck.

"Thank you! Thank you! Thank you all for coming to my first official concert!" shouted out the Foxy Lady, "My name is the Foxy Lady and this is the first time I have used my superpowers to their full extent! But hey! No time like the present! This is a little song I like to call *'Purple Haze'*

Purple Haze! Beyond Insane!

Is it pleasure? Or is it pain?!

Down on the ceiling! Looking up at the bed!

Seeing my body painted blue and red!"

Reality shook, quaked, and convulsed at the pounding of (Jim's) the Foxy Lady's sounds. It quivered, shivered, and cracks in the fabric of the universe itself began to form.

"By Allah!" cried the Red Jaw.

"Buddha!" cried the Flaming Calm Before the Storm.

"Oh my Atheism!" cried Mr. Strong.

Emperor Coil shouted, "He's not just a reality shaker! He is a reality breaker!"

Portals and doorways to another reality were unlocked by the cracks made by the Foxy Lady's music. Fantastic, otherworldly, kaleidoscopic vistas were gazed upon in these holes in existence and streaming forth into the world was...What else! Purple Haze! It ringed forth, plaguing the American troops with strange, surreal wonders – as if their lives weren't surreal enough.

One warrior, however, snuck through the four superheroes' line and sprang onto the Foxy Lady. The Foxy Lady saw him and swung his instrument, smashing his guitar on the American warrior's head. The guitar splattered its scattered pieces, broken.

An awful, dead silence enveloped the land. The cracks healed, the portals and doorways closed. Then the Foxy Lady simply pulled out the other guitar from his back, "Aw! There's plenty more where that came from! We're just getting started! Here's Voodoo Child!"

The entire army screamed in terror and fled into the desert. The samurai narrowed its eyes as the fleeing legions swarmed about its feet.

The samurai then brought out its most powerful and feared attack. Lasers flared forth out of its eyeballs and came out of its beak. The three beams converged at just above its snout, then the combined ball of light sparked up, cutting a ray through the air, as the wolf-squid-parrot samurai moved the laser's path to aim it at the Foxy Lady.

"Aw! You want to play that game, do ya!? Well, I think I can play that tune too!" mumbled the Foxy Lady and took off his fox mask. Portals to the other universe were created in his eyeballs and he opened another as he dropped open his mouth. A heat ray of purple haze shot out of the three portals and combined at his nose, similar to the giant samurai, beaming out in one big laser.

The two lasers hit directly at one another. Their powers surged as they pierced each other, but the Foxy Lady's purple haze was stronger and blasted forward. It outdid the giant samurai's laser, hitting the titanic monster. The 50ft tall giant wolf-squid-parrot samurai exploded in a burst of colors, butterflies, and flowers. The Foxy Lady raised his two fists in the air.

"Huh? What do you know?" said Mic. "This one time, the fox did beat the wolf."

The rest of the morning, the four-plus-one-more super-heroes celebrated their victory. The Flaming Calm Before the Storm danced and played with Red and Mic at the base of the rubble of the half-destroyed walls.

On top of the crumbled stone sat the Red Jaw (Maryam), Emperor Coil (Yi), Mr. Strong (Ray Burroughs), and finally the Foxy Lady (Jim). They were laughing and having a great time. Yi (Emperor Coil) sighed, "Phew, I thought we would never survive there. I'm sad that we can't do this everyday."

Jim (the Foxy Lady) asked, "Why? What do you mean?"

Ray Burroughs (Mr. Strong) explained, "The threat is gone. No reason for our team to stick around."

Maryam (The Red Jaw) said, "Yeah, we were planning to disband after this."

"Disband?! After this?!" cried Jim (the Foxy Lady), "I've only been in this town for a few days and I can see the crime rate is skyrocketing, and I've traveled these desert wastes and they're not good out there either. We cannot disband, we merely have to change from army busters to crime fighters."

Maryam (the Red Jaw) looked at everyone else sitting on the rubble. She lay her arms on her lap and her head on her hands and said decisively, "Continue."

Epilogue

A month after the famous Bata Taun battle. In a nightclub beside Ray's bookstore.

A regal, formally dressed, Japanese man sat by a table in the back room, just next to the dance floor in which the people were moving wildly. An equally regal, formally dressed, Canadian man walked by and sat next to him.

"Prime Minister Eisaku Satō," said the Canadian.

"Emperor Lester B. Pearson," greeted the Prime Minister.

"Have you read over the reports?"

"Yes. We, as the Canadian-Japanese Union, must choose our reaction to these superpowered vigilantes carefully and very seriously."

"This 'Foxy Lady' could be quite dangerous."

The two settled down as the room became quiet.

An announcer came up on stage, "Hello everybody! Hope everyone's having a great night! Now here we have a lovely father and two son band from the desert waste. Please give it up for Jim! Red! And Mic...*The Jim Experience!*"

The crowd cheered and Jim, Mic, and Red came on stage. Mic went to the drums, Red to bass guitar and Jim went to the front, being lead guitar.

"Hello, everyone." said Jim, "I want to say a couple of things. First: this music is inspired by the Foxy Lady who without her, or him, we wouldn't be here today. Secondly: this performance marks an important time for me, it being one month since I've had a drop of liquor to drink."

The crowd cheered at that.

"And thirdly: I've learned a lot about myself. I've learned to accept some things about myself, learned not to deny things about my identity. However, without further ado, we're going to play you *Are You Experienced?*"

The party and the performance went over very well. At the end, Jim had his guitar set on fire. No one knew how, though. Most thought it was stagecraft, but they never noticed one particular lady standing calmly amongst the hubbub.

GHOST
Milton Davis

One

A cold drizzle settled on Seaboard Industrial Boulevard, ushering in another miserable January night in Atlanta. The lights still burned at *Gentech*, a small genetics laboratory tucked behind a cluster of naked maples – an odd sight for a Friday night. Bryce St. George sat at his desk inside, wrestling with a genetic sequence that played hard to get. The brilliant Jamaican loved the challenge; it was something that was rare in his life in the outside world.

Bryce was a blessed man. At twenty-eight, he stood six foot four, carrying two hundred and twenty pounds of natural hard muscle on his bones. He was a gifted athlete who excelled in sports throughout his life, earning a football and academic scholarship to college. After graduating he turned down the physical challenges of pro football, soccer and basketball for the mental challenges of genetic engineering. With dark chocolate skin, dreadlocks that lifted over his head then fell to his broad shoulders like a lion's mane and deep green eyes, Bryce was a woman's dream. If his looks didn't capture her at first glance, his deep, melodic patois usually sealed the deal.

The glare of car lights interrupted his scientific scrutiny. He looked up from the stereoscope and recognized the red Honda Accord pulling into the parking lot. A knowing smile creased his face. Briana had returned to 'surprise' him. He went back to his desk and pretended to be busy, ignoring her clumsy attempt to quietly open the front door. He kept his back turned as her heels clicked across the vinyl floor. Warm, honey-brown hands slipped over his eyes.

"Guess who?" she purred.

"The cleaning lady?" he answered.

"Bastard!" she exclaimed as she smacked him on the head.

Bryce spun his seat around to view his boss' latest assistant and his soon to be latest conquest. Briana posed in a black trench coat pulled tight against her body.

"You ready to play?" she asked. She opened the coat slowly, revealing a sheer chemise, then eased onto his lap. Their kiss was wet and full.

"Not here," Bryce whispered. He picked her up suddenly and she yelped. He carried her into Lenny's office and her eyes widened.

"We can't do it here!"

Bryce smiled. "Yes we can."

He was placing her down on the sofa when he noticed Lenny's monitor. Instead of the usual screensaver of his boss' family, there was an unfamiliar emblem flashing.

"What's this?" Bryce went to the screen. "Vanguard?"

This was something new.

"Bryce?" Briana sat up on the sofa with a frown. Bryce flashed a smile, then sat at Lenny's computer.

"Give me a minute, Bree. I need to check this out." Bryce's fingers flashed across the keyboard as unfamiliar data streamed past his eyes.

"Lenny, you naughty boy," Bryce whispered. He jumped out the chair, ran to his desk and returned with a flash drive. He plugged it into the computer and began downloading files.

"What are you doing?" Briana asked.

Bryce turned to her and began to remove his shirt. "The question is *who* am I doing?"

They nestled onto the sofa, the room illuminated by the flashing monitor lights.

***

Leonard Steinberg arrived at Gentech Monday morning, just as the snow flurries began to fall from the blanket of gray clouds overhead.

This is too early for this kind of weather, he thought.

Snow usually came to Atlanta in February, sometimes as late as March. It was the reason he moved down from upstate New York years ago despite the wailing of his family. Gentech was the type of business you could run from anywhere in the country and at fifty-five, Leonard had his fill of shoveling snow and grueling drives to vacations in south Florida. Georgia was an excellent compromise as far as he was concerned. Besides, there was Bryce, who refused to relocate any further north than Atlanta. Gentech was nothing without Bryce.

The building was empty; Bryce and the other technicians usually didn't arrive until after nine. He hummed as he shuffled to his office, briefcase in one hand and the *Journal-Constitution* stuffed under his arm. He opened his office door and was assaulted by the aroma of *Glade Morning Mist.*

"For God's Sake, Bryce!" he barked. He looked at his sofa, his pale face crinkled as he imagined what had taken place the night before in his office. He knew Bryce used his office as his office tryst station; he knew that Bryce *knew* he knew. But Bryce also knew his own value to the company.

"I'll have to call the upholstery cleaners," he mumbled. As he sat his briefcase down, he noticed his monitor still on. His pale face became paler.

"No, no, no," he stammered. He sat in his seat and hit enter. Vanguard options jumped on the screen and he dropped his head. He didn't log off yesterday. Bryce and Briana had been in his office. Maybe they were too hot with each other to notice. As he logged off the system his phone rang.

"Gentech," he answered.

"We have a breach," the voice said.

Leonard took the receiver away from his face and cursed silently.

"There was no breach," he replied. "I forgot to log out, that's all."

"This was not log error. This was a breach. Files were entered and downloaded. Important files. Sensitive files."

Leonard's head began to sweat. He waited for the next words.

"I need names and information."

"He's too valuable," Leonard replied. "Everything you have from me, he created."

"No one is too valuable. Everyone is expendable, including you. Besides, the project is nearly complete. I need names and information."

Leonard pulled up Bryce's file on the screen. He gazed at it for a moment, regretting the terrible act he was about to commit.

"I'm sorry," he whispered. He opened the secure e-mail and attached Bryce's file.

"Anyone else?"

Leonard closed his eyes. "Yes, a woman, but she's fairly new. I'm sure she wasn't involved."

"That's not your decision to make."

Leonard attached Briana's file to the e-mail and clicked Send. There was a moment of silence before the caller spoke again.

"You have a week to shut down operations. Your new facility will be in Sao Paulo. No more mistakes."

Leonard rubbed his head. "Yes, I understand."

"Goodbye, Leonard."

The caller hung up. Leonard placed the receiver down, dropped his face into his hands and cried.

Two

Malik Cooper sat in the stall of the NSA building, staring at a picture of Tisha and the twins. He was doing it for them; giving up a storied career as a deep cover agent for his soon to be family. He rubbed his head, brushing his close cropped hair back and forth and sighed.

"It's the right thing to do. The best thing to do."

He exited the bathroom and marched to Sheryl Jennings' office.

Sheryl saw Malik enter and ended her phone conversation immediately.

"Sit down, Malik," she said, gesturing to the chair before her mahogany desk.

"Thanks for seeing me, Sheryl," Malik said.

"So there's no changing your mind?"

Malik shook his head. "No, Sheryl. I need to do this."

Sheryl leaned back in her chair. "Need to?"

"Don't try any psycho-talk on me today," Malik warned. "I'm quitting, effective today."

"She must be something."

Malik took the picture from his jacket and placed it on Sheryl's desk. "They are."

Sheryl picked up the picture and smiled. "You'll make a fine family."

They stood together as if on cue and shook hands.

"When does your flight leave?"

"This afternoon."

"You'll be missed, Malik. You're the best."

Malik shook Sheryl's hand. "Thanks for everything, Sheryl. I won't forget it."

Malik left the NSA building for the last time. He was heading to Atlanta to start a new life, a *real* life. The deception and killing was done. He had no regrets. He was in a cab heading for Ronald Reagan Airport when his Android buzzed. He looked at the message and grinned.

How long does it take to quit a job? Longer than it takes to get fired from one, LOL!

His phone chimed and he answered.

"What's up, Bryce?"

"Nutten, bruh. When you comin'?"

He must be at home, Malik thought. Bryce always fell into patois when he was relaxed.

"My flight leaves at 1:10."

"Good. I'll meet you there. We'll go to the *Patty Hut* and get some good food in you. There's a new sister working there that will give you a righteous welcome home if you talk to her right."

Same old Bryce. "Got to pass, St. George. My ladies are waiting on me."

"So?"

Malik laughed. Bryce never gave up.

"So, I can't. I'm engaged, man!"

"All the more reason, my brother. Your days are numbered!"

"I tell you what; we'll hook up tomorrow, okay? But no women for me."

"Cool, bruh. Tomorrow, at Two Urban Licks. Peace."

Bryce sat down his iPhone and focused on his desktop screen. The files were almost done uploading. If they contained a fraction of what he glimpsed in Leonard's office he had hit the jackpot. His project needed some enhancing and the new data could be the perfect addition.

The computer chimed. Bryce hit enter and the contents of the file were revealed. His cool countenance dissipated as the data emerged before him.

"Either I hit the lottery, or I'm in serious trouble," he whispered.

He picked up his phone and speed-dialed Kandace.

"What?" she answered.

"Meet me at the lab, Kitty. I got something to show you."

"I can't. I'm at work, and I told you to stop calling me Kitty."

"Fake sick or something. You really want to see this."

"I'll stop by at lunch. It better be good."

Bryce smiled as the sequences danced on his screen. "It's lovely, Kitty. Really, it is."

***

Leonard was cleaning out his desk when the black Infiniti FX45 eased into the Gentech parking lot. He looked up, watching the occupants exit from the vehicle as sweat formed on his forehead. He had made the announcement earlier that morning to his employees then stood silently as they reacted. Some cried, others cursed him out, while some just shrugged and asked for their severance. Bryce didn't show; Leonard shuddered when he thought of what had happened to him.

The four men entered the building. One man was tall and pale, his fading red hair flecked with gray. He looked about with piercing green eyes that finally settled on Leonard. The other three were dressed identically, long black wool coats with black hats and shades, their faces obscured by their turned up collars, their hands covered by black leather gloves. They walked with a fluid grace that reminded Leonard of the dancers at the Atlanta Ballet. They studied everything in the office but seemed uninterested in Leonard.

They entered his office. The red-headed man took off his gloves and extended his hand, his expression cold, despite his smile.

"Leonard? I'm Leif Thorvaldsen. I'm from Vanguard."

Leonard shook Leif's hand; the appendage was as cold as his face.

"Hello Mr. Thorvaldsen. You came sooner than I expected."

"Time is of the essence, Leonard. I suspect the dismissals went well?"

"As well as something like that could go."

"Any takers to relocate?"

Leonard scowled. "No."

"And Mr. St. George?"

"What about him?"

Thorvaldsen's expression shifted to serious. "Was he here?"

Leonard looked puzzled. "I thought you..."

"No. We didn't. The address you gave us led to an empty warehouse."

Leonard detected the implication in Thorvaldsen's voice.

"That's the address he gave on his application. It's the only one I have."

Thorvaldsen tilted his head and the other men moved closer to Leonard.

"Bryce has worked for you, how long, five years and you never checked him out?"

Leonard became defiant to hide his fear. "The man did his job; damn well, I might add. I had no reason to doubt his credentials."

"I see. Where is his office?"

Leonard led them to Bryce's office. Thorvaldsen's companions scoured it, examining every part and piece. Leonard wasn't sure, but it looked like they smelled the personal items. The men finally finished, then returned to Leonard's office.

"It seems your man Bryce is into more than just genetics," Thorvaldsen said.

He reached into the coat and extracted plane tickets.

"All the arrangements have been made. We expect you to be out of the country by midnight."

Leonard took the tickets. "Thank you."

"And I'll need the employee files."

Leonard was stunned. "Why?"

"That's none of your concern." Thorvaldsen nodded and his companions quickly dismantled Leonard's computer.

"Enjoy Brazil, Leonard."

Thorvaldsen and his men left the office, climbed into the Infiniti and sped away. Leonard dropped his head and closed his eyes.

"God forgive me," he whispered.

Three

Bryce stepped out of the cab in front of the *Vortex Bar and Grill* at Little Five Points, the usual lunch spot for him and Kandace. He trotted through the cold air into the gaping mouth of the skull entrance, finding himself among Atlanta's fringe culture and the best burgers in the city. Kandace waited for him at their table, ponytails sticking out from the sides of her head, with loud red lipstick announcing her full lips. Her mocha legs extended from beneath the table, her manicured feet wrapped in a pair of knee high leather platform boots. Her black skirt was so short it seemed she wore nothing below her tight black jacket.

"Still rocking the punk look I see," Bryce commented.

"You like it," she purred. She leaned toward him as he sat and they kissed. They were friends with benefits, as some like to say.

Kandace's face became serious. "Now show me what you got. I don't have a lot of time."

Bryce took out his netbook, logged in, then slid it across the table. Kandace took one look at the screen and whistled.

"Damn, boy!" she exclaimed. "You are in so much trouble!"

Bryce leaned back, folding his hands behind his head. "No, I'm not. Leonard won't touch me. He fires me and Gentech folds. I'm the Ace of Spades at that place."

Kandace peeked up from the screen. "I bet you didn't go to work today, did you?"

Bryce smiled and shook his head.

"Damn fool." Kandace pushed the laptop back. "What are we going to do with all this?"

"I figure we can enhance Ghost with it. Tweak it a bit."

"Some of this stuff looks promising. You going out tonight?"

Bryce frowned. "Got to. Funds are getting low."

A waiter came by but Kandace waved him away. "I can't believe you. You make six figures and you still can't keep a dollar."

"I'm living life, baby. I didn't hear you complaining when we went to Shanghai last month."

Kandace smiled. "Yeah, that was fun."

She looked at her watch. "Shit! I gotta go. I'll see you tonight."

She stood and Bryce's eyes got big. "Damn! I see you now!"

"Kiss my ass!"

"With pleasure."

As Kandace walked out the Vortex, a black Infiniti FX45 cruised by. Four men were distracted by her briefly then refocused on their task.

"Are you sure he's here?" Leif asked.

His companions nodded in unison.

"Too many people. We'll pick him up tonight."

The FX45 sped away, merging into the lunchtime traffic.

Four

Some habits are hard to break, especially the ones that have saved a life. Malik sensed the exact angle the Delta 727 took as it made its final approach to Hartsfield/Jackson International Airport. He knew where all the exits were located, the number of people on the flight sorted in his mind by sex, gender, age, nationality and sexual orientation. He noted the location of the Homeland security marshals and the other undercover agents on the flight. Most of all, he noted that he was coming home.

His mind shifted from deep cover mode as landing gear met tarmac. Atlanta had always been a haven for him, a stop between assignments. Here he was an international businessman with a comfortable home in the

Sugarloaf subdivision, surrounded by other successful professionals. His neighbors never came calling and he never complained, using his time to rest, heal and review his next mission. That all ended one fall Saturday morning when he decided to take a run and found himself stride for stride with a lovely divorced lawyer that changed his life.

Malik jumped from his seat the moment the plane parked at the A gate. He grabbed his overnight bag from the overhead bin and pushed his way through the other passengers, ignoring their silent and vocal complaints. He was on the train in minutes, a smile growing wider on his face with every second. By the time he stepped off the escalator at the main terminal he was practically giddy. His ladies were waiting, Kelly and Michelle holding a lime green sign with the words 'Welcome Home, Daddy!' scribbled in red marker. Tisha stood behind them, her welcoming smile and sparking eyes letting him know that this was all real.

"Hey queens!" he exclaimed. The girls dropped the sign and rushed him. He scooped them up into his arms and they assaulted his cheeks with kisses.

"Hey, Daddy!" they shrieked.

Tisha picked up the sign and sauntered to them. He leaned to her and they kissed lightly for the sake of the girls.

"Hey, baby," she said. "You really did it."

Malik smiled. "I told you I would."

Tears welled in Tisha's eyes. "Come on, let's go home."

So this was normal life. He had a beautiful wife, two gorgeous daughters, and a well-paying government job with liberal holiday time. There were no covert missions, no life threatening dilemmas and no close calls. So when his cell phone buzzed and he saw it was Sheryl, he almost jumped for joy.

Tisha looked up from her book.

"Who is it, baby? Bryce?"

"No. It's Sheryl," Malik said with a frown.

Tisha rolled her eyes.

"I thought I was retired," he said.

Sheryl laughed. "You are. How's peacetime treating you?"

"Can't complain. What's going on?"

"Bryce St. George. You know him?"

Malik lost his smile. "I do."

"Our agency received a report on him. Seems he's involved in a situation that may have national security implications."

"Bryce? I doubt that. He's not perfect but he's not a spy."

"I didn't say spy. When was the last time you two talked?"

"A few days ago."

Malik hesitated asking the next question. He knew the answer could draw him back into his old life.

"What do you have, Sheryl?"

"I can't tell you, Malik. You don't work for us anymore."

"So why did you call me?"

"No reason; just thought you'd like to know. You take care, Malik. Tell Tisha I said hello."

Sheryl hung up. Malik stared at the phone. Sheryl was trying to lure him back. This must be a deep one, one that required his expertise. He glanced upward, thinking about the ladies whose life he was a part of now. He put the phone in his pocket. He'd do a little digging and call Sheryl if he discovered something. He'd begin by calling Bryce.

Five

Bryce ordered two Spanish Fly burger plates and a large Coke. He had to fill up if he was going out with Ghost. His funds were extremely low which meant his night run would be longer than usual. The waitress smiled, working her hips as she left his table. She wasn't his type, but apparently she thought she was. The punk look only worked for him when Kandace wore it; she was so fine she would look good in a potato sack.

He stuffed down the meals then leaned back in his seat, unbuckling his belt. He called the office but got no answer. That was odd; Lenny was always at his desk and always took his calls. He shrugged it off and texted Malik. Malik didn't respond; he was probably with his 'queens' practicing fatherhood and married life. The boy was truly in love. He got that dumb look whenever he talked about Tisha and he took to the twins as if they were his own. Bryce was jealous; he'd had plenty of women, but none that made him consider settling down. He was a good time to them as they were to him. They desired him, but they didn't care about him. Well, Kandace did, but she was different.

He ordered a Steakhouse Burger to go. The waitress brought him his receipt and her number; the receipt he kept, the number he tossed as soon as he stepped outside. He caught the MARTA to Clairmont Road then transferred to the GRTA shuttle to Gwinnet County. He got off at Gwinnet Place Mall; he could walk to the hotel from there. Kandace gave him the key and the room's number a couple of weeks ago. She rented the room for a month as always. Inside was the usual set up. He went into the bathroom, closed and locked the door. The Skin floated in the nutrient filled tub, a thin, translucent wonder of genetic biotechnology. Bryce stripped naked then slipped on the suit. He waited as the loose material tightened, pressing against him like a second skin. The tingling swept his body as the contacts pierced his flesh in a million places, connecting to his blood vessels and nerve endings. He walked to the bed as the tingling subsided, pulling back the sheets to find the tablet. Kandace had updated the blotter. There was a suspected drug house only a few blocks away.

"Perfect," Bryce said. "This shouldn't take long."

He opened the desk drawer and took out the loot bag. The Skin activated and he watched as his hand and the bag disappeared. By the time he reached the mirror he was completely invisible.

"Showtime."Bryce looked out the window, then slipped outside. He was cold but not extremely so; the Skin adjusted to the temperature by increasing its flesh to fat ratio. He boarded the bus, standing between the unsuspecting passengers with a smile on his face. He wondered how they would react if the Skin failed and a naked man suddenly appeared between them. The bus reached his stop, the entrance to a neat middle class neighborhood. The Mexican drug boys were hiding their stashes in rented homes close to the interstate these days. The police were onto the scheme but it was still difficult to spot the weed among the flowers. Bryce strolled by the stake out car, walked up to the non-descript two story house, then went around to the back. He was climbing over the fence when a patch of grass lifted and two men emerged. This was even better; the house was a decoy. The real stash was underground.

Bryce slipped into the hidden chamber before the men closed it. It was well lit; he bypassed the stacks of bagged meth and weed and went straight for the money. He opened his loot bag, filling it with money. He wasn't greedy; it would take them a while to notice, and when they did, they would blame each other. He closed his bag and waited. The men returned an hour later, grabbed a few bags of money and left. Bryce left with them. He followed them to the undercover stake out car across the street from the house. The officers rolled down the window and took the money. So much for law enforcement.

Bryce hit two more drug houses before calling it a day. He went back to the hotel and stripped off the Skin. He transferred the money into a backpack and caught a taxi back to his condo. His phone rang while he cruised down I-85.

"Speak," he said.

"Bryce, it's Briana."

Bryce grinned. "What's up, baby girl?"

"Something's wrong. I went into work late today and everything was gone."

Bryce's smile faded. "What do you mean 'gone?"

"I mean gone, empty. No desks, no lab equipment, no computers, nothing."

"Somebody broke in?"

"No, Bryce. Everything was moved. I tried to contact Leonard but his phone is disconnected. Bryce, I'm scared."

"Where are you?"

"I'm in the lobby at your place."

Bryce took the phone away from his mouth to curse. "Look, stay right there. I'll be there in a minute."

"Okay, Bryce. I'll wait for you."

Bryce tapped the window between him and the driver. The driver peered at him through the rearview mirror.

"What?"

"Change of plans," Bryce said. "I need you to take me to the airport."

The cabby frowned. "I thought you said..."

"Just do it, okay?" Bryce texted Kandace, leaving her a message worked out between them a long time ago. GET GONE, it read.

Bryce sunk into his seat. The good thing was over. It was time to go home.

Bryce had just closed his phone when the taxi jerked right.

"Where the hell did you learn to drive?" he shouted.

The taxi jerked again. Bryce looked to the left out the soiled window and saw a black Infiniti FX45 speeding alongside them, the windows sliding down.

"Speed up! Speed up!"

The driver didn't need any encouragement. The taxi lurched forward, throwing Bryce back into the seat. The driver wrenched the wheel and they cut across three lanes of traffic, jumping off the next exit. The taxi barreled down the exit then stopped.

"Get out!" the driver yelled.

Bryce's eyes went wide. "What? No!"

The taxi driver turned his head, his grizzled face full of anger.

"Get the fuck out! I'm not getting killed over a fare!"

Bryce unzipped his back pack and took out a handful of money.

"It's yours man, all of it. Just get me to..."

Bryce heard a crash and then he flew into the taxi shield, smashing his face against the plexi-glass. He fell back into his seat, dazed, his ears ringing from the explosion of the airbag. The passenger door opposite him flew off the hinges and a man in a black coat, black hat and feral eyes reached in and grabbed him by the collar. Bryce's response was automatic; he reached into his back pocket, pulled out his straight razor and slashed, cutting the man's wrists and neck in one fluid motion. The man howled as he fell back. Bryce reached back and opened the opposite door. He fell into the street; someone lifted him to his feet.

"You cut my friend," the man said. Bryce was suddenly airborne, landing on the curb.

"Stop," another man said. "We need him alive until we find out what he knows."

Bryce rolled onto his back. The man was coming for him. He was dressed like the other man, possessing the same cat-like eyes. The man reached for him then jerked; a fountain of blood spewed from his hat.

"You wrecked my cab!" the driver shouted. He held a Glock in his trembling hands. He was spinning to his left when he was engulfed in white light, his body shaking and smoldering. The light dissipated and the driver collapsed in a smoking heap. Bryce looked to his right. A tall, pale man with red hair stood a few feet away from the driver, his glowing fingers smoking. The man looked at Bryce with a frigid grin and started for him.

He was impeded by another cat-eyed man. The man spoke in a language Bryce didn't understand; the red-headed man frowned.

"Let's go," he said. He stared at Bryce for a moment, his fingertips glowing as he raised his hands. A siren wailed in the distance; the man lowered his hands and walked quickly to his dead companion. He lifted him like a broken doll, tossing him into the FX45. His companion appeared with the man Bryce had sliced and threw him inside as well. They jumped into the SUV and sped away.

Bryce didn't have time to process what happened. The police were coming. He staggered to the taxi for his backpack, stuffing it into his heist pouch. He stripped off his clothes and donned Ghost, disappearing as Atlanta's Finest exited off the highway.

Six

Kandace took a long drag on her joint, bobbing her head to Janelle Monae while DNA sequences mutated and twisted before her glazed eyes. Beyond the screen, a vat of nucleic acids simmered, prodded by minute changes in temperature. It was simple, but then again it wasn't. Genetic engineering was almost like cooking with calculus. The thought – and the joint – made her burst out laughing. The laughter stopped when the new genetic codes emerged on the screen. Molecules twisted and turned in unfamiliar patterns, forming paths that almost blew her high. This was brilliance, engineering far beyond anything Bryce ever dreamed up. She realized her partner was an amateur compared to whoever developed the sequences spinning before her.

Her iPhone pulsed in her pocket and she answered.

"Get gone." it read.

"Damn it, Bryce, what you done got into this time?" Kandace didn't budge. If Bryce was in trouble he'd be coming to her. Their lab was in the safest place in "the A," deep within an abandoned industrial complex and protected by the best thugs money could buy. They didn't realize that the money they took was probably theirs, but they didn't ask. If the guns didn't scare anybody off, the smell did. Genetic engineering was a funky process, literally.

It was almost time. Kandace struggled out of her chair and staggered to the edge of the pool. The skin was taking shape, its crinkled form rising from the muck. She had no idea what it would be capable of; Bryce fed her the formula this time, so she had to trust him. Thinking of Bryce reminded her he hadn't showed up yet. It had been at least an hour since he called. Bryce was never late. Suddenly her high was gone. She paced, rubbing her hands together.

"He's in real trouble; which means I am, too!"

She ran back to the control board. Thirty more minutes before the skin was ready. She slipped into the back room and changed into a pair of baggy jeans, big shirt, huge jacket and a Braves hat. She was going butch for the next few days until she found out what was going on with Bryce. She reached into the back of the closet and took out a backpack heavy with bills. Further in the back was her FN-P90 pistol. She secured it under her jacket and trotted back to the pool. The skin was as ready as it was going to be. She took it out, her nose crinkling with the smell, then stuffed it in a small plastic bag. It took her fifteen minutes to dump the pool and shut the lab down. Her thugs appeared as she emerged from the steel door.

"Here." She handed them a backpack. "Nobody comes in here unless they're with me. There's another one for you when I get back."

They took the bag and stepped aside. Kandace rambled down the metal staircase and disappeared into the night.

Seven

Leif Thorvaldsen looked out the canopy of the private chopper as it descended on the platform surrounded by stunted evergreens. He hated Albania but understood the logic in locating Vanguard headquarters in the decrepit country. As the poorest country in Europe, the government was easy to persuade and eager to ignore anything that seemed questionable.

He glanced to the rear of the chopper. Two body bags filled the small space. His surviving assassin watched over them, his face showing little emotion. This was a botched operation, two prototypes dead and nothing to show for it. There would have to be modifications.

The chopper landed and was met by a military style truck with no markings. Two men in Vanguard security uniforms ran out to meet them.

"Sir," one said to Leif. "Mr. Constantinedes wishes to see you immediately."

"I'm sure he does," Leif replied. "I brought the bodies back. Take them to the lab for autopsies and genetic analysis."

The man glanced at the remaining assassin. "What about him?"

Leif looked at the surviving assassin and frowned. "He's defective like the others. Dispose of him."

No sooner than he gave the order did the other man extract a handgun from his jacket and shoot the assassin in the head. Leif nodded and went to the truck. Another vehicle emerged from the woods, a Black Hummer with chrome wheels. Leif entered and was taken immediately to Vanguard HQ. The squat gray building hid under a clump of old oak trees surrounded by a triple barbed wire fence. Observation towers rested at fifty foot intervals. The facility resembled a prison, and in a way it was.

After an extensive security check they entered the compound. The Hummer worked around the main building to another building in the rear, a two story structure that resembled a traditional office. Lucy Lundy, Leif's assistant, met him at the door.

"How did it go?"

"Terrible. I need you to pull up the genetic sequencing on my computer. Ask Himmel and Stryker to link up as well."

"Modifications?"

Leif glared at Lucy and she took a step back. She was brilliant, but sometimes she angered him with her naive questions.

"I'll see to it right away, sir," she said and hurried away.

Stephan Constantinedes, a rotund, olive skinned man with fading black hair, waited at his desk when Leif entered his office.

"What the hell, happened, Leif?" he snapped.

Leif sat before answering. "The prototypes failed."

"You failed," Stephen corrected.

Leif ignored the jab. "The prototypes performed well, physically. The problem is mental capacity. We need to increase their decision abilities."

"That will make them more difficult to control."

"If we plan on using them as assassins it's a risk we'll have to take."

Stephan leaned back in his chair. "Maybe we could implant a destruct module."

"We would have to."

"What about the man who escaped?"

Leif frowned. "Apparently he's a man used to trouble. He had a plan, which caught us off guard. I contacted our inside people. Apparently he has a friend that recently resigned from Deep Intel. We've informed the friend of

Bryce's situation. We expect him to lead us to him."

"Don't screw up," Stephan warned.

"We won't. We'll be using normals on this operation."

"I want you there personally."

Leif nodded. "Of course."

Stephan waved him away. Leif held his composure until he was out of the office, then his hands began to smolder. Of course he would go on the operation. He had a score to settle with this Bryce character.

Eight

Bryce sauntered down the cargo ship gangplank, his relaxed gait disguising his fear. His eyes darted back and forth as he searched for anything suspicious. He managed a laugh as his feet touched the concrete. He was home, but not the way he imagined it. He dreamed of stepping out of first class to the admiration of his relatives, a rude boy done good. Instead he was slinking back incognito, hiding from whomever it was trying to kill him. It was just the way his grandma told him it would be.

The docks swarmed with people but the three he expected stood out among the rest. They were dressed simply; blue jeans and t-shirts, each shirt representing a different American baseball team. They wore shades, their dreads spilling from under their baseball caps. The tallest of the three walked up to Bryce and shoved him.

"So, you come back now, huh cousin?" he said.

Bryce shoved him back. "Yeah, me come back."

"What trouble you got?"

"Deep trouble."

His cousin grinned. "I guess you need to go deep, then?"

Bryce nodded. "As deep as I can."

"No problem." The men turned and walked away, Bryce trailing behind. They led him to a battered Toyota extended cab. Bryce climbed into the cab with his cousin. The other two jumped in the truck bed.

"Grandma said you'd come back like this."

"Shut up, Nathan," Bryce barked. "Where you taking me?"

"To the countryside, up into the mountains. I got some Maroon friends who will keep you company for a while."

"I need you do something else for me." Bryce gave Nathan a piece of paper.

"He's a friend of mine. Tell him where I am. When he gets here bring him to me."

Nathan looked at the paper. "I don't know, cousin. If he ain't blood you can't trust him."

"Just call him. He's the only one that can get me out of this."

Nathan shook his head. "You must be in some deep shit."

Bryce rubbed his forehead. "Yeah cousin, I am."

***

The black Lexus SC400 cut across eight lanes and streaked up the West Peachtree exit. Five cars spun as the car zipped down the one-way street the wrong way, then cut over to Spring. The wild drive ended at the parking lot of the *W*, the young valet dropping and shaking his head, his dreads swishing from side to side.

Kandace stepped out of the Lexus in an outfit that labeled her either an actress or a stripper. The valet's humor was shut down by his hormones.

"Damn, girl! How much?"

"Shut the fuck up and park my car," she spat.

The valet shook his head. "Why you got to be like that, K?"

"Because I can. Now park my damn ride."

Kandace strutted through the entrance, happy with the commotion she was causing. After three weeks waiting for Bryce to contact her, she figured he was in too deep. Whoever was looking for him was probably looking for her, too. But she wasn't about to spend the last days of her life hiding in the hood. If she was going out, she was going out right. She jumped on the elevator with a tall young brother sporting an indigo silk suit. She'd seen him a few times in the building, and now he was seeing her. Every inch of her. He looked her up and down a few times and frowned.

"A little over the top, don't you think?"

Kandace grinned. "You criticizing me and you don't even know my name."

"Kandace, I believe," the brother said. "My name is Jaleel."

"Well, Jaleel, I was about to ask you to come by tonight for a drink, but since you think I'm over the top I'm sure you wouldn't want me on top."

Jaleel grinned. "I can always make exceptions."

"I bet you can."

Kandace stepped off the elevator. "Nine o'clock. Take your vitamins."

The first thing Kandace did when she entered the room was check her cell. She didn't know why; maybe from force of habit. There were no calls. Bryce was still M.I.A. The second thing she did was go into the hall bathroom to check on the skin. It hung over the bathtub, swaying with the air conditioning flow.

"I might as well," she said. She stripped off her clothes and donned the skin. It hung loose for a moment then slowly fitted itself tight against her skin. She felt like she had a bag over her head then the feeling dissipated. But the real shock hit her when she looked into the mirror. She was invisible.

"Damn," she whispered. She reached out at the blank mirror and a bolt jumped from her fingers. The glass shattered.

"What the hell?" A wave of fatigue hit her; she was suddenly famished. She peeled the skin off and stumbled naked into the kitchen in a desperate search for food.

"This skin ain't right," she said as she dumped a box of corn flakes onto a plate and ate with her hands.

"This ain't right."

Nine

The cargo plane landed with a thud on the dirt runway, miles away from the tourist destination of Montego Bay. Malik jostled in his seat, but his expression didn't change. He was destroying his life for a friend. He could still see the look on Tisha's face when he announced he was leaving and refused to tell her where he was going, why he was going and how long he would be gone. The words that spewed from her mouth were meant to hurt and they did.

His response was clichéd. "Trust me, baby," he said. Even he didn't believe them when he said them.

The cargo plane taxied to a stop before a tin metal building. Malik gathered his things then walked toward the cabin. The pilot, a scruffy looking, red faced German, looked back at him with a sly smile.

"Should I wait?" he asked.

"No. I have another ride," Malik replied.

"All you have to do is make it worth my while," the man said with a wink.

Malik sneered. "If I see your plane here five minutes after I leave I'll come back and kill you with my bare hands."

He reached into the duffle, took out a stack then tossed it at the pilot.

He went to the rear of the plane and climbed out. The pilot was off the ground and gaining altitude before Malik reached the shed.

"I'll be taking that from you now," someone said.

Three men emerged from behind the shed, guns in their hands. They wore jeans and t-shirts, their heads crowned with dreads. The man in the middle, a short, wide man with bulging muscles, stepped toward them.

"Drop the bag and put your hands behind your back,' he ordered.

"This is a shitty way to treat a friend," Malik remarked as he did what he was told.

"You're Bryce's friend, not mine," the man replied.

One of the other men stepped behind him and tied his hands together. The other came with a blindfold.

"Come on," Malik said. "Really?"

"Shut your mouth," the short man said. The lanky man tied the black fabric over his eyes. They led him to a vehicle then hoisted him in the back. He lay on a bed of straw.

Malik didn't know exactly where he was but he knew which direction they traveled. He was trained to know such things. They headed west following a winding road that climbed into the highlands. They were either headed to Maroon country or somewhere near. Bryce was making a good try at not being found.

The truck halted after two hours. Malik heard the truck door clang.

"C'mon boy," the short man said. "My cousin been waiting for you."

Malik slid to the edge of the truck and was helped to the ground. His hands were freed and his blindfold removed. He stood in the middle of a camp surrounded by marijuana fields. There were four buildings; one serving as some type of office while the others were warehouses for the illicit harvest.

"Man, I ain't never been more happy to see you!"

Bryce ran to him from the office and they bear hugged.

"I didn't think you was gonna come," he said.

"I may have lost my marriage over you," Malik said. "But we're boys, so I'm here."

"Come on in, man," Bryce said. "You must be tired."

The office was neat and orderly despite its remote location. Bryce was a stickler for organization. A man with secrets had to be organized to remember them all.

Bryce sat in a huge chair then lit a blunt.

"I'm in some deep shit, bruh. Some real deep shit."

"So what's new?" Malik replied.

Bryce extended the blunt to Malik but Malik waved him away.

"I figured it must be serious. I've never seen you run from a jealous husband."

Bryce shook his head. "I wish that was all it was. I think it's got something to do with my job."

Malik sat up. "What did you do, Bryce?"

"I was working late and came across something that was interesting. I downloaded it."

Malik was puzzled. "You work for a mom and pop lab. The worst they can do is fire you."

Bryce laughed. "They couldn't even do that. I'm the brains of that place. Fire me and you might as well lock the doors. But we do work for some heavy hitters. I think I might have taken something from one of them and they ain't happy about it."

"What happened, Bryce?"

"I was on my way home and got jumped by some weird shit."

"What's that supposed to mean?"

Bryce took another toke. "It means just that. I don't know if they were men or dogs or what. All I know is they were strong as hell and trying to kill me."

Malik scratched his head. "This has something to do with genetics."

Bryce nodded.

"Look Malik, I figured you could look 'em up, then threaten them so they leave me alone."

Malik cursed the day he let Bryce know his profession.

"It doesn't work that way, Bryce. I can't just terrify folks just because you're in trouble."

Bryce seemed distracted.

"Shit, I need something to drink. Clarence!"

Bryce assumed that was his cousin's name.

"Clarence!"

"Look Bryce, I ..."

Bryce stood up, then stormed by Malik. He was pissed, no doubt about it.

He pushed the door open then turned to face Malik.

"Why you come here? Huh, Malik? You come all this way to tell me you can't help me?"

Malik walked outside.

"Look, man. I'm..."

He saw Bryce's cousin lying behind him in a pool of blood.

"Bryce get back in!"

"What are you talking about, fool?"

Bryce's head exploded into flesh and bones. Malik ran into the building when something hot streaked across his forehead and threw him inside. He hit the ground hard on his back, slamming his head into the floor. His world was heat and stars just before he passed out.

When he finally came back to the world his head throbbed, light flashing in his head with each pulse. He couldn't move; his eyes were open but he could not see. He didn't know how long he lay there until his sight returned. The building was black except for a faint beam of light entering through an open window. He moved his head and pain flashed but he was determined to move. He slid his hands to his sides, then pushed himself upright, his eyes clenched to the pain. He touched his head; the wound had stopped bleeding, the blood caked over the crease.

Malik grabbed the door, then stood. Bryce lay before him, his head destroyed.

Malik opened the door then stumbled to the nearby building. He needed a weapon, something to defend himself. He opened the door, revealing stacks of weed. He searched it from corner to corner but found nothing. From there he went to the next building, searching it as well as he could. He paused, sitting hard as his head spun, making him nauseous. He was about to continue his search when he heard voices.

"Make sure they're dead!" the voice said. "Every last one of them."

He had to escape. If he killed any of these men, whoever sent them would know the job was not complete. He eased to the ground, then crawled across the dirt into the nearby foliage. Malik continued to crawl deeper, flinching every time he heard a shot. They were shooting everyone again to make sure the job was complete.

"Burn it," he heard someone say.

Malik continued to crawl away. The sound of crashing wood was replaced by the roar of a huge fire. As he reached the top of the wooded hill, he dared to look back. The entire compound was in flames. Malik took a hard look at every person involved. He wanted to remember every face so there would be no doubt in his mind when he hunted them down and killed them. One man stood out, tall with sickly white skin, gray eyes and red hair. Malik couldn't be sure, but it looked as if his hands were glowing.

Malik faded into the brush. He had to find out what the hell Bryce did to bring a high level hit down on him. This wasn't underworld; this had the precision of a military operation. The only way he could find out more would be to reopen old contacts. He'd be reneging on a promise, but he had no choice.

"Damn you Bryce," he whispered. "Damn you to hell!"

Ten

Kandace checked her phone again as the RV pulled into *Smit's Garage*. It had been two weeks but still no word from Bryce. He told her to run, but he didn't tell her what the hell she was running from.

"That's your baby," the man standing next to her said. "I told you it was sweet."

Tamarious' hand brushed her ass. She elbowed him hard in the ribs.

"Shit, girl!" he said through his clinched teeth.

"Watch your damn hands," Kandace said. "I paid you, and money is all you gonna get. Unless you make me shoot your ass."

"Aight, aight," Tamarious said as he rubbed his side. "She'll be ready in two weeks."

"Two weeks? Mothafucka you told me one week!"

"I lied," he replied. "Really though, we had some parts come in late. Ain't never done a mod like this one."

"Well, hurry up," Kandace said. "I got places to be."

"Where you trying to go?"

"None of your damn business. Just fix the bus."

"Aight, aight."

Kandace strode back to her car. Her phone played Bryce's song. She pressed the phone to her ear.

"It's about damn time! Where the hell you at?"

There was silence for a moment.

"Who is this?" the unfamiliar voice asked.

Kandace pulled away from the phone, her face crinkled.

"Who is this?" she asked.

"Are you Kandace?" the man asked.

"Look, I don't know what's going on, but if you stole my boy's phone..."

"Shut up and listen to me very carefully. Bryce is dead. The people who killed him are coming after you. If you want to stay alive you'll meet me as soon as possible."

"Bullshit!" Kandace said. "I'm off the grid. I don't need no help."

"Yes, you do. If you don't come to me, I'll come to you."

"Try it," she said. She dropped the phone on the pavement then stomped it to pieces.

Kandace marched back to Tamarious' office.

"Change of plans, I need that bus right now."

Tamarious took off his headphones. "Really? I'm still fleshing out the interior. Wait till you see the bed!"

Kandace tossed the backpack on his desk. "Here's the rest of the money. Give me the keys, now."

Tamarious unzipped the bag, then took out a handful of hundreds.

"I need to count this," he said.

Kandace whipped out her P90. "Give me the goddamn keys!"

"Shit!" Tamarious tossed Kandace the keys.

She scrambled into the cab, started the RV, then barreled out of the parking lot, sideswiping two cars along the way. She didn't give a shit. She was sure Bryce was dead and whoever killed him was coming for her. She would head west; yes, that's what she would do. She had no family out there so no one would know to look for her. As soon as she was settled she'd change her hair, change her clothes then leave the country. She had enough money to lay low for a few years and let things settle, whatever 'things' were. Or so she hoped.

"Fuck you, Bryce," she yelled. "Fuck you!"

Malik watched the RV careen out of Smit's Garage, into the street, then onto Interstate 20. He stuck his phone into his pocket and then pulled down his helmet's visor. He knew the call would cause her to panic and run. He started his Harley then eased into traffic. There was no reason to hurry; the RV was as conspicuous as a cherry in a bowl of milk. As he exited onto the highway he felt his phone vibrate against his thigh. A wave of guilt caused him to shudder. It was either Tisha or Sheryl and he couldn't speak to either one. He'd called Sheryl as soon as he got out of Jamaica and asked her to trace Kandace's phone. When Sheryl asked why, he wouldn't give her any details. Sheryl did it anyway but made him promise to fill her in as soon as he confirmed the threat. Tisha was a deeper matter. Someone tried to kill him, and when they discovered he was still alive they would try to kill him again...or someone he loved. He had to find out who killed Bryce and why before they discovered he was still alive.

He trailed the vehicle for ninety miles before it exited in Oxford,

Alabama. Malik followed it to a hotel parking lot, then watched Kandace scurry into the hotel. He cruised up to the RV; it took him 5 seconds to unlock the door, then climb inside. He settled behind the driver's seat then waited. Moments later the door opened and Kandace climbed in.

"Shit!" she said. "That damn bathroom was nasty as shit!"

Malik reached around the chair, then grabbed Kandace's throat.

"Motha..."

Her voice faded as she fell unconscious. Malik eased her out of the seat, tied her hands and legs, then propped her up in the passenger seat. He found the key in her bag and then hurried outside to his bike. He wiped it clean, then re-entered the van. Before he could get in, two feet smashed into his face. He fell out of the van and his head struck the pavement hard. He lay stunned for a moment, then sat up shaking his head.

"Help! Help!" Kandace screamed. "This motherfucka is trying to kidnap me! Help!"

Malik climbed into the van again, anticipating the same attack. He wasn't disappointed. He dodged the kick then caught Kandace's legs under the knees. He flipped her into the space between the seats. As he sat in the driver's seat he pulled out his gun.

"Stop moving or I'll kill you."

Kandace struggled to sit up.

"Bullshit! You gonna kill me no matter what I do! Just like you killed Bryce."

Malik lowered his gun. "I didn't kill Bryce. If I had come to kill you, you'd be dead already."

"How do I know? I don't know who the fuck you are," Kandace spit back.

"I'm a friend. Someone he knew much longer than you," Malik said. "So what are you to Bryce?" Malik asked.

"A business associate," Kandace said.

"What kind of business?"

Kandace sat up then grinned. "So you his boy and you don't know?"

"No," Malik said. "All I know is that whatever it was made him run to Jamaica and get killed."

Kandace's smirk faded. "Bryce was a thief."

Malik sat silent for a moment, letting the words sink in.

"What kind of thief?"

"Bryce had this kind Robin Hood shit going on. He stole from the rich and gave to himself."

"What rich?"

"Drug dealers mostly."

"So what part did you play in this?"

"I scoped out his hits. I also kept the gear in shape."

Malik looked puzzled. "What gear?"

Kandace hesitated. Malik raised his gun.

"What gear?"

"It's in the back," she said.

"Show me."

Kandace rolled her eyes. "My goddamn legs are tied."

"Hop," Malik said.

Kandace glared at Malik as she stood then hopped to the rear of the RV.

"In there," she said, gesturing with her head. "He calls it *Ghost*."

Malik shoved her to the floor, then opened the door. A grin came to his face as he looked inside the room.

"A stealth suit," he said.

"What you know about that?" Kandace said.

"More than you realize," he answered. The agency was testing prototypes. Apparently Bryce figured it out. Which was probably why he was killed.

"So, who killed him?" Kandace said. "I figured one of the drug boys figured things out."

Malik stepped into the room to inspect the suit.

"It wasn't a drug hit," Malik replied. "Too professional. I'll bet money it had something to do with this suit. Bryce had to steal some deep tech to make this. Whoever he stole it from killed him. And now they're looking for you."

"You ain't them?" Kandace said.

Malik came out of the room with the suit.

"No. Like I said, Bryce was my friend. I'm going to find out who did this and why."

"And what about me?"

"I don't know."

Malik stepped back into the room.

"Don't go anywhere," he said.

"Fuck you," Kandace replied.

Malik closed the door, then took off his clothes. He and Bryce were about the same build so the suit slipped on easily. There was mesh where his eyes and nose were located which allowed for easy breathing. He looked into the mirror; the suit's construction reflected light in a way that made him invisible, at least visually. Malik was about to take off the suit when he felt a slick secretion flow between the suit and his skin. It was immediately followed by the sensation of a million tiny needles pricking his flesh. He hurriedly unzipped the suit and began taking it off. By the time he was done, he was exhausted and bleeding all over. He wiped himself off before dressing, then opening the door.

Kandace grinned. "You put it on, didn't you?"

Malik nodded.

"Felt like it was eating you?"

Malik shook his head. "Bio-attachment. This is some real advanced tech. I wonder where Bryce got it?"

"From work," Kandace said. "He called one day, excited about some modification he wanted to make. Gave me the formulation."

"So, you're a scientist?"

Kandace grinned. "A biologist, to be exact. Masters in Microbiology. Don't let all this fool you."

Malik looked over Kandace with new respect. He'd let his prejudices get in the way. He thought, at the least, Kandace was Bryce's lookout, at the most, another one of his conquests. However there were more pertinent questions. Why was Gentech developing this type of tech? Most importantly, who were they developing it for?

"I need to make a call," he said. He took out his phone and dialed Sheryl. To Malik's surprise she answered him immediately.

"Malik, get off this line," Sheryl said. "Your friend was in some real deep shit. Get another phone and call Moses."

The line went dead. A tightness formed in Malik's stomach. What he feared was probably true.

He untied Kandace. She immediately tried to hit him; he blocked the blow, then wrapped her in a painful strangle hold.

"Listen to me carefully," he said. "Both of our lives are in extreme danger. If you want to survive you'll stay with me until I figure this all out. If not, I'll let you go and walk away. Do you understand?"

Kandace nodded her head. Malik let her go and she rubbed her neck.

"You're not going to kill me?" she asked.

"No," Malik said. "Bryce dragged us both into this in his own selfish way."

"So what do we do?" Kandace said.

"We follow your plan. We head west until I hear from my contact."

Kandace climbed into the driver's seat. Malik took the passenger's seat, tucking his gun in his holster as he sat. Kandace started the RV then drove to the I-20 exit. As they entered the highway, Malik tried to understand how this was happening. The life he planned was now on hold until he could figure out this mystery. He was on assignment now; he slowly blocked Tisha and the girls out of his mind. There was no future now, only the mission. He looked at Kandace.

"So tell me about Ghost," he said.

CAPES AT THE END OF THE WORLD
Rorie Still

I'm sitting on top of the world,
sitting on top of the world,
sitting on top of the world.
And I don't know what to do.
They didn't figure out a way,
to remove the bomb or stop it from exploding.
We have 48 hours.
What do you do when your job is to save the world
and you can't?
At what point does it seem foolish
to be a hero?
We're all going to die anyway;
whom am I trying to fool?

Somebody save me!
What do you do when you have an endless night?
Not one where the stars shine bright,
But your nightlight is broken and you're drowning in shadows?
What do you do when your twinkling star has burnt out and died?
What if you were that star?

Why didn't I stop them from setting the bomb?
Why didn't I stop the bomb?
Why can't I stop it now?
I just *can't*.
No one can.

We are all going to die.
Seriously, like all of us,
I'm a superhero,
And this is the end of the world.
With my purpose gone,
what is my worth?
Someone once asked me:
"What would the end of the world feel like?"
Well, when your job is to save the world---
This end of the world mess;
This crap feels a little personal

I need a oneness
Because right now my mind is split to death, split to grips.
I just watched arson go down
It was an empty barn that the girl set on fire,
But it was still a *crime*.
Yet
I felt something close to *nothing*.
My guilt was buried deep
I need to get loose Woman!
Woman, if thou art loosed?
Can I follow thee?
Free me from this pit of agony

I'm sorry to be kvetching for my last two days on Earth.
It's supposed to not just be about me
But like I said,
This crap is starting to feel *really*
Personal
Like it's-all-my-fault-Personal,
Like God-kicked-me-out-the-wrong-side-of-the-bed
And-then-dragged-me-down-a-flight-of-stairs-Personal.

I thought about starting to drink after I got the news about the bomb.
I was in Tokyo then.
Blabber Buddy was *supposed* to have the bomb thing.
However,
she was only one person.
She couldn't take the guilt.

I wonder why I can?
My guilt is not direct guilt;
maybe that is where I can find some solace---
(Lie)
if I don't find it at the bottom of a bottle first.

But
That would be too easy;
so cliché and pointless.
Nevertheless, I do finish
my first and only drink.
Hey, who said I could have a little sway as I run,
because that is what I do---
I run!

Personal life
Personal crap
It does not matter
I should have stopped it
I doesn't matter that the fault
"technically" lies with Buddy
I'm a *speedster*
I've stopped so many things
Why, when it mattered,
Didn't it take?
Why wasn't I a HERO
When I *needed* to be one?

I stroll the streets,
well, strolling for me.
I've been to so many places
and never really saw them.
I always had somewhere
I had to be:
London
Beijing
Houston
Have you heard of Johannesburg?
Yeah, I saved it from that canaried Large Largo
with a sharp NY accent and an attitudinal problem.

Not now.
I can see it *all*
because it does not matter.

So I go see Paris
The Eiffel Tower looks like it's crying
as the rain runs down its eyes and its legs.
The metal tower sighs in the wind,
both carrying an inexplicable burden
and relieved of one.
It is free
It no longer has to stand for France
representing its people.
Standing for France's creativity, freedom, and its life---
All in one.
It's just a lonely, hollow pole.
Liberation lies in its emptiness.
I know the feeling;
I go.

I sit besides the gargantuan glass pyramid, adjacent to the Louvre.
For clarity's sake, I stare at it;
I hope it will give me
Some answers,
But it remains
Silent.
The silence aches with minutes I don't have left,
The minutes I could have given to the Earth
If only I had been faster!

I stroll
I blaze
I'm at Mount Kilimanjaro
It's *big!*
The swell of it dwarfing me as I stare up at it from the bottom.
I run up
like Mercury to lightning
I rocket up a wall to the sky,
landing on the floor beneath it.
The top of the mountain.

Though the end of the world
Mt. Kibo still has nothing to say,
Though it could at least mumble
a prayer of fiery possibility,
but isn't everything busy
at a crossroads
facing east, giving gospel while humming,
chanting useless syllables,
hoping for everything,
saying nothing?

I yell at Kibo to say
Something!
Anything!
as the cool clouds blow across my face,
Choking me.
Still, *nothing.*
No one home in the homeland;
I leave for home

Philadelphia has never been this quiet.
Philadelphia,
has NEVER been this quiet.
I love/hate it.
It is the sound of silence
before the blaring of bells at a funeral.
So I mourn
and I prepare to say the world's eulogy
In the middle of City Line. It will read with sparks and kickback:
two bullets piercing a temple.
A period at the end of a LONG sentence.

What does the end of the world feel like?
It feels *totally* personal
if *you* were supposed to stop it.
Buddy *thought* she was the one
The Lady Who *Didn't Live*
The Lady of silver wand and swifter feet
LIES

Nope it wasn't them
It was *me*
But I was *late*
Because I stopped to help someone else
Someone I *knew*
Ha! Wow!
What did it matter?
Did it ever matter that we fought back?
Fought back against the flames that
Repeatedly scorched our community?
Does it matter that is why *I* fight/fought
To avenge all the Black and Brown
Bodies that were untimely laid down
That at my core
I fought and ran to raise them up
And doing so raised us all up?
Did it matter that I kept us safe,
Kept the world safe, <u>ALIVE</u>
To keep us ALL safe?
WELL IT FEELS THAT IT DOESN'T MATTER AT ALL,
AT ALL!
Because we're here
Because I didn't
Because I *couldn't*.

I tap the nozzle against my temple,
a rhythm I have learned tonight.
I cock my apology.
A trash can lid clangs against the ground.
I turn to see an elderly woman struggling for her ugly purse with a huge young man.
Whack!
He cracks her across the face!
She falls but doesn't let go of the strap.
It's just across the street
But I'll be too late,
Making it worse
And I was just
about to give my apology
Yet...

Clapping out of the shadows
Two portly young men
gallop into sight
One Black
One White
The Black boy is shorter and smaller
than the White one,
but the Black boy is pretty big.
So that is saying something
about the size of the White boy.
Actually their size stopped mattering
when I notice they don't have legs,
well, human legs,
just miniature horse legs.
This makes the mugger pause
long enough to laugh
and laugh
and laugh
The older woman faints from surprise,
letting go of the purse.
The mugger stops laughing,
a pause in his breath.
That one pause is all the boys need.

The big one pulls the older lady out of the way
as fast as his little horse legs can carry him.
The other one proceeds to kick the guts loose in the mugger.
Seriously,
This kid has viciousness to his blows
that feels unfamiliar even to him,
judging by the confusion on his face
mixed with a sick stew of rage

The mugger goes down
Then he releases the purse.
The Black boy kicks him with his tiny horse legs once more.
He is going for a second stroke when the big White boy holds him back,
then pulls him into a hug that the Black boy pretends to not want
He tries to push him away, but his friend holds on.
He doesn't try to push him a second time.

The boys rush back, after a few minutes, to tend to the grandmother on the ground.
The White boy picks her up off the ground.
The Black boy reaches down and grabs her ugly bag.
But before they leave
the boys look
at each other;
I can't hear what they say.
But their lips make it plain:
"We're heroes, no matter what the hour of day, no matter the number of them."

Racing to the equally quiet part of North Philly,
next to a doll museum
on Broad Street.
I have the same quiet inside me again.
No false Kibo in my chest,
trying to light a destroyed furnace.
I try to apologize to humanity again.
However, I see the dang groundhog's shadow.
The same science happens again,
except this time
it is two male robbers and a much younger lady.
She looks scared but isn't giving up her lunch money yet.
The robbers also have a tool of apology,
but they aren't trying to apologize.
I wait forever for fate to intervene
as it had before.
Someone who wouldn't mess up this little scene
and I can keep my train running early
to its final destination.

But oh!
Someone calls action too soon!
The young lady moves forward.
Bang!
It hits her in the shoulder.
She goes down.
Crap!
My fist crosses the first mugger's face

before I realize I've dropped *my* gun.
My sway makes me stumble a little and the second guy
gets in a couple of good licks.
I licked my bloody lip and looked at him
Smiling,
Smiling at the end of the world

Copper can function like coffee.
I take them both down in less than four seconds.
Though the young lady is about my size,
and my upper body strength
isn't what it used to be,
because I had stopped feeding my fervent metabolism about five hours ago,
I pick her up
and run for the nearest emergency room.
Only one is open.

Sirens are going off in my head.
The closest one is *across* the city;
I am thankful for the punch of adrenaline
as I speed across Philly.
I slide to a stop on the dirty floor of the *Hospital of Philadelphia.*
The doctors are watching television,
even as the young lady leaks on me.
I clear my throat.
They turn and look.
Some look like they want to help
but just don't see the point.
The doctors actually turn back to the television.
In horror, I see my reflection
mere seconds before
I scream at them
With all the fury of
an ancient Kibo
Reversing time.
Exploding in released fury.

I don't know what I said to them
but the doctors hop to,
wheeling the bleeding lady away from me.

One doctor briefly turns back to me,
eyes shining:
"Thank you, for saving her."
Striped in the woman's blood
I sit down in a hard plastic chair.
I'm not all better;
we have three hours left

On the forgotten television
Is some movie about Paris.
It was raining there, too.
Wait!
It isn't a movie.
It is a news report.
Someone lit the tower
and that nameless person had planted a flag that read
"Viva la vie, the world."
The cops were coming for her,
so she sat smiling.
Well, the tower isn't empty
Anymore.

I put my head in my hands.
I want the young lady to *live;*
She deserved to...
She had fought
And I...
I had fought for her.

During the 2016 #tonyawards
Frank Langella, upon accepting the award for LEADING ACTOR IN A PLAY,
spoke on the #pulse nightclub shooting.
He said, "When something bad happens, we have three choices:
We can let it define us,
We let it destroy us,
Or we let it strengthen us."
With this, on that night after that bad thing,
Hope didn't fly out the box.
It lit a fire and warmed the room.
It warmed the world.

Using copper-colored fingers
I bang my pockets for change.
I don't really have time to
Worry about the blood.
Zipping to the nearest snack machine
I use all my change;
buy all the snacks.
I need to be fueled
Because
I have at least three hours left.

Even the end of the world
doesn't have to be
the end of
Everything.

WHERE MONSTERS ROAM
Dennis R. Upkins

It had not been the best week. For starters, my car was still stuck in the shop. By no means am I a mechanic but even I knew it didn't take five days to replace a timing belt. Regardless, I was sentenced to taking the bus and being surrounded by the kind of element one usually avoids. A few rows ahead, some homeless drunk snored in his seat. Sadly, he wasn't even the worst of the passengers. To my right, some little Mexican girl fidgeted while her mother combed her hair. Christ, and we wonder why this country is in the shape it is in. Rolling my eyes at the pair of illegals, I resumed cleaning out my purse and chatting on my cell. As I explained to Lesley, my car – and border jumpers – was the least of my problems at the moment.

"I'm completely over the situation," I said. "I know I raised her right. Hell, part of the reason I even moved us to Chattanooga was to make sure she was in the right environment. This is on her."

"I can only imagine what you're going through, Nora," Lesley said. "These homosexuals won't stop until they've brainwashed all our children. They already control the media. Have you heard from Ginny?"

"No," I said. "Last time I spoke to her, I laid down the law. I told her that lifestyle would not be allowed under my roof. That's when she decided she wanted to go live with the deadbeat."

"Oh, I bet Hank is just loving this," Lesley hissed.

"You should've heard him," I said. "So damn smug. He just relished telling me how he was going to sue for full custody."

I felt an uneasy feeling I was being watched. Behind me sat a black man who appeared to be in his mid twenties. His brooding gaze alternated between me and the iPhone he texted on. Dressed in a blazer, sweater, cargo jeans and riding the bus, his chosen profession couldn't be more obvious.

"I have got to get my car back," I continued. "I never realized how many lowlifes use public transportation."

The black passenger's eyes narrowed. He clearly didn't appreciate being called out. Served him right for eavesdropping. I met his scowl with a smirk and returned to my conversation.

"You be careful, Nora," Lesley said. "You heard on the news about those dead bodies they've been finding downtown."

"Oh don't remind me," I said. "Wild dogs or something. Listen, I'm coming up on my stop. I'll talk to you later."

***

It's amazing how alert your senses are when you're on a deserted street. My breathing, the clanking of my high heels, the slight breeze and the occasional buzz from the overhead street lamps were all blaring. I was the only soul out at this hour, or so I thought. I glanced back and spotted another figure in the distance. It was the drug dealer on the bus. He must've followed me. No doubt looking for payback for his perceived slight. Damn it. I clenched my purse and quickened my pace. He increased his stride as well. He was hell bent on catching me. I wasn't going to let him.

"Miss!" he yelled from a distance. "Hey Miss!"

I dashed right and ducked into an alley. It would be a dead end, given the luck I was having this week. Two men leaned against a wall. Their pasty skin practically glowed in the dim backstreet. The first man was wiry and possessed spiky auburn hair. The second man was far more imposing. With a hefty frame and nearly seven feet tall, he was practically a mountain.

"What's up sweet thing?" the larger man asked.

"I need your help," I cried. "This black guy is after me!"

"Don't worry," said the smaller man. "We won't let nothing happen."

The larger man sneered, "He's not gonna get the chance."

Their faces morphed. Ridges protruded, their eyes shifted to a jaundiced shade. They growled and brandished their fangs. I had seen enough movies to know what they were but my mind wouldn't allow me to believe it. While I prayed it was panic and a trick of the light, deep down I knew better.

"She looks tasty, Morris," the smaller one said.

"Lars, I was thinking the same thing," Morris sneered. "We should take our time with this one."

I shrieked.

"I love it when they run," Lars squealed.

I nearly tripped twice in my heels as I scrambled to escape. I was too scared to look over my shoulder. I reached the edge of the alley when the black man appeared and blocked my path. His scowl was still present. He stared past me. His expression never shifted. No fear, no surprise, yet he clearly saw what I saw. That's when it hit me. He wasn't shocked because he was in on it. He had lured me here to be murdered by those...those..I still couldn't bring myself to say it. Seconds passed and I realized that neither side advanced. Morris and Lars snarled. Fangs and claws were ready. But they weren't staring at me. Their attention was focused on the man behind me.

"Brecken!" Lars growled.

The black man glanced at me, "Get out of the way!"

He shoved me into a stack of garbage bags and charged at the two men. Brecken dodged a swipe from Lars' claws and landed a right cross. He flicked his wrist and an invisible force hurled the vampire across the alley. A blue dumpster slid and pinned the pasty predator against a brick wall. My unlikely savior was some kind of...wizard?

Morris whipped behind Brecken with inhuman speed and delivered a vicious backhand. The large vampire belted the wizard in the stomach and hoisted him over his head. Brecken twisted himself from Morris' grip and landed nimbly on the ground. He kicked the vampire's legs from underneath him and Morris crashed on his back. Before the vampire could recover,

Brecken removed a stake from underneath his blazer and plunged it into the demon's chest.

Morris released a guttural cry seconds before he disintegrated into a pile of ash.

"Son of a bitch!" Lars yelled. He pushed himself free from the dumpster. Before he could pounce, the wizard discharged a golden beam of light from his fist.

Lars screamed in agony before he was reduced to ashes as well.

Lying in a pile of trash, I remained stiff. My heart raced. I barely caught my breath.

My savior, on the other hand, casually removed a pair of glasses from his blazer and put them on. He surveyed the area to make sure all was clear.

"Brecken to Ebony," he said, pressing a tiny device in his right ear. "Targets have been neutralized. I'll be in shortly. Brecken out." He adjusted his glasses. "This is the last time I go hunting when my bike is in the shop," he said. "Hopefully this is the last time I visit this godforsaken town. You should get home, Nora."

My eyes widened in shock, "How do you know my name?"

He tossed my wallet next to me. "You left that on the bus. That's why I was trying to stop you."

"Were those..."

"Yes. Been hunting those two all week. They've been racking up quite the body count all around town, or rather had been."

"What are you?"

"Not a lowlife."

"I thought..."

"Oh, I know exactly what you thought," he said evenly. "You made yourself loud and clear on the bus. And you wonder why your daughter wants nothing to do with you."

"Excuse me?"

"You know, most gay kids turn out to be pretty awesome. We often go on to do some amazing things. A few of us become wizards and battle demons. Even though it occasionally means saving the lives of other monsters."

"You have no right talking to me that way," I snapped. "Just where do you get..."

Brecken had vanished. There was no sign of him anywhere. I would've almost thought I imagined the whole thing if it wasn't for the strewn dumpster, the two mounds of ashes and my soiled clothes. It had not been the best week, though suddenly all of my problems didn't seem to matter. With broken high heels in hand and reeking of garbage, I limped for home.

BLUE SPARK vs. THE GENTLE GIANTESS
S. J. Fujimoto

The bicep rose slowly, small but solid and tough. Fingers clenched, tensing the arm further and forcing the bicep to rise. Having reached the limits of what the body could do naturally, the nanomachines powered up and rushed in. Blue light shined under the skin, energy rushing through veins. The arm quivered, creaking as the bicep bulged out dramatically, rising like an ebony mountain. The rest of the arm followed, muscles expanding like balloons, electric blue veins pumping intense buzzing power. Every muscle was swelling, arcs of electricity dancing up and down the fantastic body.

"Aw *yeah...*"

No matter how many times Susan Wright enlarged her muscles it still amazed her. Standing before a full-length mirror in a gray sports bra and black trunks, the 23-year-old SCAR agent willed her body into going from athletically slim to utterly ripped in seconds. Heart pounding and sweat beading on her forehead, the transformation ended and she admired her enhanced figure. All that was missing was her costume.

"*Suit On!*" she commanded and lit up with bright blue light. The nanomachines spun through her system, weaving around her body. When the light faded, Susan stood tall and proud in an electric blue costume that showed off her musculature, a power symbol in white emblazoned on her ample chest. A blue mask covered her eyes and cheeks while her hair and eyes turned the same color, her once neat hair now wild and spiky.

Flexing her arms, she flashed a dazzling white grin. "Now *this* is a superheroine," she said.

"Very impressive, Wright," said Colonel Wood. Susan glimpsed her superior approaching in the mirror and turned to face her with a salute. Wood returned the gesture smartly.

Colonel Nia Wood was a short but sturdily-built middle-aged Black British, looking sharp in her blue uniform with the official badge on her left shoulder, a white jagged lightning bolt in a black circle with SCAR emblazoned below. She looked somewhat youthful for her rank but boasted several battle scars across her face.

"Colonel."

Wood inspected Susan. "It's all rather strange to me, but if your 'superheroics' bring in more funding and recruits for SCAR then I'm on board with it," she said.

Susan grinned and planted her hands on her steely hips. "Hey, what can I say? The public notices when a super-powered sister in a cool costume comes charging in to stop supremum bad guys."

"Especially when those suprema are also costumed," said Wood. The colonel allowed herself a smirk. "When I founded SCAR, the UN treated us as a bit of a joke, but now that we're seeing 'super criminals' plundering bank vaults, they understand I was right all along."

She turned to leave. "Keep up the good work, Corporal Wright. Or should I say Blue Spark?"

Flexing her arms for the mirror again, Susan felt a sudden rush of energy and sparkled with blue electricity. She looked fabulous, invincible even. No wonder the media ate her up whenever she put in an appearance as Blue Spark. Speaking of which...

Susan dug her smartphone from her gym bag and opened *AllGallery* in the Internet browser, her favorite online art community. As usual for the Maidens of Muscle group, the updates focused mostly on fanart to Blue Spark. It was a little surreal to see herself in all kinds of styles, from photorealistic paintings to colorful comic book art. In all of them, the Blue Spark was either posing coolly or stopping bad guys. Some made her even more muscular, and a few daring ones depicted her in varying degrees of undress; heated debates raged across the Web on the appropriateness of this. It was kind of freaky but Susan figured she was already a sex symbol to them, and she couldn't really complain since the media often criticized how "unfeminine" her muscles looked and that she would look better slimmed down. Forget that; she was proud of her muscles and loved the fandom that appreciated her.

She tapped the next thumbnail and the screen filled with a lurid digital 3D image of her breaking a burly boxer's spine across her knee, his eyes bulging grotesquely, his mouth twisted into an agonized scream. She was modeled with a sadistic grin as she killed the man. Susan blinked; disquieted by the joy her depiction seemed to get out of the brutal beat down. It was a very skillful work too, which made it worse. The artist had put a lot of effort into it, putting in details like graffiti on an alley wall in the background and trash-filled puddles at her feet. A sordidness practically oozed from the screen, and Susan had to grimace. Sometimes killing was unavoidable but she never *enjoyed* the act and a significant threat was needed before she would even consider lethal force as an option.

Morbidly curious, she checked the comments.

Love her expression here. Classic!

Now THAT'S how a woman shows whos boss!

HOTNESS!!!

Dude, your my favorite artist EVAR

"OK, not what I was expecting..." she muttered. Searching related pictures, she found similar works where she was crushing men to death between her legs or punching them hard enough to shatter ribs. Eroticized killing and injuring done in loving detail, and she was at the center of it. Ugh...

One picture she stumbled upon was different, if still objectionable. An extra buff and powerful version of Blue Spark stood triumphantly glowing on a sunny beach, towering over a trio of cowering men bathed in the same glow. Two were extremely skinny and draped in oversized fitness outfits. The third was much more muscular but only on his left side; he was staring in shock as his right arm appeared to wither away to skin and bones. The artist, TheDrainiac, had written about the picture:

Hey guys! Here's another strength-drain pic, this time with real life superheroine Blue Spark! These jocks thought they could hit on her but she taught them a lesson they'll NEVER forget!

Susan sighed. While she had a number of powers, several of which were still unknown to her, she doubted she had anything like strength draining, and even if she did, she wouldn't be comfortable with using it no matter how much she liked to expand her muscles; draining someone's strength, even a criminal's, simply wasn't moral.

The comments didn't find anything wrong with it though.

And our favorite jungle goddess gets even BIGGER!

I love the size difference so funny

More bluespark please

Jungle goddess? Oh god, she had racist fetishists drooling over her.

Susan was about to close her browser in disgust when her eye fell on one last comment:

I'm literally queasy seeing this garbage. I hate strength-drain enough when it's done with fictional characters, but to drag the good name of Blue Spark into this is unforgivable. How dare you degrade this woman, who uses her incredible strength and power to defend the innocent, for the sake of your fetish "art"? If I could I would delete every piece of foul trash you posted and smash your computer so you'd never stink up this site again. I'm serious.

Susan raised an amused eyebrow. "Whoa man. Talk about going too far in the opposite direction." The username of the poster was TGG09. Checking TGG09's gallery, Susan found a lot of sweet digital art of a hugely muscled blond white woman giving flowers and cuddling gently with smaller men. TGG09's journal was anything but sweet though, consisting of endless angry rants about how cruel the world was, frequently linking to trashy tabloid news articles on murder. The art was really quite nice after all the S&M, but the artist needed a hug.

Susan closed the browser with some relief and soon was taking a hot shower. Slimming back down to her normal size, she changed into her blue SCAR uniform and beret and prepared for the rest of her day. Maybe it was time to post a gentle request to her fans to not draw her killing people.

***

The stylus moved down the tablet perfectly, as if Doug's hand was guided by an unseen force. Simple lines merged together to form the outline of his next scene. It was one of those exquisite moments where his art was the only thing in existence; he was merely the vessel for the art, the tool of its creation, something every artistic being entered while in the midst of a creative day.

Suddenly Doug's zone came crashing around him, his stylus slipping and running a long line right through the center of the picture, as what sounded like a cannonball slammed into his living room. Clutching his narrow chest in shock, Doug cautiously left his office and peeked into the living room. His apartment door had been torn off the hinges and hurled into the kitchen. He gaped stupidly at the sight, trying to come up with an explanation for what he was looking at, when a huge figure stepped from the kitchen. Doug stared at the giant and his knees went weak, stumbling back a step.

It was a woman, one whose shoulders were level to his head, and Doug wasn't a short man. Her hair was a pale blond and her eyes a steel gray. She wore a brown LCPD uniform that was tight on her even though it was larger than the largest men's size. She was beyond any bodybuilder for sheer vastness of muscle, the image of his most wild fantasies come to life.

Doug raised his trembling hands, hardly believing what he was seeing was real. "M-ms....?"

She looked down at him with utter contempt, disgust even. "So you're Doug Loew," she sneered.

"You...know my work?" he managed to stammer.

"Unfortunately," the woman spat. She was so muscular that her frame blocked the doorway, but Doug could hear people leaving their apartments to see what was going on. She approached him slowly, her footsteps shaking small objects around the apartment.

Doug backed away down the corridor, his awe beginning to turn into fear. "Hey! Hey, wait...!"

He backed up into the office. She ducked to enter and blocked the door. Slowly, deliberately, she cracked her knuckles. Doug paled as he began to contemplate that this was his final night alive.

With sudden savage fury she grasped his computer's CPU and crumpled it in one hand like a used tissue. Smoke and sparks popped from the ruined machine and Doug threw his hands over his face protectively, watching through his fingers in stunned horror.

She tore the monitor off and smashed it against the wall, then knocked his tablet to the floor and flattened it under her bootheel. Thousands of dollars worth of computer and art equipment gone in seconds. Doug let out a despairing sob as she grabbed the front of his T-shirt with a fist almost the size of his head and raised him to her eye level. He tried to beg for his life but couldn't find the words.

"Quit your whining!" she ordered. "I'm not gonna kill you! I'm just gonna throw your ass in my own little prison. It's more than you deserve for making the world an uglier place!"

Carrying him with a surprisingly light touch, she smashed the window open and punched a good section of the wall out too. Some of the curious tenants and a concerned police officer came into the office in time to catch the woman getting ready to leave, Doug tucked under her massive arm. "Don't worry!" she bellowed at the frightened tenants. "There's a new heroine in town to keep you safe, the Gentle Giantess!"

She launched herself from the hole, her mighty leap carrying her far into the night-shrouded city, Doug screaming all the while.

***

Her uniform neatly pressed, Susan strolled into the meeting hall for the superpowered agents. As usual, it was just her and Wood. One day soon, hopefully, they would have more people interested in using superpowers for protecting the world.

"Good morning, Wright," said Wood, reading a tablet. As always she wore heavy brown gloves. They really stood out when she held her tablet.

"Good morning, ma'am." Susan got a plate with scrambled eggs, sausages, and orange slices, taking a seat across from Wood.

"Check the news yet?" Wood asked.

"No ma'am."

Wood slid the tablet toward her. "Take a gander. Looks like we have an assignment for you."

"Cool." Susan peered at the article, chewing her sausages. There was a photo of a white male with neatly trimmed brown hair, a beard, and a mustache, his plastic glasses almost comically oversized and with a big goofy grin.

ANIMATOR KIDNAPPED BY NEW SUPREMUM

Doug Loew, 35, was carried away into the night by an unknown supremum attacker.

Susan frowned as she read the rest. "'The Gentle Giantess', huh?" It looked like yet another case of a rogue supremum. It seemed getting superpowers out of nowhere caused people to go a little wild. She moved to the eyewitness descriptions. An extremely muscular woman? Great; the only other buff woman out there and she's a kidnapper. The public's view of muscular women was bad enough already; Susan really didn't need this.

"Witnesses say she claimed to be a super*heroine*, but her actions don't point to that," Wood commented.

"Might be a vigilante," suggested Susan. "The witnesses and coworkers say Loew's an upstanding guy, but it's possible he wronged her and when she became a supremum she saw her chance to avenge herself."

Wood nodded. "She made a point to destroy his computer and tablet. What do you make of that?"

Susan considered it. "Maybe he had kiddie porn or nude photos of her and she wanted to destroy it; but if he did, she just destroyed the evidence. Wouldn't she rather have him turned over to law enforcement?"

"Or he knew something about her that she didn't want to get out." Wood paused and frowned, steepling her fingers under her chin. "Do you recall there was another kidnapping involving an assailant with super strength a little earlier?"

"Oh yeah," said Susan, snapping her fingers. "That producer guy who vanished and had a huge hole torn into his house."

"Ed David," Wood said as she switched to a news article about the David story. "Big time sitcom producer. Someone extremely strong tore his house apart and abducted him. Still working on the case, but if the kidnapper was also this Giantess then we might be able to get some insight into her."

"A sitcom producer and an animator..." Susan thought about it but drew a blank. It didn't make sense; who would want to kidnap these two? David's kidnapping was logical since he was wealthy and could be ransomed, but Loew was just an ordinary guy from what they could tell. And that was assuming they were captured by the same person; super strength wasn't too unusual amongst suprema.

Wood stood up and brushed her uniform off. "Our people are investigating. Go take a look at it."

"Can do! *Suit On!*"

Electricity crackled and Susan transformed into Blue Spark. She flashed a cocky smile. "I'll go assist the investigators in case the cops are harassing them. Gimme a call if there are any emergencies nearby that need solving."

***

The Las Costas Police Department tended to be reluctant to work with SCAR – a United Nations organization that employed a black woman with superpowers – so sometimes they needed some persuasion to cooperate. Blue Spark just stood in Loew's ruined office, massive arms folded, as SCAR investigators and cops looked for clues and questioned the other tenants. She stayed quiet and her enhanced hearing picked up on the conversations around her. The cops paid her a wide berth but they quietly shared their findings with SCAR.

One cop, a wiry white guy, stumbled past her. She glimpsed his face for only a second, but it was enough to see his eyes narrow, his lips curl just a little. Her eyes narrowed back. Even if he couldn't do anything to her, the guy brought back bad memories.

A SCAR investigator, Hank Ramírez, leafed through a portfolio of animations cels. Blue walked over to take a quick look with him. Not much to see, just various cutesy animal characters.

"Hey, I know these guys," Hank chuckled. "My kids watch some of these shows."

Some of them were so wacky that Blue had to smile. This Loew guy was really good. Hopefully he was all right.

Hank flipped to the last cel and paused, his brow furrowing. "OK," he said, "either there was a really big mix-up or Loew was making more than cartoons."

He pulled out a picture tucked behind the last cel and handed it to Blue. Her eyes widened in astonishment. It was the *AllGallery* illustration of her draining strength from the beach guys.

***

Doug squinted at his surroundings. He was only able to tell it was day by the tiny amount of light that made it through boarded up windows too high for him to reach. Over to the side, his fellow prisoner sat slumped in a beat up folding lawn chair, rubbing his balding head.

He guessed they were in an abandoned warehouse, probably near a dock based on the sea air he sometimes got a whiff of. They had been locked in what looked like an office, some cots, chairs, and even a *Porta-Potty* provided for them. He paced around, his stomach growling. He felt grimy and needed a shower after sleeping in his clothes. He supposed he had a lot to be thankful for though; it could be a lot worse.

Ed sighed and looked blearily at him. The producer was an older guy with a lot of white in his mustache, beard, and hair. He wore a rumpled orange Hawaiian shirt and jeans. He was there when the Giantess locked Doug in the night before. Doug had seen the story of Ed's kidnapping a few days earlier on TV, and he had to wonder what that maniac wanted to do to them.

The lock clicked and the door swung open, the Giantess filling the frame with her massive bulk. She ducked to enter, holding a pair of greasy brown paper bags. The smell of hamburgers and fries hit Doug's nose and his hunger suddenly became a yawning abyss. He needed food *now*.

She tossed the bags to the floor with a sneer. "Got you some lunch," she muttered. "I hope you're not vegetarian."

"No ma'am," Doug said quietly as he took one of the bags and opened it. He looked up at the Giantess again and even though she had kidnapped him, he couldn't help but admire the towering blond Valkyrie. She could have a steady career if she role-played this kind of domineering criminal for guys like him rather than actually being one.

Ed stood up, an expression of terrified awe on his face. "L-look," he stammered, "I've got a lot of money. I've got connections. I can make you a star! Just let us go!"

She shot him a furious glare and Ed fell silent, backing away. Doug winced, his eyes darting between them.

"Keep your filthy money," the Giantess growled. "Ed David, you are as guilty as any criminal for the trash you peddle."

"I—*what?*" Ed retreated behind his little chair but the Giantess made no move toward him.

The Giantess folded her arms. "The TV series you produce celebrates cruelty and cynicism, teaching viewers that cancer patients are funny and that women hitting men is acceptable."

Ed gaped at her, so bewildered that he forgot his fear. Doug was astonished too. All this to complain about TV shows?

"Lady," Ed sputtered, "I produce *comedies*. Don't you...don't you know it's not real?"

The Giantess stiffened, her mouth twitching, her gray eyes narrowing to slits. Doug shrank back, terrified he was about to see a man beaten to death. Fear returned to Ed as the Giantess slowly approached him, her arms held stiffly at her sides.

"Listen you," she whispered. "What you do is portray the most morally indefensible and evil actions as harmless entertainment. The radical feminist garbage you put out wallows in double standards. A man hitting a woman? Evil. A woman hitting a man? Funny, empowering, even sexy. You love to show men as gross losers utterly beneath women, that women can bully men with no repercussions."

The accusations struck Doug. In addition to the sheer hypocrisy, the choice of words was horribly familiar.

She turned to him next. "And you, Doug Loew, or should I say TheDrainiac?"

Doug's heart rang in his ears. "I knew this would be about that," he offered weakly.

"You're even worse than David," she spat. "Your so-called art glorifies – *sanctifies* – bullying and abuse towards men, treating evil as something to get off on. You just love to show women stealing strength from men to bulk their own muscles up, never considering that this is just another form of rape, but I guess in your world, men can't be raped. You claim it's harmless fiction, but it's not. It's misandry."

Doug backed away, raising his arm futilely. Were his life not in danger, he would have been laughing at the Giantess' over-the-top dialogue. Seriously, how many times could someone say "evil" in a conversation with a straight face?

"Even if it's not your intention," she whispered almost sadly, "depicting rape against men as entertaining is as bad as real rape. You're a rapist, Loew, and I have to punish you."

Doug swallowed fearfully, knowing just who it was who had captured him.

***

Susan examined TheDrainiac's gallery. Yup, there was no mistaking it; the illustration from Loew's portfolio was the same as in the gallery. It was possible that Loew was just a big fan of TheDrainiac's work and just happened to hide a piece in his portfolio but she was pretty sure they were one and the same; the investigators were requesting TheDrainiac's data from *AllGallery* so there would be no doubt.

She scrolled through the comments until she found TGG09 again and entered the account. This time she looked at TGG09's journal entries more carefully. The earliest ones complained about various misfortunes in between mentioning progress on artwork and stories. Past a few years worth of entries TGG09 grew gloomier, describing her getting laid off and unsuccessfully looking for a new job. She ranted about the evils of smoking, drug dealers *and* users, and big business. Finally she started making screeds about art of muscular women she disliked.

It just sickens me to check my muscle women art groups and find them full of perverse garbage where women beat up, maim, torture, and kill men so maniacs can get off to this. Everyday I'm seeing this and I can't take it anymore. I've contacted the AllGallery moderators to better enforce their rules so this smut can be thrown in the trash where it belongs.

A follow-up post showed that, for her efforts, not only was no art removed but TGG09 was warned by the moderators for harassing artists. Some of the reply posts supported her but mostly she got people telling her to chill out.

If you don't like it, look away sweetheart.

Its only fetish art. Learn to live with difference!

Until there's actually an epidemic of violent muscle women abusing men, I can't take you seriously.

TGG09 simply got more extreme, cumulating in her last post to date.

The First Amendment wasn't written to support this evil and restrictions of free speech must go into place. We must work together to ban this filth. I'll prove that it's not harmless, that we must be vigilant in our entertainment. I've been laughed at for daring to make a stand, but I'll have the last laugh. I truly believe that the supervillains we're seeing today were created by being desensitized as youths by our corrupt entertainment business and I aim to expose it. The purveyors of this sewage will go to jail right alongside the criminals they helped create. You'll see I'm right. You'll see.

Susan rubbed her eyes with her palms, sick of reading. TGG09 sounded like every supervillain cliché in the book, but if she really was a supremum would she have been capable of carrying out her claims? She did sound angry enough, and if she got powers while especially troubled...

TGG09. Susan looked at the user name, tapping her finger against the desk, She was more convinced than ever that the *AllGallery* artist was their suspect.

***

Seagulls cawed and circled lazily overhead as a cool breeze blew through the night, sending Jen's blond hair flying. Leaning against the rusted railing, she focused on the dark pier, trying to remember what it was like when it was still open and full of life. People laughing and eating ice cream, kids with balloons and playing arcade games. She smiled and clutched her worn coat closer. That was so nice. What a shame it had to close down.

She shivered in the cold. It was time to leave. Turning from the sad pier, she headed to the sandy path home, a few weak street lamps bathing the way in yellow light.

A buzzing hum filled the air, and a blue light overpowered the yellow. Squinting, Jen turned around, shielding her eyes. A glowing blue figure stood there, powerfully muscled, arms folded, crackling with electricity.

Jen gasped and couldn't suppress a loud giggle. "The Blue Spark! Oh, I am such a fan!"

Blue Spark nodded in acknowledgement. "Thanks, it's always nice to know I've got fans!" She peered around the dock, her short hair an almost luminescent blue.

"Pretty lonely here tonight. You aren't afraid of muggers?"

Jen grinned. "Nope, not with heroines like you out." Chuckling some more, she looked Blue Spark in the eye. "So...what are you doing here? Out on patrol?"

"I'm here to catch a criminal," Blue Spark answered. "Just wanted to ask some questions. Your name please?"

"Jennifer Zander. Call me Jen, if you want."

Blue nodded. "So Jen, you hear about the recent kidnapping?"

"How could I miss that?" Jen sighed. "Every time I turn on the news it's kidnapping, murder, rape..."

"Sure seems that way sometimes, Jen," said Blue. "It's why I'm a superheroine. That and because where I grew up the cops...weren't too helpful."

Jen coughed. It was obscene to hear a superheroine insinuate something bad about the police. Well, Blue was black and sometimes a racist cop would make the rest look bad, but it wasn't fair to paint them all with the same brush. Growing up, Jen had wished to join the police so badly.

Really show the bad guys who's boss...

"Y-yeah," Jen said.

"Well Jen, I thought you could help me out here," Blue said. "We've been doing some searching yesterday, and we have a pretty good idea of what the kidnapper's like."

"Oh, really?"

Blue nodded. "Yup. We found one of the victims was harassed, bullied even, online by someone very troubled, someone who lost a job and couldn't find a new one, someone who seems very depressed and decided to blame the media and violent art for the world's problems."

Jen's eye twitched. Bullied? *Bullied!?* That wasn't bullying, that was justice. How could Blue not see that?

"I can blame the media for problems too," Blue said. "We make so many movies and TV shows here in Las Costas, yet it's all about white people unless it's crime dramas. When I was a kid I almost never got to see anyone that looked like me fighting monsters or exploring space. And don't get me started on how women are treated, both on and off screen! Yet this person complained that *men* are getting the short end of the stick. Not even men of color, just men in general. Can you believe that?"

Jen bit her tongue, wanting so badly to explain how men are constantly depicted as bumbling and less down to Earth than women and how unfair that was.

"Well this someone," Blue continued, "used to work at a warehouse along this very pier, a perfect place to hide kidnapping victims. Someone who hated the victims and with access to a place to hide them. Sound familiar, Jen?"

Jen froze, realizing where this was going.

"And before that, this someone used to work as a programmer, having the right knowledge to pick up a few hacking skills; just enough to do a little hacking on *AllGallery* to learn the identities of rival artists. All we need now is evidence that this person is a supremum." Blue smiled but her gaze was like steel. "I have a feeling I'm gonna get that evidence very soon now."

Faster than any normal human, Jen whipped her arm out and struck Blue across her broad shoulder. Blue grunted, taken by surprise at the speed and strength of the attack, clutching her shoulder.

Jen turned and ran toward the warehouse, determined to keep her prisoners secure.

Light exploded all around her, blinding Jen. She shielded her eyes as huge lights shined on her from every direction. *"Freeze! Put your hands in the air"* a woman commanded over a megaphone.

Jen whirled around, confused and trying to get her sight back. "Wha...?"

"No point in running, Jen." Blue strolled up, her mouth a hard line. "We already freed Loew and David. You're coming with us."

Jen's teeth clenched so hard they went numb. Hot, queasy anger erupted inside her and she let it out in a strangled cry. She took fistfuls of hair, strands tearing off. "How...why...?" she gurgled. "How could you *idiots* do that?"

"Hands in the air, now!" the lady ordered again.

Jen's hands tightened into fists. Blue took a defensive stance, knowing what was next.

"Muscle Expansion!" Jen snarled, and her body instantly exploded with bulging sinew. The thin little woman became a hulking behemoth in seconds, bones and muscles stretching as her height increased to over seven feet. Her clothes melted away, replaced with the brown uniform for the LCPD.

Blue backed up as Jen spread her vast arms joyously and laughed. "Say hello to your new heroine, guys!" she declared. "Call me the Gentle Giantess!"

***

Wood watched the suspect transform through her binoculars and shook her head. Definitely another rogue supremum. Zander even materialized a costume for herself; some kind of psychic manifestation common to suprema.

"Secure the area but don't fire on the suspect!" she ordered her soldiers. It wasn't likely their shots would have much effect on Zander now that she transformed. All they could do was keep people away from the area.

***

Blue couldn't help but marvel at her opponent. Jen had become a perfect recreation of her own *AllGallery* character. She had fought some strong suprema before but this was the first woman with muscles comparable to her own, maybe even a bit bigger. She gave a whistle.

"Hey, do we have to fight, Jen?" she asked, hands raised. "Can't we just trade bodybuilding tips? I'd *love* to know where you work out."

Jen growled, her eyes gleaming dangerously. "Sorry Blue, but if you're not with me, you're against me!" She made a clumsy lunge that Blue sidestepped.

"Who said I'm against you?" Blue asked. "I wanna help you! We could use guys like you at SCAR. You just have to, you know, stop kidnapping people for making stuff you don't like!"

"I don't *need* help!" Jen stomped petulantly, the impact forceful enough to shake the ground. She grinned and curled her massive arms. "I don't know how but I'm a supremum now. I don't have to rely on anyone else! I can finally make a difference!"

"No one knows how suprema are made," Blue interjected. "You'd help the world so much more if you let SCAR examine you so we *can* know."

Blue circled around, Jen following her, breathing heavily. "How'd you find me anyway?" Jen demanded.

"Now that's an interesting question." Blue wagged a finger. "SCAR got a lucky break at Doug Loew's apartment, finding some of his fetish art, which matched the style of TheDrainiac. *AllGallery* admins confirmed that TheDrainiac and Loew were one and the same, and I noticed the user TGG09 harassed him a few times. TGG09. Short for *the Gentle Giantess* 09? That got me wondering, and another confirmation from the admins brought you to our attention, and what do you know! Jennifer Zander used to work at the pier warehouse, maybe even keeping the keys after it closed down. Just the place to hide a pair of kidnapping victims! Some agents scouted the place out while you went on a walk and found signs of habitation. Then I arrived to distract you while our guys extracted David and Loew, and here we are!"

Blue allowed herself a smirk. "You're not cut out for the life of a supervillain, so you really ought to give up now."

Jen's eye twitched. "I...am...not...a *supervillain!*" she bellowed, and slammed her foot onto the ground hard enough that it quaked beneath Blue.

Thrown off balance a bit, it was enough for Jen. Blue found a right hook swinging toward her head, and ducked. A left hook followed. Strafing to Jen's right, Blue was ready to retaliate.

"*Blue Knuckle!*" she called out, and her fists sparked with blue electricity, enough to seriously burn a normal human. A flurry of punches rained over Jen's right arm and side, each blow exploding in a shower of sparks.

Grunting, Jen swatted at Blue in a wide arc, retreating a step.

Blue twisted to her right to avoid the hit. She threw up her hands, her palms facing Jen.

"*Blue Buster!*" she yelled, and quick bolts of blue electricity launched from her hands. The bolts struck Jen directly, popping on her chest and stomach, each one capable of rendering a common criminal unconscious.

Jen let out a cry, more annoyed than hurt, and raised her arms to protect her face. She hunched down like a linebacker, then launched forward. Picking up speed, she was coming up much faster than Blue expected.

Blue ceased firing and stood her ground, tensing up. Right before Jen could ram her, Blue sidestepped her while throwing her left arm out, grasping Jen's left elbow. The momentum let Blue swing around, slamming into Jen's chiseled back where she threw her other arm around Jen's neck. Moving from the elbow to the wrist, Blue yanked Jen's left arm behind her back. Jen growled, twisting her head around, veins bulging from her thick neck.

"Give it up, Jen!" Blue demanded. "You may be strong but you lack technique! You can't win here!"

Jen responded with a weird strangled cry but managed to turn her head enough to glare hatefully at Blue, and suddenly flipped backwards. Blue's back smashed into the ground while her front was crushed by Jen's back, knocking her for a loop. It was enough time for Jen to roll off and deliver a hard stomp on Blue's solid stomach. A shocked gasp escaped Blue's mouth, the wind forced from her lungs. Jen might have been unskilled but she hit *hard*.

Jen chuckled, eyes twitching. "No one's...gonna stop me..." she wheezed, "from saving the world!"

"Hey, nothing wrong with dreaming big," Blue grunted, and Jen ground her heel into Blue's stomach.

"Laugh while you can," Jen sneered. "Once I lock up everyone responsible for cruel, cynical media, everyone will see how much better life is without them. You won't see any more supervillains if everyone had wholesome entertainment that promotes good values!"

Blue gurgled, the pressure on her stomach absolutely crushing. Each breath was torture. She reached for Jen's leg, her fingertips brushing Jen's pants.

"And life'll stay wholesome with every piece of media judged before release, and if it glorifies what's wrong with humanity then it's garbage unfit for consumption!" Jen sighed wistfully. "It'll be so wonderful! Media free from rape, bullying, abuse, drugs, misandry, radical feminism, and other poisons. And if I have to lock you up too, then so be it!"

Even through her pain, Blue rolled her eyes. Misandry and feminism, truly the world's foremost ills. Yeah, right. Blue found it telling that racism apparently wasn't on Jen's radar. Plus, she loved the word "wholesome" more than anyone had a right to. Well, what do you expect from someone play acting a vigilante cop?

She planted her hands and feet on the ground and pushed down as hard as she could, forcing her body up and throwing Jen's leg off. Unbalanced, Jen stumbled backwards as Blue got to her feet.

"*Blue Knuckle!*" Going on the offensive, she tore into Jen with her sparking fists, her electrified blows strong enough to shatter the bones of an ordinary human, yet Jen was merely bruised. The stunned supremum could only accept punch after punch to her head; arms raised uselessly, her eyes wide in shock as blood streamed from her nose and lips. Blue's anger bled away. All she could feel was pity.

One more left hook and then Blue delivered a blow with all her strength behind it to Jen's left cheek, launching the Gentle Giantess' head rightward, her mouth twisted into an almost comical lopsided oval. Currents of electricity sizzled and sparkled through her hair, strands standing on end. She staggered back, trembling, her head stuck in that position but her astonished eyes stayed on Blue.

Blue stood in place, waiting for Jen's next move.

"Jen," Blue breathed, "please, just stop. I don't *like* hurting people, but you're not giving me much alternative."

Slowly, painfully, Jen moved her head back into place, sucking in air through her bleeding mouth, her nose broken. She raised her shaking fists and gurgled something unintelligible but furious.

Blue thrust her palm into Jen's face. "Blue Buster," she muttered, and unloaded a shocking blast point blank.

Jen shrieked wetly, all her hair shooting straight up, spasms jerking her muscles. She might have withstood multiple Blue Buster bolts to her body from a distance, but one up close to the head was another matter.

Smoke curled from Jen's hair.

Blue withdrew her hand.

Jen stood trembling, and for a moment, Blue was ready to give her another shot, but Jen's eyes rolled up and at last, her knees buckled. She landed heavily on them. The rest of her followed, her face planting itself in the sand. Her vast body shuddered violently and then her muscles and uniform melted away, the Giantess going back to ordinary Jen Zander.

Blue checked the woman for signs of life, and, aside from superficial wounds and shock, she was all right. She let out a deep breath, glad Jen didn't die from her injuries.

SCAR troops came scrambling over soon after, securing Jen with handcuffs, although no one was sure if they would hold if she broke out of her daze. Blue would have to escort the big lug to containment.

Wood came running up, a thin smile on her lips. "Cracked the case before anyone was hurt. Splendid effort, Blue."

Blue grimaced. "Yeah, I did, but have you read the information on Zander? Her life's been one disaster after another for the longest time. Bullied as a child; worked as a programmer for a small software company that laid her off after a corruption charge. After that, the only work she could get was at the pier warehouse and she lost her job *again* when the pier closed down. She tried to get into the police numerous times but was rejected for psychological issues. She made art of herself buffed up to feel strong, but entering female muscle art circles introduced her to the BDSM stuff and it reminded her of being bullied. She was about to lose her apartment when she became a supremum. No wonder she lashed out at the world. I wish I could've talked her into getting help."

"A pity she blamed all the wrong people," Wood mentioned. "Still, she really was a Gentle Giantess. She could've killed David and Loew so easily, yet didn't harm a hair on their heads. Perhaps there's hope for her."

Blue watched as soldiers and investigators loaded Jen onto a stretcher. "Yeah, maybe."

"One day," Wood said wistfully as they walked to a waiting ambulance. "One day, SCAR will be filled with superheroes following your example. There's bound to be suprema who want to use their powers to help society, not harm it. It's our job to help them adjust to their new lives and use their powers in a responsible manner."

"Yes ma'am." Blue gazed into her palms and willed tiny arcs of electricity to dance across her skin, tingling pleasantly. Placing her hands close together, the arcs bounced between them. Even though she wasn't a supremum herself, her nanomachines made her supernormal and from the moment she was able to weaponize them, she had no doubts about using them to protect her community and offer an alternative to the police.

Blue focused on the SCAR logo on Wood's uniform. Supernormal Containment and Regulation. That meant dealing with suprema, paranormal phenomena, even extraterrestrial contact. It all sounded so bizarre when she had signed up, but now more than ever, SCAR was needed, and Susan Wright was proud to be a part of it.

GOTTA GO!
Aurelius Raines II

Although he hated ironing, Steph was calmed by the sight of the wrinkles disappearing under the hot weight of the iron. Although he found the fractal elegance of a wrinkled, white shirt fascinating, the uniformed plane of order had its own satisfaction. His father had taught him to be patient with ironing.

"Order on the outside makes order on the inside."

His father would say this while Steph watched his sinewed hands patiently smooth and press the laundry. Now, Steph said it aloud to himself because he wanted to hear some sound besides what he heard on the television.

... four alarm fire on the 14th block of Springfield Avenue. Fortunately, no one was killed in the blaze although a 52-year-old man was rushed to the hospital because of smoke inhalation. The Chicago Fire Department is credited with a speedy response to the fire.

As his anger began to take like a fungus on bread, Steph repeated the mantra to himself.

"Order on the outside makes order on the inside."

What really happened?

The fire was consuming the building and the firefighters, their station only five blocks away, had not arrived. It had been 15 minutes. Steph knew because he had heard the call go out on his police scanner. Within 3 minutes, Steph put on his gear, grabbed his fire kit, and was racing toward the fire on his *Ninja*.

When he arrived, there were no cops or fire trucks, just people outside in various states of dress looking at the flames and looking for each other.

"Did anyone see Mr. Boykin?" a 40-ish woman in pajamas kept asking people. When she saw Steph pull up, she ran to him, the flopping of her slippers a humorous contrast to the tragedy on her mind.

"Ninjaman! Ninjaman!" Steph would have preferred another name but when people saw him in his black outfit and mask fighting four armed robbers outside of a restaurant, he reminded them of a ninja. The bike didn't help. It could have been worse. He heard one astounded onlooker yell "Bruce Leroy" after an uppercut that had lifted a two-hundred pound man off his feet.

"Ninjaman! I think somebody still inside."

"Where?" Steph asked as he reached for his modified gas mask. It was air-tight and had two small canisters of compressed oxygen.

"Third floor. He stay in the back apartment"

Steph saw that most of the windows on the third floor had smoke and a distant glow. The first story seemed smoke and fire free. He assessed the situation and secured the mask on his face as he walked and then ran toward the house. He charged up the stairs. The smoke felt like running into a wall. Steph was instantly blinded. He withdrew a tomahawk from his thigh and stretched it in front of him so he wouldn't really run into a wall.

"Mr. Boykin!"

Steph thought he heard a cough. He ran the tomahawk along the wall and felt it slide against a doorway. He heard the coughing on the other side. The door was not hot but it was locked. Steph stood back and focused. His densely muscled leg became a battering ram. The doorframe splintered as it gave way to Steph's unusual strength.

Mr. Boykin lay on the kitchen floor next to the wheelchair. In his haste to escape, he'd tipped over and now he was trying to crawl to the back door. If he made it, he would have found the wooden porch stairs already in full flame.

Boykin could not breathe. Steph made the decision to take him out of the side window in the kitchen. He took a huge breath and held it. His body instantly balanced his cellular respiration so he would not need as much oxygen, but he had to move fast. He put the mask on Mr. Boykin's face.

Steph knocked out the window with a few powerful blows from his tomahawk and then tied a length of nylon around the refrigerator. He then picked up Mr. Boykin and threw him over one shoulder. The old man had wasted away in his late years, so he was easy to carry. Holding Mr. Boykin in one arm and the rope wrapped around his other, Steph lowered them from the window. The refrigerator acted as a counter weight as it tipped over and slid across the floor to the window and they glided to the bottom floor.

Steph stayed with Mr. Boykin until the EMS arrived. 20 minutes after the call. 20 minutes to answer a call 5 blocks away.

"Order on the outside makes order on the inside." Steph remembered his father's voice – as soft and insistent as pouring water.

Let it go, Steph. Let it go.

***

The next night, after work, Steph wanted to stay in. Construction work was hard and loud. He thought it would be nice to sit and paint for a bit. He liked to paint. But it was late spring time and the streets were warm. His mind could not forget the people who would be injured or killed tonight. On the way home from work, he'd seen Rhonda walking from the store, bag in one hand and baby in the other. Steph made small talk. He was wearing shades so Rhonda did not see him notice the bruise peeking from under the sleeve of her peach baby-tee. Steph made small talk, played with the baby a little and went on like nothing was wrong. Steph made a note to go talk to Duran.

And since he obviously wasn't going to paint tonight, there was no time like the present.

***

The tavern had a large tinted window so Steph could see Duran drinking at the bar. Bearded and well-muscled, his marine tattoo became more restless the more he drank. His tattoo was a knife through the globe

126

and a swooping eagle with a banner that read *Death Before Dishonor*. Two tours in Afghanistan and Duran drank too much.

When he emerged from the tavern, he was unsteady on his feet and clumsy in reaching for his keys. Steph's gate was easy and his voice lacked all authority.

"Duran, let's talk."

Despite Steph's attempt to be disarming, Duran tensed up. His twisted hair almost stood on end.

Duran cursed. "What you want?"

"To talk." But Steph was under no illusions. Duran was bad at talking and as Steph closed the distance, he'd already resigned himself to what was coming next.

Duran was emotional and drunk. But he was also well-trained and combat tested. So Steph was not taken off guard.

***

Steph's father explained everything to him after he'd been suspended from school for an unusually bloody fight when he was ten. In his calm voice, Saul told Steph about the history of violence in his family. It turned out that the men and women in his family had come from a long line of people who liked to fight and were naturally good at it. The story that came down through the generations was that a long time ago, Sundiata Keita, a wealthy king of the Mali empire, had the idea that men, like dogs, could be bred to have special qualities. It was his ambition to have an army of elite and loyal *sofa* – warriors – that would serve to expand his territory, so he bred men to have the highest levels of strength, speed, agility, affinity for reasoning, tactics, and reflexes.

Generations later, by the time of the reign of Mansa Musa Keita, the Mali Empire was home to a race of genetically superior warriors. But their natural ability and training was not enough to save the empire. Many of them managed to escape capture by enslavers but a few of them found themselves in chains, their robust and hearty nature a curse that made them sought-after merchandise and incapable of dying during the dark horror that was the journey to the Americas.

After generations of escapees, rebels, soldiers, street brawlers, boxers, and imprisoned men, Steph's father, Saul, had sought to put an end to the violence. A godly man, he did everything that he could to live a life of peace. He even left Steph's mother – who liked to see Saul fight and would create opportunities to see him break a man with the same soft hands that caressed her skin. It broke Saul's heart anew every morning that he woke alone.

But Steph felt that times like these needed a man of his skill set. He went to his grandfather, who owned a bar and a two-flat. Tall, lean, and missing teeth, Steph's grandfather was jovial and a bit mean. But he was eager to teach Stephen what he wanted to know so that the old ways would not be forgotten. So, at 14, Steph learned the secrets of warfare and combat that every *sofa* had learned since The *People Of The Book* lived peacefully in Al-Andalus.

***

So, when Duran's massive fist snaked out in an attempt to remove Steph's head, Steph had already moved slightly out his reach.

Steph's counterpunch to Duran's ribcage was almost enough to break a rib, but certainly enough to make it hard for Duran to lift his right arm. Steph did not know why he knew that Duran would rather charge him than punch with his left hand; he just took it for granted that he would. So when Duran let out an animal grunt and charged Steph's midsection, Steph was already out of the way. He grabbed Duran's shirt collar and redirected Duran's momentum while sticking his leg across Duran's shins to send him sprawling. Steph caught the muscled arm and locked every joint in Duran's arm from the wrist to the clavicle.

"Now can we just talk for a minute?" Steph asked, again, holding Duran's arm perpendicular to his prone body with his foot between Duran's shoulder blades.

***

First, Duran admitted that he'd stopped going to his support group because of his new job's hours.

"So how is the new job, man?"

"Lost it. "

"Drunk?"

"All the time,"

And they talked like that for hours. People did stare at the teary-eyed ex-marine sitting on the high curb next to Ninjaman, just talking. Only Steph noticed the other people. Duran spent much of his time back on a rocky mountain, taking cover from Taliban fire, holding a dying twenty-year-old while he bled out from his missing leg. The boy screamed like an animal until he couldn't. Duran was never rescued from that mountain, but here he was, getting drunk and using the internet and laying next to his wife while the rest of the world burned without him.

The ink of the sky began to dilute. The birds began to awake. The conversation had migrated from the curb to Steph's bike.

"You know you can't go back home, right?" Steph said abruptly.

"But I..."

"Don't go home, Duran," Steph handed Duran a wad of bills.

"This should give you a few nights at the Holiday Inn on Cicero. The address is in there. There is a meeting tonight at 6:30. Be there."

Duran looked at the money in his hand. Steph did not bother with threats. This man had seen death and, he was sure there was a part of Duran that would welcome an end to everything.

"Don't say 'thank you' just fight for your family. Don't fight your family. You know Rhonda is not going to leave you. She can't stand the thought of raising the baby without you. Just do right by yourself..."

Steph turned on the bike. The roar was loud and abrupt in the morning quiet,

"...and you will do right by her"

***

Steph sort of understood why the news never talked about him. The city was full of heroes. Many of them wore costumes. Some of them even seemed "special." None of them seemed to spend much time in *his* neighborhood. So Steph understood that someone like him, doing things for people and not asking for anything, did not fit the story that they were used to telling. And the emergency services wouldn't talk about a black man in black that saved people from burning buildings or stopped drug dealers with conversation and relationships as well as his fists.

So when Steph started seeing stories on the news that Crusader was waging "a one-man war on drugs" on the South Side, he instinctively knew that the Crusader was white and was busting heads.

The point was made more dynamic from the calls he was getting from mothers. He had a number of informants all over the neighborhood. A tweet would tell him where he had to be or when someone needed him.

Sylvia, a security guard who lived in an apartment building on an "active" block had a front row seat to a lot. When she came home late, she would see all kinds of things. She had two boys, 14 and 8, and her husband was stationed overseas. She was invested in a safe place for her family. Tonight's tweet was as short as it was urgent:

@helpthishome: tariq is hurt. need you now.

Ten minutes later he was in Sylvia's living room.

Her 14-year-old, Tariq, a boy with close-cut hair, and a chubby body, lay on the couch, curled and holding his arm. Sylvia held a plastic bag full of ice on it. She did not look at Steph when the 8-year-old, Jayvyn, let him in.

"He won't tell me who did this to him." Sylvia prided herself on being calm in bad situations but her voice was salted with worry.

As Steph walked toward Tariq, the boy flinched.

Steph stopped moving. His voice was calm. "Tariq, I know you're scared, but we are here. I can help you. You have to tell me who did this to you and I will make it so they can't do it again."

Tariq sobbed. He had always put on a macho front. He thought it his responsibility to be the man of the house when his father was deployed – being a man, to Tariq, meant never smiling and always putting on an air of stone resolution. But something had broken that façade, and that broke Steph's heart.

Steph took off his mask and knelt by the couch.

"Look at me, Tariq. Just tell me who did this to you. I give you my word..."

Tariq looked at Steph's face. He had only seen Steph, once. He'd watched him walk through a pimp right under his bedroom window. The guy had a gun and everything, Ninjaman ended up hitting the man with his own gun. By the time Tariq had the mind to get his phone and record the action, Ninjaman was gone and the pimp was tied up and waiting to go to jail. The pimp didn't go to jail but Tariq never saw him again. Tariq fantasized about what the face under the mask looked like. It was a normal face, like everybody else's.

"He was wearing blue," Tariq whispered.

"Did he have a red cross?"

"Yeah. On his chest."

"What did he say to you?"

"He wanted to know where King Lou was."

"What did you tell him?"

Tariq was quiet.

"Tariq."

"He hurt me." He sounded, so much, the child.

"I know."

"I told him he was at Club 63. I don't know."

"Okay. I got you, man."

Steph turned to Sylvia.

"Can you get him to the hospital?"

"He won't go. I can't get him off the couch," said Sylvia. The panic in her voice was becoming harder to mask.

"I'll send for an ambulance to come get him."

"I can't afford..." the panic slammed against a thin sheet of cool ice.

"Don't worry about it. I owe you and somebody owes me. They'll take care of your boy."

Steph walked to the door.

."Where are you going?" Sylvia asked.

"Me and Crusader need to have a sit down and come to an agreement."

"Agree your foot in his face, for me!"

Steph almost smiled.

***

Steph was sure that King Lou was not at *Club 63*. Club 63 was a reggae club and there was nothing about King Lou that liked small clubs that played Shabba Ranks when they wanted to go old school. But that made no difference. Crusader didn't know that and his "informant" told him King Lou would be there. So Steph knew that's where he'd find Crusader. Crusader did not know enough to know that any information he got through torture was no good. Why would anybody allow you to keep terrorizing them when they could just tell the torturer anything to make them stop? That's what Tariq did. Tariq would have told Crusader that King Lou was on the moon if he thought that would end the pain. And Crusader had no better sense than to believe a scared 14-year-old in pain.

Steph pulled up in front of the club. He figured that Crusader would probably pick high ground to do surveillance on the club. Sure enough, peeking at the building across the street, he spotted Crusader's head just over the edge. Steph knew that his direct approach was probably a mistake. There was no element of surprise.

That was okay.

"Crusader! We need to talk,"

No movement.

"King Lou is not here! I can help you! But not while you are up there!"

Steph's call drew attention. A group of men that were talking near an apartment doorway stopped to see what was happening and if they would have to run. People came to their windows, their TV's turned down. Those who were stepping out of the club for a smoke ducked in to call their friends. People pulled over cars.

By the time the Crusader used his cape to glide from his rooftop, the street was full of people. Steph had an audience.

Crusader spoke first. His voice was altered, like it was going through a filter.

"I've been watching you. I think we are on the same side. Welcome to the fight."

Crusader extended his hand but Steph did not take it.

"You broke the arm of a fourteen-year-old,"

"Necessary evil. He was protecting scum because he was scared of it. So I gave him something new to fear: Me."

"And he gave you bogus information because he was a scared boy. So what did you achieve, here?"

"Vengeance. Vengeance against those that would swallow this city whole. There are so many of them!" Crusader's cowled face did not hide his scowl.

"Man, I'm telling you, you hurt a child!"

Order on the inside makes order on the outside.

"He was protecting scum! So that made *him* scum."

"Scum? He was on the honor roll! Twice! He watches *Star Trek*! Voluntarily!"

"It doesn't matter. This city is sick. These people have tolerated it long enough. It is my job to cleanse it! Help me."

"Tolerated it? Man...you gotta go."

"I can't be stopped. I am justice."

"Man, you come straight outta a comic book. Maybe you can do some good somewhere, but there is no place for someone like you in this neighborhood. You gotta go!"

Steph saw the phones. He was no good at theater, perhaps another reason why the news ignored him. But he wanted people to see what was going to happen next.

Crusader squared up. His combat stance was subtle...elegant. "Ninjaman, I know you are a protector in this neighborhood. With you by my side I know that we can clean up this cesspool for decent people."

At this moment, Steph decided three things:

I have to take a more active role in my branding. Ninjaman can NOT be my name.

There are enough people around us and it is time to work.

A thousand years of breeding to be a sidekick? No.

Steph went for Crusader's throat with a knife hand. Crusader blocked the blow and simultaneously used the same arm to swipe an elbow at Stephen's head...also blocked.

Steph's mind was a calculator, analyzing each move and response; measuring angles and creating a profile of Crusader's fighting style. Crusader had weapons. Stephen just wasn't sure what type; probably non-lethals. Still, with all of the people around, he would have to make sure Crusader's hands were too busy to use them.

Crusader let launch a series of kicks. They were easy enough to stop. So that meant that they were a setup for...

An uppercut came at Steph from the right. Crusader was definitely a southpaw. He tried to hide it. This was a good asset to keep hidden against a skilled fighter, but Steph had trained for this. He crossed his arms to trap the punch and shot out his right fist which connected with Crusader's chin and sent him spinning.

The Crusader wasted little time in coming with a backhand blow that did not take Steph by surprise. Steph stopped it and was about to counterstrike when he heard a clicking sound. Something black and hard was around his left wrist and before he could stop his right hand from crossing it, a black metal band clicked around his right wrist. His hands were shackled. In the moment it took Steph to realize what was happening, the

Crusader had put everything he had into a punch straight to Steph's solar plexus. A starburst of pain went off in Steph's middle. His diaphragm forgot how to help him draw breath. The problem with a shot to the solar plexus is that the sudden loss of air and the ability to breath made the victim panic. Not Steph. He knew this trick and this pain had been useful. Steph fell to his back but instantly kicked his feet over his head so that he rolled backwards and he was on his feet again. Steph stood with his hands before him, below his mid-section.

***

His grandfather named all of the men in Steph's family who had been to jail.

"They put these cuffs on you and they make your hands useless. You gotta learn how to fight with them on. We been doing it since slavery. And we still gotta do it to this day."

After Steph's hands were tied behind his back, one of Grandfather's other pupils, a 13-year-old girl from up the block, began to lay into him. Grandfather laughed while Steph ducked and dodged this girl's cobra-fast fists.

"You gonna rope-a-dope forever, hmm? You wastin' food, ain't cha? Get those arms up front. It's just pain."

Her speed and endurance made Steph wonder if she was family. This kept up until the girl was winded and Steph learned to dislocate his shoulders and swing his arms over his head to bring his hands in front of him. He spent a year learning how to turn shackled hands into an advantage.

***

Crusader moved in to capitalize on a stunned Steph. Steph's hands stopped Crusader's blow at the elbow while Steph kicked into Crusader's hip. This caused the Crusader to bend forward. Steph drove his knee into Crusader's face and then grabbed a device from his opponent's utility belt. It was small with two buttons. Steph took a chance on the bottom button and the shackles released. He had a moment to pull them off as the Crusader began to recover.

Then Steph had an inspired moment. He crossed his hands at the wrists and stood ready.

The Crusader noticed his hands and hesitated, reevaluating before he attacked. Crusader let loose with an axe-kick, high and powerful. Steph stepped into it and his "bound wrists" snapped up to catch the kick before it could bring its momentum downward. Steph used Crusader's compromised balance to push him backward. He went down.

Crusader popped up. Steph saw his hands go for his belt again – throwing knives. There were people everywhere.

This time Steph kicked the inside of Crusader's knees to break his stance to throw him off balance while his hands slammed into a nerve-cluster between the biceps and shoulder muscles.

Crusader's arm fell limp, too numb to use the knives.

Steph blocked a reflexive punch from Crusader's right hand and then deadened that arm also.

This would force Crusader to use those high-kicks.

When he did, Steph cut off circulation to Crusader's legs.

***

He remembered his first lessons consisted of him trying to lay one punch on Grandfather while the 66-year-old bartender swept Steph's legs from under him. He remembered his grandfather's tooth-starved grin,

"You can't fight if you can't stand, hmm?" He chided as Steph fell time and time again. "What you got yo feet in the air, fo'? Hmm? This a fight, not a date."

Steph was never sure if it was the mocking or the desire to learn that kept driving him to his feet. All that mattered was that he kept getting up.

Crusader felt his legs go numb and he became unsteady. He tried another strike but it was clumsy and slow because he had not regained feeling in his arms, yet.

Steph let the punch slide over his shoulder as he brought his arm around Crusader's front and wrapped it around his neck. Using his hip as a fulcrum, Steph lifted Crusader off his feet and brought him to the ground in a choke hold. Crusader struggled and slapped but he had no strength or leverage.

Steph applied pressure to Crusader's carotid artery. He looked up at the cameras. Still applying pressure, he held his "bound" wrists in front of him.

"Even shackled, we are strong. We are not scum, a blight, gangsters, whores, bums, killers, sloths, or problems to be solved. We are people and we will heal *ourselves*. You are welcome to help, but if you come here to hurt us, to imprison us, to terrorize us..."

Steph felt Crusader's body go lax and released him. Crusader flopped to the ground like a pancake sliding from a pan.

"...you gotta go!"

***

At 6 a.m., Saul got up early and swung his legs over the edge of the bed. He picked up his Bible and opened it to a bookmarked page.

Lord, I know that people's lives are not their own; it is not for them to direct their steps. Discipline me, Lord, but only in due measure.

This was his thought as he made his bed. Surely the answer to his problem had not been within himself. All he knew was violence. It was in his DNA. Even now, he was compelled to continue conditioning his body so that it would be ready to fight. He turned on the television to the morning news, as was his custom and began a set of 100 push-ups. His mind counted in the background as the television news told of man's shame. He stopped in the middle of number 67 when he saw an amateur video with the caption "Chicago's New Villain."

"Onlookers shot this video as the Crusader was assailed by a mysterious attacker. It is unclear what the motive for the attack was but citizens are concerned about this new level of violence in Chicago's beleaguered Englewood neighborhood. The assailant has been called 'Ninjaman' by locals who say that they do not know who he is or where he is from. Police are currently investigating."

Saul saw the man in black choke out the Crusader as he looked at the camera. It looked like he was saying something but the sound of the video was muted as the news anchor talked out the side of his neck. But Saul saw the man in black's eyes and knew that he was looking at his son, Stephen.

He thought on this as he finished the set and then stood up. Something in Saul told him that his son would not be able to resist. There was a part of Saul that was disappointed. There was a smaller part of him that was so proud that it made Saul shine on the inside.

"But...*Ninjaman*? We can do better, hmm?"

NEW ELEMENTS
M. Haynes

The fifth command of the Mystics demands that we "Seek to do the greatest good for all your lives", and that's what I planned to do when I joined this team. It was so inspiring to interview the generation of Elementals that took out A.G., and now I get to be a part of them. To hear them talk about how difficult it was to beat her, how much they struggled, I couldn't believe that people like them cared that much, and now I'm one of them, using my powers to help protect the world. It's a big change, but I'm excited about it. The Mystics command it of us, so it will be done.

-Kiara

"Aurora Baris Mal!" Kiara yelled, firing bursts of yellow light energy toward the android racing toward her friend M. The android fell, face first, far enough from M for him to shoot a bolt of electricity at it, effectively shutting it off.

"Thanks!" M called back to her.

Kiara smiled at him and turned around just in time to be met with another android firing more laser blasts at very close range. The light from the blast brightened Kiara's already bright skin and her bushy black ponytail as well as M's afro before it connected with both of them. Both stumbled a bit from the force of the blasts, but thankfully their reinforced Skin Armor (Kiara's blue blouse and M's denim shirt) blocked most of the blasts. She turned toward the firing android and cast another spell in its direction, this time causing a series of bright lights that blinded the android and rendered it unable to see to aim any more laser blasts. M took this opportunity to send another wave of electricity at it, stopping it completely just like the first one.

The super-powered teens known as *the Elementals* were locked in a battle with a group of androids they had discovered terrorizing a small community in their native country, the Great Lands. During their quest to rid the Great Lands of the remaining androids, the mayor of the town called Quten called them with a report of androids in the vicinity, so their leader, a Fire Elemental named De, rounded up M, Rod, Mo, Jas, Lucas, and Kiara to go check it out. Almost as soon as they entered the town to investigate, they were jumped by at least a dozen of the androids they were looking for.

"Rod? Where are you?" De yelled over the sound of the android's powerful laser attacks hitting the building he was hiding behind. He hated to be using it as a shelter, especially since it was clearly still being rebuilt, but it was either that or take the lasers himself, and being that his Skin Armor was nothing more than jeans and a red muscle shirt, he wasn't sure how long he could do that.

"I'm coming!" The Water Elemental was busy pulling water from the nearest source he could sense. He figured there were some puddles or something nearby, but when he noticed the portable bathroom in the distance he yelled to De, "You might not wanna let that touch you!" as he sent the...liquid rushing past him. Rod's attack doused the three androids threatening to crush De with debris, and while they were distracted, both he and M pelted their attackers with their element-based abilities. Rod pulled on his jeans and ran back toward the others to try to help out. Not far from the three boys, his sister Jasmin "Jas" Reno was struggling a little bit against the androids attacking her.

"Go away, already!" Jas yelled, spinning her arms around her and sending another powerful gust of wind toward the two androids that pursued her. The androids seemed to be heavier than she anticipated, and refused to be blown away. They opened fire, and when Jas stopped her wind to duck out of the way, they ran closer. There was clear frustration in her round face as she flung out her arms again and the androids this time had to struggle to power through the windstorm. Jas planted her boots in the dirt below her and shifted her weight so that she could strengthen the gusts, stopping the androids' movement completely and making them excellent targets for Lucas to use his own laser hand to pick them off. He willed one of his brown strands of hair to become a scope so he could snipe the androids from a safe distance.

"Nice shooting!" Jas said.

Lucas just nodded and turned what was his laser hand into a blade and ran to help the last of their team, the Ice Elemental Mo, who struggled the most out of them.

Mo had been trying to encase the androids around him in ice, but unfortunately he had not yet mastered using his power to freeze things without the help of some body of water.

Lucas, however, was more than capable of helping him, so when an android knocked Mo off of his feet, Lucas was able to counter by slashing at the machine with his (now sword shaped) hands.

Mo looked up at Lucas with gratitude, but before he could do anything further, the final android among the team started shooting laser blasts off in every direction. The attacks sent most of the Elementals running in every direction to avoid getting blasted, but one stood through the onslaught and pitched a well-timed and very powerful fireball at the android, stopping its attack and the machine itself.

"Nice shot, man!" Mo said to De.

"Thanks! I have been working on my..."

"What's wrong with you, what were you doing with those androids? Playing house?" Rod snapped. As the rest of the Elementals gathered in the middle of the street with De and Mo, the black t-shirt and jeans-clad hero confronted his teammate.

"I have been practicing powers, you know, trying to get better! You should try it sometime," Mo said angrily. He tossed the blonde hair out of his face and continued. "There's no reason you should be stealing whatever that was from a toilet! But I guess you can't help it, huh?"

"Just like you can't help making folks have to come save you all the time right? Just like how you're too sorry to do anything but cry to your boyfriend or whine to us all the time? Ain't that right?" Rod shoved Mo so forcefully that the latter fell onto the ground, and it took De and Jas grabbing Rod to keep him from doing anything else to Mo.

"Calm down!" De yelled as he looked from Rod to Mo. On both sides of him, M had stooped down to help Mo up, and Jas was trying to calm Rod. "We do NOT have time for this right now!" Both Rod and Mo continued to argue as Kiara and Lucas, two of the more reserved Elementals, looked on.

"Do they ever stop trying to kill each other?" Kiara asked Lucas. Kiara had only been with the team for a few months, but she had seen plenty of Rod and Mo's fights. Even when she interviewed them at the end of the previous year she had sensed the tension between them.

Lucas shook his head. "They get better sometimes, but most of the time they hate each other's existence." Kiara shook her head sadly. She could hardly believe sometimes that these were the same people who saved their world not even a year ago. As she turned her focus back toward De in the center of the chaos (as he often was) she noticed that he was finishing up one of his "teamwork" speeches.

"...and we can't keep letting this stuff happen! We still have androids to get rid of in case you two forgot!" Though De was a year younger than both of the people he was yelling at and two years younger than Lucas, the team had long ago elected him as their leader, and his ability to keep them grounded in stressful situations made them all respect his authority. Sure enough, Rod and Mo (finally) started to look slightly remorseful and stopped yelling back and forth. De sighed and turned to the smallest of the group. "What did we learn, if anything?"

"I only got to one of them, but it still says what all the others said," M held up a small circular device. "I didn't see any of the signals that Don told us to look for, but I sent the info to him just in case. He said he would be calling once he had a chance to analyze it."

Don, the Elementals' resident technology expert, had stayed behind to help coordinate the true purpose of this mission. Knowing that any androids still active in the Great Lands had to be getting orders from somewhere, Don gave the Elementals a device of his own creation that he hoped could track the signal that the androids were getting their orders from.

Almost on cue, the phone in Mo's pocket began ringing. Mo reached for it and he immediately perked up when he answered.

"Hey," Mo said. He smiled and nodded for a moment before he held the phone away from his ear and in his hand. He pressed a button on the side and his enhanced phone projected a hologram of Don small enough to sit just above the phone screen. The other Elementals moved in to get a better look at the tiny image of Don's chunky frame.

Don was as good-natured as ever. He turned so he could wave at the Elementals with both hands before he explained why he called in the first place. "So, I looked at the data M sent, and as far as I can tell, the androids are still acting on normal orders," he explained.

"But how is that? A.G.'s gone, so what orders are they following?" Jas asked.

"There's a possibility that the programming is so absolute that they can carry it out even without A.G. directly leading them, but that doesn't explain what they are actually *doing.* I can't figure out why they would be attacking cities randomly. There has to be a reason," Don continued.

"Maybe they're claiming places for the Empire?" De suggested.

"But why Quten? It ain't like it's a big city or anything," Rod gestured to the area around them. Sure enough, the town of Quten was noticeably calmer and quieter than many of the other cities in the Great Lands. It didn't have the flair of a place like Rumas, Rivera, or even the expansion projects of Black City.

"Does Quten have any major history?" De asked M and Kiara. M's knowledge of older Elementals and Kiara's work as a journalist made both of them De's go-to sources about the history of Colorius.

M answered first. "Nothing that I know of. The closest important location to us is Cree Glen, and even that was only important because it was where the old Water Elemental Issa first lived when she got to the Great Lands."

"Why does that sound familiar...?" Mo wondered out loud.

"You're probably thinking of the Creature Glen, where the villains from *Frame and Lock* used to train. We watched that show last night, remember?" Don answered.

"Oh yeah! That was a good one. Do you remember how the-"

"I think Kiara has to speak," De interrupted the two. "Go ahead, Kiara," he said with a smile.

Kiara smiled back. "I can't remember us ever doing a story on Quten. As far as I know, nothing major has ever happened here, but it might just not have been big enough to make it to our news stations."

De sighed. "Well, I guess we have something. We at least know that some random person isn't controlling them."

"Yea. I'll keep looking at what I have but who knows if I'll find anything more. You guys should come on back anyway, we have a big day tomorrow," Don reminded them.

"Oh, right! I forgot all about *The Unveiling*!" De looked at the others to signal it was time for them to head back.

Mo said goodbye and hung up from Don, and five of the seven Elementals headed out of the town to De's convertible and Lucas' compact car for the ride home.

"You have got to do better with the time management, oh fearless leader," Jas joked, she had hung back to help him get the androids in one spot. De approached her and she showed him the time on her phone. It was the early evening and it would take the two cars at least two hours to drop everyone off at home.

"I know, I know," De admitted.

"So what time are we gonna meet up in the morning?" she asked. She had already started to set an alarm on her phone.

"Well the Unveiling is at noon and six of us will have to travel, so seven?" De suggested.

Jas nodded and the two joined Rod and M already sitting in De's vehicle. Since the four of them lived in Black City and the other three all lived in Rumas, this would be where they would part ways.

"See you in the morning," Lucas said and drove away with Kiara and Mo waving goodbye. The others returned the gesture and De started his car to speed them all back to their homes.

***

"There should be a manual for this stuff. Nobody explains all the work that goes into being an Elemental, let alone the leader. I thought this was all about saving people, but it seems like we spend all our time making appearances,

doing interviews, and kissing babies. It's hard enough trying to keep Rod and Mo from killing each other, keep M from smothering me in my sleep, and make Kiara and Jas feel welcome while still trying to get rid of all A.G.'s goons. Now they want us to do it all in front of cameras? That's just too much. If I had known it would be all of this I probably would've let M keep thinking he was the leader. *sigh* Guess it's too late now."

-De

"Now, why don't we get to go on an adventure to another continent?" Jas asked De over the phone. She held it out as far as her arm could go so both she and Rod could see De's exasperated face on the screen.

"Because, the Shrine of Kashiro is the only place that we know for certain has water around it, and since-"

"-since I gotta be around some water you just stuck us here," Rod finished. De looked slightly sad for his friend, it wasn't the first time Rod's slow developing powers had hindered him.

"Can I just say I'm perfectly fine with leaving him here and coming to one of the places you guys are?" Jas looked serious, but burst into laughter when De actually started to consider switching her with someone else. "It's okay. We'll be okay. Just take pictures! Bye!"

As soon as Jas hung up Rod looked at her seriously. "You really could go if you wanna."

Jas shook her head. "No, it's fine. Besides, we probably need to talk about stuff anyway. You know the facility is out this way, why don't we go see J when we leave? He called yesterday and said he gets out in a few months."

"I don't care," Rod lied. Truthfully, the idea that his best friend was finally getting released from the detention facility made him anxious in a lot of ways, but there were too many other things on his mind to give too much thought to Javari Meadows.

Jas nodded. "Alright. Well, can we at least go in? I'm about to pass out out here," she was using her powers to keep a steady breeze blowing over herself, but because she requested that her Skin Armor be made to compliment her shape, she was still quite warm. Rod agreed and the two walked a little faster so that they could enter the oasis-like entrance to the Shrine of Kashiro.

Immediately it seemed as if the temperature got more pleasant inside the gates of the Shrine. Just like its three sister shrines across the world, the Shrine of Kashiro was built to house a powerful national treasure and was home to a number of monks dedicated to worship of the Mystics and protecting the item. Today, however, the Shrine was also home to a number of media personalities and journalists. In fact, it was a number of them, and not the monks, who greeted the two Elementals at the gates.

"Rodrik!" "Jasmin!" "Over here!" "Tell us how you feel today!"

"Are you excited?"

The chorus of reporters and their flashing cameras ambushed the siblings inside the Shrine, but it was Jas who composed herself first to answer.

"Well, we are definitely excited. It's not every day we get to witness a gift from the Mystics themselves. We look forward to meeting the Guardian Beast and hope that you all are excited too!" she waved to the cameras and dragged her brother past the rest of them asking questions into the main building of the shrine. "Maybe we can hide out in here until the actual Unveiling," Jas suggested.

Inside the building there was a small foyer where a number of monks were busy preparing for the event. Men and women in brown robes carried chairs to and from the antechamber, and several others shouted instructions to each other. None of them noticed the two Elementals, so Rod had to stop one to get their attention.

"Oh! Friends! Hello! The Unveiling will be starting momentarily. We just have a few more things to get ready. If you would like, you can enter the chamber. HighPhoenix is already inside." Rod and Jas exchanged looks, and when it was clear neither of them had any idea who or what a HighPhoenix was, they both walked cautiously into the chamber.

"Oh!" Jas gasped.

"Wow..." Rod breathed.

Inside the antechamber stood what looked at first glance to be a large and colorful humanoid bird. The bird stood about nine feet tall on two talons, and several sets of wings protruded from its back. The blonde plume on its head seemed to coordinate beautifully with its mostly red feathers and golden wings, and it became clear that this must have been the HighPhoenix that the monk outside spoke of. The bird turned its head toward the Elementals and spoke, not through its beak, but inside their minds.

"Hello Elementals."

"Umm, hey," Rod said back.

"Can I just say that I am SO glad I stayed here?" Jas said in awe. She approached HighPhoenix and the monks surrounding it carefully, as though afraid to offend or frighten any of them.

"Well, this just got really interesting," Rod said as he walked behind his sister.

***

"J would probably laugh if he saw me right now. Three years ago I woulda been in here trying to snatch everything I could put my hands on, but now, I'm in here representing the whole country as one of the 'Elemental Heroes'. He'd laugh and ask me how I got so lame so quick; tell me that if I didn't start grabbing some of this stuff he would. Sometimes I miss those days. I mean, we got more money and stuff now for sure, but it was fun back then, I can't lie. I don't know. I ain't going to that facility but maybe I'll see what J talking about when he get out...nah. I bet not. Jas, Ma, and even De already gave me speeches about 'being better' now. Too bad I don't feel better, but it's cool."

-Rod

"...and we of course have Elementals, like young Rodrick and Jasmin here, to thank for ridding us of the A.G. problem," the newly elected president of the Great Lands, Harvey Bradley, spoke to the crowd from a podium right beside HighPhoenix. "Without their efforts, our entire continent would still be in the clutches of the androids, and the Orange Scepter that HighPhoenix now protects would still be in the hands of a mad dictator. We owe these young heroes extreme gratitude!" he led the crowd in a roaring applause, and both Jas and Rod gave a quick wave of gratitude.

After the actual unveiling of The Unveiling, several of the reporters asked HighPhoenix how she – it was revealed that the Guardian Beasts all had some sort of gender expression – planned to serve the people of Redd Continent, and the council of leaders from the various countries all gave speeches, with President Bradley being last. After the applause for Rod and

Jas stopped, President Bradley finished his speech.

"But perhaps the largest thanks goes out to you, the people who live and work all over Redd Continent. Without your tireless efforts to keep our nations moving smoothly, we would have fallen with A.G., but thanks to you, we have risen stronger than ever! Thanks to you, we can welcome HighPhoenix to the list of beings dedicated to our success and thanks to you, we continue to move toward the dreams that our Mystics had for us when they formed our world! You, my brothers and sisters, are the true heroes here, and HighPhoenix, the Elementals, the nation leaders and myself exist to serve you! Thank you, and may the Mystics keep you all."

The thunderous applause that followed President Bradley rang throughout the antechamber for a full minute before the olive skinned monk at the podium could get their attention.

"He's good," Rod said and Jas nodded as the room finally quieted down.

"We thank you all for coming to The Unveiling, and we hope that the people of Redd Continent, as well as our brothers and sisters in Bleu, Sylver, and Golde Continents will all be able to rest a little easier knowing that four Guardian Beasts are keeping watch over the shrines to ensure that no living creature gets his, her, or its hands on one of the Mystic Items ever again. The Orange Scepter is safe here with HighPhoenix, and with the Elementals protecting the rest of our world we can continue to grow. Thank you all for your time, and have a good rest of your day." The monk left the podium, ignoring the questions from the crowd, so Rod, Jas, the nation leaders, and HighPhoenix took this as a cue for them to leave the stage as well. HighPhoenix had left through the back exit (the only one large enough for her) and the rest of them walked slowly to the front entrance.

"Well that was cool, I can't wait to hear what-" Jas started, but she was cut off by screams and an explosion. She and Rod turned around to see the table the leaders were sitting at destroyed, the actual leaders and the crowd running, and a number of androids rushing into the building. As people tried to file out of the doors, their way was blocked by more androids pouring into the antechamber.

"Great! Just great," Rod groaned. He looked outside at the small lake. He would have to bring the water through the chamber's high windows if he wanted to be of any help taking out these androids. Jas was similarly in a bind. Any wind she created in such a closed space could risk harming the people inside it.

"Media-civilians, out of the way! Our leader requires the leader-civilians alone!" several of the androids spoke at once to threaten the media and other onlookers. Jas and Rod backed against the wall as well, biding their time until they could relax.

"Where are the national leaders?" the chorus of androids asked. When no one responded and President Bradley and the other nations' leaders didn't budge, the androids continued, "Kill them all, then." The androids filed in front of the citizens and all raised their hands to unleash laser blasts.

Rod and Jas looked at each other. They would have to act now. But before either of the Elementals could react, there was a terrible screeching sound that brought everyone to their knees.

HighPhoenix had glided back into the chamber. Rod took this chance to bring the water he had been focusing on into the chamber and used it to wash over the still dazed androids. Jas screamed as loud as she could for the civilians to run, and as they raced out of the building she was free to unleash her wind powers on the room. She spun her arms in front of her as fast as she could, getting the wind to mix with the water Rod spun and created a whirlpool-like effect that kept the androids off their feet.

"Keep that up and they should fall apart!" Rod encouraged his sister, and sure enough, the androids started to break up from the extreme force of the swirling water and wind. This wasn't fast enough for HighPhoenix, it seemed, as the Guardian Beast took this moment to aim the Orange Scepter at the spinning androids. A blast of silver energy, larger than even what Rod remembered A.G. using, erupted from the Scepter, instantly destroying all the androids it touched. Jas and Rod stopped their efforts and looked at HighPhoenix.

"*You Elementals need to deal with these androids. Now,*" was all she said.

Though it was obvious that both of them were disappointed at not being able to finish the androids themselves, neither of them wanted to anger the nine foot being capable of something like what they had just seen. "Yes ma'am," was all they said instead.

***

"See! This is what they get! This is what happens when you remove the true leader from power. They put De in charge and look at what happened! We've been fighting androids for over a year and there are still enough of them to go to all four continents and mess up The Unveiling! Those folks in Sylver Continent were lucky Lucas and I were there; otherwise, the Guardian Beast would've never beaten them! Maybe they will finally realize now that they made a mistake and put me back in charge. They know they need me now!

-M

M walked into the Elementals base of operations – the Rackson family manor – with Lucas Rackson right on his heels. "Hold up," Lucas said when they reached the top of the hill the huge house sat on.

"What's wrong?"

"There are too many cars here," Lucas pointed toward the long black car and the four cars parked around it. "Somebody else is inside."

M looked from the manor to Lucas anxiously. "What should we do?"

"Go in, but be ready," Lucas answered, and he swung open the front door. The moment the two of them stepped into the foyer, they could hear arguing from upstairs. They could make out Rod's voice, but he was arguing with someone who (for once) wasn't Mo. Now, more curious than anxious, M and Lucas started walking up the stairs and headed to the upstairs study, where Rod and President Bradley were arguing while De, Mo, Kiara, Don, and Jas listened.

"-this aint our fault-" Rod tried to explain.

"Yes it is! If you had destroyed these things when you were supposed to none of this-" the president jumped in.

"When was the last time *you* tried to get rid of an android army? Oh, right, NEVER, because your sorry police-"

"The police force has nothing to do with this-"

"Yea, they do! If they actually DID something then maybe-"

"Okay already!" Lucas yelled. The shock of hearing Lucas raise his voice shut up both Rod and the president and brought all attention to him. "Why are you here?" he asked the latter.

President Bradley adjusted his fitted suit before he answered. He looked a little uncomfortable now having this over six foot new opposition, but still held his ground. "I come on the behalf of myself, the presidents of Grandia and Phorbes, the king of the Underground Kingdom, and the primes of the Sky Nation and Teratitra to demand that the Elementals rectify the remnants of the A.G. situation."

"What do you think we are doing?" Lucas asked

"I understand that you all are...routinely destroying androids-"

"So you think we're just playing around?" Lucas interrupted.

"Let him talk," De finally spoke, much to the added frustration of both Lucas and Rod.

"Thank you, Derren." President Bradley adjusted himself again and addressed the room as a whole, ignoring the dirty looks Jas was throwing his way. "I understand that you all are making progress, but what happened today should have never taken place. I am certain, by now, the leaders in other continents are probably all trying to set up a meeting to discuss how all of them were embarrassed in front of the media. How did you all let a bunch of androids get to the shrines? You were supposed to have taken care of this! The previous generations would have never let something like this happen!"

"You're not helping at all, President Bradley," Kiara said quietly. Luckily it was she who spoke, since by this time, all the others looked ready to pounce on the new president.

President Bradley noticed. He sighed and tried to talk calmly. "It has been very difficult, for me particularly, to calm the general public after what happened with A.G. People are terrified of their toasters now because they are certain they will rise up and try to enslave them. Just when we got people believing in us again; just when things seem to be back on track, a bunch of androids try to kill media personnel from around the world. I'd be surprised if they don't call for all of us elected leaders to step down by the end of the week," he sighed again and looked around the room for sympathy. He got none. "You all might not understand it, but it's not easy running a country."

"Try saving one," Rod spat.

"Well you should understand, then, that you have to keep working to save it. Please, you all have to finish off these androids, quickly, so that things can go back to normal. The world is depending on you." There was real pleading in his eyes, but he had long since killed any chance he had at getting sympathy from the Elementals. Instead, he just turned and walked out of the room, leaving the eight of them to discuss what had just happened. As soon as the door closed behind President Bradley Rod started cursing, and both Jas and Lucas nodded their agreement.

"I don't like him either, but he's kind of right, we gotta finish what we started, and fast," De let the others vent their frustrations before he spoke. "We need to get rid of these androids. Fast."

"And how do you expect us to do that? We don't even know where the ones at the shrines came from, how are we supposed to find the rest of them when they're probably all over the planet?" M countered.

"Sparky is kind of right," Rod pointed out.

"Actually, I know where the androids are," Don spoke for the first time since he had arrived at the manor. He kept his face buried in the screen of his most trusted electronic device, but he finally looked up at this exact moment.

"What are you talking about, Don?" Jas asked.

"Well, when Mo and Gancta were finishing off the androids, I told them to leave one to escape, and I slipped a tracking device on it," he lifted up his device so that everyone could see the single flashing dot on the screen. Behind the dot was a faint map of what looked like Redd Continent.

"Wait...is that still here?" Mo asked, looking closer at the screen.

"Yea, it actually looks like it came to Phorbes. I'm willing to bet that's where whoever is giving them orders is!" Don explained.

"So if we go there-" M started.

"-we can stop whoever is giving out the orders!" Jas finished.

De perked up and looked around at his comrades. "Looks like we have another mission, guys! We might be able to actually do what Bradley wants us to do, and before the end of the night too!" He pointed to the not-yet-set main sun outside the window on the other side of the room.

"Speaking of President Bradley, I kind of feel sorry for him. I know journalists are going to be ruthless with him after what happened today. It's going to be hard out there for him," Kiara said sadly.

Most of the rest of the room was having trouble sharing Kiara's feelings, but De looked thoughtful.

"Lucas, why don't you go help him out?" he suggested.

"What?" Lucas almost yelled at the suggestion.

"Your dad and aunt are already talking to press trying to smooth things over, it may help if they have one of us speaking with them," De explained.

"Having one of us that is directly related to the previous generation is pretty good too," M added.

Lucas opened his mouth to argue, but as far as he could tell, De was right. As much as he didn't want to go anywhere with his father, it would make the most sense if he, the oldest of the current generation and the blood relative of two of the previous generation's most famous members, went to talk to the cameras. Lucas sighed and nodded.

"So, Don, can you keep a track on that thing until we get there?" Rod asked.

"I sure can! It will be easier than the wimpy setting of *Xtreme Brawls*!" Don said excitedly.

M laughed. "We'll take your word for it."

***

"All of this is my fault. Well, no, that's not true. Dad is the one who created the android that would become A.G., but that makes me guilty by association, right? He created the android because he knew the money he would make could really help us out. So that kind of makes it my fault, right? Plus, President Hammock only found out about my dad making androids because he made Lauryn first. And that wouldn't have happened if he didn't miss Mom so much. I should have been there for him more so he wouldn't have had to make all this stuff. That...that is my fault."

-Mo

"Mo? Mo! MORGAN PETERS!" Don yelled over the phone to get Mo out of his daydreams.

"Huh? Oh, sorry, what is it?" Mo asked.

"You guys are close to where the signal is coming from. Where are you guys?" Don asked again.

"Don wants to know where we are," Mo informed the others. Kiara answered from the front seat.

"The last sign I saw said we were approaching the Western Oasis. Looks like we're pretty much here now," she said. Sure enough, the sandy roads of Phorbes had turned green, and trees and a large body of water replaced sand dunes and rock formations outside of the car.

"You heard that?" Mo asked. When Don answered he continued, "I don't know why you didn't just come with us. It would have been easier and I wouldn't have to stay on the phone for hours at a time."

"Oh, you know, I had to stay here and coordinate, you know? It's hard to see the whole picture when you're really close to it, you know?" Even though this was a regular phone conversation and Mo couldn't see Don's face or expressions, he still felt like the inventor was lying.

"Sure. Anyway, call De or M in the other car so they can know too," Mo suggested.

"Will do!" Don was so relieved to be done with the conversation that he hung up without saying goodbye. Mo started to feel a little jilted, but now was not the time. They had a mission to complete. He peered out of his window and looked around at their new lush surroundings. He even saw what looked like a large old rest stop a little down the road from where they were, right before a small community of houses. This would be a good place to hide.

"I'm going to park here so we can take a look around," Kiara said to Mo and Jas. She had whipped Lucas' car off the main road and focused on trying to park. "Hopefully we can find out where the-"

"LOOK OUT!" Jas screamed suddenly. Kiara looked back at the road to see a group of androids racing toward them firing lasers at both cars. Kiara swerved to try to dodge some of the attacks, but one of them managed to tear through the backseat of the car, blasting through one door and carrying Mo out of the other one.

"No!" Kiara yelled. She slammed on the breaks and leapt out of the barely stopped car to rush to Mo's side.

For once, De's dangerous driving skills worked to his advantage, and he was able to throw his car in reverse and avoid much of the damage. After yelling at De for nearly breaking their necks, Rod and M leapt out of the car and using the water from the oasis, started the attack. Jas soon joined them by creating a powerful gust that stopped more of the androids from coming out of the shabby building that they were using for a "base." Kiara and De, however, were tending to their fallen teammate.

"Is he okay?" De asked. Kiara dropped Mo's hand and breathed a sigh of relief.

"He's just knocked out. He was sandwiched between the two doors so he's hurt, but he's okay. Aurora Baris Mal!" she roared at the android that slipped past the others to approach them.

"We gotta help!" De said once he saw the android hit the ground. Kiara nodded, and the two of them joined the fight. Thanks to their closeness to the oasis Rod was able to send quite a bit of water over the seemingly never-ending flow of androids, making it easier for M to hit them with bolts of electricity, or Jas to create concentrated wind to tear them apart. When De joined the fight he immediately began pitching fire balls at every android he could see, and Kiara was casting spells as fast as she could.

"Where are all these things coming from? It's so many!" Jas complained.

"They're coming from that little hut thing!" M answered.

"Well it's coming down!" Jas broke away from the onslaught and raced toward the building that the androids had poured out of. A few of the nearly two dozen machines outside had seen her and tried to follow the Air Elemental, but one had her back.

"Octoren Lumes!" Kiara yelled, sending no less than eight beams of light from her fingertips and directly into the androids. The four machines glowed yellow and collapsed into a heap behind Jas, and the younger Elemental raised her own hands, and immediately the building stared to shake and sway from the strong wind pushing against it. The other androids were dropping like flies thanks to the combined attacks of De, M, Rod, and Kiara. Even Mo started to stir and lumbered over to help out.

"Jas, bring it down!" Rod encouraged his sister. Though no more androids were coming out of the building, he was under the impression that if the building fell so would the androids. Jas agreed, and a particularly powerful gust took the roof off the building. At that moment, a single figure came running out of the building, flailing his arms and screaming at the top of his lungs. Jas stopped her wind to better hear his surrender.

"Stop, stop! I'll call them off! We won't do anything else! Just stop!" the figure, in its tight buttoned shirt and short buzz cut looked desperate enough to catch the other Elementals attention as well. Only three of the androids remained, and as soon as "I'll call them off" left this new figure's lips they immediately ceased their attack. The six Elementals walked closer to this figure, and upon closer inspection Mo realized something.

"You're an android!" He yelled, pointing at it.

The android nodded. "Please, do not harm my sisters and brothers any further. We are all that are left," he explained. "I'll do whatever you want."

Rod barked out a laugh. "I swear I love these smart ones. They always help us out."

Kiara looked confused. "'Smart one'?" she repeated.

"Yea, when we were fighting A.G. we found out she made some smart droids to live with regular people and spy on them. This is definitely one of them," M knocked on the android's leg to emphasize his point, and the smart droid grimaced to hold back its frustration.

"Mo, can you call Don? Maybe we can get him to do some tech stuff over the phone and check this story out," De suggested.

"Good idea," Mo agreed. He pulled out his phone, but instead of bringing it to his face, he held it out so that the tiny Don hologram could be seen by all of them, including the smart droid.

"Hey guys, what's going on?" he asked.

"Oh nothing major. We're just killing the last androids," Jas said with a grin.

***

"This. Is. AWESOME. Who would've thought I would be here, in Phorbes, fighting androids as an Elemental? I still can't believe it myself, I'm not exactly

the 'hero' type, but then again none of us are. I guess that's what makes it work, we're all insane kids with crazier powers. But we're here! It gives a great distraction from all the other headache, I gotta admit, but sometimes I wonder if...no, it will be fine. I mean it has to be, right? We can handle anything, can't we? If the boys could beat A.G., then a little argument is nothing, right? I mean, we are Elementals. Yeah, it will be fine. Besides, that's not important right now. We have stuff to do and I REFUSE to be the one to hold everybody back. Sorry Mom, we'll have to figure this stuff out later, I have a job to do!"

-Jas

"So what you got?" Rod asked Don. The latter had spent the last fifteen minutes pecking away at his holographic computer sitting in his holographic chair and getting on everyone's very real nerves. The silence from the inventor made them nervous almost as much as the trance-like state the last smart droid was in as long as Don's device was plugged into it.

"Alright! Got it!" Don announced.

"Great! Now what is 'it'?" De asked.

"Oh, right, sorry. So basically he was telling the truth. These are the last few androids. They were here supposed to be waiting for the people who have been controlling all of them, but apparently once you guys showed up this guy got to work cleaning house."

"What does that mean?" Mo asked.

"Basically, he sent a signal to who they were working for telling them not to come, and he erased all memory of what they were doing in the first place from himself and the rest of the androids. I can use the signal to see what they were reporting to each other, and the last thing they all have is basically a memory wipe," Don explained.

"So...so...." M said, struggling to keep up.

"That means this was a waste of time," Jas sighed.

"Not entirely," Don said. "I did get an image of the two people the androids were working for. It was almost literally burned in all of their memories with the word "Boss". It was probably there to remind them not to kill the two of them should they find them. It's pretty smart," he admitted.

"So what is the image?" De asked.

"Hold on. I'll transfer the image to my computer so you guys can see it." Don got up and walked out of the "frame" of his hologram and a minute or so later the image changed to a three dimensional image of two people, a short dark woman with purple hair and a taller light man with curly hair. Kiara gasped loudly.

"I know them! Their faces are plastered all over the papers, that's the Prudence Kids!"

"Prudence...kids?" It was now Jas' turn to be confused.

"The Prudence Kids are the ones who started all of this...they're the ones who reprogrammed A.G. in the first place to make her into a killing machine," M explained. Mo and De both looked at the images with utter disgust. Off screen, they heard Don speaking.

"Kiara's right. These two are the ones behind all of this."

De gritted his teeth and looked at the others. He had a sudden flash of anger at seeing the Prudence Kids that was only intensified when he saw his foster parents in his mind, the nice older couple that was killed by A.G.'s androids before he joined the team. "Well, we know what we have to do next," he growled.

"Umm, why? Look man, I get you want revenge and stuff, but we did what the government wanted us to do. We stopped the androids. I say we take some time off and take care of ourselves for a little while," Rod said.

"This is our duty as Elementals! I can't believe even you would be so selfish!" Mo snapped. Instead of getting angry, Rod actually laughed.

"You caught up in revenge too kid. Think of it this way, where would we even find these two? The cops been looking for them for months; they pretty much gave up. I mean, we're better than them but still. Besides, without A.G. or androids they can't really do anything to us. I'm just saying that we shouldn't jump right back into some stuff so quick."

"I kind of agree with Rod," Don admitted. He had walked back into the frame to look around at the group. "We all could use some time off, I think."

Kiara was next. Her answer was simple. "De and Mo are right. It's the 5th Command. We have to do what we can to help. Technically the 4th one too, 'Value others' well-being'."

Jas looked from Rod to Kiara and back. "Well, I joined you guys to help people. We find the Prudence Kids and take them back to jail we're helping a lot of people. We should do it." Rod looked a little surprised that his sister would go against him, but when he saw the look in her eyes he knew there was no changing her mind. Instead, he and the others all looked at M.

"Oh so now my opinion matters?" he snarled.

"Just say what you gotta say, Sparky." Rod shot back.

"Well..." M held out the word for dramatic (and annoying) effect. "I think we need to call the President."

"I don't need him telling me a decision to make!" De argued.

"I'm with him on that," Rod agreed.

"Not for that dummy. Think about it, if the Prudence Kids really are behind the androids still wrecking stuff, this is the government's fault. They let them escape prison and stopped trying to find them. It's their fault that people are being hurt, so unless they want the rest of the world to find out, they would have to help us find them. We get the government on our side, it will be nothing to find the Prudence Kids. It probably won't be a long journey again with them backing us."

"Okay, I actually love that idea," Rod admitted.

"And it works another way too. I mean it was another government official who ordered A.G. be created in the first place. This is just as much their fault as anybody else's," Don pointed out.

"So, does this mean we're going with it? Finding the Prudence Kids?" De asked hopefully.

M sighed. "I can't believe I'm saying this, but...I agree with De. Let's do it."

Kiara grinned. "Guess I should get ready to do another special piece on this. I wonder...could I interview myself?"

The others laughed, but in all of their minds, they came to the realization that they had just signed themselves up for another mission, another journey to continue their duty as Elementals.

REAL MONSTERS
Nora Anthony

Smokey eye shadow, check.

Konda flipped the black shiny hair that cascaded down the middle of her back.

New weave, check.

She puckered her thick lips, applied the wine red lipstick. Eye shadow, mascara, and foundation, all from the *Walgreens* on Main Street, were scattered on the bathroom sink.

Tonight was the night. She was gonna get Freddy.

"Shut up!"

She heard the voice echo from under the bathroom floor.

A young man. She sniffed the air. A few young men. Teenagers. In the apartment right under her.

Who lived down there?

Then she remembered; Ms. Jean, the old Haitian woman that would leave leftover bread hanging on Konda's door. She was sweet.

In a few breaths, Konda was downstairs, bursting down the door.

She stared into the shocked eyes of three boys, tall and skinny. One of them with tattoos on his eyelids licked his lips.

"Ya'll better get out of here now. You hear me?"

"Who says?' One of them pulled out a gun, and cocked it.

Crap. Where's Ms. Jean?

She heard her whimpering in the kitchen.

Good. She's out the way. And I don't smell any blood.

Before the bullet left the gun, Konda had disarmed him, kicked him on the floor and cracked his spine.

She couldn't prevent the next gun from firing off, but she grabbed his arm and jammed her elbow up his nose. More cracks and screams before he fainted.

The other two ran out the door, but they were too slow. Konda knocked both of them out in the hallway, a little gentler this time. She didn't want any dead bodies around. That wouldn't be good for her.

She stood up, felt her lipstick, her make up. No sweat, as usual. She didn't think anything could make her sweat anymore.

She stomped back into the small apartment, carrying out the remaining young men and tossing them out in the hallway. "Ms. Jean? Did you call the police?"

"Yes!" Ms. Jean hobbled out of the kitchen unharmed. She looked at Konda wide eyed. "You beat them up? You skinny thing, that never eats?"

Konda laughed, hesitantly. "I eat." *Just not in the past few days.* "I do karate. Keep the men away, you know." Konda frowned. "Are you really okay?"

Ms. Jean sighed sitting down on her couch. "My son was right. I need to move back in with him in Westchester. Spring Valley isn't safe anymore." She rubbed her arms.

"Make sure he comes and gets you tonight, after the police report."

"I will." Ms. Jean frowned. "And where are you going, with that hoochie dress?"

"Hoochie? It's not hoochie, it's nice. I'm trying to catch a man tonight, I need something black and tight, right?"

"Not if you want a *good* man!"

Konda grinned. *I'm not looking for a good man.* "I'll keep that in mind. Take care! The police should be coming soon." She could hear them running up the creaky stairs to the third floor of the apartment complex.

Konda sauntered back up to her apartment.

She froze.

There, standing in her empty living room, was Rachel. Her pierced lip lifted up in a smile. " Where you going?"

Konda pressed her lips firmly together. "None of your business." She went into the bathroom and continued to get ready.

"I'm not coming," Konda said in her bedroom, as she rubbed lotion down her legs. Her skin was dry and getting a little pale. It would return to its flawless state after she ate something.

"You need to. " Rachel was still standing in the living room. "You can't keep doing this."

"I have to." *I can't not do anything with my powers.*

Konda walked out of the room in her heels, her black purse hung on her shoulder. She turned to the black woman with short curly hair and bright teeth. "Get out of my house."

Rachel sighed. "I'll be around, if you need me."

"I won't."

"When was the last time you ate? You're gonna need us, Konda. After tonight, you'll be coming back with us."

With that, Konda walked out the door and slammed it behind her.

Who she think she is? I'm not joining their colony. I'm not living with other people like me.

She was going to keep moving from town to town in New York, saving people and disappearing, putting in a new weave or wearing her normal hair out, changing her wardrobe, where she hung out and who she spoke to.

She was looking for monsters. Before she found her apartment, she lived on the streets, the cold nights not bothering her skin, shooting, smoking and snorting the dope that would never alter her brain just so she could find the pushers, the suppliers, the traffickers.

Freddy was a bonus. He pushed drugs and got runaway girls into his sex trafficking ring.

A real monster, Konda repeated to herself, as she walked into *Fire and Ice.*

Fetty Wap was blaring on the speakers in the club. Konda let her hips sway back and forth, slowly as she walked to the bar, an advanced replicate of the many women in skin tight dresses and heels. She ignored the eyes of the men who watched her walk by the edge of the dance floor, ignored the whistles and murmurs of desire.

Konda was used to the compliments by now. Before she changed, she wasn't ugly; just normal. Her skin was sepia brown; she had a thin frame with wide hips and small breasts; she thought her eyes were too small for her face and her hair was always in need of a touch up. But after, her skin glowed. Men couldn't help but look at her. It didn't truly matter if she couldn't get the right rhythm to sway her hips or if she wore makeup. Something in her made her irresistible.

The hard part was the people. She connected with people too easily, even if she only needed information from them. The red eyed women hooked on crack and the rot-mouthed men were mothers, sisters, brothers. They looked like monsters, but they were only broken creatures.

Like me, she thought, but she silenced herself and ordered a Moscato. It used to be her favorite drink, but after the change, she couldn't taste the sweet drink or feel the buzz.

She drank it anyway.

She saw Freddy further down the bar, talking to a few of his men. She could see the grills on his bottom teeth.

She began her walk by them, but kept her eyes on him only. Made him believe she wanted him.

He smiled at her. "Aye; come here."

Konda obeyed. She walked over to the overweight black man, let him pull her onto his lap. "You new? I never seen you before."

"Yeah. I come from here, there." Konda smiled her bright large teeth at him.

She spent the most of the night on Freddy's lap, kissing his small ears, whispering into them.

She smelled meat; hamburgers. Konda bit her lip.

"What, you hungry girl? Freddy can feed you."

Konda giggled. "I bet you can." She nibbled on his ear, careful not to bite too hard.

Freddy ran his thick fingers through her hair, and kissed her.

It wasn't as disgusting as Konda thought it would be. It was enjoyable...tasty.

"I want you," Konda whined. "Now."

With a quickness, Freddy and his men left the club. Konda and Freddy fooled around in the back of his truck. She was careful not to be too hard, too rough with him. He was large, but she could easily break him.

She had no doubt that he was enjoying the feel of her skin, the way her lips tasted. She was irresistible; so much so that he told his men to go back to the club at her request, that they'd need complete privacy for what he was about to do to her.

They made it into his large colonial house, and into the bedroom.

She pushed Freddy onto his bed, stood over him, began to strip him as he grinned almost comically at her.

She drank in that look in his eyes, that powerlessness he had slumped into.

She could smell him. Soft; salty; delicious.

Konda let herself black out.

He truly was delicious. She swallowed his torn ears and lips easily. She chomped on his brain to stop his screaming and let herself indulge in his face and neck. The microscopic canines on her bright white teeth allowed her to chomp through his chest, stomach, torso, then finally his legs and feet.

The warm rush was running through her blood, her heart pounding, her muscles flexing and rejoicing at the new energy. Finally, after days of starvation, she was fed!

With bright eyes and glowing skin, she walked into the bathroom to wash all of the blood off.

She had a few hours before someone knew something was up. She kicked off her heels and ran out the house, all the way home.

She wasn't winded at all when she made it back to the old apartment complex. She was walking into the hallway when she smelt someone delicious.

She was still hungry? No way.

She walked into her apartment, to see Ms. Jean, cooking on her stove.

"You left your door unlocked. You can't tell *me* I'm not being safe."

"Ms. Jean," Konda grimaced. She was losing her vision. Why wasn't Freddy enough? She swore she locked the door.

"Get out, get out before..."

Konda blacked out.

When she awoke, she saw Rachel looking down on her.

"Ms. Jean!" Konda scurried around her.

Torn pieces of Mrs. Jean's lime Mumu were scattered across the bare floor. The beef she cooked was still simmering in the pot.

"No. No, I didn't..."

"You did. What did I tell you about starving yourself?"

"No...not again." Konda rocked back and forth on her knees, revisiting the memories of when she first changed, became infected...*evolved*, as Rachel would say. Her dad, he was just there and was worried because she wasn't eating and she blacked out and he was...

"Konda," Rachel grabbed her shoulders. "You need to move. Now. Come with me. We can take care of you! You'll be properly fed..."

"No! I'm not just eating humans. I can't do that."

"But you are."

"I'm not! People like Freddy...they deserve it. I'm doing the world some good. It's the only thing I could do."

"But you ate the old lady."

Konda staggered up. Black eyeliner ran down her cheeks, her face a purple and black mess of cheap makeup. "You left my door open." She grabbed Rachel by the neck. "You killed her."

Rachel didn't move. She only squeaked out, "You're the one who ate her."

Konda slammed her into the wall. It cracked.

Rachel coughed and picked herself up. "It will happen again. It always does."

"Get out. Get out before I kill you, you stupid..."

"You know we can't die."

Konda crumbled to the floor. How she wished death was possible. She was beautiful, strong and immortal. But her beautiful immortal body craved flesh, and it would find it, whether she wanted to or not.

Konda dug around for her street clothes. "So I just hole up with you and the other sick. Prey on people." Her eyes kept blurring from the tears. *Poor Ms. Jean. What about her son?*

"Better than torturing yourself like this."

Konda was in faded jeans and an oversized hoodie in no time. She ripped her weave out, so her short, broken hair stuck out every which way. "I still can't do that, Rachel. I'm still human, I can't...I can't think of myself as anything other."

Rachel looked concerned. "You'll only make yourself crazy thinking that way."

Konda shrugged. "Fine with me." She scanned the apartment, made sure it was barer than before.

She slipped out of the window and climbed down to the ground. She knew Rachel would follow her in a few minutes. The leader of the Evolved Colony told her to follow Konda as long as it takes, to do whatever it takes to bring her to the colony. *To be united,* Rachel had said. *To be among our own.*

They could take over the world, for all Konda cared. She knew she had to keep consuming the real monsters, eradicating their existence.

Even if she was a real monster herself.

GLASCOCK
Cynthia Ward

Under the curving glass sky, a young woman reclined on a hotel balcony. She was alone. She wore a white bikini which emphasized her dark, flawless skin, yet she was obscured from upturned gazes by an arabesque parapet. Save for the tiny crystal glittering just below her shapely lips, she wore no jewelry. However, diamonds adorned the cigarette holder angled in her left hand and the dataspex lorgnette upheld by her right.

Her balcony faced the main building of Bokassa's Palace, a casino resort renowned throughout Human Space. In the distance, the subtly groomed grounds rose, lush in tropical colors. La Rivière Infinie Congo flowed upward, following the outer curve of the Stanford torus.

The young woman's dataspex weren't fixed on any of the space station's storied sights. Instead, her lorgnette was turned toward a large swimming pool, which glittered between hotel and casino. More precisely, her app was focused tightly upon one of two men seated poolside. The men faced each other over round pasteboard playing cards, which had been fabbed by the table between them. Though alone on the balcony, the woman spoke quietly, now and again, in Galactic Standard KiSwahili.

She resumed murmuring. "He's holding an ace, two threes--"

"Fascinating." A man leaned close to the woman's ear, whispering almost inaudibly as his thumb covered the tiny crystal just below her lower lip. "I understand now why Richard Glascock is playing Go Fish by the pool, instead of baccarat inside the casino."

The woman laid down the lorgnette and turned on her divan to face the man, fully revealing her classic Somalied 'Usub features. She occupied the room alone. However, she didn't appear disturbed to find a tall, dark man regarding her from a distance of mere inches, while covering her crystalline adornment with his thumb.

She swept her gaze over the man, taking in the dark, sharp eyes, the amused smile, the rugged face. His vest and swimming trunks bared a pleasing breadth of shoulder and symmetry of muscle. He seemed a few years older than the young woman.

Meeting his eyes again, she smiled, in a manner far from unfriendly. "Did you climb down the wall of my hotel, or merely break into my room?"

"That's a professional secret." The man glanced at the card players. "I'm devastated to learn the wealthiest diamond merchant in Human Space is dishonest. How much has Mr. Glascock won?"

The woman's smile widened. "Two hundred twenty thousand AU since they began play."

The man leaned closer, his thumb still covering the crystal below her lip as his own lips brushed her ear. "I would be even more devastated to learn you were involved with Mr. Glascock."

"As a freelance employee only," said the woman. "The owners of the space station demand strict adherence to Elemental Revivalist Christian morality. Therefore, I am paid to look beautiful on a man's arm and, when Mr. Glascock visits, to peer on occasion through a binocular app."

"I cannot express my relief," the man murmured, gazing deeply into her dark, appraising eyes. "I should hate to think a gambling Mecca operated in the absence of morality."

Keeping his thumb over the tiny crystal below her lips, he raised his head a little. She tilted her lorgnette so he might peer through. The app adjusted itself to his gaze, sharpening the image of the thin, pallid, light-haired card-player, who sat facing the balcony.

"I believe," said the man on the balcony, "it's time for Crystal Dick's luck to turn."

The woman's smile grew sly. "I believe you might be right."

The man brought his lips close to hers, and, brushing the edge of her lower lip with his thumbnail, he removed the crystal from below her lips and held it to his own.

"Mr. Glascock!" he said to the micro-crystal, a lab-cultured Aurigan transmitter.

The pale card-player jerked in his seat. He began to look up.

"I strongly recommend that you keep your eyes on your cards, Mr. Glascock."

The pale player went rigid. He lowered his head. His gaze fixed on his hand with an intentness not previously displayed.

"I'm assisting you now," said the man on the balcony. "But the rules of the game have changed. You will ask your opponent only for cards he doesn't hold, unless you'd like me to contact casino security. Would you like me to contact casino security?"

The pale player gave his head a quick shake.

"Very good," said the man on the balcony. "You will start by asking for the queen--"

When the pale player found himself down two hundred twenty thousand AU, the man on the balcony said, "Game over, Mr. Glascock."

Glascock flung down his cards.

On the balcony, the man holding the Aurigan crystal transmitter squeezed it between his thumb and forefinger. The crystal shattered.

The woman smiled at him, seductively. "Do you have a name?"

He held out his hand, and she placed her hand in his.

"Bhamu," he answered, as he raised her to her feet. "Jangano Bhamu."

"I'm Tai Msasi."

She led him into her suite. He took her into his arms.

Enormous mirrors deflected sunlight through the glass inner rim of Bokassa's Torus. The mirrors began slowly to turn. Night seeped into the space station. Electricity and neon flared across hotels and retail structures, amphitheatres and nightclubs, restoring artificial day.

Bhamu and Msasi sat up in her expansive bed. Light came faintly through a slit between the heavy curtains drawn over the glass balcony door. The light reached the bed and nightstand. The rest of the room was lost in shadow.

Msasi reached for the cigarette pack on the nightstand. The pack lay next to a miniature flechette pistol. Bhamu had removed it from his vest while disrobing.

As Bhamu lit Msasi's cigarette, the glow revealed a man, broad and still and besuited, watching them.

The woman gasped. "Oddlot!"

Bhamu lunged for the flechette pistol.

The besuited man moved with equal alacrity. His arm flexed, snapping forward with the swiftness of a New Murri dandarabilla snake. The long, bent object he'd been holding flew from his hand.

The boomerang struck Bhamu's temple. He sank down on the bed as if rendered boneless. He did not stir.

***

Bhamu was not unconscious long. But, when he woke, the man was gone. Every light in the room was ablaze. Tai Msasi's nude form glittered.

***

"She wasn't turned to crystal."

The speaker, a whip-thin, blade-faced older woman known to her subordinates as Alif, extended a long arm across her desk. On her palm rested a small, elegant case of deep purple Alzubran burlwood. From the case, Jangano Bhamu selected a cigarette. He leaned back, placing it between his lips and touching an Alpha Cepheian crystal to the tip. Though the crystal was cool in his hand, the tip of his cigarette glowed red. Smoke rose in a thin line. Bhamu did not enjoy the taste of Novo Brasilian tobacco – he favored Yeniturkish – but it could have been worse. The Director of the Special Intelligence Service preferred Newmerican tobacco, which Bhamu despised.

Looking at Alif, he raised his brows. "Not crystal?"

Alif said, "She was turned to diamond, Agent Za."

He drew on his cigarette and looked meditatively out the window of Alif's office. He was no longer in Bokassa's Torus. He was now on – or, more correctly, inside – his homeworld, a vast Dyson sphere known as New Zanzibar. To be more specific, Bhamu sat inside the tall, bland high-rise known to the public as the home of the Ministry of Agriculture and Wildlife. It was a plausible identity; immense swathes of New Zanzibar's interior were given over to the cropland, rangeland, and carefully cultivated wilderness that sustained the sphere's several hundred quintillion residents. However, much of the interior surface was occupied by the single, enormous city of New Trantor. The window behind Alif offered Bhamu a view of the district of Steel Town, the gleaming governmental soul of the ecumenopolis. Though seated in an office over one hundred stories above ground level, Bhamu couldn't see the upcurve of the cityscape. Despite certain romantic images featured in New Zanzibarean tourism ministry advertisements on the InterPlanetNet, the beginning of the Dyson sphere curvature was millions of kilometers distant, and therefore out of sight.

"Interesting," Bhamu said, at length. "I'd not been aware that a process existed to turn flesh to diamond."

"It *was* a secret of the New Zanzibarean defense ministry," Alif replied. "It is no longer."

"I see." Bhamu did not comment on the obvious danger such a leak posed to New Zanzibar and its allies. "This process would be a threat to Glascock and other diamond traders, I suppose."

"Perhaps," Alif said. "Perhaps not. Diamond manufactured by human or alien processes has never previously threatened the market for naturally occurring diamonds of the first water."

She reached into the burlwood case, which now rested on the authentic Fomolhautean hardwood of her desk, and selected a cigarette. Bhamu knew very little about the head of SIS--New Zanzibar's Special Intelligence Service-- but he knew better than to offer her a light. She deployed her own Alpha Cepheian crystal, then smoked for a moment, studying him.

"Our concern is not for the state of the natural diamond market," she said finally, "although of course we wouldn't care to test the theory that creating diamonds from flesh wouldn't affect the interstellar economy."

"Then there's a concern beyond the obvious."

"Of course there's a concern beyond the obvious, Agent Za. You wouldn't be sitting in my office if there wasn't. The threat is immediate, and grave."

"I'm afraid I fail to grasp the nature of this threat."

"Part of our concern is that the process also works in reverse."

"Ah," Bhamu said. "I can see where that would be a threat to the interstellar diamond market, and therefore to economic stability."

"Would that this was the full extent of the threat," Alif said. "But this reverse process doesn't only convert diamond to flesh. It also works, with equal swiftness, on certain metals."

"Gold and other precious metals?"

"When applied directly, as with an aerosol dispenser, or an explosion, it dissolves most metals, Agent Za."

Involuntarily, Bhamu glanced out the window at Steel Town.

"You comprehend, I see," 'Alif said. "Glascock has come into possession of a secret more threatening to us than fusion was to Old Earth."

"Glascock possesses," Bhamu said, "the means to dissolve our graviton generators and our great world-city, and most every other urb in Human Space."

"Which would be catastrophic enough," 'Alif said. "But that's not all. He can dissolve the transsteel of which our sphere-world itself is constructed, and leave every one of New Zanzibar's several hundred quintillion inhabitants to die in the vacuum of space."

***

In the darkness of a planetary night from which both moons had fled, Bhamu crouched on a forested hillside. He was clad in a full-body coverall provided by Qāf, the research and development division of SIS. The coverall's smartcloth showed a shifting camouflage pattern, which harmonized with the deciduous forests of the planet New New England. Qāf Division wasn't responsible for the video-camo, but it had created the app that gave Bhamu the heat signature of a local deer species.

Bhamu wore an earpiece and a pair of dataspex. Both were far superior to any on the interstellar market. Data flickered in Bhamu's peripheral vision as he watched a small, sporty starship descend noisily to the spacefield of a palatial estate. The ship came to rest on retro-style fins and cut its roaring rocket. The rocket and fins were aesthetic. Starships circumvented the vastness of interstellar space with near-instantaneous warp drives, and landed and launched by generating anti-gravitons.

An aesthetically old-school airlock opened in the starship's sleek side. From the lock, a ramp emerged, settling on the plascrete. Soon thereafter, the airlock disgorged several individuals into the bright artificial lighting of the spacefield, and into range of Bhamu's Qāf-designed spex.

Emerging first were a pair of watchful male bodyguards. Their uniforms matched those of the private security guards Bhamu had spotted patrolling the grounds of the estate, and they bore the same weapons: 905 nm laser-rifles of New Palestinian design. The bodyguards were followed by a dozen men of varying degrees of attentiveness and attractiveness. These were clad in unflattering one-piece lavender jumpsuits of the sort favored by henchpersons, or, rather, their employers. The jumpsuit of each henchman was belted with a white sash, which held a semi-automatic flechette pistol of Neudeutchlander design.

After the henchmen, three dark-skinned young women emerged from the ship. They were so beautiful, the agent covertly watching them caught his breath. All three were clad in far more upmarket uniforms than the men. The shortest wore the sort of dress uniform associated with starship engineers, though hers came from no official space force. The other two women – one tall, the other downright stunning – wore the sort of blazer, tie, and slacks favored for over a millennium by civilian starcraft pilots. Each carried the traditional pilot's cap under one arm. The stunning woman had a voluptuous figure and a gorgeous Hausa Sáabóo face and a civilian captain's insignia. Her right hand rested on an accessory less commonly associated with private aviators: a flechette pistol.

Bhamu tore his gaze from the lead pilot and forced himself to study the man who followed her out of the starship. This man was dark and powerfully built, of average height, with black, wavy hair that fell to his shoulders. His features were pure New Murri, though he wore an elegant cream lace agbada and deep red fila in the latest New Yoruban style. In his left hand he held a large boomerang. He was the man Tai Msasi had identified as Oddlot before she died.

The New Murrian was followed by two men. One was a beautiful, willowy young man, dripping with diamonds and dressed in the height of New Mumbai fashion. He had one bejeweled brown hand draped negligently over the elbow of the other man. This man appeared some years older. He was tall and thin, with the pale, straight hair and bony, pallid face of a New New Englander. He was Richard Glascock, and he was retro-stylishly attired in a revival of TwenCen Western men's fashion, complete with analog watch, diamond cufflinks, diamond-accented tie clip, and an absence of further ornamentation.

Behind Richard Glascock and his arm-candy, a fourth woman stepped from the craft. She had the straight black hair and round tan face of Xin Zhongguo. She wore the silk slacks and long jacquard jacket of a wealthy Xin Zhongguo businesswoman without an air of comfort. Hastening to the unoccupied side of the diamond merchant, she leaned close and began speaking intently into his ear.

Bhamu began to hear a woman's voice in his left ear. When the airlock had opened, he'd released a nano-drone. It featured an Aurigan cultured-crystal transmitter and the freshest in Qāf Division anti-detection measures. It followed Glascock's party, sending Bhamu's earpiece the clearest conversation possible.

"We're prepared to pay very well--" the black-haired woman was speaking the Běifānghuà Mandarin of Xin Zhongguo "--for use of the formula--"

"Of course you are," Glascock replied in the same language, its tones tinged with the nasal accent of New Boston. "Only the New Zanzibarean government and I have the formula. And New Zanzibar wouldn't sell it to you at any price."

Bhamu began to move stealthily down the wooded slope.

On the spacefield, Glascock smiled at the Xin Zhongguo woman. "You're in luck, Madame Zhang. I'm willing to fulfill your government's fondest desire at a bargain rate. I will charge your government only slightly less than everything."

Zhang ignored his witticism. "We should like to begin Operation Slam Dunk in one Galactic Standard week--"

Zhang's voice cut off as she, Glascock, and Glascock's arm-candy rounded the corner of a large warehouse.

No building should have been able to block the nano-drone's transmission. It was possible the nano-drone had failed. It was also possible the Glascock estate's datanet had a counter-surveillance measure unknown to Qāf Division.

If the latter was true, the datanet might have detected the nano-drone-- and reported it to Glascock.

Abandoning caution, Bhamu sprinted down the dangerously rough hillside. He could only hope the sounds he made would be drowned by the henchmen's tramping footsteps, or mistaken for a deer running through the woods.

Emerging from the forest, Bhamu sped like a gazelle across the spacefield. He appreciated its modest dimensions, but not its bright lights. He was grateful to reach the shadow of a hangar for planetary aircraft.

Glascock's party had disappeared around a corner of the warehouse. Bhamu followed, advancing quietly on large squares of plascrete pavement. Peering around a second corner, he saw Glascock's group some distance ahead, rounding the corner of a greenhouse. Glascock was calmly discussing payment with Madame Zhang, and no one in his entourage glanced around. None demonstrated awareness of a security breach.

Glascock's party had progressed along the pavement without incident. But as Bhamu followed, one of the squares of plascrete gave way beneath his feet.

He stifled the impulse to curse the darkness as he plunged through it.

A sudden but not unexpected impact stole his senses.

***

Jangano Bhamu woke to bright light, and to powerful aches in head and body. He didn't change expression. He kept his eyes narrow, letting his vision adjust.

He lay on his back. He wondered if he'd been moved. He couldn't recall the moment of impact. He doubted he'd landed with his weight evenly distributed, his arms against his sides, and his legs stretched out straight.

Through barely parted lids, Bhamu looked around.

His body was aligned with the length of a rectangular tabletop. Its sides were equidistant from his arms. He couldn't see the head or foot of the tabletop unless he moved his head. He kept still.

He could see a wall to either side. The walls were pink as the interior of a Nueva Cuba conch. The left wall had a metal door, a motion detector light-switch, and a square red button. Each wall was over six Standard Meters from the table.

Bhamu assessed himself. His aches suggested serious bruises, but no broken bones. His dataspex, earpiece, concealed firearms and knives, video-camouflage coverall, and boots had been removed, leaving him in the tight-fitting black pants and long-sleeved shirt he'd worn underneath the coverall.

Bhamu felt a discernable interruption in the surface beneath his torso and head. The interruption might mean the tabletop could be separated for addition of an extender. The separation felt wider than necessary. Bhamu didn't like it.

He also didn't like the broad metal bands binding his torso and limbs to the table. Those passing over his chest and stomach also confined his arms. However, each of his legs was secured in place by a separate series of bands. These kept his legs separated by several centimeters.

A faint click drew Bhamu's attention to the door. It swung open, admitting the diamond smuggler and his diamond-dripping arm-candy. The two were followed into the room by Oddlot, still bearing his boomerang. Oddlot was followed by a dozen henchmen to be named later, if at all.

"Rise and shine, Mr. Bhamu!" called the diamond smuggler.

Bhamu raised his head and looked around.

The tabletop was pale wood. The separation divided the tabletop from head to foot. The surface was patched with large, dark stains. They bore a distinct resemblance to dried blood.

Bhamu's gaze fixed on the table's most unusual detail.

This appeared to be a diamond blade, visible between and beyond his parted feet. The blade rose a Standard meter above the tabletop. The glittering edge faced Bhamu from the edge of the separation in the table. To be more precise, the blade-edge faced Bhamu's groin.

Observing the focus of Bhamu's attention, Richard Glascock laughed. "Mr. Bhamu, it's a pleasure to see you again!" he said in Galactic Standard KiSwahili. "I regret that our last acquaintance was so unsatisfying. But you were unconscious in my lady companion's hotel room. Furthermore, my earpiece was transmitting the news that your counterpart in the Newmerican Central Intelligence Agency was rushing to your side. I found it necessary to leave Bokassa's Torus before you could wake."

Bhamu looked at him. "Pleased to meet you, I suppose."

"I suppose you believe you pleased Ms. Tsasi," Glascock returned with a smile. "But I was quite displeased that I hadn't time to reward you as I rewarded her. However, I'm a diamond merchant, so I always look on the bright side of life. And I rejoice that you've gratified me with the opportunity to introduce you to--" he gestured at the foot of the table "--a singular gem."

"Charmed, I'm sure," Bhamu replied coolly. "Now, if I might have a spot of assistance in rising from this table--"

"I'm afraid I must disappoint your hope, Mr. Bhamu."

Glascock gestured. Oddlot turned and retraced his steps. Instead of exiting, he depressed the red button beside the door.

A faint motor noise began, drawing Bhamu's attention to the foot of the table.

The diamond blade began to move rapidly up and down. Simultaneously, it began to proceed up the channel in the table. Its advance was less frantic than its up-and-down motions, but still distressingly rapid.

Bhamu's efforts to escape the metal bonds pinning him in the blade's implacable path met with no success.

Looking again at Glascock, he spoke levelly. "I suppose you expect me to talk."

"No, Mr. Bhamu," Glascock countered, with a smile. "I expect you to scream. I expect you to beg for mercy. And – in the most exquisite possible gratification, at least for my dear partner and myself – I expect you to die in the most prolonged and terrific agony."

Bhamu gave the approaching blade another glance, then addressed Glascock in Běifānghuà Mandarin. "You're making a grave mistake."

The revelation of Bhamu's familiarity with Mandarin caused no alteration in the expressions of Glascock or his companions.

Glascock's rejoinder was in the same language. "I never make a mistake when it comes to self-gratification."

"If you kill me--" Bhamu took another glance at the blade, which advanced as relentlessly as a jigsaw "--you'll never know what I know."

"I know what you know," Glascock said, cheerfully. "I was, after all, the one who turned Ms. Tsasi to diamond."

"I know about Operation Slam Dunk," Bhamu said.

Glascock turned to one of his henchmen and switched to KiSwahili. "Security missed a listening device, it seems. Institute a scan and destroy it, along with whoever is responsible for the slip-up." He turned back to Bhamu, his smile undimmed, and spoke in Mandarin. "You've overheard a few words, and conveyed nothing to your associates. My estate – which is not a small property, Mr. Bhamu – is surrounded with jammers that prevent local, interplanetary, and interstellar communication."

Bhamu shrugged. "Take the risk, then."

Glascock watched the diamond blade sawing through the remaining centimeters toward the Bhamu family jewels.

Finally, Glascock spoke. "Oddlot."

Oddlot depressed the button.

The blade froze, millimeters from Bhamu's skin-tight pants.

Bhamu exhaled. A trickle of sweat ran down his left temple.

Movement caught his attention. He turned his head. He saw Glascock gesturing at the New Murrian.

Oddlot smiled, raised the boomerang, and threw.

That was the last thing Jangano Bhamu remembered.

***

Bhamu's eyelids twitched, then parted slightly.

He was lying on the plump silk pillows of a white and lavender couch. It occupied a tiny but luxuriously appointed stateroom. He felt, more than heard, the rumble of a starship engine, speeding the craft far enough from the planet to safely engage the warp drive.

Bhamu's bruises throbbed. His headache had grown more severe. He still wore his black garments, and his boots were back on his feet. His body was free, his limbs unconfined.

He didn't move, because the stunning Hausa Sáabóo woman in the lead pilot's uniform stood facing him. An Aurigan micro-crystal glittered just below her lower lip. She no longer had her pilot's cap. Her right hand no longer rested on the butt of her flechette pistol.

Instead, it aimed the business end at Bhamu's heart.

"We warp in twenty minutes," she said.

"What service!" Bhamu said. "Even on private starships, I've never seen a pilot leave the cockpit to deliver the warp-jump warning in person before."

Her gaze swept his body in its skin-tight garments from head to toe, then returned, with equal slowness, to his eyes.

He said, "Like what you see?"

"Glascock might," she said. "But he refuses to hire women who do."

Bhamu smiled. "Are you sure?"

"I'm sure you need to meet the rest of the flight crew." The pilot raised her voice, though doing so was unnecessary when communicating by Aurigan micro-crystal transmitter. "Amaka, Paloma, if you could step into the guest cabin for a moment?"

Within moments, the lock on the cabin door made a heavy sound. The door opened, admitting the two lovely women Bhamu had last seen exiting Glascock's starship with the lead pilot. The new arrivals smiled at the pilot, unperturbed by her drawn pistol. Then they looked curiously at Bhamu.

"Paloma Castaña and Amaka Farai," the pilot told Bhamu, "are the copilot and engineer." She glanced at the women. "Ladies, this gentleman is Jangano Bhamu. Please tell him the nature of our relationship outside of work."

The women burst into laughter, and spoke simultaneously. "She's our wife."

Still laughing, the copilot and engineer departed. The door closed itself behind them. The lock clunked.

The pilot smiled at Bhamu with the sweetness of poisoned sugar.

"Now, where was I?" she said, in the tone of someone who has forgotten nothing. "Ah, yes. I hadn't concluded Mr. Glascock's message. He wishes you to know we're warping to Novaya Russika, where he owns another estate. There, Mr. Bhamu, he will make you talk."

"I've lost track of the number of times I've heard that," Bhamu said. "This time, I might talk. If, that is, the attempt is made by you."

"Don't hold your breath," the pilot said. "I'm not the sadist at Glascock Diamonds, Limited."

"And how would you happen to possess such an intimate piece of information about Mr. Glascock, if you have no interest in men?"

"It doesn't remain a secret when you drag a dozen henchmen in to watch every time you torture a corporate spy."

"You believe I'm a corporate spy?"

The pilot raised one shoulder in a negligent shrug. "You were spying on the most successful diamond merchant in Human Space."

"You've made a reasonable deduction," Bhamu said. "It's also dangerously incorrect."

"Mr. Bhamu," said the pilot, "I don't care what you are. You trespassed on Glascock's estate. Prepare to die."

Bhamu shifted on the luxurious couch until he lay on his side, head propped on one hand. The other arm, also bent at the elbow, rested on his upper side. The hand dangled, its fingertips grazing his stomach as if to draw attention to his abdominal muscles. His skin-tight garments revealed the muscles of torso and limb with such fidelity, the pilot seemed unable to believe her eyes. At least, she seemed unable to remove her regard from the landscape revealed by his change of position.

"You've been gracious enough to introduce me to your wives," Bhamu said. "Might I know your name, as well?"

With apparent effort, the pilot moved her gaze up his torso. She studied his face, considering. She studied his body again. She looked him in the eye.

She answered. "Kitty Splendour."

"Splendid," said Bhamu. "Would you like to purr?"

"Did I mention my pistol fires tranquilizer darts?" she asked. "Allow me to demonstrate."

She demonstrated.

***

When next Bhamu awoke, he lay in a stone cell with an iron door. The cell was unfurnished. The tranquilizer dart had been removed from Bhamu's chest, but he was still clothed and unbound. He rose from the chilly floor.

Pacing, Bhamu silently counted his steps. The cell was almost twice as long as he was tall; in width, it was five steps narrower. The door had a small, barred window, set a little lower than the level of his eyes. The door also had a detention lock, with a keyhole and no key.

Bhamu looked through the window.

He found a brightly illuminated corridor. It was lined with a series of iron doors identical to his. His door was the only one with guards.

The two men noticed him promptly, and targeted his face with 905 nm laser-rifles.

One grunted. "Step away from the door."

Returning to the center of the cell, Bhamu lay down on his side, facing the door. He narrowed his eyes until they were not quite shut. Then, pressing his hand to his skull, he began groaning like a man in pain.

The guardsmen looked through the window.

Silently, they studied the prisoner. They assessed his condition. They assessed the features revealed by his skin-tight garments.

Finally, the guardsman who'd spoken earlier said, "Shut your pie-hole, prisoner."

The groaning continued.

The guardsmen continued to watch the prisoner's behavior and examine his body. The prisoner made no move to rise. He rubbed his head and gave an occasional groan. His eyes did not open; nor did they ever quite close.

Eventually, the talkative guard said, "Oddlot's boomerang hit the prisoner pretty hard. Maybe he's badly hurt."

"He's faking," said the other guard. "Glascock's physician examined him and gave him nanomeds for the blow."

"We'd better make sure. We're under orders not to kill the prisoner, on pain of death."

"We're not killing him."

"If he dies," said the first guard, "will Glascock agree with you?"

A new voice rose, smooth and dark as Novo Brasilian honey. "If you enter the cell and the prisoner escapes, Glascock will kill you. Very, very slowly."

Bhamu recognized the voice.

"Open his cell and remain on alert," the voice continued. "I'm transferring the prisoner."

The lock thunked. The door opened. Bhamu remained motionless.

The new voice said, "Stop play-acting and step out of the cell, Mr. Bhamu. Don't make any sudden moves, unless you're eager to take another nap."

"I've rested enough for one day," Bhamu said, and exited the cell slowly.

He found three muzzles aimed at his chest. He smiled at the newcomer.

"Kitty Splendour," he said. "A pleasure to see you again."

The pilot made a come-along gesture with her flechette pistol. "We're returning to the ship, Mr. Bhamu."

"Wouldn't it be easier for Glascock to torture me in a cell?" Bhamu asked.

"There's been a change of plans," Kitty Splendour said. "Your masochistic pleasures must wait. Get moving. And keep your distance."

He did as she ordered.

"Don't try anything funny," she added, falling in behind Bhamu. "You're in a building full of bodyguards and other employees of Glascock Diamond, Limited."

Bhamu assessed the sound of her footsteps. She was close enough to shoot him, but not close enough to let him overcome her before she fired. He would have to wait for a better opportunity before attempting escape.

He said, "Why are we leaving so soon?"

"I have no orders to give you information."

"You don't need to, Ms. Splendour." He looked over his shoulder. "You're going to overfly the planetary capitol of Novaya Rossika and drop a package from the ship's hold."

His words appeared to astonish the pilot.

But her pistol didn't waver, and her face swiftly regained its stony expression. "As always, Mr. Bhamu, you fail to amuse."

"Wouldn't you like to know what your boss is planning to drop on Novaya Moskva?"

"You grow tedious," Splendour said. "A diamond merchant would deliver diamonds."

Bhamu looked over his shoulder again. "You know he's never previously made a delivery via drone."

Her slim brows pinched in thought.

Then her face hardened. "It's none of my business how Mr. Glascock chooses to conduct his business. Now, silence yourself, Mr. Bhamu, or I'll do it for you."

***

Kitty Splendour escorted Bhamu to a starship stateroom. It appeared identical to the one he'd occupied on his largely unconscious trip to Novaya Rossika. And, as before, he and the pilot were the only ones in the room.

"Get on the couch, and stay there," the lead pilot said, with a twitch of her weapon. "We take off shortly."

He moved toward the couch. "I have urgent information, Ms. Splendour," he said. "You would do well to listen."

She said, "Silence."

So he maintained silence as he laid his hand on one of the white and lavender cushions and swung. The plump pillow knocked her pistol aside. Dropping his makeshift weapon, Bhamu sprang like a panther.

As they crashed to the floor, the breath was knocked out of the pilot. As she lay stunned, Bhamu's left hand pressed her gun-hand to the floor, with the muzzle pointed away from them. Keeping her body pinned with his weight, Bhamu pulverized her micro-crystal transmitter between his free thumb and forefinger, then reached for her left arm.

As he acted, his lips brushed her ear. "I was trying to warn you," he said, his voice barely audible. "In the right hands, anything is a weapon."

He spoke his next words even more softly, as he pressed his body even more firmly against hers.

The pilot whipped her left arm away from Bhamu's reaching hand. Then, with the speed of a KwaZulu Entsha cobra, she swung. Her fist struck his temple.

"You're beyond tedious, Mr. Bhamu," Kitty Splendour observed as she pushed Bhamu's limp body aside. Arising, she holstered her weapon and straightened her blazer. "When the flight is over," she added, "I shall ask Mr. Glascock's leave to torture you personally."

***

Bhamu stirred. Glancing around, he found himself alone. He sprang to the door and tried the handle.

Inaudibly, he mouthed, "Unlocked."

Smiling almost imperceptibly, he cracked the door and peered into the starship corridor.

It was empty except for a uniformed Glascock Diamonds guard. He stood just outside Bhamu's stateroom door. The guard wore a sidearm and dataspex. By the sounds spilling from his earpiece, the guard was watching porn.

Lunging through the door, Bhamu knocked the preoccupied man unconscious. Dragging the limp figure into his stateroom, he assumed its uniform and firearm. The latter was, unsurprisingly, a flechette pistol; no one wanted a firearm that shot anything more forceful than a dart or 905 nanometer laser-beam on a spacecraft. A bullet or higher-frequency laser could breach the hull. The pistol was a model which fired tranquilizer darts exclusively. Perhaps Glascock still wished to preserve Bhamu for a vigorous round of torture.

Bhamu stepped into the corridor.

The starship was a small, swift, elegant Sunstar cruiser, of the Mark 007 class favored by the ultra-wealthy. Remarkably dependable, it was also used by SIS. Familiar with its layout, Bhamu proceeded vigilantly in the direction of the hold.

Its entrance was an airlock. It was unguarded, and both massive doors were open. Peering warily through the open chamber, Bhamu saw Richard Glascock and his boomerang-toting factotum. They faced aft. They stood at the control panel of the enormous cargo airlock, which was set in the floor.

On the floor between the men rested a small cargo drone. Some of its operational lights were red. Most were green.

A small bomb was attached to the drone. The bomb showed three glowing red numerals. The numerals were counting steadily down, signaling less than five minutes to detonation.

The countdown held Bhamu's attention a moment too long.

Swift as a New Murrian needletail, the boomerang knocked the flechette pistol from Bhamu's hand.

Smiling with sadistic pleasure, Oddlot let his returning boomerang fly past his head as he flung himself toward Bhamu. Bhamu tried to leap aside, but he was slightly off-balance from the blow, and the other man was quicker than his powerful build suggested. He closed sinewy hands on Bhamu's throat.

Smiling even more sadistically than his factotum, Richard Glascock said, "Only render Bhamu unconscious, Oddlot."

A new voice said, "Sounds like a plan."

Shock suffused Glascock's features as his lead pilot stepped into the hold and fired her pistol.

Involuntarily, Oddlot watched his boss collapse.

Bhamu's palm drove into Oddlot's face. The New Murrian's head snapped back and his eyes glazed. However, his hands continued to tighten on Bhamu's throat.

As Kitty Splendour aimed at Oddlot, a man's voice came into the hold. "Why is this airlock open?"

The henchman followed his question and his flechette pistol through the airlock and immediately dropped, shot by Kitty Splendour.

She wheeled to fire at Oddlot, and found that Bhamu had struck again, driving the edge of his palm into the side of Oddlot's head.

Oddlot's eyes rolled up and he released Bhamu.

As Oddlot sagged, Splendour shot him.

"Making sure he stays unconscious," she told Bhamu as she hurried to his side.

He crouched beside the drone and its little blinking bomb.

"They activated the explosive," he told Splendour. "Unfortunately, I don't know how to stop it from exploding."

"Neither do I." She drew a shaky breath. "And the explosion will release the metal-dissolving formula. It'll devour our ship and enter the atmosphere."

Bhamu had filled her in quickly, when he'd pinned her to the floor. Then he'd made a request. She'd followed it, pretending to knock him unconscious.

"Clearly, the government of Xin Zhongguo met Glascock's price," Bhamu said now. "There must be enough formula in the bomb to destroy every settlement on Novaya Rossika, Xin Zhongguo's archenemy."

"Paloma!" Splendour called, addressing her co-wife through the replacement micro-crystal transmitter by her lip. "Depart Novaya Rossika at top speed, but don't warp."

As she spoke, Bhamu carefully opened a small compartment on the bomb, just below the digital clock speeding through the remaining seconds.

"I see three wires in there," Splendour said. "Wouldn't yanking one loose disarm the explosive?"

"That," Bhamu said, "or cause it to detonate."

"Kitty says you're a secret agent, Mr. Bhamu," said Amaka Farai, striding into the hold. "Why are you so clueless about a bomb?"

Before Bhamu or Splendour could object, Farai slipped her fingers between the bomb and the mini-drone.

The bomb clicked.

Bhamu and Splendour tensed.

"It has an off switch," Amaka Farai said. "Oh, don't look so surprised. I'm an engineer."

Jangano Bhamu exhaled.

Kitty Splendour exclaimed, "I love you, Amaka."

***

As the starship cruised toward the warp point, Bhamu reclined on the stateroom couch. Clad once more in his skin-tight black garb, he was as gracefully relaxed as a Kirinyaga Mpya caracal. He had made a deal with the pilot, the engineer, and the copilot. They had agreed to take him, the now-confined Glascock and Oddlot, the bomb, and the formula to New Zanzibar, in exchange for amnesty and new employment.

"She's bisex, I know it," he muttered. "But inconveniently devoted to her wives."

"Devoted, yes," Kitty Splendour said, stepping through the cabin door and letting it lock behind her. "Bisex, no."

"You're preparing for warp transit and you feel the need to come to my cabin and tell me you're samesex?"

"Paloma and Amaka can handle the jump without me," she said. "And that's not what I came to tell you."

She pressed herself against him.

When their lips finally parted, Bhamu gazed deeply into her eyes and whispered:

"Why is an opposex woman in a samesex marriage?"

"Haven't you heard of a marriage of convenience?" Kitty Splendour responded. "I told you women couldn't work for Glascock unless they weren't interested in men. Paloma and Amaka aren't interested in men. But all three of us were out of work, and we're lifelong friends, and Glascock had openings in our fields. They added me to their marriage and we got the jobs."

"Splendid," Jangano Bhamu said, and pressed his lips to hers.

DJANGO UNPLUGGED
A T.A.S.K. STORY
Hannibal Tabu

T.A.S.K. created by Damion Gonzales, Zak Farmer and Conliffe Matthew

For what felt like the thousandth time, Django's bare feet sloshed through cold, viscous sewage and he shuddered at what lie hidden. The dim illumination from shattered streets above and maintenance lights along the walls followed him, reluctantly, as if wanting no part of St. Louis' municipal underbelly. In a distance, he heard the pounding of ham-sized fists on unforgiving stone and the crash of load-bearing walls. Grimly, Django gritted his teeth and trudged forward, the fate of the world in his hands.

* * *

Hours earlier, thunderous applause followed the brightly clad hero Django as he walked off stage after giving a well-crafted keynote speech at Casa Central's Anniversary Annual Awards Dinner. He walked down the steps, his bare feet padding softly as he went, shaking hands with the mayor of Chicago and other well-wishers and carrying a trophy honoring his status as an "icon of racial harmony and ideals."

Django – well accustomed to the fawning and adulation of masses – smiled graciously as he shook hands, waved and accepted random hugs from adherents. His jovial mood switched when he saw the stoic form of John Henry near the green room door, arms crossed and wearing an expression like a summer storm, sudden and unforgiving.

Django extricated himself from the crowds and followed Henry into the green room. Even after six months as T.A.S.K.'s representative from two "divine" houses, alien powers revered as gods by many human populations, Django still felt nervous around the organization's leader, a mortal in name only, with powers imbued by the planet itself matching his peerless valor and reputation.

"Did you see any of the speech?" Django opened conversationally, sitting down to grab a bottled water.

"I caught a lot of it, yes," Henry replied, still standing. "Meridian told me you'd asked him for help with it, but I barely even noticed any of his work there. Your flourishes and style, however, were very effective. You had the crowd eating out of your hand."

Django looked down smiling – he appreciated Henry's praise more than any of the *hoi polloi* outside the door. "That's kind, thank you. The good doctor gave me the idea to use what he called a 'framing device,' but yes, most of it was the rhythm and cadence of my grandfather's voice."

Getting serious, Henry said, "I wish I was here to enjoy the expensive eats. T.A.S.K. needs your help, Django."

Django furrowed his brows – for Henry to be delivering this message must imply great severity. "What can I do?" he asked earnestly, leaning forward, elbows on his knees.

"Our old friend Legacy has discovered that a very important piece of technology has been hidden under the city of St. Louis for thousands of years," Henry began. "We need you to retrieve it before Legacy's people do, but there are...let's just say this won't be an easy mission. There's a Tempest waiting for you on the roof, can you come now?"

Django stood and nodded. "I can text my people from the air, yessir."

Django followed Henry's steadfast steps to a nearby elevator, which was waiting. As they ascended the entirety of the skyscraper, passing through the residential areas after clearing the hotel section, Henry said, "This will require you to work with people, maybe even put your ego in check. I believe you aren't the hothead the media makes you out to be. Can you prove me right?"

Django hid his nervousness and nodded solemnly as the elevator came to a stop.

Henry walked confidently out, unflappable, up the ramp into the waiting transport – a sleek slice of the future on nearly silent compressed air jets, hovering above the building with a ramp placidly ready to receive.

Django wondered as the JSOC pilot ignored John Henry, seated opposite, while checking straps on Django for security. *I know he's durable, but so am I...* Django wondered.

Once the ramp was up and they began moving above the clouds, John Henry continued. "We are stretched thin with active duty response teams addressing crises in multiple locations. A nuclear threat in Sri Lanka, disaster relief in North Carolina, volcanic fallout in Iceland, mutant monsters in Tasmania and an ecological catastrophe off the coast of Somalia. You're the least committed person closest to this new challenge, because it's your day off."

Django chuckled. "Where I'm from, we don't get days off. What's the mission?"

Henry smirked and replied, "I'd love to give you more detail but..." and then Henry's face dissolved in a cloud of static before continuing, "...into Jaffna now. Glitch will fill you in and..."

Suddenly, Henry was gone, as though he had never been there. Django frowned, glancing around the suddenly empty cabin, made to carry up to 10 people and any attendant equipment. Django sighed and slid one of the digital workbenches from the wall – a fold out desk with a holographic keyboard and display – so he could email his assistant Gabriela about the change in his itinerary.

He'd been watching a "page loading" indicator for perhaps thirty seconds when the lithe young figure of the team's techno-savant Glitch appeared on the seat across from him. He glanced at her, seeing her gaze focused on something to Django's right, tapping away at a space she treated like a keyboard, but he could see nothing there. *Another hologram...* he surmised.

After a moment, Django asked, "Glitch?"

She briefly glanced his way and replied, "Oh, hi! Django, why would I have you on my... oh, I contacted you because the big guy is in the middle of the Pacific and didn't finish telling you how to save the world. Right, I remember what you need now, just one... sec..."

Django fumed, sucking in a sudden breath. "Look, I got pulled out of a favor for my grandfather and if John Henry can't deal with me himself..."

"Hold that thought, El DeBarge..." Glitch interrupted distractedly. "Just... gotta... there! Okay, I just stopped Bosnian hackers from bankrupting the EU and throwing the world economy into chaos. Now, what's your whiny holdup?"

With a frown, Django gritted his teeth and focused on business. "What is the mission?" he managed.

Glitch seemed to ignore his expression, still distracted by things he couldn't see. "Hang on, an anarchist data collective is trying to black out Manhattan for the third time today... gotta retask satellites to get eyes on Tasmania, now... oh, you, St. Louis, right. Can I assume you know something about your family history and understand the term 'Liume?'"

Reining in his rising anger at this annoying child, Django simply said, "Yes."

"Sweet," she continued, barely pausing to register his reply. "The Liume genius Kao designed something hundreds of thousands of years ago to hide Earth from a transdimensional threat even he feared..."

"*The Burning Tide*," Django interrupted. "The boogeymen haunting children of my kind."

"Sure, whatever," Glitch went on, typing furiously. "Anyway, Kao put it in the most boring place he could find at the time, made a note in case he ever had to fix it, then forgot about it. Now, his wackjob former apprentice Legacy found the note and figured he could take a shortcut to his nihilist wet dream and invite some dinner guests who have zero manners, you feel me?"

Django sat silently.

"I'll take that as tacit assent," Glitch continued, unabated. "That dull spot now has the city of St. Louis on top of it, and Legacy sent that stooge Royce..."

Django chortled. "Barely a test for my powers..."

"If you'll let me finish, early 90's Bishop," Glitch said testily, "...and somehow figured out how to duplicate that psycho two dozen times. Now there's a platoon of him, destroying the sewers, caving in streets, waking babies from their naps and generally making stuff awful. You have to get the Liume cloaking device back to T.A.S.K. HQ before the Royces destroy it and doom us all."

"What does the device look like?" Django asked thoughtfully.

"Nobody knows," Glitch fired off, her attention wandering again. "Next question!"

"How can I find this thing?"

"No idea, but if the Royces have a way, you have to be smarter than them." After a pause she looked directly at him and asked, "Right?"

Django's hands crunched the edges of the workbench. He closed his eyes, saying nothing. After a while, he said, "When do I get there?"

Glitch pulled an apple from seemingly nowhere and took a bite. "You've been hovering over the first responder triage center for thirty seconds," she said through munching. "I'm surprised we're still talking about this..."

He rolled his eyes and stood up. "Please contact my assistant and tell her I have to miss the fundraiser in LA." Without another word, Django disappeared in a flash of lightning.

Appearing in a flash of lightning below, Django began, "Could anyone please direct me to..."

"Are you out of your ever loving mind?" a bellowing voice from behind Django yelled.

He turned to see a blustery, overweight police lieutenant in an incongruous white and orange hard hat barreling towards him to waggle an index finger angrily. "We have gas leaks everywhere; you're likely to blow up the whole damned thing!"

Django took a deep breath, ignoring the hundreds of ways he could murder this small man, and remembered John Henry's admonition. "I'm sorry," Django said slowly, getting past how he'd let that teenaged technophile get under his skin again. "I didn't get a lot of information before I got here. Can we start fresh? I'm Django, from T.A.S.K., and I'm here to help."

The cop, hands on his hips, narrowed his eyes at Django before softening. Sticking out a hand he said, "Lieutenant Jack Callahan, St. Louis PD. Thanks for rushing out here. Follow me. I can show you what we know..."

Django nodded and followed Callahan into a hastily constructed mobile headquarters – a bank of communications equipment and computers on folding tables under an impromptu canopy tent. "We've got IR on 25 moving targets," Callahan explained. "The file said this guy was just strong and healed fast, this duplicate thing is new."

"That's why they sent me," Django said, leaning in to look at the screens. "You said something about a gas leak?"

Callahan nodded. "One of the first things they smashed. The whole sewer system is flooded with natural gas. We're trying to evacuate the area, but it's slow going."

Django frowned. "I can't teleport, then. That takes lightning. Hm."

"Sorry," Callahan shrugged. "Why is he down there tearing up everything?"

Django considered this and decided to be straight with the man. "Underneath your city is an ancient artifact that's protected the world from alien invasion. If Royce down there finds it, we're all in danger."

Callahan blanched, gulping audibly. "Wow."

Django spared Callahan a considerate glance before asking, "Can you guide me if I go down there? I can't see carrying a tablet..."

The lieutenant straightened up, saying, "Ah! That I know about, one sec..."

Callahan reached under a table and pulled out a large black case. Unlatching it, he rummaged around until he pulled out a transparent bead the size of a pea. "We use these in hostage situations; new military issue stuff. Mic is inside of it, and it's lightly adhesive to stay in your ear. Give 'er a shot ..."

Regarding the device oddly, Django took the small transceiver and placed it in his left ear. Callahan pulled a small microphone from the case and whispered into it, which Django heard clearly as, "Do you read me?"

"Will wonders never cease?" Django pondered, fidgeting with the tight fit.

"Not with people like you on hand to help," Callahan admitted. "Okay, lemme walk you out..."

As they walked out, a short uniformed female police sergeant, with her cap pulled over her short dreadlocks, approached carrying a disposable cell phone. "Lou, I...I think this call is for him," she said.

"Thanks, Mary," Callahan said, taking the phone from her. He looked at it oddly as she walked off.

"I'll take it, go on ahead," Django said, taking the small piece of plastic in his large hands.

"Can you hear me, grandson?" a kindly old voice came through the phone.

Django was startled to hear the serpentine voice of his grandsire Quetzalcoatl coming through a modern device. "Yes, my lord," Django said, his voice suddenly humble. "This is a surprise. I was just about to..."

"You were just about to head under the ground, to the realm of dirt and serpents," Quetzalcoatl chuckled. "I know much about what your day will be like. Just know this will be a test of your resilience, son of my daughter. Take your time, use all your powers smartly, and know I believe in you."

Django pulled the phone away and wondered at it, appreciating the gesture of having a god believe in you. "Wow," he managed. "Thank you, grandfather, I..."

"I would love to have a good long chat with you," Quetzalcoatl interrupted, "but you have a lot to do and Jim Richards will be walking up behind you. Good luck, and please turn to your right to hand him the phone."

Django turned and noted a fireman in full safety gear walking up, the name RICHARDS emblazoned across his hat. "Excuse me," Django said, unsure, "Are you Jim Richards?"

The man – two days of salt and pepper stubble on his face, eyes sunken and body covered in soot – raised an eyebrow at Django before saying, "Yeeessss..."

Django handed him the phone and said, "I don't know what is happening or why, but this is for you..."

Richards wondered at the phone – a simple purplish plastic candy bar – and took it from Django. "...thank you, then," Richards said simply, put the phone to his ear and continued on his way.

Django caught up to Callahan a few feet away, looking down into a massive sinkhole with frayed pipes and rebar extending from shattered asphalt. "This section collapsed when one of these guys smashed through a load bearing section of the sewer," Callahan explained. "Spots like this all over town. There's one about 40 yards north of here, but it ain't pretty down there.

He looked at Django – dressed in a tight red leotard with white lightning bolts across its surface, golden bracers around his ankles and wrists and bare feet – and said, "I could, uh, get you a hazmat suit, maybe some boots..."

Django waived Callahan off. "Just slow me down. Thank you, lieutenant. Pray to whatever god you honor for good fortune!"

Without another word, Django jumped down into the brackish water and started walking north, under the city streets.

* * *

Hundreds of feet away, the hulking figure of Royce plodded along through trash and human waste, glancing occasionally at the bracelet on his arm, pulsing with an otherworldly glow. He almost had to stoop to fit through the gray-green moss-bedecked walls of the claustrophobic sewer tunnels, grunting to himself as he went.

Taking a right at a corner, he glanced up to see an exact replica of himself, down to the bracelet, staring back at him.

"Oi!" the first Royce cried out.

"Oi!" his doppelganger replied.

"This is my bleedin' search pattern!" the first one growled.

"It bloody well is not!" the second returned. "You're... hell, which one are you?"

The first pondered this a moment and said, "16! Legacy said I was 'Royse 16' when we went through 'is funny machine."

"Oi, then," the second said, pulling a grubby and battered piece of paper from a back pocket. "Says right 'ere, 'Royse 16 covers Junction 243, marker 9 to Junction 256, marker 12!"

"All right, wot?" Royse 16 asked.

The second Royce pointed at a grimy bronzed plaque, barely visible in the dim illumination of emergency lights. The plaque read, "Junction 237, Marker 19."

"...oh..." Royce 16 said, hanging his head low.

Cursing and stuffing the paper back in his pocket, the second Royce said, "Legacy tells me, 'I can make two dozen of you, but only once and only for a day,' I figger, 'This'll be an orgy of mayhem the likes of which the world's never bloody seen! Is this a feckin' orgy of mayhem, 16?"

Before the hapless clone could answer, the second Royce continued. "No it's not! Everybody else from the Factory gets to blow stuff up and fight 'eroes, and I'm under this stupid city lookin' for a bloody magic rock with two dozen morons too stupid to follow a search pattern!"

16 furrowed his brow. "If we're all you, then doesn't that mean..."

"I know what it bloody well means!" the second Royce bellowed. "I'm down 'ere talking to myself! Turn around and get back to your grid, you poncy tosser!"

Grumbling, the second Royce turned around and trudged into the darkness.

Nonplussed, 16 pulled a candy bar from a pocket and started eating as he returned the way he came, heading back towards Django.

* * *

Callahan's voice in Django's ear said, "You're quiet down there, pal. Everything all right?"

"I've walked through more feces in the last minute than I have touched in my entire life," Django said through gritted teeth without breaking stride. "My visit to your lovely city could not be going better."

"Glad to hear it," Callahan chuckled, because you'll be right on top of one of those monsters in a minute. Natural gas leaks are all around you, so please no fireworks. I'd like to see the gold watch they give cops when they retire, if it's all the same to you."

Django noted the sound of footsteps and whispered, "Perhaps you should turn down the volume, both ways," the son of Shango said. "This could get loud."

Django positioned his back against the turn at the plus sign-shaped intersection of junctions, crouched slightly and pulled his fist back. Still chewing the candy bar, Royce 16 came around the corner, oblivious. Django punched with much of his considerable strength, landing a blow directly in Royce 16's abdomen. The clone spat a chunk of nougat ten feet, the breath knocked out of him. Django leapt up and smashed the back of Royce 16's head, knocking the bulk of the British man into the sewage with a messy splash. Django stood, ready for more, but saw the massive man lying still, bubbles percolating up from the water.

"Didja kill him?" Callahan asked.

Django walked around the fallen felon, eyebrow furrowed. "I don't think this is a real 'him' to kill," Django said, examining Royce 16's back.

"Whaddaya mean?" Callahan barked.

"Sheesh... could you remember you're right in my ear?" Django spat out. "Something feels different about this man. Most people... they feel like people when I meet them. I shook your hand and it was like shaking the hand of a whole person. This... even when I hit him, he felt like something was missing. Now he's probably suffocating to death, I'm taking a good look and... and it just feels like something's missing in the small of his back..."

"Chakras," Callahan said plainly.

"What?" Django asked.

"My ex-wife went really new age for about two years," Callahan explained. "Had me taking yoga, studying all kinds of eastern hoo-hah. Turned her into a wildcat in the sack, but I guess the yoga instructor thought so too...anyway, according to them, everybody has seven centers of energy up and down their spine, and the one in line with the solar plexus is the source of a person's life energy. If these guys ain't guys, no chakra there."

The bubbles stopped and Django nodded. "So I didn't just commit felonious assault pursuant to murder..."

"You put down a dangerous and unpredictable animal that literally was not human, down to the way it's disappearing from my screen," Callahan finished. "Cheers!"

Django considered this as the body began to disintegrate. "It'll be good to not hold back as much, then. What about when I find the real Royce?"

"Sounds like you'll know the difference," Callahan replied. "I read his sheet though; you'd be doing the world a favor finishing him off too. Hey, did you see anything else unusual on the guy?"

As the body melted, Django noted the bracelet's glow fading as it disintegrated. "Glowing bracelet," he said. "Disappeared when he did."

"Maybe next time grab that before you dust the dupe," Callahan said thoughtfully.

"Dust the dupe?" Django asked.

"Sorry, I'm a Whedonite," Callahan chuckled, "and you're going full Slayer down there. Long story, I'll explain later. Now, if you head due east, you'll run into two, one walking away from you and one towards, about half a click."

"Copy that," Django said, stepping away from the ooze that was Royce 16, mixing in with the detritus of the city.

* * *

Elsewhere, the original Royce was pounding through a wall when he heard a trilling sound echoing through the sewers. He sighed and fumbled for his pocket, tapping at the screen until it offered forth sound.

"Mister Royce, can you hear me?" came Legacy's voice through the touchscreen phone's speaker.

"Oi!" Royce responded.

"I'm told that's a greeting where you're from," Legacy continued, "so I'll take that as an affirmative answer. Have you and your platoon of reproductions located the stone yet?"

"No, sir," Royce responded, "I've got all of, uh, me'selves tearin' up the town, but these detector bracelets 'aven't found it in all the shyte and what not. You're sure they work?"

"Thousands of years ago," Legacy said with the rhythms of someone intending to tell a lengthy yarn, "the being who made me also created technology to hide this world from a threat even his immeasurably powerful people feared. A relentless and nigh-unstoppable horde of ravenous space monsters burning their way through entire universes. Destroying that deceptively simple stone will bring them all coming, fulfilling every one of our dreams of fire and blood and screaming in the night. The stone is made of elements not of this earth, and the bracelet you got before being duplicated can detect it if brought close enough. Just keep proceeding as you are and keep me happy."

Royce grunted. "It'd go faster if there were more than 25 of me; St. Louis is a big bloody town."

Legacy sighed, an expression conveying such exasperation that it seemed as though it could weigh down continents. "As I explained, the technology I employed is both *very* unstable and very rare. I've been saving it for seven hundred years because I cannot replicate it with the technology of this planet, nor can I stretch out its effects. Two dozen copies of any one carbon-based life form that will all dissolve in exactly twenty four hours, no more. I will check on your progress in two hours, Mister Royce. Please destroy the stone."

The line went CLICK and Royce wondered at the phone. Shrugging, he shoved it back into his pocket, slammed a fist into the wall and walked through the hole he'd created.

* * *

It took five more Royces before Django was able to secure a bracelet. The two at once turned into a legitimate brawl, knocking down two load-bearing sections and inadvertently making another sinkhole. A Buick fell on one of the Royces, shearing his head clean off of his body. The second was somewhere between laughter and shock and didn't see Django plowing into him from the side. The impact drove the larger man into a set of exposed rebar. The metal rod pushed through the Royce's throat, spraying blood everywhere.

As Django was catching his breath, three more of the man monstrosities rushed in to attack at once, piling on top of him. Django unleashed all of his strength, punching straight through a Royce's chest. Swinging wildly, he ripped off the head of a second while the third tried to get him in a headlock. Frustrated, a sizzle of current danced along Django's fist for a split second but he calmed himself, stretched out his arms and slammed his elbows back into the Royce, sending bone fragments through soft tissue and tossing the creature back 20 feet. Before Django could get to the fallen body, the bracelet and the corpse were already starting to dissolve.

Django stood, breathing heavily, arms akimbo, looking down on the wrecked bodies dissolving away. Remembering, he leapt at the last one down and snatched the bracelet off before the dissolution began. He slapped it on his wrist and watched the body begin to turn into ooze, smiling that the bracelet remained solid.

He heard the sound of footsteps running behind him and spun, fists up, but furrowed his brow when he realized they were too quick and too soft to be another one of the Royce duplicates.

A small Caucasian girl ran around the corner, her face a mask of terror. She was dressed in tatters, dirty gray and brown clothes that were stained and torn and encrusted with the filth of the sewers. She was looking over her shoulder and not where she was running, bumping directly into Django, her face slamming into his chest.

She fell on her backside and stared up at him, dumbfounded.

"Hello," Django began calmly, holding his hands out in a placating gesture. "Are you ..."

The girl screamed loudly and leapt up, fists swinging and pounding ineffectually on Django's chest. He stood there, eyebrow raised as she continued until she got winded and stopped.

"You can calm down," Django said slowly, "I'm one of the good guys...the way I look notwithstanding."

She looked at him, wondering. "You're not one of those monsters! Can you help me? They squashed my squat and killed my boyfriend Jimmy!"

Django recoiled, aghast. "You *lived* down here?"

The girl sucked her teeth and glared at him. "Look, I'm gonna keep running if you wanna sit here and judge me; ain't nobody got time for that!"

Django looked down, realizing the issue and started again. "I'm sorry, I'm sorry. I can help you. My name is Django, I'm with T.A.S.K., which is like…"

"I've seen a television," the girl spat out, "I know what T.A.S.K. is. I'm Erin, can we get out of here?"

"Hang on one second," Django said, put a hand to his ear and asked, "Callahan, can you hear me?"

"I hear you, Jamie Foxx," Callahan said. "If you backtrack and head to your left, which is due east, I can have some uniforms come get her to safety."

Django nodded and said, "Erin, I just spoke to the police. They're coming to get you out of…"

Erin cringed, shrinking back from him.

"Listen, listen, it's okay…" Django said, reaching out to hold her shoulder. "You can trust me. Nobody's mad at you, you won't get arrested. We just want to stop these guys. Look at me." He held her eye contact and said, "I can help."

Erin looked skeptically at him, and said, "I guess you're my best choice, Magic Mullet. Let's go."

She walked behind him as he led the way, frowning at all the jokes leveled his way. "How long have you been living down here, Erin?" Django asked after a little while, trying to change the mood.

"Really?" Erin laughed. "We're on a date now? Is this what we're doing?"

"I'm sorry," Django said through gritted teeth. "People have been telling me I'm not exactly open to people, so I wanted to try and make you feel more comfortable…"

"Get me out of the sewers filled with giant smashing monsters," Erin muttered. "Get me completely dry for the first time in six weeks. Get me a meal that doesn't taste like something somebody else ate. Then I can try this 'comfortable' you're talking about."

Django was about to respond when he heard an angry voice yelling "Oi!" from behind. He turned to look and saw the silhouette of two of the Royce clones running towards them.

"Erin," Django said calmly, "you're gonna keep running in the direction we were walking. Run hard. There will be cops who will get you out of here, get you cleaned up, get you a meal. I'll make sure you're taken care of, I promise, but you have to run, NOW!"

Erin's eyes went wide and she sprinted away. Django started to power up before he inhaled a whiff of natural gas and recalled why this was all taking so long. Ducking under the haymaker of the first, Django swept his foot, tripping the second, who fell face first into the feces-laced water. The first one was quicker than Django expected and smashed the hero in the back. Django fell into the water as well and saw Erin stop to look back at him.

"RUN!" he yelled as the second Royce rose and the first pounded his back again.

Erin fretted a moment and yelled, "I'll never forget what you did for me, Black Jesus!" She then ran as quickly as possible away from the fight.

Django rolled out of the way of a punch that smashed a foot down through the sewer floor. He performed a Capoeira kick to the knee of the other Royce, who was trying to move into a better position after wiping himself off somewhat. Django flipped to his feet before the one that got some punches in could free himself. He leapt up, then drop kicked the clone in the face. The Royce dissolved into muck. The remaining Royce leapt angrily but lost his balance, and Django was able to evade him easily, punching the side of the clone's neck, silencing it forever. Pulling himself from the wet newspaper and clinging trash, Django smashed a foot down on the head of the fallen clone and watched it dissolve as well.

"Callahan..." Django breathed heavily, "the girl..."

"We got her out," the cop's calm voice returned. "They're getting her some cocoa. We'll make sure she's cared for. You okay down there?"

"How... many... left?" Django asked, clearing his throat.

"Lemme see what's on the heat map here," Callahan said, his voice drifting a bit as he reached for something away from the microphone. "Seventeen."

"SEVENTEEN?" Django asked, incredulous. "Seventeen more of these things... spirits above..."

"If it makes you feel better," Callahan offered, "None of my boys could handle one, and you've taken down eight."

Django chuckled. "Thank you for trying to make me feel better, Lieutenant. Okay, what's next..."

"Well, if you turn left at the next junction instead of going straight like the girl did, you'll find three standing together in about fifty yards. Follow that and you'll be heading in the direction of most of them."

Django boggled but replied, "Copy that. I'm en route."

"The city of St. Louis thanks you, Django," Callahan said sincerely. "We've completely evacuated the area, but it'd still be nice to avoid blowing it all up..."

"Yes, I can smell the natural gas more heavily down here," Django said. "I should be fine, but I want to hurry..."

"For a lot of reasons, I get it," Callahan finished for him. "I'm here if you need me."

Django trudged onward.

* * *

Some miles away, the original Royce walked up to find four of his duplicates standing together in a large open area where multiple sluiceways with ten foot wide openings dumped sewer water into a large centralized room.

"Oi!" they all said as he approached.

"I can see why I'm an acquired taste," Royce muttered. "What are you nutters standing around for?"

In unison, they all pointed at his wrist without a word. He looked down and saw that it was glowing bright red. "Blimey!" he said, "best we got was a sassy pink!"

All four held up their wrists to him and showed the same. One walked slowly back and had the brightness of his bracelet fade slightly.

"I get it, I get it, ye're all bloody brilliant," Royce said. "It's under the ground; get to it!"

All four started pounding at the ground simultaneously, water splashing furiously around them as they went. Royce stepped off to one side, out of range of the waterworks, and fumbled with his pocket to retrieve his phone. He sat down in one of the sluiceways, his feet hanging freely like a child at a holiday dinner table, and waited.

"Mister Royce?" Legacy's voice came through, like a serpent in the night.

"Oi!" Royce replied. "The bracelets worked. Four of, uh, me are digging for it now."

"Splendid!" Legacy replied, clapping his hands a little. "I was worried that the losses you've incurred would be an issue."

Royce took the phone away from his ear and wondered at it a moment. "Losses?"

Legacy sighed and said, "Ah, perhaps I should have given you some way to communicate with your simulacra. Nine ... wait, no, ten of the duplicates have ceased to exist. Let me see here... ah, local law enforcement notes that a member of T.A.S.K. is on hand, a Liume demigod of some sort... Django."

"Which one is he?" Royce asked.

"Let me call up his file; one moment, Mister Royce..." Legacy said distractedly. "Oh, my, he's impressive. Sixty ton bench press, that's why he's making his way through... oh my, two more gone, that's almost half. He can use lightning but I'm not seeing any indication of that..."

"Gas leaks," Royce grunted. "Smells like the crack of a fat man's arse down 'ere, but my people worked utilities enough for me to notice. Musta busted something open..."

"Hm. Well, as long as he doesn't destroy you, all the remaining duplicates should remain functional."

"Bloody fat chance of that," Royce muttered.

"You are indeed impressive, Mister Royce," Legacy agreed, "But he is stronger than you by a factor of four. Can you marshal your numbers and use your military experience to defeat this divine antagonist? Oh, he's speeding up, there went three, no, four more. Sixteen of twenty five, gone."

"I got four more 'ere with me," Royce noted. "No easy way to get to the rest. Don't wanna send one out to warn 'em, lose the numbers. He prolly got a way to find us, so he's 'eadin' 'ere. Gotta set a bloody trap..."

"That's that dangerous mind I found so delightful," Legacy said proudly. "Well... oh, seventeen ... he's on his way. Don't fail me."

The line went CLICK and Royce mulled over the situation. He looked around, seeing far too many entry points to protect. He hopped down and waded over to the duplicates surrounded by a circle of shattered stone as they pounded their way into the ground below.

"Oi! OI!" Royce yelled as he approached. One tapped the next and in seconds they had all stopped, looking at him.

"Company's comin' 'ere," he said grimly. "Seventeen of us gone. T.A.S.K. guy called Django. Can't use 'is lightning, but strong as four of us."

They looked at each other and then back to him before one said, "There's five of us."

"Exactly," Royce nodded, pointing at the dupe. "The three left out there, prolly dead or on their way. You four keep doin' this, I'll dig into a wall and wait. We'll overpower 'im."

"Dogpile!" another duplicate smiled, cracking his knuckles.

"You got it," Royce agreed. "Take turns. Three dig, one watches. Oi!"

Three turned back to smash at the ground while one climbed to the top of the pile of rubble, nodding. Royce walked back to find the biggest patch of wall and started smashing at it, carving a nook for himself to lie in wait. He muttered to himself, "Bossin' people around's too much work!"

* * *

It had been ten minutes since Django had finished off a Royce clone as he trudged faithfully in the direction Callahan had suggested earlier. He stopped and listened, hearing faint but rhythmic pounding ahead.

"Callahan, are you there?" Django asked, his voice low for no good reason.

"Got you on my screen, yessir," Callahan said. "Science geeks up here are complaining about seismic activity, what's going on down there?"

"I can hear loud rhythmic sounds ahead," Django said, putting a hand against a wall. "I'd guess they found the right place and are trying to get down to it. Any idea how many are left?"

"Looks like the last five of them are about six hundred yards ahead of you," Callahan noted, "four together and one near a wall."

Django sighed. "An attempt at an ambush. They know I'm coming but don't know about you. Hm... you're sure the area is completely evacuated?"

"...yeah, nobody is within 500 yards of where they are," Callahan said uneasily, "but the gas company says one of the ruptured mains is right in the junction where those five are. We really like this city, you know, with roads and buildings..."

"I'm trying to factor that in – plus saving the whole planet from being eaten," Django said, starting to walk again. "Can you tell me about the layout, where the last five are? Where is the gas main, and where are they?"

Callahan "hmm"ed while he watched his screen. "If you keep going the way you are, you'll come out facing the four guys in the middle and be just over the head of the one next to a wall. The gas main will be to your right at your 4 o'clock position."

Django considered this as he walked. "Can you call the T.A.S.K. main desk and ask them to connect you to my assistant, Gabriela Gomez? I am going to call in a favor from my grandfather and get enough gold to pay for whatever I'm going to break, but Gabriela will know how to make it all work on paper. I hope ten tons will be enough..."

Callahan audibly gulped. "I'm... I'm gonna get everybody to pull back some more, you okay for a few minutes?"

Django wearily said, "Thank you, yes. It will take me some time to walk that far."

Callahan dropped the mic and Django could hear the lieutenant anxiously yelling as he got further away.

With only the dim light of far off points and the moist sound of his own footsteps for company, Django, covered in slime and trash, marched on.

* * *

Bored, Royce pulled out his phone and started tapping at it. Typically, there was almost nothing on it. "Luckily, coverage is never a problem with Legacy," he chuckled and downloaded a game called Temple Run. Despite his huge fingers, he was able to nimbly guide the tiny on-screen character past various obstacles and hazards.

"Oi!" Royce squealed as he turned at a particularly hazardous curve.

"You're pretty good at that game," a friendly voice from above said.

"'s funny," Royce responded, never taking his eye off the screen, "I end up with a lotta free time between murders and what not, so..."

Royce looked up from the screen, his character suffering from this lapse in attentiveness, and glared around. The lookout was glaring angrily away from him, the pounding of the other three continued unabated. Then, he looked up to see Django – bedraggled hair hanging down towards the ground – smiling and waving.

"Hello!" Django said confidently before leaping off to the right.

"OI!" yelled the lookout, noticing the flash of motion.

"All by yourself, huh?" Royce asked, standing up.

"Seven," Django smiled. "Like seven shining lights. Perfect."

The other Royces were clamoring out of the hole as the first one said, "Wot's this all about?"

"Just wanted to make sure you'd survive this," Django said, leaping at Royce and kicking him hard in the solar plexus, sending him flying dozens of yards and skidding off the sewer walls.

As the others started his way, Django yelled, "The police have evacuated and I am standing near a gas leak! I can teleport away from here before you can get me, and the lightning will ignite the gas! Walk away now, and nobody else has to get hurt!"

Far off, the first Royce stood up, laughing. "I never get hurt for long, and I don't give a toss what happens to these blokes. Neither do they, right boys?"

Cracking knuckles and walking over menacingly, the duplicates all nodded.

Here goes nothing, Django thought to himself, as he held out both hands and sent blasts of lightning at the oncoming duplicates. As skin and clothing was seared off of torsos and faces, they slowed but continued to march.

Just then, the gas ignited with a huge KABOOM! The duplicate in front was destroyed instantly, and both Django and the rest were hurled in different directions. Singed but unbowed, Django rose quickly to punch through one, two duplicates' chests and ducked out of the way of a haymaker from the last one. Django pulled his arm back before being grabbed and held aloft by the real Royce.

"That trick won't work on me, boyo!" Royce yelled, swinging Django around and around his head before slamming the hero through the knee-high water into the ground. The dupe kicked Django in the ribs and Django lashed out with a massive lightning attack, incinerating the clone instantly and singing Royce.

Royce staggered backward, allowing Django time to recover somewhat. Django drew his fist back and wrapped his fist in lightning, uppercutting Royce so hard that the man flew upwards, smashing into the sewer roof, and then falling right into a full two-fisted blast of lightning from Django, which sent him flying across the empty space. Django teleported just then and appeared where Royce was falling to punch him again, then teleported a final time to rush to catch the man with a last uppercut, felling the huge villain unconscious into the brackish water.

Breathing heavily, Django stood over Royce, waiting for signs of motion. After a moment he said, "Callahan, can you hear me?"

Callahan responded, "Jesus, yes, it sounds like World War Three down there! You okay?"

"Yes..." Django said tiredly, "if someone can help with containing this monster. He may not stay down for long, and T.A.S.K. needs to contain the site."

"Your pal Glitch said she was sending Kraken already," Callahan answered. "That the guy from all those TV shows?"

"That's him..." Django said, plopping down against the rubble the Royces created. "I'll just wait here."

Callahan said, "Minimal damage up here, just a couple of houses knocked down. You saved us all, so let me be the first to say 'thanks.'"

Django smiled wearily and grunted.

* * *

Hours later, John Henry stood next to the much drier and calmer Django while Kraken – who somehow had gotten a transparent Armani clean suit with extendable segments for his tentacles – supervised the excavation.

"The winch will have it up here in a minute," Kraken yelled back over the sound of the heavy machine. "Royce did most of the work for us, so that's helpful."

"I'm sure Django will send him a gift basket in that supermax prison," Henry chuckled, patting Django on the shoulder. Django grunted in reply and took a sip of coffee from an SLPD travel mug.

The winch reached the top and they all strained to see what Kraken was bringing up. A plain surfaced, opalescent oval emerged and Kraken confidently settled it into a nesting of flexible foam inside a huge crate he'd specially designed to contain this item. Once enclosed, Kraken activated the multi-combination lock and smiled at them.

"All done!" he said cheerily. "This thing is awesome – it's broadcasting a signal based on the biology of the Burning Tide, making the whole solar system invisible to them. I can't turn it off of course, that'd be crazy, but I can't wait to get some readings off of it."

Kraken cheerily pushed the floating crate on to a platform, which lifted the artifact and the scientist up to street level.

"You did great work here, Django," Henry said, arms crossed.

"Thanks, John," Django smiled, standing. "There was a girl... I'd like to..."

"You work with T.A.S.K. now," Henry interrupted, waving a hand. "We don't just show up, knock down some walls and fly off. In addition to what social services is going to do for her, we've assigned a T.A.S.K. social counselor to keep tabs on her and help her stay on the right path."

Django pondered this. "I wish we could do more ..."

Henry raised an eyebrow. "Do you have some other ideas?"

"Maybe ..." Django said thoughtfully. "Maybe ..."

"Well, for now you should teleport up to the Tempest," Henry said. "I'm told your assistant has a full calendar of things you should be doing. We've got this under control."

Django nodded, stood back and disappeared in a flash of lightning.

* * *

Two weeks later, Erin was sitting on her bed in a foster home on Florland Drive as her roommates Tanisha, Rocio and Courtney danced to a Becky G song. Erin glared icily at them, her homework undone on her lap. She rolled her eyes and chucked the notebook on her pillow.

Suddenly, she heard screams from downstairs and wondered what idiocy her foster sisters were getting into now. After a moment, she heard her name mixed in with the screams and decided to find out what was the problem.

Erin lazily strolled down stairs and was stunned to see Django standing in the front hall, two of Erin's "foster sisters" fawning over him.

"Hey!" he said excitedly.

"Wha... you..." Erin stammered.

"I found out about you, Erin," Django said. "That you were an honor student, that your parents were killed in a tornado, that you had a bad time in a group home. I...I'd like to do more."

Erin walked closer. "You saved my life, even when I was kind of a jerk to you."

"I acted like you were a stereotype," Django replied. "Not cool. So, I called in some favors. Everybody in this foster home who keeps up good grades and stays out of trouble is going to college, free, on me. Simple as that."

Erin's eyes welled and she clasped her hands to her mouth while the other girls screamed. "That's..."

"My people sent me out to help people," Django smiled. "That takes more than my fists. The T.A.S.K. counselor is going to be there for all of you, and you will have every chance to become a hero in your own life."

Erin ran over to hug him, and he smiled.

"I don't know how to thank you!"

"Find somebody to save, one day," Django said. "Deal?"

Erin rested her head on his chest and said, "I promise."

NIKIA THE PANDORA
Lance Oliver Keeble

One thinks of the strangest things when they're tied up. Especially when it's not for pleasure. You find yourself asking, *How did I get myself in this predicament?*

Smack! The sound echoed in the dark dank concrete room used as a dungeon. Nikia abruptly awakened by a rush of pain across her face, it was her nemesis, the Black Russian, who would, for the next hour, be taking out his frustrations on her. Nikia was tall, her skin color of newly creamed coffee; covered with freckles head to toe. Her hair was thick with large curls. Her multicolored locks where black and brown with blond streaks in the winter and red streaks in the summer. Her Afro framed her face, hiding ears. As a child she was teased for her freckles and wild hair, a product of African and Irish slaves coupling. As an adult, men and women alike pursued her. Today she'd been captured.

Nikia was tied to a large oak cross, bound by abrasive thick manila rope – how apropos. Actually, it was called a *St. Andrew's cross*. It was quite uncomfortable.

Nikia had started her day happy. This was her last year as this city's heroine. She had fallen in love. She was getting married soon. She looked forward to retiring and being a mother. She looked forward to transferring the Herculean task of heroine to a new female child, a new generation of the unknown and unseen protectors of earth.

Whack, came the hand of her enemy, as he stalked back and forth, talking trash to her. Nikia contemplated her escape.

"You fuckin' bitches are all the same!"

Nikia was not; she was the ultimate woman and she inherited superior power and the proverbial virtues of womanhood, including persuasion, persistence and endurance to the tenth power to name a few. Nikia was all the positives of womankind packed into a single human being. Even her tolerance for pain was unmatched. No man could endure what a woman was created to endure. Childbirth is that ultimate example and proof. Still, Nikia wasn't enjoying this thrashing.

Black Russian is a drink containing vodka and coffee. It's also the name of the asshole standing before Nikia monologuing and hitting her. His true name is Peter Nieves Gannibal. Peter's family was transplanted to Russia many years ago. He was a descendant of an Afro-Russian nobleman, military engineer and general who was kidnapped as a child and presented as a gift to Peter the Great who raised the child in the Emperor's household. Russia was Peter's homeland via kidnapping.

Whap! He hit her again and stood in front of her in grand fashion. Hitting her rapidly proved that he was a sadistic twat. His long trench coat flowed like a flag as he breathed heavily through his mask, bragging about finally winning, finally getting the upper hand, finally ridding the world of her kind.

Nikia Lynott was an Eve, an Anesidora. Americans called her Pandora from the Greek mythos. It was much deeper than that. They were descendants of Lilith, Lucy, Mawu – the real Eve from over 150,000 years ago. Not the biblical Eve most people are familiar with; the true Eve born of the earth, the motherland, where it all began.

Pow! That one hurt.

Black Russian was a super soldier, genetically engineered through years of fetus tampering. He had high intelligence and astute strategic skills but there were some qualities that the lab boys neglected to enhance. His fragile ego and poor common sense were just a few of his vulnerabilities.

Nikia finally focused her swollen eyes. She looked Black Russian up and down. She couldn't hold in a snicker. He looked ridiculous. His costume combined the Russian flag and the African flag; it was the South African flag, more or less. Emblazoned on his front torso was a green "ч", for the word "черный". It was outlined by yellow and white. The red, blue and black colors framed the rest of the body suit and mask. He finished the ensemble off with a black trench coat. To Nikia, he looked like a combination of a Mexican wrestler and a gay version of Blade.

Wham, he didn't like her giggling. What was she giggling about?

His vehement hatred made no sense to her. Maybe he was simply a misogynistic jerked who resented the women who apotheosized creation? Maybe he wanted to kill her because of his need to erase his historical truth. The Freudian psychology of it didn't matter much. What mattered was that Nikia wasn't going to take too many more of those slaps across the head and face. She was a mystical being bestowed with magical powers of life and death, good and evil. Her human side was ready to kick this motherfucker's ass. That shit hurt.

Nikia didn't like Black Russian either. Not because he denied his blackness; not because he ignored the thousands of years of oppression while claiming Afro-pride; not even because he dated only Caucasian women – dating someone you preferred was no crime, but to belittle and hate on Black women to justify a choice, Nikia found deplorable. He was a hot mess of conflict and contradictions. Even so, Nikia disliked Black Russian because he was always trying to kill her.

Pop! That was a solid backhand. Black Russian should have been the antithesis of all that prejudice. Instead, he embodied it. His name was a play on words *and* a cruel irony. In Russian, they loved him; he could have had the honor of being Russia's Super-man, their Captain. See, Russia wasn't too kind to Black people, but they loved their celebrities. Black Russian could have been a trailblazer. He let his powers and abilities get to his head. He became a villain instead.

Nikia used her powers for good. It was her obligation. Her kind had been cursed after releasing evil to the world. They spent generations tracking evil, capturing it, and putting it back where it belongs. Unfortunately, evil begets evil, so the responsibility, the curse, is an eternal circle, never to be broken until the end of time.

Crack! He hit her again. Nikia was growing weary. She looked past Black Russian to see the Pandora's Box on the table behind him. The box, the pithos, was more like a jar or an urn that had evolved into a locket the size of her palm. It was an egg-shaped jewelry box made of gold and ivory. Historical glyphs adorned the sides. They changed and moved as the Pandora coursed through time and history.

Nikia spit blood. Her thoughts seemed to be all over the place, but she was now focused on the box. If only she could open it telepathically. The clasp was a traditional looking one but it was a modern touch lock that could only be bypassed by an Anesidora. The internal hinges secured the lid so that the user could control how much she opened and closed it. She could control the volume of good and evil that she released or captured. Legend was that the powers used to control the box itself were hope, faith and trust.

Bam! He taunted her. "Do you want your precious weapon? You're powerless without it, aren't you?" Black Russian chortled.

"It's not a weapon." Nikia spoke through her bloodied mouth.

Hope lied deep within the pithos. It was a great responsibility, one a Pandora never took lightly. If used properly, the wielder could dole out exactly what was needed for each adversary. For example, if it was an evil water monster, then a fire dragon might appear. Equally, if the person was inherently good, then some other sprite would appear, causing the opponent to succumb to reason.

But, it wasn't the only pithos. Nikia had been adorned with many. Her costume, though in constant flux, was a combination of the Greek robes of her predecessors. She modernized her look by wearing black leggings and soft boots. She was covered with jewelry, bracelets, anklets, toe rings, rings on her fingers and necklaces of various lengths. Nikia's plethora of adornments sported hidden compartments, lockets and charms – all miniature pithos. Contained within the *mini-urns*, were seeds of hope, faith, truth and the deadly whims of a Pandora. The Pandora stayed prepared.

Smack! Black Russian was so preoccupied with torturing Nikia that it was only a matter of time that she would find a way to defeat him. Nikia wiggled her hands and wrists, readying herself to open a locket on her bracelet with her fingertips.

Black Russian foolishly continued his diatribe, never noticing.

Nikia interrupted him "What's the matter Black Russian? You really don't have the balls to kill a woman, *do* you? You profess to hate me but I don't believe you. I think I remind you of your mother. Maybe it's an Oedipus thing? Do you secretly love me? Maybe that's why you go out of your way to find women who are the opposite of her."

Bang! Black Russian struck Nikia again. "What did you say?" he spat, with fire in his eyes.

Nikia pressed on, "Your mother, she was the bench mark, wasn't she? The catalyst, you couldn't please her no matter what you did? Your Russian blood overrode your Black blood, didn't it? Maybe you love white women and hate black women 'cuz..." Nikia paused and looked down from his eyes to his crotch and continued, "...ya' just don't measure up."

Black Russian was incensed. He turned around and flipped over the table and kicked the chair. He punched a wall, cracking the concrete. Nikia was witnessing a full-blown tantrum from this man. He eventually came for Nikia. He was ready to kill her.

Touching the lock was all she needed to do. The small pithos swung open quickly, and the first demons appeared. Demons of self-hatred swirled around Black Russian, tormenting his mind. They brought to light every loathsome doubt and thought he had about himself and his people. He screamed, swinging wildly. His fists merely wisped through the demons. They swirled, dissipated and reappeared as smoky apparitions, more wretched and abominable than before.

With a subtle flick of her fingers, she tapped another charm and the sprites of pride appeared while the demons returned to their urn. Multitudes of the small creatures that bore the faces of long past freedom fighters beset upon the Black Russian, overwhelming him.

Black Russian fought at them, cursed them, but nothing he did could sway or slow their taunts and tortures. They crawled up his body, seemingly tearing at his skin. When each arrived at his head and face, they bore through his ears, eyes and mouth. His anguish was an incredible sight to behold.

Nikia, the Pandora, was not finished yet.

Nikia's final salvo was an army of women, led by Black Russian's mother. These women bore the faces of every woman of color he had ever known – relatives, friends, classmates, colleagues, even the women he rejected, slighted, insulted and harmed. They were armed with weapons from every era of war – spears, knives, swords, pistols, rifles, and machine guns. Wave after wave, they marched in battle formation, riddling his body with deft blade strikes and bullets of every caliber. When it was over, Black Russian was bleeding, lying on the floor in pain and dying.

Moments later, the room cleared, leaving just Nikia and Peter. She was still trussed up and vulnerable on the large X shaped cross and Peter, the Black Russian, remained on the floor, a shivering mass of a broken man. There was no more bravado or brash cockiness, just a shell. When he finally looked up at Nikia all he saw was his mother's face.

Peter, the Black Russian, silently wept. He gazed at Nikia who bore his mother's face.

She gave him a stern look and spoke in his mother's voice. "Peter, why are you lying on the floor like that? Be strong; learn from your mistakes son. Get up, come over her and untie your mother. I got things to do baby!"

Peter rose, he checked his person and found no physical injuries. He calmly walked over to Nikia and released her, without speaking. He watched as she gathered her things and headed to the exit.

She turned, walked back to him. From her tiptoes she kissed him on the forehead and spoke again, "Now you behave yourself boy."

Peter's silent tears continued to flow as he watched his long since dead mother exit the dungeon.

The door slammed shut. Nikia stood on the other side, bruised but back to her old self. She triumphantly departed, never to be seen again.

SHADOWBOXER: NEUTRAL CORNERS
Adeatoyshe J. Heru

"Alright, Curtis...how about a three piece?"

A right jab. A left jab. A second right.

"Nice. Nice. Okay. Work the body."

A strong right to the middle, followed by a second, a third, a fourth.

"Yeah, yeah. That's it. Just like that."

A left to the middle – hard enough to actually budge the bag this time.

Clayton smiled.

"What," the fourteen year old asked the much larger man standing behind the punching bag, "Why you got that look on your face?"

"Nothing. No reason," Clayton lied. The truth was that he was proud of the kid. Curtis Barrows didn't have much going for him. He was small for his age, not much of a student, he got next to no attention from the girls, but he had one thing in his favor, something Clayton knew all about: the boy was a fighter.

"You sure," Curtis fired back at his trainer and mentor quizzically.

"Yeah. Hundred percent. Tell you what. Let's wrap it here for the day. You've put in some good work?"

"Thanks, Mr. Cassidy."

"C'mon, Curt. We've been over this. It's 'Clay' or it's nothing. Got it?"

"Yes, sir."

Clayton's face went rigid with annoyance.

"I meant 'Clay'. Yes, Clay."

"Good. Now get out of those gloves, get packed up, and head home. You know your folks are going to worry if you're not home by the time that street light turns on."

"Tell me about it," the teen replied, offering his hands out to Clayton to pull off the gloves so that he could get to work on the tape on his hands underneath.

Clayton obliged and, with a strong pat on Curtis' shoulder, said, "You really are getting it, man. I've seen a huge improvement the last couple of weeks. You keep this up and you'll be something dangerous."

"Thanks, that means a lot coming from the champ."

Clayton laughed in spite of himself. He hadn't been anyone's "champ" for about two and a half years, not since running afoul of some gangsters put an end to all of that and set him on his current path. He couldn't really complain, he told himself. After all, if things hadn't shaken out the way they did he wouldn't be here, in his own gym, working to set kids like Curtis on the right track. He wouldn't be the man who spends his time outside of the gym making his city safer, one punch at a time.

"Go on, head on back and get your stuff. You're losing daylight."

Curtis took off in a hurry, a bundle of energy after spending an hour and some change wailing on a bag that weighed three times his own weight.

"Matter of fact, all of you need to be winding down," Clay called out to no one and everyone in the *Ring Leader Gym and Fitness Center*, his place of business, home, and base of operations, "It's coming up on closing time. You don't have to go home but you need to get your butts out of here!"

A chorus of "You got it, Champ;" "Sure thing, Clay;" and other affirmations, came flooding over him. He ran a tight ship and every patron of the Ring Leader knew good and well that Clay only had to say something once... if at all.

All at once they dropped gloves and weights, started putting away equipment and gear, and went about the business of making themselves scarce so that Clayton Cassidy could put his gym – his baby – to bed.

He started his walk toward his office, passing poster after poster and fight card after fight card. He was featured on a few of them – well, more than a few of them – and he'd done very well for himself. A guy his size, with his strength and range, shouldn't have been able to slip past all of those blows but he did. And he made it look easy, like his opponent was boxing his shadow.

He smiled for what had to be the thousandth time that day.

That was a good life. But this... this was a good life too.

The only thing stopping it from being *great* was the endless parade of self-destructive, self-hating, and overall selfish jackasses that wanted to turn his town into a warzone day in and day out.

He hadn't started his "retirement" taking those folks on. That hadn't been part of the plan. It just... happened that way. But here he was, a man on a mission, with nothing to lose but his temper.

And the longer the gym's doors stayed open, the longer it was going to be before he could get to work.

"Hey Boss Man," a voice broke his reverie.

It was Rudy Gray, the gym's manager and one of Clay's first students and patrons. He was a good man with a good head on his shoulders but a right hook that left a lot to be desired.

There are some things even a champ can't help, Clayton mused.

"What's got you in such a good mood, man," Rudy inquired, noticing the obvious wry grin that passed over his long time friend and employer's face.

"Nothing, Rude. Wassup?"

"Nothing crazy. I just wanted to let you know I can stay a bit later today to lock up in case you, you know, you need to get an early start on those extracurriculars of yours."

Clay's smile faded.

"What have I told you about talking about that in public; even the gym?" Clay admonished through clenched teeth.

"Sorry, man. I forgot."

Clay shot his friend an annoyed look. To his credit, Rudy didn't shy away... much.

"But the offer still stands," the younger man started again, undeterred by a little browbeating.

Clay softened his expression as best he could. He liked Rudy. He had to in order to spend most of the daylight hours with him and to cut him a check every two weeks. But more importantly, he trusted the young man. He trusted him to run his business when he wasn't around, to represent him and the gym with the clientele, and most importantly, to tell him about his second life as Shadowboxer, Bay City's Punishing Pugilist.

Clayton Cassidy, former heavyweight contender and the most talented prized fighter of his generation, moonlighted as the black-clad nocturnal vigilante feared throughout the city for his relentless pursuit of justice and a haymaker that could drop a raging bull. He helped the weak and disenfranchised, the preyed upon of the city, punch above their weight.

"I appreciate it, man, I do. But it shouldn't take too long to get everything squared away and head upstairs for a bite to eat before hitting the town. You go on home. Get some rest. You gotta be back here early in the morning anyway."

"Alright; you're the boss. Hit the town a few times for me too, while you're at it."

"Will do, Rude," Clayton chuckled. "Will do."

The two friends shared a handshake and a quick hug and then Rudy made his way back toward the door where his bag waited for him. Clayton watched him and the last patrons make their exit and then turned to take a look at his gym.

The former fighter had every reason to be proud of the place. He had spent the lion's share of his winnings to buy the property, fix it up, and outfit it with some of the most state of the art equipment on the market. It took a while to get everything he thought he'd need to have Bay City's number one gym and fitness center but he put up the money and the gym hasn't had a single slow day yet. In fact, business was so good that he thought about opening up a new location or two in the next year.

But the ellipticals, speed bags, weights, and such weren't the only pieces of equipment he had brought in. Just twenty-five feet below, in the Ring Leader's sub-basement, which just so happened to be missing from the building's plans, Clayton had constructed a mini command center – a hub where he could not only store his costume and equipment and lick his wounds after those particularly rough nights, but also where his satellite uplink to the Crusader's Guild of America's supercomputer was housed. From his hideout, he was able to conduct his war on crime away from the prying eyes of friends, family, customers, and building inspectors.

He was serious about cleaning up his city. He had lived there his entire life. It had taught him how to fight and, more importantly, given him a reason to.

An hour later, the gym was locked up tight. Clayton had enjoyed a quick meal of broiled chicken, wild rice, and asparagus, and made his way down to his hideout via the secret elevator in his bedroom closet.

The room lit up when he stepped off of the elevator, acknowledging his return. A fairly large space – outfitted with computers, a first aid station, a shower, a twin bed, and just about everything a vigilante on the go might need – he didn't really need the lights to navigate his way around it. Even if he had not memorized the room's layout, his one superhuman ability – his power to see in absolute darkness – made light sources unnecessary for him.

It wasn't an ability he bragged on all that much. Not that he was ashamed of it, mind you. In fact, this super power had saved his life, and the lives of others, time and again. He could see clear as day in the dead of night. A cavern a mile underground would appear as bright as Main Street at midday to him.

What he hated was how he came upon his gift.

Back in his boxing days, back when he was a young upstart with a very real shot at the title, he made a few wrong turns after meeting some even more wrong people. He was asked to throw a fight; he threw some hard punches instead. For his trouble, he was drugged, just in time to test positive for performance-enhancing drugs and to lose his shot at the belt.

What no one counted on, not Clayton or the monsters that ruined him, was Clayton having an adverse reaction to whatever they shot him up with. He lost his vision for a few days but it slowly returned and it was better than ever, especially at night. Consumed with rage and having gone too long without hitting someone that deserved it, Cassidy hit the streets in a ski mask and beat the truth out of his assailants.

A few nights of "rough housing" later and he put everything back in place. But he couldn't deny how good it felt to make those crooks face the music. It felt better than anything, even being in the ring. That was when he decided.

He wouldn't give up fighting but he would give up fighting for just himself. He saw, first-hand, how dark the city's shadows could get. Someone had to be there to stand guard.

Snapping back to the present, he made the short walk across the room and stood in front of the fifty-five inch high definition monitor. A few keystrokes on a keyboard to his right and he drew up a glowing blue digital map of Bay City, his hometown and stomping grounds. Another press of a button and the map changed, some of the blue portions changing to red to indicate emergencies, crimes in progress, and the like. Ten "hot spots" overall.

"Another quiet night in the BC," Clayton muttered to himself as he scrolled through each of the incidents. Three house fires, two fender benders, four bar brawls, and a 911 call for an elderly woman complaining of heart troubles. The local authorities were already on scene or on their way to each of the locations.

He was actually relieved.

His city could be a brutal and unforgiving place; the kind of town that hits below the belt and never waits for the bell. Good parents and boxing had spared him the brunt of it but he knew better than most that this was a land of no return more often than not.

Since there wasn't any situation that demanded his particular skill set, he figured he'd take to the rooftops for a patrol. Usually, he ran into the most action when he wasn't headed to any crisis in particular. And, unfortunately, he never had to venture too far afield from the Ring Leader.

He tapped a couple buttons and got a read on Bay City's weather forecast for the night. With winter right around the corner he wasn't surprised to see that it was going to be a cool night.

"Good thing the suit's got some insulation," he said to no one as he made his way over to the closet. He pressed his right hand against the biometric reader and waited patiently as it scanned his fingerprints, body heat, pulse, and other unique biological rhythms to verify his identity.

He would have been just as happy to keep his suits in a footlocker but the Crusader's Guild insisted that members keep their costumes and gear under lock and virtual key. That way, even if someone did stumble upon his hideaway they'd have to work extra hard to get at any weapons or gear he kept down there.

The automatic door slid open with a quiet hiss and its internal illumination revealed his collection of costumes, all hanging and waiting on him.

"Alright. Time to hit the town." He chuckled at his favorite pun.

He stripped his tee shirt and shorts, taped his hands, and slipped into the all-black bulletproof body suit he wore every night. It fit like a glove and, even though it took him a while to get used to throwing uppercuts, jabs, and crosses in formfitting pajamas, he couldn't argue with the way it stopped a nine-millimeter round, fired from ten feet away, in its tracks. The suit's ebony coloring made it even easier to sneak around in the dark city and take down the criminals without them being any wiser.

He slipped on the full-face mask as the finishing touch. He wiggled and flexed his fingers in his gloves, reassured by the additional weight in the knuckles.

He took inventory of his utility belt and pouches, noting his standard issue Guild grapple gun, lock picks, spare keys, cash, and first aid kit were all in place. He learned early on that he needed more than his fists out there on the street... even if it wasn't much more than his fists.

Satisfied that he was ready for the night, he turned and made his way toward the back of the room. The hideout had a secret exit to match its secret entrance. He pressed a combination of buttons on the keypad next to the reinforced steel door and made his way out to the tunnels beyond.

Unlike the room behind him, the tunnel ahead was pitch black, with absolutely no light to guide someone making their way through the passage. The best they could hope to do without a flashlight was to stumble forward on the path as it sloped upward. However, thanks to his night vision, he could see even better in the tunnel than he did in the room behind him.

He had a few dozen yards before he got to the end of the tunnel but he wasn't in much of a hurry. He used the walk to the end of the passage to psych himself up, get his mind focused on the task at hand. It reminded him of every walk to the ring from the locker room. The only difference on nights like these as opposed to nights like those was that he wasn't facing one man in the boxing ring; he was taking on the entire city.

The tunnel ended after about a minute and terminated in a door identical to the one at the entrance of his hideout. Once again punching in a code and shouldering the big metal door open, he found himself standing in a dark alley with his exit obscured by a pair of dumpsters and their overflowing detritus.

The city's brisk night air wrapped around him and carried the smells of the city to his nose – garbage, stagnant water, fast food.

The distant sounds of Newtown Street welcomed him. Cars and buses mainly. It was still too early for the usual rabble to flood the street but there was a high possibility that a few early birds were out and about.

Night after night of starting his evening like this had drilled a number of healthy habits into the vigilante. He scanned the dark alley to make sure he was unobserved. He quieted his breathing to listen for anything amiss in the space around him. He made sure to not move the boxes, lengths of wood, and garbage too much so that he didn't risk exposing the tunnel door.

Completing his "pre-fight" ritual, he reached into his utility belt to withdraw his grapple gun. He took aim at the edge of the building overhead and pulled the trigger.

Pfft.

The gun's CO_2 cartridge discharged and sent the sturdy hook and line flying toward the ledge.

Clink.

The hook seized the rooftop.

Whizz.

He hit the button to retract the line and felt the rush of having his two hundred and thirty pounds ripped off of the ground and pulled skyward.

A fraction of a second later and he was standing on the edge of the building, the alley below him, and the city stretching out for miles on end. He could see the *Ring Leader* a block and a half away from his perch. It was actually one of the shorter buildings in the neighborhood. Still, the bigger buildings that made up Bay City's skyline were farther away from the inner city, titans made of metal and glass standing watch over the city's commerce and tourism.

"Alright, let's get this night started."

Shadowboxer broke out into a run, heading full tilt for the opposite side of the building. Every patrol started like this: a lung full of air, a heart full of determination, and a leap of faith.

He bounded from the building and fired the grapple gun again.

The gun's hook latched onto a fire escape across the street and he let his momentum carry him into a wild arc above the street below.

The black figure sailed upward, retracting the hook on his ascent, and fired again without missing a beat. The hook met his new target without trouble and he repeated the process until he had climbed over ten stories and come to rest on one of his favorite ledges overlooking the city.

Shadowboxer called all of Bay City his home but his neighborhood, the place where he laid his head, was his favorite part of the city. He was born and raised there. He went to school there. He fell in love for the first time in that neighborhood. He had his first heartbreak in that neighborhood. His patrols carried him all over the city, from Oxonburg to Rickettville to Crystal Heights, but he always made sure to focus his attention and energy on his little slice of the city before he pushed on to see what new danger the city had to throw at him.

He made up his mind to spiral outward tonight. That way, he'd get a chance to peer into every alley on his way out to the bigger city beyond.

Descending from the building toward the city below, he went to work.

The first forty-five minutes were quiet. Well, as quiet as you can expect swinging above a city by a cable eleven stories above the street.

He landed quietly on a roof to catch his breath and check the CO_2 cartridge on the gun when he heard a noise below.

"Leave me alone," came a woman's voice.

"Why you gotta be like that, ma," a man's voice countered.

"Be like what?" she shot back. "I was minding my business. You fools came at me."

"Fools?" a second man asked. "Haha. See? This is the problem with these females, Teddy. They got big mouths and nothing to back it up."

"True, true. Haha."

"I said, leave me alone!"

Shadowboxer approached the edge of the roof above the scene and peered down into the gloom of the alley. It was about what he expected. A pretty young woman, alone, being approached by a handful of guys that looked like they didn't know how to speak to a woman, let alone show her a good time.

The crime fighter couldn't stand a bully and he liked five of them even less. He fought the urge to descend on them immediately, but reminded himself that he hadn't lasted this long by just jumping into a fight without sizing up the competition.

Five men: two heavily muscled and over six feet tall, one on the soft and pudgy side but even taller than the other two, and two shorter men, one with a runner's physique and the other with the build of an amateur bodybuilder.

He didn't anticipate any trouble but he knew he'd have to keep his eyes open for any weapons they might carry.

"C'mon girl. Be cool and hang with us," a third man, the pudgy one pleaded.

"What part of 'Leave me alone' don't you understand?"

The men broke out in laughter at her frustration.

Shadowboxer, having seen enough and not wanting to run the risk of it getting out of hand, hooked his grapple gun to the ledge at his feet and leapt outward and downward to the alley below.

"Look," the short bodybuilder started, "We'll overlook how rude you're being if you just calm down and kick it with us. Damn, didn't your momma ever…"

His words were cut short as the large, heavily muscled, black-clad shape of the Shadowboxer landed heavily between the group of men and the young woman.

"I believe," Shadowboxer intoned in a voice that sounded like boiling gravel, "that the young lady here asked you to leave her alone."

Silence.

The Shadowboxer's reputation preceded him in Bay City. From one side of town to the other, folks had heard about the dark protector that wasn't above laying hands on any criminal he came across.

Everyone knew he didn't play around and he didn't do second chances.

"Y-Y-You right," the stout man replied.

"Yes, I am right," Shadowboxer menaced.

The men moved as one to back out of the alley and leave the vigilante and the young woman in peace.

"Stop," Shadowboxer said.

They stopped in unison, frozen in their tracks.

"I know your faces," he continued, "I'll know your names by the end of the night. I suggest you walk a tightrope from here on out. If you don't…"

He punctuated his sentence by driving his gloved fist into the wall to his right, leaving a fist-shaped indentation in the brick and mortar.

The girl yelped in surprise and a little bit of fear.

Even in the darkness of the alley, his face completely covered by the black material of his mask, the five toughs could see the unmistakable smile of the vigilante. Every one of them knew he was hoping for an excuse.

Without ceremony, and with no care for their fellows, all five of them turned and ran as fast and as far away as they could.

Shadowboxer was satisfied with the result and grateful for the additional protection his glove afforded his hand.

"Th-Thank you," the young woman offered to the back of the man who had saved her.

She had a very hard time hiding her fear when the much larger masked man turned to regard her.

"Are you okay," he asked, his voice much softer than it had been when he spoke to her assailants.

This had an obvious effect on her. She relaxed a bit.

"I think so, yeah."

"Good. You know, things could've gone a lot differently if I hadn't shown up when I had."

"You don't have to tell me," she replied.

With that she opened her purse and reached in.

Shadowboxer's vision let him see much clearer than the streetlight overhead would have allowed. He made out the grip on what could only be a revolver, a .38 Special. He did his best to stifle a surprised look, not even sure his mask would hide it from the young woman.

"A girl has to take care of herself out here," she stated matter-of-factly.

"Yes, yes she does."

"But still, thank you, for stepping in. Not a whole lot of men would do what you just did for me."

"It was my pleasure. Are you going to be all right from here? Do you need me to escort you--"?

"No, I'm fine," she interrupted.

"Good."

"Charise."

"Excuse me?"

"Charise, that's my name."

"Oh, okay."

Shadowboxer hadn't even thought to ask. He never really thought to ask anyone he saved, he realized.

"Nice to meet you, Charise. I'm..."

"You're the Shadowboxer," she said, cutting him off. "You're the masked man that punches people in the dead of night."

He nodded.

"Well, I appreciate everything you did tonight."

"So you've said," he retorted.

Charise closed her purse and slung it over her shoulder.

Shadowboxer stepped aside as she made her way past him toward the street beyond.

"You know, you might..." she started, but when she turned around the vigilante was gone.

"Damn."

Shadowboxer cleared the roof and launched immediately into a run. Good deeds like that, where he didn't have to throw a punch, were few and far between but he appreciated them. He didn't put on the suit to punish the people of the city but to protect them. If those five idiots could be dissuaded with a threat or two he was more than happy to settle for that. But he hadn't lied. He fully intended to look them up, learn their names, and even check out their criminal records. They got off easy tonight but he didn't rule out having to hunt them down tomorrow evening.

He knew he still had another couple hours on his patrol and had no expectations for a night full of similar encounters. Bay City almost always found an opponent for him.

Much to his surprise, the remaining hours of his patrol were uneventful. He didn't come across any scenes that needed his intervention and his mask's police scanner/communicator didn't yield any situations where the Shadowboxer's unique brand of justice might apply.

Winding his way back home, he found himself swinging past a familiar apartment tenement building. It was Yellowbrook Apartments, the seven-floor building where Curtis lived with his mother, father, and two younger sisters.

Swinging by the building from five stories above, he had a clear view of the roof and could easily make out a small assemblage in the darkness.

He couldn't shake the feeling that he was needed there.

"Let's see what we have here."

He adjusted his course and was soon swinging toward the roof of the apartment building. He made sure to approach unseen and landed on the roof with barely a sound. He tucked the grapple gun back into his belt and began the swift and stealthy approach to get within earshot of the group.

He could see them long before he could hear them and he made out a group of men and teenagers on the roof. There were twelve in total. They wore heavy coats and wool caps. Shadowboxer couldn't help but be a little surprised. Sure, the air was cooler for that time of year but these guys were dressed for the dead of winter.

"—said you were on the level," came the first voice to hit his ears. It belonged to an older man, likely one with at least a decade on Shadowboxer himself. He was large, with a bigger and even more muscular frame than even Shadowboxer's. He looked like he knew his way around a brawl and it was easy to see how most people would be intimidated by him.

Most people.

"Yeah." The voice was several years younger and sounded very familiar to the hero's ears, "I'm on the level. I mean, I'm down."

If he didn't know any better he would have sworn it was Curtis, his student from the Ring Leader Gym. But, since he had super night vision and not super hearing, he figured he'd give himself room to doubt.

Shadowboxer continued to draw nearer, taking position behind an HVAC unit about four yards away from the group. His black costume helped him blend with the shadows and he was absolutely sure that no one in attendance would see him unless he wanted them to.

"Good, good," the older man said.

"Yeah, Big G," another young voice chimed in. "My boy Curt is down for whatever. He can help us move this weight."

That clenched it. Curtis, a good kid, was on this rooftop in the dead of night with a bunch of men who didn't sound like they had anything good planned for this, or any other, evening. He searched his memory for the name "Big G," trying to figure out if it was one he had come across while reading police reports or shaking down criminal informants over the last couple of years. He came up with nothing.

"You keep telling me that, Omar, but I need proof your boy is with it. I mean, anybody can *say* they'll do that dirt but I gotta check under the fingernails. Know what I'm sayin'?"

"I got it," Curtis, instead of his friend, answered flatly.

Shadowboxer felt his stomach lurch at what he heard.

"Oh, alright. Big man here thinks he's ready to be a God of War, huh?"

"Hell yeah he is," Omar, a boy that only looked slightly older than Curtis, shot at the man.

"Alright, alright," Big G wore a wry smile on his face, "Let me confer with my associates here. See what they think of this."

With that Big G turned away from the two teens and he and his nine cohorts huddled up a couple of yards away.

Their low murmurs and ironic chuckles were all the boys could make out. Shadowboxer could hear even less from his position.

The men, all ranging from late teens to however old Big G was, kept this up for about five minutes. They'd take the time to turn and regard the boys, some pointing and laughing, others looking incredibly stern and serious.

Shadowboxer kept fighting the sinking feeling in his gut. He was immediately glad that he followed his intuition and made the detour to the roof. Now, he just had to be patient to see what he, and Curtis, was up against.

The huddle dispersed and Big G turned to regard the teenagers. His posse stood at his back, looking grim and determined and waited for their leader to speak.

"Okay, so this is how it's gonna go," he started, his crooked smile betraying him, "We're the Gods of War, right?"

He waited for the teens to answer.

"Yeah," Omar said confidently.

"Right," Curtis answered.

"Well," Big G continued, "Gods demand sacrifices. You know that much, right?"

"Y-Yeah," Curtis answered, confused.

"Damn straight," Omar retorted.

"Good, good. Since you know that, this shouldn't come as a surprise."

He held out both of his hands to his sides. Two of his men stepped forward, reached into their out of season coats, and produced a pawn shop nine-millimeter each. They placed the guns in Big G's hands and stepped back, all without saying a word and without even a change of their facial expression.

Big G stepped toward the boys and offered each of them a gun.

Omar didn't hesitate.

Curtis, to his credit, looked very unsure and tentatively reached out toward the firearm.

"Don't do it, Curt," Shadowboxer found himself muttering under his breath.

"Go on, kid, take it," Big G egged on as he gestured the gun toward Curtis.

Curtis took the gun but a look of regret immediately settled on his young features.

Dammit, Shadowboxer thought.

"Good man. Now, since gods demand a sacrifice and, well, the Gods of

War aren't looking to open up a damn intern program..."

A bout of raucous laughter exploded behind Big G, his men dropping their stern facades in order to enjoy a good laugh at the boys' expense.

"Since we're not looking to have a bunch of kids weighing us down here in the BC," the gang leader continued after his companions' managed to rein in their laughter. "We're gonna need you boys to prove who's the most down; who's the most ready to bring war to this city."

"You don't mean," Curtis' voiced trailed off as the realization washed over him.

"Damn straight," Big G fired back.

"But, but, Omar is my friend," Curtis spoke up weakly.

"Yeah, he is," Big G offered in a voice as cold and as hard as ice. "Yeah, he is."

The two boys turned to regard one another. Curtis' face was a mask of fear, apprehension, pain, all of the emotions you'd expect to see on a fourteen year old's face when you tell him you want him to kill his friend.

Omar's expression, however, was one of grim determination, like that of an executioner who just got today's assignment. He was ready to do what he had to do.

"Omar," Curtis said weakly, afraid to look his friend in the eye.

"It's nothing personal, Curt," was all Omar bothered to say.

"That's what I'm talking about," Big G said with a broad grin, "Boys, we're looking at some real Gods of War material here. Pop him, Omar!"

Omar brought his gun up to eye level, the barrel squarely in Curtis' face.

"Omar...man, don't do this," Curtis uttered, "We're boys, man."

"Omar's not a boy anymore," Big G whispered just loud enough for Curtis to catch.

"I didn't want it to end up like this, Curt. But this is how it's gotta be."

Omar tensed and got ready to pull the trigger. What happened next was something no one on the roof would have predicted.

Before Omar could pull the trigger, his gun was snatched from his hand in the blink of an eye.

Omar and Curtis turned as one to regard the dark form of the Shadowboxer, radiating menace in their midst.

The vigilante nonchalantly tossed the gun over his shoulder and out of sight.

He then reached down and took Curtis' gun. He tossed it like Omar's.

"Boys," his voice was heavy with threat and anger, "Walk away. Now."

Stunned into silence, the boys slowly stepped back from the scene, making their way toward the door that led down into the apartment building. They broke out into a run, not unlike the five idiots harassing the woman earlier that night.

Big G and the other Gods of War looked on in disbelief at the man standing in front of them. Not a single one moved a muscle, too wary to utter a word.

All of the men on the roof, Shadowboxer and Big G included, stood in silence and waited for the door to close behind the boys.

"You," Shadowboxer started, "You have a lot to answer for, friend."

Big G found his voice, "Friend? Man, I don't know you. I don't kick it with freaks in pajamas."

A couple of his men chuckled nervously.

"Now, this is how it's going to go," Shadowboxer started, "You and your boys here are going to head over to the 114th and turn yourselves in. You won't stop for drinks. You won't call your mother. You won't even put gas in your tank. What you've done here is unforgivable and you're going to pay."

A tense moment passed after Shadowboxer completed his instructions.

Then all of the Gods of War, including Big G, burst into raucous laughter. Some even clutched their sides, slapped their knees, and stomped their feet.

"You, you," Big G could barely stifle his laughter long enough to form words, "You've got to be the craziest son of a bitch I met in this town, man. You walk up here, dressed like it's damn Halloween, and then you tell me, you tell the damn God of War, that he's going to do what, now? What did he say, Vinny?"

Vinny, a large, heavyset man that looked to be in his late twenties, stepped forward to stand between Big G and Shadowboxer and forced himself to stop laughing long enough to answer his boss. "He said, he said, he wanted us to snitch on ourselves."

"Yeah, that's what I thought," Big G said in a sober tone, his voice even and measured.

Shadowboxer was far from amused.

"I'll be honest with you," Shadowboxer started, "I was really hoping that you'd answer the way you did. See, I haven't had a chance to blow off any steam tonight and you boys, you pushed me over the edge. I'm going to enjoy this."

Vinny reached for his gun. Well, to be fair, he made the decision to reach for his gun. His brain sent the impulse to the nerves in his right arm to reach for the gun. But, sadly for the gang member, the message took too long. Shadowboxer, moving faster than any of the men's eyes could follow, punched Vinny squarely in the face with enough force to send the overweight man sailing past Big G and landing at the feet of his comrades. He was out cold.

"So, I gathered from your conversation with those boys," Shadowboxer started, adjusting his glove for added effect, "That you're new in town. I guess I get to be the welcoming committee."

The Gods of War looked down at Vinny, unable to believe that any man could move that fast or hit that hard.

"Now, you boys can either step up one at a time or all at once. Honestly, I don't care."

The men didn't look like they were in a hurry, so Shadowboxer obliged.

He dashed past Big G, having decided to save him for last, and waded into the eight remaining Gods of War. The men were all in reasonably good shape but "reasonably good" doesn't mean a thing against a seasoned combatant with peak human strength, endurance, speed, and reflexes.

The only advantage they had was in their numbers and that wasn't going to last very long. Shadowboxer learned early on that he had to hit hard, hit fast, and aim to make every punch he threw what his old coach Bernard "Smiley" Cokely called a "one hitta quitta."

What started out as eight full-grown men was reduced to a pile of moaning, groaning, and bleeding heaps in less than twenty seconds.

He stood over the unconscious Gods of War. He hadn't even broken a sweat.

Bang!

He immediately regretted his arrogance, but he regretted the searing pain in his left shoulder even more.

Shadowboxer had gotten cocky. He was so used to dictating the terms of combat, of dominating his enemies, that he allowed himself to get taken by surprise.

Of course, Big G had a gun!

Hell, all of them probably had guns on them. He had just been too fast, too intimidating, for any of them to remember. Big G had nearly twenty seconds to remember he had a gun and a target too busy beating the hell out of his men to look over his shoulder.

"It's a good thing you're wearing black, man. You're already dressed for your funeral."

Shadowboxer ignored the pain. He'd been shot before, by bigger guns than that. Besides, his suit took the brunt of the hit. He'd be feeling it tomorrow but, for tonight, right at this moment, he had more than enough adrenaline to get him through.

"You should've just gone down to the precinct," Shadowboxer stated flatly.

"And you should've just minded your own damn business!"

Big G emptied the clip at Shadowboxer.

Shadowboxer proved to be a very difficult target in the dead of night, garbed in black, and moving faster than any man Big G had ever seen outside of a kung fu flick. He was out of bullets faster than he thought he'd be and standing face to face with the man that just knocked eight of his best men down like dominoes.

"Now," Shadowboxer intoned grimly, "Where were we?"

If Big G had any hope of answering, it was dashed with the lightning fast uppercut that sent him reeling.

But that punch wasn't nearly as surprising as the fact that Big G was still standing after the blow.

"Man, you got nice hands, alright," Big G complimented, spitting blood and checking his jaw, "You hit like a truck."

Shadowboxer took a step back and realized that, for the second time in two minutes, he had underestimated this man, this Big G.

"Wanna know what the G stands for?" the crook offered.

Shadowboxer didn't bother to reply.

"Ah, come on, man. You had all that mouth earlier. Now you want to be the strong, silent type?"

Big G started to unzip his jacket.

"See, I'm guessing you don't get a lot of exercise out here in these streets. You hit folks like that, they don't stay up very long. But, all of those hard punches made you soft, man."

Big G dropped his coat to the ground at his feet, leaving him in just a tank top in the chill autumn air.

"But I can guarantee you that you've never faced a brother like Goliath."

There were two things that Shadowboxer never questioned: his fists and his eyes. But tonight, facing off against this two-bit gangbanger had him doubting both. He squinted his preternaturally sharp eyes, unable to really process what he was seeing. The crime fighter couldn't possibly be watching as this man's muscles not only gained definition but also mass. He was growing before his very eyes.

In short order his mass and density had increased so much that the roof beneath his boots was starting to crack under the pressure.

"What are you," Shadowboxer asked, sure to keep his guard up in the face of this dangerous unknown.

Big G, Goliath, just chuckled, "I'm a, watcha call it, a 'Variant.' I can turn up my muscles, getting stronger and tougher. I was born like this."

Shadowboxer knew what a Variant was, a person born with superhuman power and potential. Some claimed they were the next stage in human evolution, others an offshoot of the human race altogether. But the common consensus was that they were dangerous.

And this "Goliath" didn't seem very different from popular opinion.

"So, wanna finish this, hero?"

Shadowboxer had to rethink his stance. He had tangled with a few super powered opponents in the past. Nothing too dangerous, mostly folks that tossed around lighting or controlled minds. Pretty basic stuff. For all of their powers they still had glass jaws. But he hadn't had the "good fortune" of taking on an opponent in a different weight class altogether.

But he wasn't the type to back down from any fight.

Shadowboxer lunged forward, leading with his right. His fist slammed solidly into Goliath's face. The Variant smiled.

"Really?" the strong man taunted.

Shadowboxer barely moved in time to duck a swipe of the Variant's left arm. He could feel the violent ripples in the air in the wake of the swing. One hit, he knew, would end this fight and more than likely his life.

He threw himself back into the melee. He threw lefts, rights, and uppercuts. All to no avail. He was sure to keep an eye on the bigger man's hands, avoiding his punches, swipes, lunges, grabs, and the like.

Dancing back, he had to not only catch his breath but also flex his fingers. His heaviest blows had only served to numb his own hands, even through the reinforced gloves.

"I could do this all day, man. What about you?" Goliath goaded.

"So could I," Shadowboxer replied.

Goliath looked visibly annoyed.

"What the hell are you talking about?"

"You've got me in strength," Shadowboxer explained, "And you can definitely take a hit."

Goliath cocked an eyebrow.

"But you're too slow, Goliath. You couldn't hit me if we kept this up all *week*. You're not even worth the fight."

Shadowboxer turned his back on the muscle-bound Variant and started strolling toward the edge of the roof.

"I took your men out," he continued without bothering to pay Goliath the respect of looking him in the eyes, "I put them on their backs. I might not be able to do that to you but I can promise you one thing: you won't be able to do a damn thing in this city without looking over your shoulder, waiting for me to sucker punch you back into the gutter."

"What did you say?"

"You heard me," Shadowboxer replied without breaking his stride.

Shadowboxer couldn't help but smile when the telltale thundering of a charging Goliath rang out behind him. The fool had taken the bait.

Shadowboxer proved to be much too fast and too cunning for the enraged Variant. In one fluid motion he sidestepped the giant's outstretched arms, drew his grapple gun, fired it at the roof to anchor it, and slipped past Goliath to entangle him in the high-tensile line.

What resulted was an overly muscled piñata dangling off the side of the building, stressing the grapple gun's two-ton test line.

"Let me up," Goliath bellowed, fear in his voice, "Let me up!"

"I don't know," Shadowboxer taunted, "That shot to the shoulder really weakened my grip, Goliath. I don't know how long I can hold you here."

The truth was that the grapple gun was doing most of the work. But Shadowboxer wasn't going to tell Goliath that.

"You need to power down, I have a better chance of pulling you up when you don't weigh as much."

"Alright, alright."

Shadowboxer felt the line slacken up gradually over the course of about ten seconds.

Good to know, Shadowboxer thought, gaining a better understanding of who and what he was up against.

He slowly reeled Goliath back up onto the roof. "Man," Goliath started, "Thank..."

The gang leader was interrupted by a flurry of blows. Shadowboxer hit him harder and faster than he ever dared to hit another human being.

Without his extra mass and muscle, Goliath went down like a ton of bricks.

"Bastard," Shadowboxer muttered, dragging the heavy man over to the center of the roof where the rest of the still unconscious Gods of War were.

He double tapped his mask's communicator.

"Nine-one-one; what's your emergency?" came a woman's voice on the other end of the line.

"Hi, I'd like to report some shots fired on the roof of the Yellowbrook Apartments. I think I saw the Shadowboxer up there fighting with some gangbangers and a super strong Variant. I think you need to send somebody to check it out."

"Okay, sir, can you stay..."

Shadowboxer cut the call short. He considered himself the city's protector but he wasn't too fond of getting involved with the cops. His Guild membership got him a few privileges and the cops looked the other way every now and then but, if he was being honest, he didn't quite trust Bay City's police department. There were more than a few issues to work out there.

Besides, as he stretched his wounded shoulder, he wasn't in any condition to hang around and give a police report. He needed to get home, get in an ice bath, and hit the sheets.

He had a busy day ahead and an even busier night.

"And someone's going to have to talk to Curtis about the company he keeps…"

Shadowboxer took a running leap from the building and swung off into the night.

BLACK LICORICE
Keith Gaston

Chapter One
Fallen Hero

James Baldwin once said, "To act is to be committed, and to be committed is to be in danger."

Those words couldn't ring truer; especially in my case. I was once committed to being a superhero. Using my abilities, I'd saved countless lives, and I believed I was making a difference in the world. It was all a terrible lie.

Once upon a time, I was a husband and a father. I couldn't save my family. Those who witnessed their murders did nothing but watch. I had been committed to protecting the city, but they'd turned their backs on me.

Now I'd turned my back on them.

***

Despite the warm weather, I threw on an olive drab coat I'd purchased at a military clothing outlet before heading out. I followed my ritual of hiding my face. Draped, cowl-like under the thick hoodie, it gave off a Grim Reaper vibe. The ensemble completed my appearance of looking like a war-ravaged veteran who hadn't quite adjusted to civilian life. People tended to provide a wide berth for someone who might snap at the harmless blast of a car backfiring.

Walking with my head lowered, it was an extra precaution I took to have people avoid identifying me. That was the problem these days, absolutely everyone recognized me. All thanks to an obstinate investigative reporter who discovered my true identity and aired it nationally. Not one day passed by that I didn't dream of paying a visit to the reporter's home and doing to her what my enemies had done to my family.

It would be easy too. I had the power. No one could stop me – no one but myself. Murdering her would profane my son's memory of who he wanted me to be. It was because of him I became a hero in the first place. He'd collect news clippings of violent crimes throughout the city and present them to me, insisting I could've done something to prevent those offenses. Finally I gave in to his wishes.

I fought on the side of light for years and saved many lives. Simultaneously, I'd made plenty of powerful enemies too. Being a superhero wasn't like the movies. Battles led to trace evidence being left at locations. The police and the media appreciated my help and regularly ignored any fibers, hair, or blood that could have lead straight to me. As long as I didn't cross the line they were content knowing I was out there when they needed me to beat back whatever evil threatened the city.

Faith Copeland, an ambitious reporter, had changed that implicit agreement. She had aspirations of becoming world renown and, blinded by her greed for fame, she sought the truth of who I was. It took time and resources that most people didn't have, but finally she found what she sought. When her employers rejected her story to protect me, she released everything on the web, including the school my son attended.

Some of my minor enemies, who'd never had the power to hurt me physically, heard the news. What Copeland told the world gave them a way of hurting me and they'd jumped at the opportunity, descending on the school like a plague. My wife, Catherine, was walking our child, Xavier, to the car like she had done every weekday when my enemies surrounded them. Those bastards could have made my family's death quick, but they didn't, because they wanted me to suffer.

I'd found their battered, blood-soaked bodies lying in the street. The crowd had caught footage of every second of the attack on their cell phones and posted it online commenting on how tragic it all was. Not one of them had even shouted for my wife and son's attackers to stop, let alone lifted a finger to help. My persona as the Night Siege died that day with my family. Copeland got her fame at the cost of my wife and son's lives. One day I may not be able to hold back the tide that raged inside of me – one day I may not want to.

Someone bumped me. I didn't even register the collision. It is his shout of pain that snapped me out of my thoughts. He rubbed the shoulder that collided with mine, his face a mask of pain and anger.

"Dude, watch where you're going," he spat. "What are you wearing under that coat, an armor suit?"

"I'm sorry," I replied before striding away from him.

The last thing I wanted was to attract any undue attention. I jaywalked, ignored the speeding cars going both directions, and made a beeline toward the only party store within walking distance of the place where I was living. I'd dodged oncoming traffic with practiced skill honed over years of fighting bad people. It was second nature to me and I scarcely gave my actions any thought.

When I reached the opposite side of the street, I realized the grave mistake I'd made. The man who bumped into me stared wide-eyed with disbelief. So had a few other passersby who'd witnessed my little evasive dance through heavy traffic.

Real dumb, I thought, *I shouldn't have done that.*

When I had an identity to protect, I went out of my way to hide my abilities, always conscious of not giving myself away to anyone. I had less of a reason to do that these days, since everyone knows me. Still, there are times, like today, I'd like to remain incognito. After a few seconds, those who'd witnessed what I'd done lost interest, perhaps more inclined to thinking I was the luckiest person in the world, rather than some has-been superhero.

I let out the breath I'd been holding and continued my way to the party store. The bell over the door alerted the person behind the counter that someone had entered. Tensing as if ready to reach for a gun, Ilyas, the owner's son, glared in my direction.

"It's me," I said, removing the hoodie from my head.

Ilyas grinned, extending his arms wide in greeting, shouting, "Assalamu Alaikum wa Rahmatullaahi wa barakato." "Peace and mercy and blessings of God be upon you."

"'Sup," I replied. He was part of the select few people I spoke to of late. As much as I detested conversing, it was impractical to believe I could make it through everyday life without *some* human interaction. Even folks with superpowers had to eat. "You keeping your grades up?"

He looked crestfallen. "I'm not doing so well in a couple of my classes.

My father is furious." Ilyas hoped to be a doctor someday. He was the first person in his family to attend college, so his parents were pressuring him to maintain his grades.

"Sorry to hear that."

I grabbed a gallon of milk, a package of cheese, and eggs out of the freezer. Checking the expiration on the items, I'd noticed the milk and cheese's due date ended in two days. Not a big deal since I'd likely finish them before that time. After gathering a few more items I took them up to the counter and placed them in front of the struggling college student.

Ilyas scanned the barcodes pulling up the prices. I glanced around the magnitude of candy until my eyes fell on the section with the licorice.

"We're out," Ilyas said.

I cut a glance his way. "What do you mean, you're out?"

"The truck with supplies is behind schedule today. It was supposed to be here an hour ago. We're low on everything. We ran out of black licorice the last time you were here," he explained. "But we have plenty of other colors. There's blue, red, and green for your choosing."

"I want black."

"You're the only customer who buys black licorice. No one likes black licorice. Everyone's favorite is cherry red."

Picking up the expiring cheese I considered throwing it through a wall but calmed myself. "B-L-A-C-K," I spelled out.

"Sorry, Night Siege."

My fingers closed hard around the package I held. Compressed cheese burst out of the edges spattering to the floor. "Don't call me that. I'm not that person anymore."

"It just slipped out. I didn't mean anything."

I blew out a breath. "I know; I'm sorry. Just don't call me that. It brings up too many unpleasant memories. Okay?"

Ilyas flashed me a nervous grin. "Sure, sure; won't happen again, Mr. Calderon."

Something akin to a smile worked its way to my face. I really hadn't meant to snap at him like that. "It's Tyson. Call me Tyson; I keep telling you that," I said, adding a little mirth to relax him. We both looked down at the crushed cheese. "I'll pay for that."

I needed to get another package to replace the one I'd destroyed. Sauntering down one of the aisles, I cursed inwardly for letting my temper get the best of me. It was just an innocent mistake and I was ready to throw him through a pane glass window.

The bell rang as the door swung open just as I made it to the freezer at the back of the store. From my angle, I couldn't see who'd come inside, but I heard three sets of footsteps. I replaced the hoodie over my head to obscure my face and searched for a package of cheese not expiring in a couple of days.

"Can I help you find anything?" Ilyas asked the newly arrived patrons.

"You can," one of them replied, "You can give us what's in the register." The all-too-familiar clickety-clack noise of a shotgun being pumped reverberated inside the store.

"Geez," I mumbled, "Not now."

Dropping the package of cheese that I'd been scrutinizing, I debated whether to let things play out or entangle myself into the affair. It wasn't my business if the store was robbed, but if Ilyas got hurt, when I could've done something, would only compound the guilt I already lived with.

I started back down the aisle. The store-clerk came into view. He had his arms raised over his head, gawking in my direction. His horrified eyes plead for help. Muscle memory had instinctively kicked in and kept my strides stealthy.

As I'd suspected, three men had come into the store. They all wore hoodies. They stared shamelessly at Ilyas, which gave him full view of their faces. The hoodies were obviously to make them look more ominous to their victim, though it left the trio vulnerable because they were unable to spot anyone standing off in their peripherals.

I could have taken them down easily, however I wanted to end the entire matter without using my abilities. The last thing I wanted was media attention. The neighborhood may have gone into the toilet, but it was where I called home. Once journals caught wind of where I shopped, it'd only be a matter of time before they found out where I stayed.

"Hurry up and open the register," the one with the shotgun demanded. Apparently he was the trio's leader.

His hands shook, though not from fear. The discolored veins in his exposed skin were a dead giveaway; he suffered from after effects of Noricloregion, a failed drug trial that was conducted years ago by the pharmaceutical company, *CorrectivePrim.* The Noricloregion drug was supposed to be a vaccine to slow aging. Instead test subjects either died after a week of use, became chronically sick, or gained superhuman abilities.

I was one of the lucky ones and fell into the latter category. Along with my hyper-cellular regeneration ability and body becoming impenetrable to most attacks, my intelligence, strength, and endurance had all increased. People started calling us 'Superiors'. After my son talked me into becoming a hero, I developed a suit and devices to help me battle crime.

The shotgun bearer's orange veins told me he wasn't so fortunate. Those who survived the drug test, but didn't gain powers, became living incubators for a new organism that fed on their bodies. The extremely contagious virus was spread through intercourse or blood transfers. The virus ravaged its host's immune system and the only thing that kept it in check was an expensive illegal narcotic called *Impervious.* Unsubstantiated rumors said that CorrectivePrim created the treatment, but kept it off the shelves because more profits were to be gained in the black market for the drug.

The infected typically became irrational, with bouts of pure insanity without regular use of Impervious. The veins on the man with the shotgun had nearly become neon, which meant he'd been without treatment for days. Still, I was hesitant to jump into action and risk an army of reporters at my front door.

"Go to another store to rob," I said, getting the trio's attention. "There's a gas station just down the street."

They whirled on me. The biggest of the three circled around and pressed his pistol to the back of my head. The sclera, the white portions of the eyes, had turned dark yellow in all of them, as if they suffered from jaundice. Each of them suffered from the effects of Noricloregion. The one behind me hit me with the butt of the pistol. I didn't even flinch. He yanked my hoodie off revealing my face.

The one with the shotgun started and then grinned as he recognized me. "Well, well, well – lookie wha' we got here. A has-been superhero. I heard you offed yourself. Guess rumors was wrong." His teeth clattered constantly as he spoke like he was gnawing an invisible corn on the cob.

"I don't want any trouble. Just go rob someone else," I urged him. There was madness in his yellow eyes and I doubted I was getting through.

He pressed the shotgun to my chest. "But I likes dis store. Why don'cha run your ass off while my crew finishes up here?"

Glancing at Ilyas I read, from his expression, that was an option he didn't want happening. I blew out a breath, knowing where things were headed if I stayed and then looked at the shotgun bearer. "Okay, I'll go...just don't hurt him." I pointed behind the counter. The crestfallen look on Ilyas's face told me I'd destroyed any remnants of hero worship he had for me. "H-he's good people."

The third man carried an auto-pistol and spoke for the first time. "He won't feel anything after he's dead."

The shotgun bearer pushed his weapon harder against my chest. "Yeah, what do ya care about dis fool anyways? He ah friend?"

"No. I don't have...friends. I don't let people get close to me."

"That's right," the one behind me shouted, "'Cause being close to you gets them killed, like your family. That's why you went off the radar ain't it?"

"Don't talk about my family again," I said through clinched teeth.

The bastard kept on talking. "Killed your wife and your son right in front of a crowd at some school."

I lost it then. Lightning fast, I grabbed the shotgun holding it in place while I turned sideways exposing the man in back of me to its barrel. The bearer instinctively pulled the trigger. The blast blew a hole into the big robber's chest, yanked him feet off the floor and sent him sailing backward into the aisle.

Snatching the weapon out of the shooter's hand, I spun it around, pumped it and then pointed it at him. "I told you to walk away. Why couldn't you just have listened to me?"

My enhanced hearing heard the third man's finger tightening around the automatic pistol's trigger. I snatched up the milk I'd left on the counter with my left hand and flung it at him with blinding speed. The carton exploded in his face on impact. His pistol went off, the round striking my arm holding the shotgun. I barely felt the bullet that hit me, but it was enough to cause me to inadvertently pull the trigger.

Thunder erupted, leaving a dead crumbled body on the floor in a pool of his own infected blood in front of me. Exposed to the air, the virus attacked his corpse, consuming his skin until there was nothing left but bone. I glanced over my shoulder into the aisle where the other one had been shot and saw that the same thing had happened to him.

I knew I should have felt something, but all I could see were those villains who'd taken the life of my wife and child. I gave them a chance and they'd gotten what they deserved.

"You shouldn't have done that," the third robber said, wiping milk from face. "That's Detonation's little bro. He's gonna kill us both, man!"

Detonation was a Superior like me, though our powers were very different. He had the ability to make any inorganic object he touched detonate like a bomb. The size of the object didn't determine the yield of the explosive reaction. Detonation controlled it all somehow. He could also transfer his powers through the ground to nearby targets and blow up objects from a distance. Of all the Superiors, he was one of the most powerful.

"Great," I mumbled. And I thought the media was the worst of my troubles.

Chapter Two
Detonation

Darryl chewed nervously on his fingernails in a corner of his prison cell. Even knowing the building was heavily defended, and two guards had been posted around the clock outside his cell, he feared for his life. His initial appearance in front of a judge, to advise him of his charges, was in an hour.

The distant sound of thunder caused him to stop biting his nails. He stared beyond the barred window and up at the blue sky. Not a single cloud was in sight. Darryl jumped to his feet and backed away from the glass.

"He's coming," he gasped.

"Stay calm prisoner. No one can get to you here," one of the guards assured him.

Darryl spun around to face the men, his face a mask of terror. "Don'cha understand who you're dealing with? I ain't safe in here, man!"

The shorter of the two, an Asian man, laughed. "The Chief of Police had security tripled. We've taken every precaution possible to stop anyone from getting to you and that includes a Superior." He jabbed one arm between the bars and shoved Darryl away. "I doubt he even comes. You're not worth all this trouble, prisoner."

"He'll come and kill us all."

"Let him try," the larger guard barked. He had a head the size of a basketball and a face only his blind mother could love. "Superior or not, a bullet to the skull will kill him just like it would anyone else."

Darryl scrambled back to his place on the bunk, folded himself into a ball in the shadows and resumed his nail biting. "Bullets can't stop him," he muttered under his breath. "Nothing will."

There was another clap of thunder but much closer. Darryl heard shouts and weapons being fired. The two guards stiffened and then stared into his cell with disbelieving looks.

The Asian guard ripped his radio from his belt. "This is Li! What's going on?" The radio squawked once, went dead. "Hello? Is anyone there?" Another squawk followed by screams.

"What the hell?" the larger guard said. "You don't think Detonation really came do you?"

A nearby explosion somewhere in the building answered his question. The men instinctively reached for their sidearm only to find empty holsters. Guns weren't allowed in lockup. All they had on them were Tasers, extendable asp batons, and pepper spray. In concert, they cursed under their breath.

"Get me out of here, man," Darryl shouted.

The smaller guard whirled around on him, glaring through the bars, baton in hand. "Shut up, I'm trying to think!"

Prisoners in all the cells erupted into a mad frenzy. They taunted the guards, hollering the two were about to die. They pushed their arms between the spaces in the bars reaching out, clawing for the two men. All the while, more explosions and screams could be heard drawing ever closer to the lockup.

"Screw this, we need to get out of here," the bigger guard asserted.

His partner peered about, wild-eyed, already slowly retreating away from the entrance leading into the lockup. "Yeah, yeah, you're right."

Getting up from the bunk, Darryl rushed toward the men, his hands gripping the metal shafts that kept him trapped inside. "Don't leave me here, man! Don't let him kill me!"

The smaller guard raised his baton readying to strike out at Darryl. A noise like kindling wood from a fireplace assaulted everyone's ears. From up the corridor, the hinges and bolts securing the metallic door for lockup glowed orange, then crimson. Everyone froze in place and stilled their voices. A sulfurous odor, that Darryl was all too familiar with, filled his nostrils. His knuckles went white as his hold intensified around the bars.

The shimmering metal pieces ignited simultaneously with an earsplitting bang. With nothing to hold it in place, the door pitched inward and crashed heavily to the floor with a thud that resounded through the detention area. Engulfing the entire doorway stood a huge, black silhouetted figure of a man. Behind him, fires burned.

Detonation strutted inside the room and into the light. Six-three, built like a heavyweight boxing champion, and dark complexioned, he was a sight to behold. The man, sporting dark tinted shades, stared about casually. Clad in a black, skin-tight, long-sleeve t-shirt with a designer silver colored tattoo print, his clothing seemed to have been painted on his sculpted upper body. A chain was wrapped around his neck with a metallic gray crucifix that hung prominently from it. His loose fitting sweatpants had a tattoo print that matched the one on his shirt running lengthwise down one leg. Unblemished silver Jordan's sneakers completed his ensemble.

"You know who I'm lookin' fo," Detonation said with a voice deep and silky enough to make James Earl Jones envious. "So don't make me ask."

The white guard, who was nearly as impressive in stature as Detonation, must have sparred a couple of rounds with his courage and won, or, more likely, with insanity and lost. He looked unmoved by the threat standing before him. The guard snatched the baton from the catch on his belt and pointed it like it was an accusing finger. "Don't move!"

"What are you doing?" the smaller guard demanded. "He'll kill us both."

"You got that right," Detonation said, his grin broad and menacing.

Spasms of irritation crossed the big guard's face. "He's just a thug. We can take him."

Detonation lifted a hand and gestured for them to come. "Bring it then."

The big man charged down the corridor, and his partner reluctantly followed.

The prisoners hooted and hollered, calling out for the guards' blood to be spilled.

Darryl watched, unable to look away, because he knew he'd soon share the guards' same fate.

When they closed in on their target, the taller man brought the baton high, intending to swing it down like a hammer and crack Detonation's skull. The shorter man, thrusting his baton like it was a sword, aimed for the gut.

Detonation moved with the speed and agility of someone accustomed to battle. He grabbed both batons mid-strike. The guards' steel sticks immediately glowed crimson, making the same crackling sound as the door bolts earlier. The men tried to release their grips from their weapons, but it was too late. The batons had become superheated and melded to the insides of their palms. They screamed with a mixture of pain and horror.

Detonation loosened his hold.

The pair stumbled backward.

"What did you do to us?" the white guard yelled through gritted teeth.

"10-9-8...," Detonation replied.

The guard gawked, mystified. "What th--?" Then he glanced down at the crimson glow of the baton, realization dawning on his face. He and the other guard spun on their heels, racing away down to the opposite end of the corridor, trying to shake their weapons free of their hands.

"...3-2-1," Detonation said to their backs.

The batons exploded with loud pops. They weren't large eruptions – not meant to kill, but maim, blowing off their hands and part of their arms. The white guard staggered against one of the cells, staring in horror at the charred nob that ended at his elbow. Some of the inmates reached through the bars taking hold of him, tearing at his skin, while others clasped at his throat to choke him.

The Asian guard fell to his knees, then all the way to the floor, his body locking into the fetal position.

Somehow Darryl had managed to will himself away from the bars and deeper into his cell. He retreated back into his corner and crawled under the bunk hoping he could hide in the shadows. Squeezing his eyes shut he wanted to pray but he didn't know which god to beseech, so he said nothing.

"Darryl," a deep voice said. "Open your eyes, bruh. I want you to see me."

He forced his eyes open, his face stricken. Detonation stood on the opposite side of the bars. "I-it wasn't my fault, man!"

"That's why I'm here. To find out whose fault it is," Detonation said.

He placed a single finger against one of the metal shafts. In an instant, all the bars glowed. It sounded like a small firecracker going off as metal turned into ash, raining down to the floor. Glancing down at his sneakers, Detonation inspected them and then frowned looking up. "Now see what you gone and made me do, bruh? My Jordan's are dirty."

"I-I'm sorry," Darryl pleaded from his hiding place.

"Oh, now you got apologies?" Stepping over the pile of ash and into the cell, the big man slowly made his way to the bunk as if he had all the time in the world. "Too late for that, bruh."

From his angle, all Darryl could see was Detonation's smudged shoes as he approached. His pants suddenly felt wet and warm as his bladder emptied. "There's wasn't nothing I could do, man! Nothing!"

The mattress above him sunk in the middle as Detonation sat heavily on the bunk. Detonation was quiet for a period, then he made the sound of blowing out air. "I spilled a lotta blood today bruh, and I ain't in any mood for your whining."

The strong scent of weed reached Darryl's nostrils.

"You're gonna tell me what happened to my little bro today," his tormentor explained, "And then you're gonna die."

***

Detonation swaggered through the station with significantly less trouble than when he entered. The survivors of his attack watched him leave without uttering a single word of protest. They were either too scared or too hurt to stop him. He paid little attention to the mayhem he'd created, because his thoughts were elsewhere.

"Night Siege," he muttered through gritted teeth.

Their paths had never crossed before, but that hadn't meant the former superhero wasn't, from time to time, a complication for him in the past. In the early days of Detonation's rise to power in the city, plans had been in place to grow his criminal empire by having his crew take out other gangs. More than once, Night Siege's interference crippled his campaigns for power, significantly slowing his takeover of the rival gangs.

When the superhero became too much of a problem, Detonation decided enough was enough and had intended to end Night Siege once and for all. Then providence stepped in as a glory seeking journalist had done what so many had attempted to do in the past, but failed. She brought the superhero down to his knees by revealing his true identity to the world. With Night Siege out of the picture, there was no need to seek him out. The city, deprived of its hero, left nothing to stand in Detonation's way and his power and influence grew in a short time.

As fate would have it, however, it seemed that Detonation's decision to let the broken hero live had come back to bite him. He didn't have any real affection for his little brother, Carlon. The fool was addicted to Noricloregion, though that was no fault of his own. The drug made his brother weak and Detonation couldn't afford to have weakness around him, not when he was building his empire. He shunned his little brother, leaving him to fend for himself on the streets. Still, they were blood, whether he liked it or not, and even Detonation knew better than to ignore someone murdering his kin. He would look weak in the eyes of those he command.

Night Siege therefore had to die.

Chapter Three
Night Siege

It wasn't something I did often, but under the circumstances, I made an exception and went to a sports bar to have a drink. I came in with the intention of drinking myself into a stupor until the police picked me up for the deaths of those two men in the party store. Unfortunately, my accelerated metabolism was keeping me sober. I nursed a single beer instead.

The sports bar clientele were all staring at me with recognition, whispering questions about where I had been all these years and what had happened to me. My enhanced hearing heard it all though I tried desperately to tune them out. I should have left the hoodie over my head to cover my face, but I was likely going to prison soon, so I figured, what the hell. Now, I regret that decision.

At least no one was brave enough to approach. The whole time I sat at the bar the stools to either side of me remained empty, even though the place was crowded. I suspect they recalled old news reports of me fighting in public and putting dozens in the hospital. What had set me off then was that someone had innocently tried to console me after my family was killed. I wasn't in the right frame of mind, blaming the entire city for not helping them. I took my anger out on those closest to me and paid the price with three weeks in a cell. No one had the heart to press charges against me and the police had no choice but to let me go. I went off the grid after that, living like a hermit ever since.

Because of necessity, I only interacted with a handful of people, like Ilyas. I should have known the day was going to be a bust after I found out the black licorice hadn't been delivered at the store. Now, there were two bodies; well, what was left of their bodies, questions about their deaths from cops, and the looming possibility that another Superior might come after me.

Then the newsflash happened.

All the screens on the sports bar televisions broadcasted various stations reporting a prison being attacked earlier by Detonation. The aftermath of his destruction looked like a scene from the Terminator. He left few survivors, but those who lived to talk all reported that my name came up while the killer questioned a prisoner – the thief with the automatic pistol from the store.

That was not good.

The whispers in the sports bar became loud and accusing murmurs. They were already saying it was my fault that those guards and police officers were dead. How I shouldn't have crawled out of the hole I'd been hiding in. All it took was a sixty second clip for the public to condemn me. I spun around on my stool eyeing everyone in the place, daring someone to blame me to my face. The entire sports bar went silent, but it wasn't because of me. All eyes were turned to the televisions. Detonation filled all the large screens, his hands glowed crimson and he flexed his fingers as if he were cracking his knuckles.

The video feeds switched to a helicopter view that panned out to show police cruisers racing toward him from all directions. Detonation stood his ground in the middle of a street in the business district. Uniformed officers worked to cordon off the area, working desperately to push back a cell phone clutching crowd more interested in recording the event than seeking safety.

I was reminded of how this city watched as my family died, chronicling the brutality of their deaths forever on mobile devices. Unable to bear witness any longer to what was happening on the screen, I turned my attention back to my glass, allowing the barely touched beer to become my world, desiring nothing more than to get drunk.

A collective gasp circumnavigated the room. Something bad had happened. I concentrated harder on my drink, staring into the brown liquid as if it would reveal answers to questions I'd yet to ask. I saw the faint image of my son's face in my glass. Squeezing my eyelids shut I tried not to think of him because it hurt so much.

The piped in music ceased and what little filters I had to block some of the patrons was gone. I feared what I knew was coming. The televisions had been muted before, leaving closed caption to describe the events on the screen, but now gunfire, explosions and animated narrations flooded the sports bars.

"...the criminal, Detonation, killed several officers as they..."

"...bullets are exploding harmlessly against Detonation's skin..."

"...the police are unable to stop the Superior..."

"...several cruisers exploded..."

"...can no one stop him?"

I refused to acknowledge the mayhem being broadcasted, to become a witness to it; and I refused to see what the liquid in my glass wanted to reveal to me. The city let my family die. Whatever the villain did to this wretched city wouldn't be my fault, it'd be theirs.

Finally, the gunshots and explosions ended. For a time I wondered if the sound had once again been muted, but I the voice of a newscaster shouted, "Detonation is gesturing for a camera crew to approach him! It appears he wants to speak!"

Typical. I shook my head. Why do they always want to talk? Why can't they do whatever dirty deed they have to do and then call it the day? But no, they always want to announce their bold plan to the world.

Obviously, one of the news crews was brave enough to move toward him because Detonation's voice came loud and clear across all the screens. "You know who I am! You know what I can do! My little brother was killed today," he roared. "Blood has already been spilled, and more will come..."

Here it comes.

"...unless Night Siege comes out of the hole he's hiding in to face me!"

The many stares I sensed on my back felt palpable. I didn't acknowledge his words; I didn't acknowledge their gazes and kept my eyes shut.

An anchorman detailed Detonation's movements as he stepped off the blacktop street and onto the asphalt sidewalk toward one of the taller buildings. He described the Superior's glowing hand slapping the surface of the large structure. Loud crackling noises, like embers in a fireplace, spewed from the sports bar's speakers.

Despite myself I opened my eyes to stare up at one of the screens. An orange and red radiance spread throughout the building that had been touched, racing all the way to the top in a few seconds. His powers had literally turned the structure into a destructive weapon.

"Those inside are trapped," Detonation announced. "If anyone tries to get out or enter, the building will explode, not only killing everyone inside, but taking out the twenty square blocks surrounding it!"

I didn't doubt what he was saying. At one time I had planned to confront him, so I'd studied his abilities. He could control the amount of energy released. The bigger the object, the stronger he could make his explosions. If Detonation wanted to, he could destroy the entire city with just his touch.

"You have three hours to face me here, Night Siege, or countless people will die..." Detonation paused for effect, "...just like my little brother. Just like your wife and boy!"

I wasn't even aware that I'd reacted until I heard the crack of straining wood. Looking down, the side of my fist had impaled the bar, crushing a section of it. The ripple effect had caused fissures to run lengthways, in both directions on the floor, stretching from end to end. My drink had somehow survived my outburst.

The bartender gaped. I craned my neck over my left shoulder and slowly panned to the right. Everyone stared expectantly in my direction. Had their memories really been that short?

I whirled around on them. "You got something to say, then say it," I shouted.

"He wants you," one of the patrons explained.

"So?"

"People are going to die," another customer said.

I gave them all incredulous looks. "People die every day. It's not my problem."

"But you're a hero," the bartender said behind me.

"*Was*," I corrected him. "I'm not anymore." I pointed indiscriminately at faces in the sports bar. "I won't lift a single finger to help. All of you made sure of that. I'm going to watch this city burn and do nothing just like all of you did when my family was being slaughtered."

An uncomfortable silence filled the room. I knew what they expected of me, but I wasn't that guy anymore. Especially now, not on this day. Scooping up the drink from the bar, I drained the glass.

Putting my back to the crowd, I stormed out of the place, breaking the spell of quiet. Behind me, with fetid breaths, my name was being vilified as much as, if not more than, Detonation's. A part of me couldn't blame them for their anger. I understood their passion. When those people watched my family being murdered, it did more than simply make me give up my life as a superhero, the experience broke me to the point of impassiveness. Even knowing that, I couldn't bring myself to forgive any of them for doing nothing.

Pulling on my hoodie, I once again returned to my private world of obscurity and isolation. I'd stepped out of that world once already and I ended up taking two lives, which in turn, led to even more deaths, with Detonation running amok in the city looking to settle a score.

All I wanted was black licorice, not trouble, but trouble always had a way of finding me. Questions swirled rampant in my mind: Why had it been today of all days? What had I done to the universe to make it place a bullseye on my chest? Was it guilt I felt? Was I blaming myself for what a madman was doing? I found myself adrift in a sea of my own making and I saw no way out of my predicament.

I should have been paying more attention to where I was walking; I narrowly avoided crashing through a store window. Stenciled on the large glass was *Helen's Bakery*. Staring inside, I saw that the shop was empty. It appeared to have been hastily abandoned. Cash sat on the counter, boxed cakes ready for pickup had been dropped to the floor. Only then had I realized that many of the businesses on the block were left much the same. Glancing over my shoulder at the sports bar I had been, the patrons were rushing to their vehicles.

I'd been so lost in my own thoughts, that I ignored everything going on around me. What did I expect? A powerful Superior was threatening to blow up half the city if I didn't stop him. Of course people were going to try to escape. The roads out were likely already choked with vehicles. People would be trapped on the highways as much as all those innocent folks in the building that Detonation had touched.

"It's not my problem anymore," I said to no one.

"Yes, it is," a small voice countered.

I spun around to face the bakery. A boy stood inside the shop. No, not in the store, but on the glass, like a reflection. It was my son, Xavier. I glanced down to my side, ready to pick him up and never let him go, but no one was beside me. It was only my overactive imagination making me see my boy.

I returned my gaze to the glass. Xavier's reflection remained. I dropped to my knees, resting one palm against the pane. "Xavier? Is that really you?" It couldn't be of course. My child was dead.

"Daddy," he said. It sounded so real. He laid his palm against mine and it felt real to me. "You have to help them, daddy."

Tears ran down my cheeks. "They let you and your mother die," I protested. "They don't deserve my help."

"You're a hero, daddy."

His words, so simple, so innocent, struck a nerve. "No, I'm not! That's not me. Maybe it was never me."

"You're one to me," he said.

"But I-I wasn't there to save you... H-how can you still think that?"

Another voice said, "We don't blame you."

I stared up in disbelief. My wife, Catherine, stood beside Xavier. She got down on her knees, placing herself almost eye level with me. For a long time I couldn't find words to say. It couldn't be real; but the pleasant scent of her favorite perfume told me otherwise.

"You have to save them," she said.

Perhaps the Noricloregion in my blood system had finally broken down and was affecting my mind. They were buried six-feet under the earth. There was no coming back from that. I closed my eyes, counted to ten and opened them again. Catherine and Xavier were still there. If my mind was truly slipping into madness, I wasn't sure it was a bad thing as long as my family was back with me.

"Catherine," I said. "Are you real?"

"As real as I need to be for you, Ty," she replied. "I'm always by your side. We both are."

Her answer left me with more questions, but I couldn't voice them. All I wanted was spend as much time as I could with my family.

"You have to save them," they said in unison.

My gaze went to the ground. "They let you die."

Her arm came through the glass and touched my chin, lifting my head up so I could look her in the eyes. "You didn't let us die, Ty. They didn't let us die either. What could they have done? If they helped, they would have died that day too."

I took her hand and brought it to my lips. "I love you both," I told them.

"I love you, daddy."

"I love you, Ty."

And just like that, they were gone. All that remained in the glass was my own reflection. Had it been real? Could it have been my guilt or the Noricloregion in my bloodstream that created them?

Did it matter?

I turned my attention in the direction of the business district. In the distance, a single, tall structure shone red and grew brighter by the minute like it was building up to critical mass.

Chapter Four
The Panagis

I fastened the last of the straps on the combat vest. The suit felt snug in some places. I must have gained a little weight. Need to lay off the TV dinners and donuts at night. Doing a quick inspection, I made sure I'd collected everything I needed for the coming battle. The deadline was almost up.

Years ago, I had everything put away into storage under an assumed name. It took time to gather my old outfit and gear, but it was necessary. If I had any chance of beating Detonation, I needed to be prepared. Flexing my fingers in the gloves it felt strangely natural and unnatural at the same time.

The Nanoskin I'd developed was made of a resilient material much stronger than steel yet elastic enough to not restrict my movements. The micro-tech integrated throughout the clothing's synthetic and natural biopolymers made the suit perfect for combat with other Superiors. My enhanced strength, endurance, and hyper-cellular regeneration made sure I wouldn't go down easy in the middle of a fight. Oh, the arsenal and gadgets I kept on my hip and in various pouches helped too.

I blew out a breath. "Okay, I can do this. I can be a hero again." I didn't sound convincing to myself. Despite the vision, or whatever, I'd experienced earlier, I still didn't feel the city deserved being saved. That was a problem. If I couldn't get my mind into the game, I might make a mistake that could cost me my life as well as those trapped by Detonation.

Picking up the face mask I wondered why I should even bother with it. Everyone around the globe knew my identity. The mask hung loosely over the side of my palm. "It's for my protection, not concealment," I explained. Slipping it on over my head, the micro-machinery went to work and the material instantly hardened. My disguise resembled an Extreme Motorcyclist's skull mask, except that my version was filled with useful technology.

An inner display appeared on the tinted goggles giving me an updated status report for the suit. Even after all these years collecting dust, the gear had maintained a small charge. Once I stepped out of the dimly lit storage container and into the sunlight, the solar cells would start collecting energy. Draping the hood over my head to finish my ensemble, I had once again become Night Siege.

***

Detonation was a cold-blooded killer and couldn't be trusted. If I turned up early to face him, he'd likely destroy the building and its occupants anyway, though he might spare most of the city. His home was here and despite his threats, he wanted to remain in the city where he'd spent his entire life, to rule its criminal underground with an iron-hand. A number of bad guys wanted to rule the world, while others like Detonation were content with just a small piece of it.

Confronting him head-on had to wait until after I got his prisoners out of the building. I rode a motorcycle through the dark underbelly of the city's sewerage systems to both avoid the escaping outgoing traffic from above and equally for stealth. The bike roared inside the deep tunnels like some great cave dwelling predator. With the headlight glowing on full blast, I zoomed past scurrying things hidden in the shadows that were better left in the dark.

There were stories of creatures living under the city, mutated by illegal dumping of chemical waste from various large companies; one of which was the same pharmaceutical conglomerate that had conducted human testing on me and others. Some of what lurked in that darkness stared back with intelligence and malice, a deadly combination if they somehow became fixated on a particular target. I hadn't posed any danger to them, so they left me alone, and I extended them the same courtesy.

Several minutes later, I was directly underneath the *Panagis Building*, staring up at a series of pipes and ductwork running lengthwise across the ceiling. The structure was one of the oldest buildings still in operation in the city. Back in the day, subbasements in buildings were common places to hide the conduits and pipes that provided water, power, ventilation and heat. Much of it was no longer utilized because of advancements in technology and energy conservation.

I performed a fifteen foot vertical leap and hooked my hands around a pair of rusted pipes. The metal creaked and groaned in protest of my added weight, but held in place. Hand over hand I worked my way to one of the large ducts like a kid on a playground's monkey bars. There was a sealed plating used as an access for maintenance workers. I swung my legs up and kicked the entry open. Climbing into the dark duct, night vision automatically engaged on my mask and I stared into a network of shafts that stretched in four different directions. It was a good thing I wasn't claustrophobic, the space was compact and confining, though maneuverable as long as I kept low.

"I need a path to the subbasement above," I whispered into my suit's onboard AI.

A white computer-generated line appeared ahead of me to lead the way and I began crawling on all fours. After several minutes of working my way through level terrain, the line I was following abruptly turned upward. I rolled over onto my back and stared up the shaft. Maybe sixty yards at the end I could scarcely make out a hatch door. All I had to do to get there was to climb up a smooth metal surface caked thick with a half century of old dust and rust.

There were pairs of evenly spaced holes leading to the top, evidence of a ladder once being affixed to the wall. Would have made things a lot simpler for me if it was still there. As always, I had to do things the hard way. "Great fun," I grumbled. My voice reverberated through the conduits like I'd shouted across the Grand Canyon.

Standing to my full height, I stretched out my arms from side to side and braced my palms against the metallic interior. Applying some pressure to verify my hands wouldn't go clean through I was relatively sure the wall could endure my climb. Lifting my legs, I gripped the sides and scaled my way up.

I made it to the top easily enough but at the cost of sounding like a marching band's drum team going full blast. Stealthy I was not. Planting the soles of my boots against the interior wall, I held myself in place to work on the hatch door. As the access resisted my efforts to open it, the door creaked loud enough to wake the dead. I made a mental note to carry oil from then on, assuming I would live through the imminent battle. Eventually the latch gave and I pushed the hatch open.

Heaving my body up and out, I saw that there was no need to worry about stealth. Four huge turbine fans spun at full power, obviously compensating for the energy field Detonation created around the Panagis. Little good it did. His power climbed incrementally, increasing, with time, to eventually reach critical mass, while the fans had an upper limit. There would be no compensating, only death, unless I could get the people out.

My display showed me the way out of the basement. There were stairs and a freight elevator. I positioned myself behind equipment with a vantage point that gave me a clear view of the stairway door. As I suspected, Detonation had the building on lockdown. There was no way he could monitor the entire building by himself. So he brought in a contingent of his thugs to make sure those trapped inside stayed that way.

A man I recognized stood guard – Zero Point. He could create energy vacuums, taking empty space and filling it with some type of quantum power field, essentially giving nothingness mass. I'd fought him before, several times in fact. It often led to long battles, the decimation of several hundred thousands of dollars' worth of property damage and lives. Something I couldn't afford in the building, not with Detonation hovering outside.

Moving toward the elevator, I saw that it too had a guard – Oil Slick. I didn't have any run-ins with him during my hero days but I was aware of his powers. He had transmutative abilities; his flesh could transform into a black oleaginous liquid. Both Zero Point and Oil Slick were formidable on their own; if I was to fight them collectively, I'd be heading down a world of hurt.

It wasn't like I had much choice; I was on the clock and time was ticking away closer to the deadline. I'd have to hit them hard and fast and hope for an outcome that didn't include my untimely demise.

I launched out of my hiding place and charged toward Oil Slick at full speed. He barely had time to register my movements before I was on top of him. I slammed the sole of my shoe into his stomach and felt his ribs cave under the pressure. Instinctively, his defenses kicked in and his body got underway to liquefy. The melanin in Oil Slick's skin and eyes went from brown to black, but he still hadn't fully transformed. I clutched his throat with one hand, twisted my body, and hurled him like a baseball across the room.

Zero Point seized me within a quantum field. I knew what he intended. He either meant to pull my limbs apart simultaneously or crush me to the size of a golf ball inside the containment field. Oil Slick's fully altered form careening at him put a damper on his plans, however. Black ooze hit Zero Point full on with the force of a fire hose. Two hundred and fifty pounds per square inch took Zero Point completely by surprise and sent him sprawling backward off his feet.

He hit the ground with a wet slap and skidded another twelve or more feet before he stopped sliding. Oil Slick's oily form sank deep into Zero Point's eyes, nose, and mouth. The quantum field that trapped me faded. I had to move before either of them could recover.

I ejected a vile from my utility belt, cracked the seal and lobbed it into the black pulsating mass. It was a powerful anesthetic. In Oil Slick's gelatinous state, the sedative would have little effect on him, but Zero Point was a different story. The anesthetic spread through the oil and entered Zero Point's every orifice.

The black mass oozed away from Zero Point's unconscious frame, forming a large ungainly pool next to him. A bubble formed in the center of it and grew until it stood nine feet tall. It loomed over me. What I imagined were eyes and a mouth molded itself into what was supposed to be a face.

"I'll kill you for that," Oil Slick bellowed in a wet, inhuman voice.

I ran in the other direction. There was no way to defeat him by throwing a few punches and the gadgets I carried were not intended for an enemy like him. As expected, he pursued me. Oil Slick was fast – too fast. The only thing that kept me ahead of him was my enhanced speed, though eventually I would slow. On the other hand, he wouldn't. His liquid body took up every inch of the corridor behind me, while the bulk pushed down its center. It looked as if the dark itself wanted to consume me.

"You cannot escape me," Oil Slick yelled.

Escape wasn't the idea. I burst through a metal door and rushed into the room I had entered through the conduits. The explosive sound of the giant turbine fans became the entirety of my world. I whirled around to face my opponent just as he came flooding through the door like a black tide.

"I have you now," he screamed with that eerie, wet voice.

My reply came in the form of chucking flashbangs in front of him. He reacted instinctively to avoid the small blasts. Though flashbangs weren't commonly known to ignite paper or clothing, it didn't mean it wasn't flammable when it came to vapors or liquids. Oil Slick, in his transmuted form, was defenseless against flames. It wasn't my intention to set the man on fire. If that happened, he would trigger the very explosion I was trying to prevent Detonation from doing. What I wanted was to get him mad as hell, while at the same time maneuvering to a specific side of the room.

Satisfied with his placement, I stopped my barrage. I whispered to my internal AI, "Hack into the building's system and shutdown the fans pronto."

<Initiating,> was its response.

That was step one. Step two would be harder. First things first, I had to make sure Oil Slick was completely enraged. "Oh, are you scared of a little fire? Poor baby."

He howled and flooded toward me. Okay, he has been properly enraged. I leapt to one side of the room, away from his flowing black mass padding down in front of the center fan. Air shoved at my back, threatening to push me, but I held my ground. Oil Slick's size seemed to double and he opened his mouth wide enough to swallow me whole, which was likely his intent. He surged forward.

I sprang up above the spinning rotors and landed on a slight ledge housing the turbine fans. The blast of air slowed Oil Slick's progress as he pressed on in my direction. "Anytime with those fans," I whispered.

<Task complete.>

The rotors slowed and then stopped. The room grew eerily quiet except for the disgusting sloshing of my opponent's movement. No longer deterred by the air flow, Oil Slick slammed his mass hard against the fans and wall. Large buckets of his oily physique were spread across the three fan housings and gushed inside. Oil Slick's perverted face stared up at me grinning with triumph.

"Turn them back on," I commanded.

<Initiating.>

Oil Slick screamed as the gigantic rotors spun. The fans violently wrenched him inside, ripping him asunder as he was distributed across the three individual housings. The more rapidly the blades rotated the faster he was drawn in. His nightmarish wet shrieks will follow me to my grave. Even though his transmuted body was oil, he was still human and as such was never meant to be shredded apart. Bit by bit, the fans spat out black splotches, caking the floor, ceiling and walls, but I knew the smudges would never reconstitute again – Oil Slick was dead.

Running up the stairway I ran into more of Detonation's henchmen and, one by one, I took them down fast and hard. There weren't as many as I expected which I suppose was a good thing. The problem was, the floors were empty of the building's occupants. It wasn't until I'd nearly reached the top floor that I discovered where everyone was.

On the empty floor just below the top, I'd tapped into the building's security cameras. What remained of the Superiors had assembled the hundreds of hostages in one area. Smart. Once Detonation was ready to blow the structure, his people could evacuate and lock all their victims on a single floor to prevent them from escaping.

I picked out three Superiors, all minor leaguers. They could handle a crowd of people without powers with little trouble. I on the other hand, might prove to be more troublesome for them. Though I had to be careful, too many innocent bystanders could be hurt if I went in too hard.

After conducting a quick search of the offices on the floor, I managed to find a spare business suit. It was a few sizes bigger than me, but that was a good thing. I slipped the clothing on over my uniform and put on a pair of nerdy glasses. The simple disguise worked for Clark Kent, so I figured what the hell. I didn't bother with changing my boots. With the number of people taking up tight space on the top floor, I figured my feet would go unnoticed.

Getting on the occupied top floor was easy; all I had to do was knock. The Superior guarding the door on the opposite side yanked it open, blinked with surprise with his mouth gaping wide for a few seconds, and then hustled me inside without uttering a word.

It astonished me that not one Superior bothered at any point to send updates to make sure the perimeter was secure. They didn't see a reason to since they had the power to make sure the perimeter couldn't be breached. Well, surprise, surprise, it *had* been breached. I rocked the guard at the door with a solid elbow to his right temple, followed by a knee to his groin to knock the fight out of him. He doubled over and collapsed to the floor.

Those who witnessed what I did joined in the fray and pounded on him with their feet. Apparently, they didn't care much for being imprisoned. Go figure. I slipped into the throng and made my way toward the second target. It went much the same. By the time I made it to the third Superior, the commotion from the crowd had drawn her attention.

She was called Dragon's Breath. It didn't take a genius to guess what her ability was. Smoke sprayed out of her nostrils and the sides of her mouth as she sought out a threat to target with her powers. She looked nervous and angry. It was only a matter of time before she blew her flames into those closest to her. The mass around me thinned. I glanced over my shoulder. The panicked crowd rushed the exits. In minutes, the first of them would be in the lobby, making their escape outside. If any of them went out the front door, Detonation would spot them and follow through with his threat.

I sprang over the crowd, making myself visible. Dragon's Breath's burning red gaze locked onto me. She opened her mouth wide; flames shot forth.

I protected my face with my arms. The oversized suit I was wearing turned into cinders. My uniform was fire retardant and remained relatively unscathed by her assault. Fire retardant, however, didn't mean it was fire *proof*. With enough stress, it would burn away, exposing my skin.

The red of her eyes died and Dragon's Breath flames let up after a few seconds. She appeared to be winded. Perhaps using her ability was like blowing up balloons, needing to draw oxygen into her body before she could go again. Though her attack had done me little damage, I couldn't say the same about the surrounding area. The level was in flames, causing the sprinkler system to rain down on everyone, sending the already panicked crowd into a frenzy.

If she used her powers again, the sprinklers might not be enough to control the blaze. Once again I was faced with a terrible decision. Her eyes turned crimson again. Smoke spewed out of her opened mouth and I could feel a wave of heat hit me. My leap placed me within arm's reach of Dragon's Breath and I took full advantage of it. I clutched her throat and squeezed, closing off her air passage, leaving no place for her flames to go.

In my haste to save the people inside the Panagis, I'd lost track of time and quickly realized my error when the timer on my suit went off. Dragon's Breath's stomach expanded like a frog's cheeks as the pressure built inside of her. I rushed to the windows and stared down at the ground below. Detonation stood in the middle of the street and turned to face the building.

I glanced at my captive. Her eyes bulged in her sockets in the same fashion as her bloated stomach. "Sorry lady, times up for the both of us," I said, before taking a step back and hurling Dragon's Breath through the inch-thick pane glass window.

Chapter Five
Critical Mass

Detonation frowned. With seconds left on the clock, there was still no sign of Night Siege. He'd expected the hero to make some grand entrance, declaring how he was the protector of the city or some muck like that.

"Well," he said, to the police and news crews brave enough to stay, though they kept their distance. "I guess your hero really is a coward!"

A tangle of murmured voices, coming from where they shouldn't, caught his attention. He spun around to face the glowing building. A crowd that had come flooding out of the elevators and stairways filled the lobby of the Panagis and rushed for the exit.

"Son of ah..." The distant sound of shattering glass forced him to turn his attention above.

A ball of fire rocketed straight at him. Detonation bounded to his left, narrowly avoiding the projectile. The road quaked with a deafening explosion. His power shielded him from hurtling shards of molten asphalt and concrete, igniting everything that touched him into harmless sparks.

Once the ground quieted and the smoke thinned, he got to his feet and dusted himself off. The pulverized spot he'd been standing at had become a smoldering crater. He approached the pit, staring inside. A woman's charred body lay broken and twisted in its center.

"Dragon's Breath," he growled.

In his peripheral, the crowd surged out of the glowing building, rushing in every direction, yet managing to stay clear of him.

The Night Siege isn't as cowardly as I thought, he considered. *How the hell did he get past my crew?*

Shouts erupted behind him. Glancing over at the news crews and officers stationed behind the cordoned off area, they cheered. All their heads were raised toward the sky. Detonation followed their gazes.

A lone figure leapt out of the glassless window Dragon's Breath had been cast from. The figure soared through the air like some graceful and noble bird. His arms were outstretched. Wing-like apparel was fastened between both his wrists and his rib cage, allowing him to pull off the aerial stunt.

Night Siege released his wings and dropped from three stories above ground. He landed, rolled and then quickly pushed himself up right in front of Detonation. He held two pistols high, tilted his chin up and said, "'Sup."

Grinning, Detonation replied, "Now that's how you make a grand entrance."

***

The liberated group ran frantically out of the office building toward the police barricades as if shelter could be found there. As long as the structure remained under Detonation's power, there was be no safe place to go. If the building exploded, he, and he alone, would be the only one left standing.

"The Panagis. Release it now," I demanded.

"Hell nah, you broke the deal, hero. I said no one was to help the people inside."

"No, you told the police they weren't allowed to help. You never said anything about me."

Detonation considered that for a moment. Cocking an eyebrow, he put on a half-grin. "Damned if you ain't right."

"You wanted me. I'm here," I said. "Free the building like you've promised."

"For a brotha 'bout to die, you kinda bossy." He glanced at the Panagis. "Nah, I've changed my mind. I'm going to kill you and still blow up the building."

"Why?"

His eyes narrowed. "Because I can. You shou--,"

I opened up with both barrels. With my enhanced speed, it seemed as if the pistols fired on full auto. He hadn't so much as twitched as bullets burst harmlessly into dust against his skin. I kept firing anyway until the guns emptied.

"Bruh, you cut me off." Detonation frowned. "Guess we're done with our back and forth banter, then?" He stuck a hand into his pants pocket and retrieved a handful of coins. Shifting through the change with a finger, he picked out one, a quarter. The coined glowed red.

"Oh crap," I muttered under my breath as he casually tossed it in my direction.

It landed with an unimpressive ping as it hit the ground at my feet. The explosion it produced was a different matter entirely. The concussive blast blew me off my feet. The pistols went in two different directions. I landed with a hard thud in the hole next to Dragon's Breath's charred remains.

Before I could collect my thoughts, three glowing pennies came soaring over the edge of the hole. I somersaulted up and out of the crater with a spin and landed on my feet before the coins touched the ground. The explosive discharge was larger than the first. Flames shot straight up into the air, akin to a volcanic eruption. Again, I was blown aside by the blast. My back slammed hard against a Mountaineer, crushing its side door and shattering all the glass in the windows.

The driver's side mirror snapped off its perch and clocked me on top of my skull. "Ouch," I cried.

Things weren't going well. Detonation had the advantage because I couldn't touch him directly. His cells absorbed light waves like a plant, transforming the light into a form of chemical energy that could be released through his glands. Whenever he touched an object, his secretions attached themselves to the material and it too absorbed light. But without a mechanism to negate the absorption, like he could do with his body, the items would go ballistic.

Detonation circled around behind a parked car, touched it with his bare hand and then placed his foot on its rear bumper. He gave the vehicle a good shove. It rolled toward me with alarming speed. I'd read, but didn't believe that another of his abilities was to fluctuate his energy from hot to cold. By decreasing the temperature of an object, he could theoretically decrease the object's mass. I wouldn't have believed it if not for the glowing red Gremlin careering at me.

Getting to my feet, I ripped the damaged car door off the SUV I had slammed into. I spun around, hefting the Mountaineer's door up one-handed, and flung it, like a Frisbee, at the rushing vehicle. The car door made a whooshing sound as it cut through the air. The Gremlin vomited glass from it's front and rear as the projectile plowed through it.

When the glowing Gremlin was almost on top of me, I planted my feet on the Mountaineer and then thrust myself upward and forward with all I had. Arms stretched ahead of me, I rocketed toward the car, passed-through the glassless front window and then out the rear.

Detonation was distracted by the Mountaineer's car door coming straight at him. I don't care how powerful one thinks he is – if a large, fast-moving projectile rushes toward you, instincts automatically kick in. He jumped to the pavement like he came off a swimming pool diving board, landing hard on his stomach. The wind rushed from his gaping mouth. His coins went scattering in all directions.

The Gremlin collided with the Mountaineer. Both vehicles exploded.

The burning husk of the smaller car overtook me and flew inches above, and past, me, landing where its journey had begun, in its original parking space, except that it was without wheels and upside down.

I hit the ground rolling, came to a stop on one knee, and secured two capsules about the size of a pack of gum from a compartment on my utility belt. Holding one in each hand, I waited for my enemy to catch his breath.

"Sorry about messing up that nice outfit of yours, Detonation," I said, trying to get him nice and upset.

He spat dirt out of his mouth. "You think you can make me look like a punk? I'm done playing with you." He spread his fingers apart and slapped both palms on the pavement. A wave of crimson energy swelled beneath him, expanding out. The air rippled around him. Even the molecules in the air surrounding him hissed.

Squandering his powers, for one final blast. His total concentration had been on killing me. He forgot about the Panagis. The energy that cloaked the building dissipated quickly. The asphalt beneath his palms superheated and liquefied. The crimson surged toward me faster.

Now or never, I thought.

Heaving the first capsule at him, it hit his wall of heated air. The reaction was immediate as the casing burst, releasing a dark syrupy gas. The chemical spread quickly across his energy wave.

"What the fu--," Detonation shouted. "Wh-what is happening?" He being the source of the power, the gas was drawn to him.

"The gas is something I cooked up a while ago, before I retired, specifically for you," I explained. "Your ability is to manipulate light into something combustible. My chemical absorbs the visible light passing through the atmosphere. That's why things are getting dark around you."

He forced out more of his power, trying to fight the gas off. Big mistake. The kinetic theory of matter states that molecules are perpetually in motion. These particles move faster when their temperature goes up, giving the gas more to consume. The more he fought the faster it worked.

The darkness drew closer to Detonation. He was submerged in the gas. It entered every orifice in his body.

I tossed the capsule containing the second compound. The vapor rapidly turned into a gelatinous crust. Smoke rose from the shapeless form. Detonation tried desperately to breathe and to free himself. He looked like a man immersed in steaming tar trying to free himself. Finally, his struggling stopped, and he slumped to the ground, no longer moving.

I regretted what I had done. It was a horrible way to go. But it was either his life or the life of the city. I didn't think I cared about people who lived here anymore. It took the ghost of my son to remind me of that.

Cheering burst out all around me. In seconds. I was surrounded, being thanked, congratulated, kissed, hugged, and asked out on dates. How I went from hermit to hero boggles my mind to this day.

Epilogue
Black Licorice

After escaping the crowd, I walked through my neighborhood, intending to go home. I was tired out by all the fighting, and conflicted by how I felt about putting on the uniform again. I wanted to hate the people of this city for letting my family die. Yet, I couldn't help seeing the fear in the eyes of all those trapped in the office building. They were helpless. Superiors, even the lesser ones, couldn't be stopped by normal people.

My thoughts were interrupted when I noticed the delivery truck at the party store. I was surprised the driver would still be running his route with the recent threat to the destruction of the city. I crossed the street, heading for the store. The truck pulled away.

The driver rolled his window down, and gave me a thumbs up. "You rock, dude," he shouted.

For a second, I wondered how he recognized me until I realized I still wore my suit. Shaking my head, I went inside the store, after returning the driver's thumbs up.

Ilyas was behind the counter. He grinned when he saw me. Then he ducked out of sight and came back up with something in his hand. "Guess what, Mr. Calderon, the black licorice has arrived."

His smile was infectious. I grinned too. "That's great news." I instinctively reached for my wallet, forgetting again what I was wearing.

"No biggie," Ilyas said.

He tossed the entire container of candy toward me. I caught it one-handed.

"It's on the house. It's the least I can do for the man who saved the city. But what is the deal with it being black? Why is it always black?" he asked.

I stared down at the licorice feeling some kind of emotion and then back up at him. "It was my son's favorite," I explained. "One day a week, after I fought some criminal, I would stop and pick the candy up. I would wake him in the middle of the night without his mother knowing. We'd sit on his bed. I'd tell him about my fight and we'd eat the black licorice together."

Ilyas went slack jaw. "My bad. I had no idea the candy had anything to do with your... I feel horrible about making you tell me that."

Placing a hand on his shoulder, I said, "Don't worry about it. It felt good finally telling someone." I popped the lid off the container and pulled out two strands of licorice. "Would you like one?"

His infectious grin returned. "I would. Thanks."

"Would you like to hear about how I defeated Detonation today?"

"Really?" He nodded. "That would be great, Mr. Calderon?"

"I'm in uniform," I said, "Call me, Night Siege."

In Need Of a Friend
Derrick Ferguson

"You couldn't hope for better merchandise than this anywhere. You're getting the best of this deal and you know it." Louis Culkin's grin was at once engaging and repulsive. It was the grin of a man who had long ago placed his morals and virtues in a box, padlocked the box shut and sunk that box into the deep black recesses of what had once been his soul.

He pushed the shivering, dark blonde girl toward the idling full-sized van. The girl wasn't shivering so much out of fear as out of indignation at being manhandled by these street thugs who looked to her to have the IQ of doorknobs.

The empty lot was only one of many located in *The Barrens*. Located along the banks of the Hopkins River were numerous industrial parks that had once been the throbbing, vital industrial hub of Denbrook. Now, the factories and warehouses were abandoned or burned out. At night, these old industrial sites turned into another world all together, the scene of nocturnal trades in drugs, forbidden computer programs, exotic weapons and human flesh.

Nineteen girls filled the van, ranging in age from twelve to nineteen. The driver and his two helpers had administered injections of a mild sedative to keep the girls quiet and compliant. In addition, all were handcuffed securely to thick iron bars welded to the inside sides of the van. They slumped on the cold metal floor, barely aware of what was going on.

"Make sure you get this one out of town as soon as you can," Louis

Culkin said, pointing to the girl he had shoved. The two assistants quickly and expertly injected her, despite her struggles.

The straw boss eyed the girl warily. "Why? What's her deal?"

"You don't want her on your hands any longer than you haveta," Culkin said. "There's a guy lookin' to get her back. Guy name of Regency."

The straw boss snorted. "Yeah, I've heard of him. Got a lotta you mutts runnin' scared, way I hear tell. Thought you Denbrook boys were supposed to be tough."

Culkin seemed put out by his associate's lack of respect. "Scared don't enter into it. Let's just say he's established himself as a major player in this town and I'd just as soon not give him an easy target, okay? The girl was supposed to be sent overseas, but with Regency lookin' for her...well, I just want her gone."

The two helpers finished their work and took the opportunity to catch a quick smoke. A tall, dark figure slipped from his hiding place under the van and, despite their being gravel underneath his booted feet, moved with the silence of a shadow on a mirror. With quick, blinding movements, his gloved hands gripped the heads of the two men and brought them crashing together. The impact knocked them out instantly and their attacker caught one of the cigarettes in midair. He flipped it into his own mouth and walked forward to confront Culkin and his associate.

Culkin was the first to notice the new arrival and his hand dived to his waistband for the Glock he had there. The stranger's gloved hand flicked out and Culkin cursed in pain and surprise as a metal spike some four inches long pierced his hand. The Glock thumped to the ground. Culkin eyed it longingly, contemplating making a grab for it with his good hand.

"Best leave it there, Lou. If I have to spike your other hand, you're going to have one uncomfortable time going to the men's room." The stranger's voice was a hearty, rasping growl full of menacing good humor. He stood six feet in height and his midnight black duster flapped around his ankles. Save for the blood-red, double-breasted vest that looked to be held shut by thick plastic latches every other article of clothing he wore was as black as midnight at the bottom of a mine shaft.

The straw boss sized up the stranger, taking note of the elaborate, intricate tribal tattoos around his eyes. "Lemme guess...Regency, right? The guy who thinks he's some hotshot vigilante out to clean up the streets, right?"

Regency relit the cigarette and inhaled the menthol smoke deeply before answering. "And you would be Kenny French. You've got quite the rep as a flesh peddler, Kenny. You've have been snatching girls from New Orleans, San Antonio, Lumberton and now here, in Denbrook. What do you do with the girls, Kenny? Where do you send them?"

"You don't want to cut yourself into this, man. You're mixin' in the bidness of people a whole lot higher up the food chain than you can ever hope to imagine."

Regency opened his mouth to answer but was cut off by a pair of high intensity halogen floodlights filling the yard with harsh white light. "THIS IS THE POLICE! EVERYBODY JUST STAY WHERE YOU ARE AND PLACE YOUR HANDS ON TOP OF YOUR HEADS!"

French took his chances with the 9mm Beretta he whipped out from his shoulder holster and fired first at Regency, then at the floodlight. Regency spat out the cigarette even as he dived out of the line of fire. He wore enough body armor to protect his torso and a body stocking of interwoven micromesh metal fibers and Kevlar IV but his head was unprotected. Blast and damnation! What in the hell were those cops doing here? Regency's police contact had assured that there would be no interference from the police in this matter unless Regency specifically asked for their help.

Culkin regained his weapon and awkwardly tried to fire it at the police, who in turn were firing back most enthusiastically. Regency leaped, grabbed Culkin around the waist and they both rolled out of the floodlight while bullets spanged and hummed around them. Culkin cried out in pain as the two men tumbled over broken bottles, wood scraps and other large pieces of garbage and debris. Culkin's noises ended as Regency's gloved fist cracked against his jaw.

The van revved up. Kenny French and the driver were inside the cab and they were making a break for it. French got hold of another handgun from the van's glove compartment and using the both of them with great accuracy, shot out the floodlights, restoring the darkness to the street. The van lurched forward, picking up speed as it surged right at the police car.

Regency leaped onto the running board of the van's cab as it rumbled past him and seized the driver by the throat. "Kill the engine!" he ordered. Kenny French shoved one of his guns in Regency's face and pulled the trigger.

Regency let go the driver and ducked just in time to keep his face from being shot off. The van hit the police car with enough force to throw the vehicle out of the way, the windows exploding as if a bomb had went off inside. Regency hit the street, bounced and rolled some six or seven feet before finally coming to a stop.

The two uniformed Municipal Police Officers – Ruiz and Patterson – fired futile shots in the direction of the fleeing van.

"Hold your fire!" Patterson jumped in surprise. Regency stood at his side, watching the van speed off in a cloud of burning rubber. Patterson had seen how hard the man had hit the ground and he would have bet his next paycheck that nobody would have been able to get up that fast.

"There are at least a dozen kidnapped girls in the back of that van, officer. That's why you need to hold your fire."

"And how would you know that, mister?"

"Because I was going to free them until the two of you showed up and queered the deal. Weren't you informed by Special Inspector Harris about this and told to stay out of the area?"

Patterson shook his head. "I dunno about all that...my partner and I were in the area on a routine sweep and saw the bunch of you standing in the yard so we decided to investigate."

"What the hell are you doing?" Officer Ruiz had her weapon leveled at Regency's head. "Patterson, since when do we have conversations with suspects?"

"C'mon, Ruiz, he had a chance to get away and he didn't. And he mentioned Inspector Harris."

"Cuff him."

"Ruiz..."

"I said cuff him, dammit! Do it now! He can tell his story down at the precinct!"

As Patterson reluctantly handcuffed Regency, Ruiz holstered her weapon and said; "I don't know who you think you are, but you made a big mistake shooting at me."

Regency sighed and the two cops heard slight clicking noises just before Regency held up the handcuffs Patterson had just put on him. "Could you not waste my time with this?"

Ruiz's hand dived for her handgun to find it gone. Patterson's holster was likewise empty. Both weapons were in Regency's other hand. "Now, if I give you back your side-arms will the two of you take just one minute to listen to me?"

It was Patterson who nodded and said, "You've got my ears, mister. Talk."

As he handed back the guns and cuffs, Regency issued swift orders. "Get on your radio and get an APB out on that van and this description of Kenny French. Caucasian male, about 27, five seven, five eight.140 pounds. Sandy hair, blue eyes, some kind of Arabic tattoo on his neck and the back of his left hand. You have three prisoners in the yard that I want taken to Special Inspector Andre Harris for interrogation right now. That should keep the two of you out of trouble for a while."

Ruiz asked sarcastically, "And what are we supposed to put in our report? That we were helped out by some mystery man who won't even give us his name?"

"Inspector Harris knows all about me." Regency turned and walked away rapidly. "You just get busy with that APB! If French gets out of the city, those girls will be lost to us." And one girl in particular would not live to see the morning if Regency couldn't find her.

***

Municipal Police Department Special Inspector Andre Harris looked up from his computer screen as his office door was abruptly opened. "Dammit, Wilma, didn't your mother teach you to knock first?"

Wilma Echavarria grinned sheepishly as she said, "Sorry, sir, but you said you wanted to be notified the minute there was any word on the girl or Regency."

Andre picked up a half-empty pack of Brightons and shook one out. "So?

You gonna make me pay for the information or what?"

"Call came in from a couple of patrol cops. Kenny French has the girl we want and a whole bunch of others to boot. Regency couldn't stop him from getting away. The patrol cops have two of French's men and a flesh peddler named Culkin. They're bringing 'em in now."

"Good. Maybe we'll get a break in this stinking case." Andre looked at his watch. It was 12:17 AM "Regency's got a little over six hours to find that girl."

"And to add to the fun, Mrs. Garritano is here and she's brought her lawyers with her."

Andre sighed and crushed out his cigarette. "Give me a minute to wash my face and fix my tie, then show her in."

***

Regency stopped his jet black 1970 Buick GSX in front of a respectable looking four-story mansion that looked as if it had been airlifted from the set of *"Gone With The Wind"* and dropped right in the middle of Denbrook Heights. Regency locked up his car, then walked up the short flight of Kherry marble steps to the front door and rang the bell. A thin Asian man in a tuxedo opened the door. The man groaned and rolled his eyes upon seeing Regency.

"Aw, c'mon man. I don't wanna have to deal with your bullshit tonight. Go hassle somebody else, wouldja?"

"I need to have words with Zuleika, so just back on up and stand out of my way." Regency shoved the Asian aside and walked on inside the foyer.

"You know I gotta put up some token resistance, man."

"You do and I'll break both your legs. I'm on the clock and I don't have time to waste dancing with you." Regency looked at the man with eyes that were dead black in color. It occurred to the man that he'd never before seen anybody with black eyes. The effect was unnerving. Add to that the unsettling fact that Regency didn't blink and the little man suddenly had the feeling he was looking into the eyes of a man with no soul.

"I'll tell Zuleika you wanta see her."

"You do that."

***

Catherine Garritano radiated wealth and intelligence. She impressed Andre and he didn't impress easy. But he knew something of her background, as it had been the subject of many newspaper and magazine articles. She had been left a near bankrupt business by her husband who had the poor grace to get himself killed after embezzling ten million dollars. His body had been found. The ten million hadn't. Through determination and hard work, Catherine Garritano pulled the company together and prospered. Today, her personal worth was somewhere in the neighborhood of seven billion dollars and her company, renamed *Epoch Futureworks*, was a major player in the fields of communications, practical technology and cutting edge research.

The company was based in New Jersey but Catherine was being wooed by Denbrook's Powers-That-Be to open a branch there. If that happened it meant jobs and a significant boost to Denbrook's economy. Andre's mandate from those selfsame P-T-B had been put to him as simply as possible: Do whatever it takes to make Catherine Garritano happy.

Catherine herself was a strikingly tall woman. Without the two inch heels, she would still have been an easy five ten or five eleven. Her mane of platinum hair looked as if she'd come from having it freshly washed and styled. Her black business dress looked simple enough, but Andre would have bet it cost four thousand bucks easy. Andre hoped she was wearing black because she liked the color and not because she was already in mourning for her sister.

At her back were her lawyers, two men and one woman and they all looked as though they hadn't been fed cop in quite a while.

"Mrs. Garritano, you didn't have to come down here. I promise you that as soon as I have word of your sister, you'll be contacted."

"Funny thing about contacts, Inspector Harris." Catherine's voice was that kind of Demi Moor-ish huskiness men found sexy. In Catherine's case, it came from years of smoking and drinking Scotch straight. "My contacts in the Municpal Police Department tell me that you've only got one man handling my sister's kidnapping and that he's not even a detective on your staff. Could it be possible that they're wrong?"

"No, they're not wrong Mrs. Garritano."

"Allow me to introduce you to my lawyers. They're from Zimmerman, Zimmerman, Fraley and Finch. You should get to know them since they're the ones who are going to destroy your career and ruin your life."

"Mrs. Garritano, I don't appreciate you threatening me."

"And I don't appreciate you being so blasé about my sister's life! You've only got one man looking for her? I'd heard that you were one of the best Special Inspector's on the Police Commissioner's staff, but I'm-"

"Mrs. Garritano, if you'll send your lawyers out of my office and sit down and talk to me like the intelligent, reasonable woman you are, I can explain my strategy and tell you something about the man I've asked to rescue your sister."

***

Regency entered Zuleika's office to find her sitting behind her Art Deco French Walnut desk, playing "Fallout 5" on her lime green PS3 while talking into a headset. Zuleika topped out at somewhere near three hundred pounds. A mixture of African, Vietnamese and Brazilian bloods gave her skin a distinct coppery tone, a natural tan envied by men and women who spent hours in tanning salons or baking themselves on the beach to obtain. Her green eyes were both delicate and piercing. Long black hair with a streak of white cascaded down her back and ample behind.

Regency walked over to the bar and helped himself to a shot of tequila while Zuleika finished her call. She removed the headphone, paused the game and said to her guest; "Thank you for not crippling anybody on your way in. I'm still paying medical bills from your last visit."

"I'm not here to make trouble, Zuleika. Quite the opposite. I need your help."

"Oh, really?" Zuleika leaned back in the matching Art Deco chair which had been reinforced to support her weight. Nobody knew how she had come to run a high-class bordello in Denbrook. There were rumors that she had been one of the most sought after courtesans in Europe and the Middle East and had known the favors of princes and potentates. "And how can I help?"

"You know Kenny French?"

"I know *of* him," Zuleika said carefully.

"I have to find him in the next five hours. There's a girl he has that will die unless I find her."

Zuleika shrugged. "Girls die in that business all the time. You know that."

"Zuleika...I know you better than that. The girls that work for you do so willingly. They come to you; you hold no truck with having children kidnapped off the street like French does. You really mean to say you would sit back and do nothing while a girl...a baby, really, is forced into a life of degradation and filth?"

***

The lawyers were dismissed with instructions to stay nearby just in case. Catherine took a flask from her purse and poured sizeable measures of Tullamore into plastic cups Andre produced from his left desk drawer. He also took a thick paperback novel from a desk drawer and passed it over to her.

Catherine Garritano looked at the garishly lurid cover that depicted a black man in a trench coat and fedora fighting four rather wicked looking ninja types while all were overshadowed by a laughing, jeweled demon's mask.

She read the title and the author's name out loud; "*The Laughing Devil: A Regency Adventure* by Lowell O'Neal. You're sitting there trying to tell me that the man you claim is going to save my sister is a fictional character?"

"Well...yes and no. You ever read any of them?"

"Inspector Harris, I'm an extremely busy woman. If it's not related to the running of my company, I don't have time to read it."

"There are five books in the series so far and except for some of the names being changed and dates and locations, they're mostly true."

Catherine impatiently ground out her cigarette in the dangerously overflowing ashtray. "Stop wasting my time and get to the point of all this. What's this book got to do with my sister being rescued?"

"Lowell O'Neal comes from a wealthy family. They're not the Rockefellers, but you won't find any O'Neal's shoveling coal. One of Lowell's ancestors was an escaped slave who made it north and became one of the first black lawyers in the United States. Law became the family profession. You may have heard of Lowell's parents. Preston O'Neal sat on the bench of the state Supreme Court and Sandra O'Neal was at one time the most sought after defense lawyers in the city. Lowell went to Harvard and graduated at the top of his class but instead of joining the family firm, he was approached by the government and opted for another kind of life."

"I take it he didn't join the Post Office."

Andre grinned and nodded. "Lowell was not only tops in law, but he was quite an exceptional athlete. That, combined with his aptitude in several other areas made him a prime candidate to be recruited into a special team."

"Black Ops?"

"The blackest you can imagine; an outfit codenamed *Omega Elite*. That's where he got the nickname Regency." Andre paused for a bit, wondering if he should tell her about the dangerous experiment Lowell had volunteered for and survived. The experiment had given him the ability to consciously trigger his adrenal glands to pump adrenaline into his system, giving him a boost to his already exceptional levels of strength, speed and agility, enabling him to perform near superhuman feats for short periods of time. He decided against it. That ability was Lowell's secret weapon. And Andre wouldn't even be telling her this much about the unique relationship between Lowell and Regency if it hadn't been for the fact he had checked up on her and found to his surprise that due to some government contracts her company had been awarded, Catherine Garritano had a pretty high security clearance. Which meant that she could be trusted to a certain degree.

"Why Regency?"

Andre shrugged. "The leader of the team then was a man named Milo Dane and he liked giving nicknames to his team members. There was one woman he called 'Hatrack' another guy he called 'The Maestro'. Dane and Regency are pretty formidable men, let me assure you."

Andre had seen for himself just how formidable three summers ago. He still got the shakes when he thought of that night when he, Regency, Milo Dane and the global instigator known only as Dillon had faced a howling thing with forty blood-red eyes in a filthy basement in The Barrens that had crawled at them over the two dozen dismembered bodies of a Denbrook SWAT team.

"After he left Omega Elite, Lowell settled in Brooklyn and wanted to fulfill a childhood dream of being a writer. Problem was the poor guy couldn't *give* his stories and novels away. He collected a stack of rejection letters six feet high and was about to go back to law when he hit on an idea. He'd always been told in his writing courses that a writer should write what he knows, so he created the alter ego of Regency and contacted me. I knew him from his Omega Elite days since two of their operations brought them to Denbrook and he pitched his idea to me. Since I was familiar with his skills, I saw the advantages of allowing him to operate here. Denbrook is a somewhat unique American city...as I'm sure you've noticed. So we turn a blind eye to his freelancing and in return, he looks out for us when we've got a difficult case.

"As Regency, he uses his considerable talents and skills to aid and assist those who need aid and assistance and then, as O'Neal, he writes up those adventures. And so far, it's worked. He's turned out four best-selling books. There's even a Regency comic book out now and the Netflix series starts next year."

"You've got to be kidding me. How does he get away with this? Don't people know O'Neal's just pretending to be this Regency?"

"First off, Lowell doesn't pretend to be Regency. Very few people who have met Lowell have met Regency and vice versa. They just don't travel in the same circles. And the few who have met the both of them are convinced they're two different men. It's really sorta spooky if you ask me. Lowell has a completely different set of mannerisms, body language, speech patterns...there's a physical resemblance, sure...but they act nothing alike. I know people who have met Lowell and then an hour later met Regency and never caught on that they were the same man.

"So you've got a self-made schizophrenic on the job of finding my sister? Is that what you're telling me?"

"Exactly. Understand something, Mrs. Garritano; Regency operates without red tape holding him back. He works fast and he does what has to be done. In a situation like this, where time is our enemy, he's the best hope your sister has."

***

"Explain to me why this girl is so important to you and maybe I can do a little something." Zuleika said, pretending to not be very interested.

Regency poured another shot of tequila and spoke slowly, yet urgently. "Elise Garritano was snatched off the street by Kenny French's boys over in the city. She was hanging out with some friends at McGee's VRcade. One minute she was there, the next she was gone. The friends called the police and Andre Harris called me. I was able to find out French was in town and snatching girls, but that is all anybody seems to know. Nobody knows whom he is working for these days or what he is going to do with those girls.

"Elise Garritano has a rare blood disorder called Pembrook's Malady. She needs to take an injection at least once in a forty-eight hour period. She can miss maybe one injection, but not two in a row. Her sister is pretty sure she skipped taking her last injection, which means that she has to have the next one. If not, she'll have seizures and go into a coma and then she will be dead soon after. I have to find her."

"This girl. She's related to Catherine Garritano, correct?"

"Correct." Regency leaned forward, his eyes crafty and knowing. "I think I can safely say that Mrs. Garritano would be most generous towards anybody helping to save the life of her sister."

"And you?" Zuleika smiled sweetly. "What would I get from you?"

"I'll owe you a favor. But nothing illegal. Nothing against the police and nothing against any innocent person."

"But you wouldn't mind if the favor involved one of my competitors."

"You insult me, Zuleika. I'm hardly a common leg breaker. You would be better off storing up the favor for when you really need it. You know I'm good for it."

Indeed she did. Regency didn't offer his favors out often. He was usually the one collecting the favors.

"Okay, you've got a deal. How do I reach you?"

"Here's my number," he said, sliding a slip of folded paper toward Zuleika. You will have something for me?"

She nodded. "I'll make some calls."

Regency came over and bent down to kiss one rounded, chipmunk cheek.

"Thank you, Zuleika."

"No, no, dear boy. Thank you."

***

Elise Garritano twisted and fought against the plastic binders holding her wrists together. This night had surpassed all her wildest dreams of what Hell must be like. She had long ago abandoned the hope that this was a dream, a mistake or some bizarre gag played on her. Outside of the filthy, semi-dark room she occupied with the rest of the captive girls, she heard curses and shouted orders. They were on a boat, she knew that much.

Elise twisted around to look at the rest of the girls. They were a huddled, whimpering mass that made an unspoken, collective decision to surrender to their fate and that made her mad. Elise had a lot more to lose than the rest of them. She was looking at certain death in a few hours.

"Hey! HEY!"

The others looked at her. Covered in muck and dirt. Eyes as wide as they could get.

"Listen to me. We gotta get these things off and get outta here!"

One girl, thin as a foal, trembling, as if seized with the ague, whimpered, "they'll kill us if we try to get away. Maybe if we do what they say—"

Elise hissed in a voice raw with anger, "We've got to get away! What if they decide to kill us all? They could take us out on the river and dump us out there somewhere! Do you wanta die? I don't! Now c'mon! Somebody crawl over here and help me get these things off!"

***

Regency drove from Zuleika's to Downtown Denbrook. He'd checked his voicemail on his smartphone and found an urgent message for Lowell O'Neal. He had some time to kill anyway while waiting for Zuleika to come through so he decided to attend to this bit of business.

He parked on Carson Parkway and swiftly walked to the Sandstone Café. An elegant, two story structure; the first floor was the dining area and bar which was usually packed with downtown workers during the week and jazz aficionados on the weekends that came to listen to The Dwayne Broadnax

Trio. The second floor boasted a balcony that overlooked the street and private dining rooms for large parties or those who wanted privacy. Regency entered the smoky café, nodding here and there at familiar faces, looking for Lowell's agent.

George Alexander waved from the bar. A slim, waspish man with a thin intense face, George looked Regency up and down and said in a dismal voice full of infinite doom; "Tell me that it's you, Lowell. You're just dressed like Regency to impress some chick."

In answer, Regency held up a finger to the bartender. "Tequila." He fished out a pack of menthol Morleys. He shook one out the pack and lit it up.

George sighed. Lowell O'Neal didn't smoke and he didn't drink Tequila. "Look, I've got to speak with Lowell about a meeting we've got with the Netflix people on Friday, so could you please do whatever head trip you gotta do and bring Lowell out so I can talk business with him?"

Regency downed his shot of tequila in one gulp and motioned for another. "I'm working now, George. I understand your concern but you cannot talk to Lowell until I'm done. You know the rules."

George groaned softly and turned back to his frosty glass of Coors. Although he made good money from the novelized adventures of his client's alter ego, he didn't particularly like Regency all that much. "Y'know, you and Lowell might want to go get some help with this duality problem you seem to have."

Regency shrugged, not really caring a poobah's pizzle what George thought. "The only one who has a problem is you, George. Try not to worry so much. Lowell will make your meeting. Trust him and trust me."

Regency's phone vibrated and he took it out, unlocked it with a swipe of his thumb. "Go."

"It's your new best friend," Zuleika said.

"Tell me something good."

"Kenny French has the girls at a private estate located at the north shore. Kenny's got the girls on a yacht and he's taking them out tonight, across Lake Erie into Canada."

"I owe you big time for this."

"Don't say that. I haven't told you who owns the estate and the yacht. Both belong to McGrath Wynne. You do know who he is, don't you?"

"I know. A member of The Society of Seven. It was just a matter of time before we bumped heads."

"You sure you want to mix it with them?"

"Got no choice. The Garritano girl is under my protection now."

"Well, if they catch you, do be a dear and forget who gave you the information? There's a love."

"I appreciate the vote of confidence." Regency answered. He cut off the connection and put the phone away. "I got to go, George. Lowell will call you in the morning."

Before George could do more than mount a token growl of protest, Regency was already leaving The Sandstone and walking back to his car, thinking about his next move. Wynne would be sure to have plenty of hired muscle at the estate and by now, Kenny French would have informed him that Regency was hunting for the girls. What in the hell would an international player like McGrath Wynne want with a bunch of high-school girls when he could have girls from anywhere in the world?

Regency had heard stories about The Society of Seven for years. Seven of the world's richest and most powerful men and women, they spent their time globe hopping, playing elaborate 'games' they made up to test and challenge each other's resources and skills. And there were other, darker rumors about The Society of Seven. Rumors of demon worship, genetic experimentation, cybernetic augmentation. They were all quite a package if even half the stories were true.

Regency reached his car, unlocked the driver's side door and climbed in. He sat behind the steering wheel for a minute, drumming gloved fingers on the wheel. He dialed a number on his phone. It was answered on the third ring.

"Yes?"

"Good morning, Lori."

"I've been expecting you to call. This is about the Garritano girl."

"I need backup. Can you help me out?"

"That's why I'm still up. Where do you want me to meet you?"

"I have to brief you and your girls on the situation first. And I need to steal a boat. Meet me at The Union Bridge Park Marina as soon as you can."

"I'll roust my girls out of bed and be right down. Nice to hear from you again."

"Same here."

"Is this going to be bloody?"

"It always is."

***

Elise Garritano led her small, frightened band up the creaking steps that hopefully led to their freedom. It had taken her almost an hour to convince them to undo their bonds and make this escape attempt.

Elise peered out the hatchway. She saw nothing except for an empty deck illuminated by the bright halogen lights. She turned around, brushing her long hair out of her face as she whispered urgently to the others; "I don't see any guards. When you hit the hatch, run and don't stop for anything. I don't care what you hear or what they say. If just one of us can get out, they can bring the cops back to help anybody that might get captured."

"You said that we wouldn't get caught!" a plump girl named Babs wailed. Her body shook so hard, Elise was afraid that she might have a heart attack right there on the spot.

"Listen to me! They can't catch all of us and if you do what I say, I'm positive that you'll make it! Now let's GO!"

The girls ran out of the hatchway, screaming and waving their arms in as much fear as distraction. Elise was amazed as Babs ran with the speed of an alley cat, despite her baby fat, arms pumping like mad. The other girls were not far behind her. Men appeared seemingly out of nowhere, shouting for the girls to stop their flight. Elise had to give the girls credit. They were so fast they were out of sight in seconds. The yacht's crew gave hearty pursuit.

Elise, her heart swelling with gratitude that she had helped the other girls escape, started to make her move. She screamed as a large hand clamped down on her shoulder. She was lifted bodily and dangled in the air as the man who held her stepped out of the hatchway and onto the deck.

The man who held her was easily well over six feet in height and powerfully muscled under the impeccably tailored Pino Salicci double-breasted silk suit. He smiled with an amazingly white set of perfect, even teeth. His rather large, square head boasted a full head of white hair that looked too good to be natural.

"So what have we here? A rebel with a cause? A teenaged Spartacus?" The man seemed to be having a pretty good time. Kenny French appeared by his side.

"Ah, Kenny. I was just wondering where you were. How did the young ladies get out of the storeroom they were locked in?"

"They managed to unscrew the grating on the lower half of the door." Kenny French's voice carried a twinge of admiration. "Then they musta got one of the really skinny, smaller girls to squeeze through and unlock the door from the other side. She woulda left some skin behind, but that's how they did it."

"I see. Which one is this?"

"That's the Garritano girl. That's the one Regency is lookin' for. My people tell me he's been asking all over where I can be found."

"And do you think it likely he knows where you are now?" Wynne McGrath held the struggling Elise at arm's length. She bit and scratched like a bobcat, but McGrath's arm seemingly was impervious as an iron beam.

"If he's as good as his rep, I'd haveta say yeah...he's most likely on his way here."

"And you really think this Regency will risk incurring disfavor with The Society of Seven over this?" McGrath gave Elise a hearty shake that made her teeth clack together painfully.

"He's not the type to give up. I say we leave the girl right here and pull out."

"But you're not in charge here, Kenny. Take her and tie her someplace on the yacht where she can be seen clearly."

"Didn't you hear me? Regency's coming for her!"

"I heard you, Kenny. I heard you."

***

The Union Bridge Park actually wasn't located at Union Bridge Park. It actually was located four miles up the Hopkins River. And the marina had seen better days since Denbrook wasn't exactly known for attracting boaters. Even in summer, the waters of the Hopkins River were just too frigid and choppy and the currents too tricky. Still, there were a number of boats docked at the Marina, many of them used for illegal activities, as Regency well knew.

Regency picked out a lean, wicked looking red and white cigarette boat with Twin 500 HP Mercruisers and within minutes had it started. He had a feeling he'd do better trying to reach McGrath's mansion by water. He wondered impatiently where Lori and her girls were as he lit up another cigarette.

"I keep telling you those things'll kill you." Regency turned to see Lori Higgins sitting in the back of the boat, a 9mm Ruger P94 pointed at his head.

"I wish you would stop doing that."

"Well, now you know how it feels when you do it to other people," Lori replied without sympathy as she holstered her weapon. "So what's the dilly-o?"

Regency summed up the situation quite accurately for the young woman, who looked nothing like the highly proficient professional warrior she was. Along with the 9mm, she also had a powerful crossbow slung on her back with a small quiver of steel-tipped arrows.

When Regency had finished, she jerked her head at an idling Lincoln Navigator. "My girls are ready. What do you want us to do?"

"Make your way to the estate and give me one hell of a distraction in exactly one hour. I should be in position by then, but if not, just go ahead and start the party. And Lori, I just want a distraction, not World War III. The primary objective is to get the Garritano girl, and any others McGrath may be holding captive, free, okay?"

Lori shrugged. "You know McGrath's not going to let this end here. After tonight he's going to be after you."

"And you as well."

"Unlike you, I intend to put a bullet in his brain the second I lay eyes on him."

***

Wynne McGrath stood on the foredeck of the yacht, watching Elise Garritano struggle against her bonds uselessly. He was smoking a thick cigar and looking inland, toward the mansion and waiting patiently for Regency to arrive. Kenny French was standing at his side and, quite frankly, Kenny French was being an annoyance right about now.

"Mr. McGrath, I'd just as soon you paid me now and I'll go on about my business."

"Pay you?" McGrath's left eyebrow raised and the corners of his mouth turned downward ever so slightly in displeasure. "Kenny, do you honestly think you deserve to be paid after you've screwed up this operation so badly?"

"Hey, you wanted girls, you got girls."

"But the specifications were simple: they were to be homeless girls living on the street, that wouldn't be missed. Who told you to take Catherine Garritano's sister?"

"Mr. McGrath, I didn't know who she was at the time. You wanted girls in a hurry and I told you that it wasn't that easy to just grab girls off the street. I had to make compromises."

"You mean you decided to get sloppy. And now you've placed my name in jeopardy and attracted the attention of this man Regency, who by all accounts is quite a formidable player in his own right."

"Y'know, Mr. McGrath, I'm really tired of having to listen to your bullshit, and I really suggest you pay me what you owe me and do it right now." Kenny's right hand crept around to where he had his Beretta tucked in the small of his back.

McGrath turned and looked at Kenny French thoughtfully. "You're absolutely right, Kenny. It's high time I paid you off."

McGrath's hands were a blur. One hand came up and around to cup the back of Kenny's head while the other drove the burning end of the cigar straight into his right eye, which burst like a stepped on grape. Wynne drove the cigar deeper and deeper into Kenny's head. The smell was truly nauseating, but Wynne McGrath merely chuckled as he twisted the cigar viciously.

The gun fell from Kenny's wildly jerking hand and McGrath whispered in the dying man's ear, "Nothing like a good smoke; eh, Kenny?" He let go of the body and let it lie there on the deck as the last few spasms of life ran their course.

The mansion exploded in a tremendous gout of flame that seemed to crack it in half. McGrath was thrown to the deck by the force of the explosion. He lay there, his mouth open in shock and horror as he watched the mansion that had been in his family since 1828 collapse into flaming rubble right in front of him.

As he shakily got to his feet, he could hear Elise Garritano's cackling giggle of triumph, the curses and shouted questions of his men and the sharp, staccato sounds of gunfire. Already, dark, choking smoke cut off his vision of what was happening onshore. Another explosion rocked the mansion and it collapsed inward on itself with an agonized groan of shattered masonry. McGrath reflected that perhaps it was time to cut his losses and get out of New York for a time and regroup. But first, he'd deal with the Garritano girl and leave her in pieces for Regency.

He turned and blinked in surprise upon seeing a tall man dressed all in black untying the Garritano girl. The man looked up and fixed McGrath with his dark tombstone gaze.

"Regency, I presume."

Regency nodded slightly. "And you would be Wynne McGrath."

McGrath stepped back over the body of Kenny French. "If you know me then you know what organization I'm a part of. I can't honestly believe you'd want to war with us."

"You think I blew up your house for fun? That is just the beginning. Here's the rest of my message." Regency rushed upon McGrath like a hot black wind from Hell's main furnace.

McGrath slipped the first couple of straight punches that Regency sent his way and came back with several impressive strikes of his own.

Regency blocked, his arms moving with an unnerving speed and precision. Regency got in close and blasted four punishing blows to McGrath's midsection.

McGrath grunted as he doubled over. Regency's right hand came up and around, in a short arcing loop that ended on McGrath's jaw, which broke with a frighteningly loud sound, as if it were brittle.

Regency's gloves had solid metal discs woven into the fabric over each knuckle, in effect giving him a set of brass knuckles on each hand and giving his already powerful punches even more devastating force.

McGrath slumped to his knees. Regency grabbed him by his three thousand dollar suit and yanked him back to his feet. He held him close while he whispered in his raspy, dark voice; "The only reason you are still alive is because I want you to take a message back the rest of those spoiled sick freaks you run with: play your games all you want but you don't play them in Denbrook anymore. You stay out of my town. You want a war with me? Bring it on. I'll give you a war so vicious it will be remembered for generations to come as Vietnam Part II."

Regency let Wynne drop and turned away, walked back to where Elise stood with Lori Higgins. Lori had her gun trained on McGrath.

"You want I should kill him?"

Regency looked at McGrath, who looked back with his mouth swollen shut and soul-searing rage in his eyes.

"No. We have a little girl who needs to get home and take her medicine."

"You're making a mistake."

"I said no, Lori." Regency looked down at Elise and allowed his anger to drain away. "Hi. You ready to go home?"

Elise nodded. "You're scary," she said in a small voice. "How'd you learn to be so scary?"

Lori laughed and answered that one; "Practice, honey. Lots and lots of practice."

"Can you teach me how to be scary like you so that people like him..."

Elise pointed at Wynne. "...can't hurt me?"

Regency picked Elise Garritano up in his arms and said; "I can do better than that. I can take you to a place that can teach you how to take care of yourself so that men like him will respect you. Would you like that?"

"I'd rather make them scared of me."

Lori howled with laughter as Regency smiled and said, "Well, in any case, we will have to talk to your sister about that. Let's go see her so you can get your shot, okay?"

Two Days Later...

"And over here we have the archery range," Lori Higgins said to Catherine Garritano and Special Inspector Andre Harris as they emerged from the hedge maze into an open area where a dozen young girls were firing arrows into targets.

Catherine took off her Penrose sunglasses and looked out over the archery range. "All this and a firing range, dojos, stables, a racetrack...one would think you were not just teaching young girls, Miss Higgins, but that you were training them to be mercenaries or something."

"*The Higgins School of Higher Learning For Girls* is dedicated to teaching girls between the ages of 12 to 19 all the skills necessary to function in the 21st Century. Not only do we provide a comprehensive academic program, we also provide a full physical regimen where we teach practical skills that they will need to compete in what is still pretty much a man's world."

Catherine smiled radiantly. "I wasn't criticizing your school, Miss Higgins. In fact, I heartily approve of everything I've seen here."

Andre said, "Mrs. Garritano, I can't think of a safer place for your sister to be. Many of the girls going to school here are the daughters of famous actors, politicians, industrialists and heads of state. The academic program is of college level. They'll be getting the equivalent of an education they'd get in Harvard or Oxford. Every one of Lori's instructors is highly trained in marksmanship and martial arts and they're fully the equals of any professional bodyguard. Your sister will not only be training her mind, she'll get training in how to use weapons and fighting skills that will give her confidence and self-respect."

"Stop, stop," Catherine held up a hand, laughing. "You're preaching to the choir, Inspector. I'm sold. There's just one other thing while I've got you both here. When do I get to meet Regency?"

***

Elise Garritano looked up from her Harry Potter paperback as the door of Lori's office opened. She had decided to wait here while her sister toured the school. She'd seen it all already anyway. Regency had brought her here the night he'd rescued her and she had stayed there for a couple of days hanging out with some of the girls her own age that Lori had introduced her to.

The man who entered the office was tall, dressed in a sand-colored Armani suit with a matching fedora. He smiled rather shyly and took off his hat, revealing a head full of small, tight 'locks. "Hi...Elise, right?"

Elise smiled back. "That's right. If you're looking for Miss Higgins, she's not here right now. She's out showing the school to my sister."

"Actually, I'm here to see you. I'm a friend of Regency's. My name's Lowell O'Neal."

"Regency! Have you seen him? How is he? Can you call him and tell him I want to talk to him?"

Lowell said, "I can't call him right now. He's a busy man and he stays on the move a lot. But he did want me to come by and tell you that he's not going to forget you and he wanted you to have this."

Lowell reached in a pocket and pulled out a ring of red and yellow gold that boasted a stylized R. He gave it to her.

"It's so pretty," Elise breathed and slipped it on her left index finger. "And it fits! How'd he know my ring size?"

Lowell shrugged. "How does he know any of the stuff he knows? Regency said to tell you that this ring means you're under his protection. Anybody gives you a problem you show that ring to him or her and it'll make it clear that Regency is your friend. And if they still don't leave you alone, he'll deal with them." Lowell O'Neal put his fedora back on and headed for the door. "Enjoy your stay here, Elise. We'll talk again."

"Wait! How will Regency know I need help?"

Lowell O'Neal turned and gave Elise a devilish grin that looked awfully familiar to her...she had seen that grin somewhere before...on another face...

"He'll know, Elise. He'll know."

***

"I want my sister enrolled here as soon as possible, Miss Higgins. Here, this is for you." Catherine passed over a check. Lori looked at it and her eyes widened.

"You sure you got the right amount of zeros here, Mrs. Garritano?"

"Call me Catherine. I added something extra for you and the members of your staff that helped rescue my sister. I like you and I want you to put my sister through the wringer, you get me?"

Lori grinned as she slipped the check into the back pocket of her jeans. "I get you. Oh, here comes Lowell."

Catherine turned to watch as Lowell ambled towards them, hands jammed in his pockets, fedora pushed back.

"Well, I do get to meet Regency after all..."

Andre said warningly, "No, Mrs. Garritano...you're meeting Lowell O'Neal."

"But you said that he and Regency..."

"I know full well what I said. But he's not Regency now. He's Lowell O'Neal and that's what you'll call him and nothing else."

Lowell joined the little group and stuck out his hand. "Catherine Garritano, right? I just met your sister. I'm glad my friend could help get her back."

"Yes...Mr. O'Neal...I thank the...both of you for everything you've done. Maybe you and I could have dinner some night soon? Or maybe Regency would be available if you're not free?"

Andre's phone beeped for attention and he said, "Excuse me" and stepped away a few feet to answer it.

Lowell answered Catherine smoothly. "I can't answer for Regency, Mrs.

Garritano. Due to the nature of his work, he's very secretive about his activities. But I'll be happy to accept."

Catherine looked up in his handsome, smiling face and wondered if he was putting her on or what. She opened her mouth to ask him point blank about Regency when Andre said urgently, "I've got to get back to Denbrook. There's a situation."

Lowell asked, "How bad?"

"Hostage situation in City Center. Twenty men; all armed; all claiming to have the entire joint wired to blow up if their demands aren't met in two hours." Andre looked hard at Lowell. "Sure would be nice if you could get in touch with Regency and ask him to help out."

Everybody looked at Lowell, who said mildly, "Well, I suppose I should go see if I can roust him up, then. If you'll excuse me..." Lowell turned and rapidly walked away.

Andre looked at Lori. "You want in on this?"

Lori grinned and said, "Why the hell not. Let's go." They hurried to catch up to Lowell. Catherine Garritano watched them go and could only think to say, "Have fun!"

It was Lowell O'Neal who turned and waved and called back, "We will!"

BRIANNA'S INTERLUDE
Jeffrey Bolden

"Do you know who that is!?" The flashes of memory of watching Bri stand up for me ran vividly through my mind. I remembered sitting in the backseat of that Accord, draped in darkness, watching this small Hispanic girl stand up to her own people defending a little black man like me. I remembered the tears nearly stinging my eyes as she pointed at me yelling, "That is a poet! An author!" I loved that woman in that moment; loved her more than anything I could remember loving anything. She was my paragon of love, and I saw God in her. And it was that night she was taken from me, and a fire in me was born.

The same fire blazed in me as I barreled forward, with eyes gleaming, toward my sister, Kara, trying to pull her boyfriend, Thomas, out of his defiant stance. But he stood strong and firm in front of the drawn police issued pistols aimed at him.

"Stand down, boy," the lead police officer shouted with his finger trembling on the trigger.

I saw the fear in the police officer's blue eyes as I ran toward Kara and her Thomas.

The wind picked up, carrying the curls away from Kara's fine features. The lines of her face furrowed in diagonal scars of pain stretching over her diamond visage as she screamed at the policemen standing in front of her much taller boyfriend.

"Tell that bitch to shut up!"

Thomas stepped forward, ready to defend his girlfriend just as Brianna

304

had defended me. He stood with his chest broad and his shoulders squared. Through gritted teeth, Thomas growled, his own visage twisting into a demon's mask as he said, "Don't talk to her like that!"

"Fuck this..." I watched those tiny pink lips form the words, that wrinkled finger press down on the trigger and all I thought about was the last time I saw Brianna. The last words I told her.

I really like you, and I hope this ain't the last time we get to chill together. We shared a smile and I stumbled to my house not realizing that would be the last time I would ever see her. It was. And now I knew what it was to stand in her shoes, defending someone else as I pushed Thomas out of the way, not knowing where the strength came from. I widened my stance and spread my arms out as bullets seared through the polyester of my favorite blue blazer and pierced my chest, my abs, my shoulder. I felt like an inferno was blazing through my thigh as another bullet ripped through my fitted blue jeans, knocking me into Kara's arms. She screamed, "Nooooooooooo," but all I could do was smile as I put my hand to my heart, pulling it away to see the dark blood coating the beige cracks in my palm as Kara whimpered one question into my ear. "Why?"

I turned my hand over to see Bri's name tattooed on the outside of my right hand and I smiled, having my answer right in front of me. I whispered with a haggard breath, "Because it was the right thing to do," and then I closed my eyes happy that the last thing I saw was the name of the reason I strove to be great.

***

"So what exactly are you working on, again?" Berna watched the calculations whizzing at a whirling speed on her thin monitor, numbers reflecting on her gold-rimmed reading glasses as she lowered it from her face and spread her fingers further at the bottom of the light-rimmed screen. With a flick of her arm, the petite Hispanic woman, dressed in a flowing white labcoat, brought up the image of double helices forming and an endless array of calculations flowing through the strands. Probabilities ran down the side bar of the image.

Savannah, Berna's best friend, stared at the screen, her youthful, sand-brown features forming a mask of malleable confusion.

"You know what you're looking at?"

Savannah's mouth hung agape, her dark brown eyes wide as they moved slowly in Berna's direction.

"This is the future, Vannah," Berna shouted, jumping up and down with her black Converses pounding against the linoleum floor, eyes alight with excitement and a large, bowing smile emphasizing the dimples underneath the sharp angles of her cheeks.

Savannah looked back at the enlarged screen, shaking her head as Berna walked around her unkempt laboratory.

Berna thrust her hand into a stack of papers and retrieved a novel of white sheets. She pulled the paperwork toward her face. Berna pinched the gold earpiece running alongside her temples, lowering the glasses over the straight bridge of her nose, eyes narrowing as she examined the figures she scrawled across the paper. "Everything is working exactly as I thought it would. My molecular machines have finally applied the correct calculations to build new DNA from scratch. I implanted the serum and science I used to manifest your powers into the DNA," Berna said as she spun on the heel of her sneaker and pinched the air in front of her glasses, bending at the knees as though she was readying her little body to take flight. "And it perfected itself!"

Berna bounded in the air, bouncing among the random trinkets and miniature cranes constantly fixing exoskeletons and robotic figures Berna had built in her spare time.

"Boosie," Berna shouted with child-like excitement pointing at the bulb protruding from the ceiling, light blue cumulus clouds forming in the half-sphere as it came to life. "Music!"

A computerized sing-song voice echoed throughout the spherical laboratory. The machines all around the girl genius' laboratory moved to a melody all of their own.

"What would you like to hear, Berna?" the half-sphere asked.

"Aaliyah! No...Selena! And no sappy shit! I want some happy music," Berna said with arched eyebrows furrowing.

The half-sphere chuckled, the blue clouds lightening into a deep pink and light blue. "Your wish is my command..."

Berna smiled at the thought of the amount of time she spent coding just so Boosie could replicate happiness, her smile spreading that much larger at her success as Selena's *Donde Queira Que Estas* began thumping through the speakers of the laboratory. The video of the late great Selena spread from the center of the enlarged screen that once held all of Berna's calculations until all that was seen was a Hispanic boy band dancing alongside the angel that was once Selena. Berna began mimicking the 90's choreography and Savannah just stared, trying to stifle laughter as she crossed her arms over her chest.

Just then, a great beam of golden light cascaded in the middle of the movement of Berna's laboratory, trumpets signaling the arrival of Thomas. Both Berna and Savannah looked up to see a being bathed in the same golden light descend upon them.

A melodic voice wafted throughout the lab. "What are you doing?"

The golden light receded, revealing a chocolate man with a strong chin and long, braided dreadlocks framing his leonine features before falling over his taut torso. He was a compact man, but his golden tinted angel wings added an undeniable girth to the aura of power that surrounded him.

Savannah felt herself paralyzed under the weight of his dark and judgmental gaze. "I smell an abomination…"

Offended, Berna's disembodied voice filled the expanse as she shouted, "What the fuck!?"

The music video scratched out and TJ's dark eyes cut in Berna's direction as she stomped over the linoleum with her fists against her hips.

"Who do you think you are, coming down here and passing judgment on my shit!?"

"I think," TJ said with an air of smug calm, "I'm the person that helped stop the Armageddon…"

Air whistled out of a pocket in Savannah's cheek as her forehead smacked against the palm of her hand. "Here we go…"

"What," TJ asked with an eyebrow raised, his lip poking out from his jutting chin as he spoke.

"Don't you ever get tired of reminding everybody of that," Berna asked, walking closer to TJ as he descended onto the floor.

His eyes darted toward the myriad of mechanics being created through automatons – wonders built out of nothing and life created out of whirs, sparks, and air. "Don't you get tired of playing God?"

Berna's eyes narrowed before the words, "You would know, huh, Golden Boy?"

TJ shrugged his shoulders as Savannah inched closer to Berna, placing her hand on the shoulder of Berna's labcoat before narrowing her own eyes and asking with disdain dripping off of every word, "What are you here for anyway, Thomas?"

TJ shrugged his shoulders, rolling his head as his dreadlocks waved to the melody of his own voice. "I'm just here to try and convince you that you are making a mistake bringing this abomination into the world."

Berna's fingers formed fists, trembling as she glared at TJ.

Savannah tried to whisper calming words into Berna's ear, grasping both of her shoulders with comforting hands. But Berna was too far gone in her own rage. Berna took one step forward and barked, "And what happens when I tell you to fuck off?"

TJ said nothing, merely raised his hand flat toward the sarcophagus-like object, pale blue light glowing from within. A crooked smile appeared on TJ's smooth features before he said with whispered malice, "Then I'll simply have to be more convincing," as a sphere of golden flame began to form in the palm of his hand.

"You fucking better not!" Berna grew red as the sphere above them gave birth to a brewing storm, complete with lightning crackling, thunder pounding, and black clouds forming in the glass half-ball.

"Stop, TJ," Savannah screamed, but TJ's smile stretched with malice, pointing at the corner of his mouth before the ball of golden flame exploded toward the apparatus that contained Berna's greatest achievement.

Berna's teary eyes followed the blaze.

"No," Berna whimpered as she watched the ball of golden flame crash into the chest of an oversized pink and white jersey.

Savannah's eyes widened as she realized just who it was TJ had struck. "Bailey..."

The flame burned away the polyester of the jersey as a petite young woman stood before them with a snarl on her face and her eyes whited out. Red kinetic energy crackled around her taut and tawny frame. Her curly afro mane billowed like the red flames dancing around her pink and white hi-tops. Her tiny fists shook with contained rage. Berna trembled at the sight of Bailey as a translucent ruby angel wing bloomed from her right shoulder. "Thomas," Bailey growled as she lowered her gaze at the angel that stood wide-eyed and petrified.

Only one word escaped Thomas' lips in a whisper. "Sorry," he said uncertain whether or not that would appease Bailey's rage.

In a flash, Bailey flew toward TJ before striking him with a crippling blow against the strong planes of his cheek. TJ collapsed to his knees, his hand slowly rising to greet the pain thumping in his jaw before he met Bailey's furious eyes with a dark and beady gaze of his own, his expression stoic.

"Stop!" Savannah stepped in between the two with her fists balled.

TJ glared at Savannah as she stood in her power skirt and blue blouse, looking down at TJ with shame painting her expression flat.

"Stop what?" TJ shouted before standing up with trembling fists. He pointed directly at Berna's chest. "She opens up the gates of hell and you tell *me* to stop? She dabbles in God's realm of creation and you order *me* to stop?" TJ reared his curled fingers back, gearing for another attack, as golden flames bloomed inside of his hand. "I won't..."

"TJ," Savannah raised her hands flat before her, voice filled with warning, as TJ extended his hand out toward the apparatus building Berna's greatest achievement.

"Not until..."

Berna screamed, rushing from her lowered stance toward TJ with her hand extended. Lightning began to crackle in the half-sphere as the lights of the laboratory flickered on and off.

"I destroy..."

The apparatus glowed brightly, just as all of the machines stopped whirring and the power went dark.

"That abomination!"

Bailey wrapped her lone angel wing around Savannah as the golden flame burst into an inferno. Berna was flung back. Bailey covered her eyes with the back of her hand. But the conflagration was halted by an undeniable force.

Bailey removed her hand from in front of her face. Berna lifted herself up from the crater her body had created. Machine parts sparked and electricity flickered, but within that darkness one being illuminated in an azure blue aura served as a beacon of light.

Berna gawked at the compact sparkling man with adoration. He hovered in the air, a tiny black man with a coltish frame, lacquered in a thin navy blue polyester coating. The tips of his fingers held jumping blue lightning which doused the golden flames. He looked down at TJ with a glowing icy blue stare that contrasted with his dark brown skin.

Berna saw the dog-shaped birthmark on his left index finger and remembered it was those same tiny fingers that taught her how to count on her hands. She remembered the little girl sitting in her beanbag chair watching as the man floating before her staggered out of the bathroom with sparkling dark eyes and a Crown Royal induced smile cascading down on her. She remembered he inquired about the cartoons she watched, taught her how to count on her fingers, and showed her that there is a simple answer to even the most complex of questions. She remembered the young man dressed in his fitted jeans, blue blazer, and red bow tie entering the church for Savannah's mother's funeral with tears in his eyes, but showing her a smile. Those were the only memories she had of the man that went on to die for the president a year later. A man that taught her about strength. And here he was again, giving another lesson as she simply whispered to herself with unblinking eyes, "Brody..."

Bailey unfolded her wing from in front of Savannah with a wide mouth and unblinking eyes, Savannah's expression mirroring her mentor as Bailey whispered, "Brody," with two tears falling from her eyes. Brody's translucent light blue angel wing beat in the air as he descended before Savannah and Bailey.

TJ backpedaled, arms cocked back as more flames danced on his curled fingers. The utter dismay on his face was replaced by sheer rage as he barked the words, "What have you done," before looking back at Berna while she still gawked at the resurrected Brody. TJ's fingers extended and he shoved the flames forward in a stream of gold, looking to devour the unsuspecting Berna.

Berna could feel the flames inch closer to her; could feel the heat of her coming end. Only the end didn't come. Those same arms that once seemed so small wrapped her in a powerful embrace. That lone angel wing shielded her from the blast, but Berna had not noticed. She was too busy looking at the hairless features of Brody's visage, noticing how he had still not lost the baby fat in his cheeks, the small straight angle of his nose, the curvature of those dark lips forming a tight line on his face, and Berna realized that she had not held on to the memory for nostalgia's sake or even because she was inspired by his memory. The epiphany that she had been in love with the young man that changed her life almost fifteen years ago dawned on her like the son rising over the Sandia Mountains and as he held her close – his slipper covered feet descending on the cracking linoleum – she couldn't help but smile at the fact that her mind had accepted a fact that her heart had always known.

Berna rested her head on Brody's shoulder, closing her eyes as he unfolded his wing and glared at TJ advancing toward him with his hand outstretched before him. His war cry summoned a gilded ivory brand, golden flames covering the white steel as he clutched the golden hilt tightly. But before he could cut the distance between himself and what he deemed the abomination, Savannah leapt through the air with a flying kick that connected with TJ's cheek.

TJ was sent careening into the already broken monitors. Glass shrapnel and electric cords fell over his naked torso.

Savannah landed with a crouch, eyes never leaving the delusional angel.

Brody set Berna down on her feet and walked toward Savannah with Bailey reciprocating his actions. "Are you okay," Brody asked with a combination of the syrupy Southern accent Berna remembered from her memories and the computer-generated voice she had created through countless hours of code.

Savannah said nothing; she just stood erect, looking up at the slightly taller man with wide eyes. Bailey mimicked Savannah's actions.

Brody's eyes roamed over the two women. Berna stood beside him and wrapped her fingers around his hand as she looked up to him, leaning into him before asking, "What's your name?"

Brody looked down on Berna, his expression never changing as his ice-blue eyes softened to a chestnut brown. He shook his head and said with a slight smile and closed eyes, "I don't know. You haven't named me yet."

"But I have..."

Brody, Berna, Bailey, and Savannah turned in TJ's direction to see him rise from the rubble, jabbing his blade into the linoleum and using it to lift himself up. "Abomination," TJ coughed out, glaring at the four of them.

Brody's eyes returned to their ice-blue hue.

TJ wiped the blood trailing from his lips with the back of his hand. He smiled and said with a deep and reverberating bravado, "And I won't stop until I destroy you."

Berna stepped in front of Brody and gesticulated the act of pushing the air as her eyebrows furrowed. "Just stop, TJ! He's not our enemy!"

"Shut up, woman," TJ roared. He whisked his hand through the air, knocking Berna off of her feet with a gust of wind. "He's not our enemy! You're right!"

Brody zipped behind the airborne Berna and caught her mid-air, setting her down slowly with his ice-blue eyes set on TJ.

"He's my enemy and the enemy of God! And as His word dictates..." TJ said with a smile as he turned in their direction. "...no weapon formed against me shall prosper."

TJ lifted his hand in the air, a golden ball of flames forming in the palm of his outstretched hand.

Before the ball could be released, Savannah raced across the cracks in the linoleum once again and surprised TJ with a kick to the solar plexus. Her foot made an indentation in TJ's torso, but he merely looked down at the crater in his chest and raised his gaze to meet Savannah's eyes. A maniacal smile curved over his chocolate features. "No weapon," he whispered before bombarding Savannah with searing flames.

An agonized din rose from deep within her.

"Vannah!" Berna attempted to jump out of Brody's hold, but Brody curled his arms and kept her in his embrace while he watched Savannah's smoking body fall into Bailey's arms.

The scent of singed flesh filled the air.

Time slowed as Bailey looked down at the unconscious Savannah in her arms. She shook Savannah's body but found her to be unresponsive. Tears formed on her dark eyes before the browns of her irises twinkled ruby red. She looked back at TJ with a shell-shocked expression as she gently laid Savannah onto the cracking linoleum. She burst toward TJ, slamming into him with her shoulder.

TJ careened through the wall behind him, with Bailey squeezing him tightly.

Berna kept her eyes locked on Savannah, unsure if her best friend, her sister was just unconscious or had met her demise.

Brody lifted Berna off the ground and walked toward Savannah's still smoking body before setting her down next to Savannah and saying with a soft tone of understanding, "Take care of your friend, okay?"

Berna looked up at Brody as he turned on his heels, leaving her to look at the lone wing beat against the air. Tears raced down her cheeks. She did not understand why it sounded as though Brody said goodbye as he took off through the rift in the wall Bailey and TJ had created.

***

Bailey carried TJ through the mauve and indigo skies above Lexington, KY. They crashed into the roof of The Big Blue Building. Blue-tinted glass cascaded down to the ground.

Bailey rained down blow after blow upon TJ's face. Tears rolled down her beige brown cheeks, her sharp teeth bared as her roar shook the walls around them. "You killed my Vannah!!!!"

Bailey continued to pummel TJ's face until it became a mix of gore and skin.

Memories of her training a young Savannah in the greenery of her Albuquerque home flooded her mind. She recalled the moments in which Savannah had held onto her, crying over the mother she had lost just two years prior. She remembered how she had cried with that little girl, relating to Savannah's loss as she too recalled the loss of her twin brother and her unborn son – the same son she now beat into the carpeted top floor of The Big Blue.

She cocked her arm back with curled fingers around a bright pink ball of crackling energy, ready to send her son back to the Heaven in which he belonged, to greet the adopted daughter he had murdered in cold blood.

"You made me do this, son! You made me!"

Bailey was halfway into thrusting the ball of energy toward his face when a small hand shot toward her arm and wrapped chocolate fingers around her lanky wrist. With teary eyes, Bailey looked up to find her twin brother staring down on her with cold blue eyes shaking his head slowly. In a tremulous tone, Bailey asked, "Why Brody!?"

Brody stared at her for a few seconds, then smiled, as if he had finally realized who he was. "Not right."

Bailey's anger receded as she stood, freeing her son. She wrapped her arms around Brody's strong torso, crying into his chest. Her sobs were drowned out by the din of the sudden winds blowing through the open ceiling.

Brody looked up to the sky, painted by the colors of the setting sun.

The sound of TJ spitting up blood echoed in Bailey's ears. She looked down at her son taking ragged breaths. Two more tears fell from her face as she said, "I'll never forgive you for this, Thomas..." Bailey shook her head slowly. "Never." She looked back up into Brody's eyes with a solemn smile. "Brody..."

He looked at her as if he understood the turmoil within her; as if he understood she could not bear the sight of the son she had miscarried sixteen years ago. Brody nodded, his lone azure blue wing beating against the wind.

In seconds, they were hovering above the downed TJ. Bailey took one last look at her son. Brody's cold gaze measured the sight of his lost nephew, and then, they were off. And TJ remained in the crater as nothing more than the angel defeated by blood.

***

Brody landed on the tiptoes of his lycra covered feet as he looked down on Bailey, feeling as though he finally belonged. He watched Bailey as she walked over to Berna, who was still crying over the body of Savannah. He felt an emotion he could not comprehend; an emotion that left his heart falling to the pit of his stomach.

Bailey knelt next to Berna, placing a comforting hand on her shoulder. Berna looked up at Bailey with tears streaming down her supple features and all Brody could do was tremble, feeling the blood rush through his temples. He placed his hand on his forehead and a low groan reverberated from his dark lips as he crashed down on to one knee.

Brody let out a scream as he bowed low to the ground.

Bailey and Berna looked back at him with concern.

"It hurts! It hurts!" Brody cried in agony. Surrounded by pain and despair, Brody found himself bombarded with memories that weren't his.

The image of a little girl sitting in the dark, watching cartoons filled his mind. He remembered teaching her to count on her fingers. The same little girl made another appearance in another memory that wasn't his as he remembered her smiling up at him at a funeral, bringing warmth in one of the saddest moments of a life he had never lived. More memories poured in as Brody screamed into the Lexington sunset. In another set of memories, Brody saw himself running toward Bailey as she pulled away a taller man that shared an uncanny resemblance to TJ; saw himself pushing Thomas out of the way and standing in front of Bailey with his arms spread wide. Only she wasn't Bailey in his memory. She was Kara. And he was Boosie. The same Boosie that took four shots before falling into Kara's arms.

Brody shook the comforting touches of Bailey and Berna off of him as he stood, still gripping the sides of his head, still screaming so loudly he could not hear Bailey and Berna crying alongside him. He saw it all so clearly that tears coated his long eyelashes. He saw himself looking down at a little girl outside of a church, containing the tears stored inside of him as he apologized to a shell-shocked little girl. An unfathomable guilt filled his heart as he recanted the fact that this little girl looked so much like her mother, his Brianna. He remembered how the only thing Brianna cared about was making the best life for her and her daughter.

Brody's eyes went light blue and the screaming stopped as a sudden and serene epiphany warmed him.

Bailey and Berna both took a breath of relief. They thought his pain was no more. They were wrong. The pain was still there; the anger; the heartache; it was all still in his heart. But along with all of those emotions, there was truth. These memories weren't his, just like this *life* wasn't. It was Boosie's life. And now there was only one thing left for him to do. *Rise.*

***

And rise I did.

A warm light bloomed from my eyes, rendering the entirety of Downtown Nashville into different shades of blue. I took a deep breath as I realized that I was alive, despite all of the gunshots I had suffered. I checked the bullet wounds I had endured to find them cauterized…every single one of them.

I looked up to see Kara, drenched in the light of purple flames, standing before me with a gleaming, purple angel wing jutting from her right shoulder. I My ears perked up as I heard Kara growl, "I won't let you get away with this…"

The police officers stood in the middle of chaos-filled Downtown Nashville, their shouts barely audible above the screams and the panic ensuing all around us, but I heard the trembling words slither out of the police officer's thin pink lips – the same officer that took the first shot. "Don't move!" The other officers stood with unblinking eyes, almost as if they were too afraid to even breathe.

A small sphere of blazes bloomed from Kara's tiny fingers.

An officer fired three rounds toward my sister.

I blinked, and the bullets seemed to slow, as though they were being sucked into a vacuum, before completely stopping in front of the violet flames flickering around Kara. The bullets fell to the cobblestone, melting into pools of metal.

I whispered, "No," as the other officers fired.

Those bullets joined the first melted volley.

Clicks of emptied guns filled the air. I smiled, picking myself up and onto my feet.

Thomas – still lying on the ground – looked up at me with wide, disbelieving eyes. I couldn't blame him. If I was in his shoes, I would have stared, not believing what I saw either. But here I was, walking with azure blue flames swirling all around me, powder blue feathers molting as I felt the presence of an angel wing beating behind me. The wounds that once seemed mortal didn't even bother me, didn't even hinder my gait as I walked toward my sister. I watched, with stoic expression, as Kara raised her right hand in front of her, the sphered flames hovering before her palm, roaring for their chance to devour the police officers.

"You will pay for what you did to my brother..." she said.

I could hear the tears coaxing the vocal chords in her throat. A ball of light warmed my hand as it bloomed inside of my palm. I stepped beside her and threw my arm around her shoulder. I raised my arm before me with fingers spread out. The ball of light surged before my palm. I felt our lone wings beat in unison. I smiled, happy to be reunited with my sister. I spoke slowly and just loud enough for her to hear me through the shouts from the police and the panic happening all around us. "We could destroy them all Sissy..."

I heard the police officers reload their clips, ready to empty another volley at us.

Kara's deep violet eyes relaxed, turning navy blue. Even though it seemed her attention was rapt on the trembling officers in front of us, I could tell I had her ear. I whispered, "We could destroy them all. But then we would have to destroy *all* those that would seek to destroy us." The flames dancing around us blended into a brilliant shade of violet as I closed the palm of my hand and extinguished the light inside it. "We would have to kill everyone, for leaving even one would leave us a lot of sleepless nights, worrying about what they would do to us. What they would do to the people that we leave defenseless." I pushed her arm down gently. The flames crackled around her fingers, dying. The sound of guns cocking filled my ears, but a gentle smile curved on my face. "Or we could uplift our people, and lead them by example. Just as we did so many centuries before."

I could see the smile that wasn't on her face sparkle in her eyes as she looked up at me before nodding her head I stared at the police officers pressing down on their triggers. My eyes narrowed as my right hand shot out in front of me. The bullets stopped in their trajectories and fell to the cobblestone in a succession of clinks. Our wings carried us backward and we scooped Thomas into our arms and took him into the embrace of the Nashville night.

And as we hovered above the gaping mouths of the police officers, I realized I would never be a great poet or the great author Brianna thought me to be. I closed my eyes, tears coating my long eyelashes as I realized just how close I was to meeting her again. But then, I realized, this was my chance to make my life into the great story she inspired me to write. And as I said just months ago, I said it again under my breath. *I won't let you down, Bri.*

A MONSTROUS JOURNEY
Mark P. Steele

Featuring the original Arrow.

Special thanks to Eric Roman; dedicated to Paul Gustavson.

The moon above shone down, but the lights of the city, even during the year 1939, gave scant allowance for the brightness above to penetrate past the hazes within the air. But the shadows deepened even so, casting a pall around the high buildings and the now-quiet waterfront warehouses, where the still of the night held sway.

A figure flitted from shadow to shadow, the night cloak he wore over the more brilliant red beneath dimming his form. The hood he wore, and the darker mask beneath, kept all but the slightest glimmer of his eyes, peering through lenses, from being seen should any be able to spy his stealthy form.

The tip he'd got indicated that something wrong – something that the police didn't wish to stake out – was going on near here. There had been disappearances among the street people of the time, and no one knew where the missing might be. Such always happened, and often, bodies turned up in the river or hidden within the scant regions of wilderness near New York. But this was more than the usual numbers. No one seemed to care when people from the Bronx, Brooklyn and Harlem vanished from the Five Boroughs, as long as Park Avenue, Queens and the brownstones of Manhattan were left untouched.

The man glanced around, his senses alert, his eyes peeled, his hearing tuned to the slightest sounds, despite the covering of cloth over them. He slowly turned his head, scanning, searching for...

And there it was.

From a darkened region off to his left, a slight moan could be heard. His eyes fastened there, trying to pierce the gloom that lingered like a veil across the city's dilapidated waterfront. He focused his eyes on the source of the moaning and stealthily, quietly headed toward it.

It was a man, dressed in ill-fitting rags, sores on his arms and legs, a putrid odor coming from the open wounds. Glancing around, the Arrow saw no traces of anyone around, no footprints of any others, simply the tracks of this man in the slight muddy traces the misty rain had left that night. These streets were seldom cleaned, and the buildup of debris in the street was sufficient enough to leave something that he could survey.

The groaning man, about 40, pale of skin, his hair brown, was quite thin, as if he hadn't eaten in quite a while. His eyes were bloodshot, and wandered aimlessly, out of focus, not appearing to be tracking anything that the world around might display. Taking his drawn arrow into the fingers of the bow hand, the Arrow stepped slowly forward, senses alert for anything around that might be a sign of danger. Gingerly, he felt for the man's pulse, listened to his breathing.

The pulse was thready but steady, slightly fast, but not strong. The man's breath came raspy, forced, as if there was something inside blocking the airway. The Arrow, though not a medic, had picked up a few things in his years and could tell, even without the aid of a clock, the basics of checking the injured. He glanced around again and, hearing nothing, leaned forward, speaking quietly:

"Rest easy, old man...I'll try and get you to help."

The man's eyes flew sharply into focus, and stared at the dark hood the other wore. A look of fear came over his face.

"No!" He reached up and pushed against the Arrow's chest. "Don't take me back there! I can't stand it! All those people...the dying...the dead...and the others..." The man's shoving was weak, not a threat, a futile act of resistance should the Arrow have posed a threat. But the fear was real.

"Shh...I'm not one of them...whoever they are." He reached for the man's hands and then stopped. A sound, a slight whisper of breeze from behind him that was from something other than the wind whistling through the city, brought his attention around. He re-armed his bow and turned round.

"NO!" The man near him pointed as he turned, and started screaming, the night pierced by the anguish.

There, framed by the street light, standing over him at almost twice his height, stood the figure of...well, it *resembled* a man, but yet it wasn't. Its limbs were misshapen, large, lumpy, as if formed by some mad sculptor from partially hardened clay. The eyes were uneven, not spaced right, and its lips were twisted and drooling. One eye was focused on the Arrow, the other looking off somewhere toward the man who lay so close. A strange grunting, soft but powerful, emerged from the creature's throat, covering the sounds of the city around them.

"Get back!" The Arrow pulled his arrow back as the monster came toward him and the injured old man...

***

Edward Richard Bowyer couldn't remember his parents. They passed on before he became aware of the world enough for his memories to start. As near as he could tell, he'd always lived at the circus owned and run by his uncles. Back in the days when Barnum and Bailey and the Ringling Brothers were making their marks, some time after the old Buffalo Bill Wild West shows had wound down, the Hillman Circus of the Stars was starting to climb. And it was due to the two men Eddie called uncles.

Though they sent white front men into towns to do their business, the owners were somewhat unusual for the 1920s. One was a "negro" – what they now call a Black man – and the other "Indian" – now called Native American. These were the men Eddie Bowyer looked up to, idolized, strove to be like when he was grown, and to whom he owed his youthful living.

But there were times...

The trapeze had been something he loved watching from his youngest days. Watching Grissom up above, with his new wife, soaring in the air with just the thin bars and thinner ropes to support them, and only the flimsiest of nets below in case they fell, was one of his favorite sights in the world. He was watching them one day, smiling and moving his arms back and forth, ignoring the cleaning detail he'd been assigned in his joy over the sight of their practice.

"Like that, huh?" Eddie looked over. It was his uncle Benny, smoking his cigar. He pulled the cheroot from his lips and pointed toward the acrobats with it. "Want to join them?"

"Oh, can I, Uncle Ben?" A gleam of excitement came over Eddie's face, and he looked back toward them. His uncle nodded.

"Hey! John! You and your bride got room for my Eddie-boy up there?" His uncle shouted, and the trap artist paused when he reached the pole, looking down.

"Sure thing, Mr. Lamont. Send him on up!"

Nervously, Eddie went to the pole and climbed up it, looking down only once, and then closing his eyes...but just for a moment. Gritting his teeth, he finished his way up, and made it to the platform near the top.

"Here y'go, bud," the trap artist said, swinging one of the bars toward him. Eddie caught it, and looked down, swaying just a bit, his throat in his mouth. "Just hold tight and swing when you're ready. Stop looking down." The man looked at Eddie, and the young man looked back, gulped a bit, and then swung out, his hands firmly gripped on the bar.

As he headed toward the trap artist he felt freed, light, as if there weren't a care in the world. Smiling, he swung toward the other, and reached him. John Grissom helped him on to the other platform, and all seemed right.

"That was an easy one, it gets harder when you have to use more than one swing. But it's a start."

"I wanna go back!"

The man frowned. "There's no one over there to help you off. It might not work out as well."

"Oh, I can do it! I saw you do it lots of times." Eddie smiled, still keeping his eyes off the ground. Reluctantly, the acrobat let Eddie turn and again grasp the bar.

"This time, think more about form. Not just getting across, but how it looks...how your motions either help you or hinder you. Grasp it tight, but don't squeeze...that can tire the arm muscles. And you don't want that!" John gripped the bar, and showed Eddie how. "Now, just stay relaxed, keep your arms straight, and when your feet hit that platform over there... don't let go right away, get your balance. Ready?"

Eddie nodded and began his arc across to the other side, but before he could reach it, he heard the shout from below:

"Running Bear!"

Hearing his "Indian name," he looked down, and...he lost it. Seeing the distance to the ground below, he froze. His feet hit the platform but he did not get his balance. Then, as he fell backward off the platform, he lost his grip and began plummeting.

He hit the net with his left shoulder, twisted and landed yet again, and eventually stopped.

"You don't go up there. I told you that."

"Oh, let him, Nick...the kid's gotta grow up some time. Better he learn now than wait." Uncle Ben puffed his cigar, staring down his son's father-in-law. Nick looked on stoically, his eyes shifting between Eddie and Ben. Then, finally, sighing, he looked up at the trap artist.

"Can you help him, Grissom? Are you one of the trusty ones?"

The trap artist nodded, smiling down. "Sure thing, Mr. Long Bow...the kid did great on his first try. I'll have him flying up here in no time!"

Sighing quietly, the tall, long-haired circus partner turned, and as he strode off, glanced over toward Eddie.

"Don't fall again!"

***

The Arrow drew back the shaft, sighting along it, aiming for one of the creature's thighs. "Stay back!" He watched carefully, trying to get some sense of what this manlike being might be.

The creature lumbered forward, arms raised, the odd sounds coming from its throat resounding off the concrete surrounding them.

"I warned you! Stay back!"

But the words were in vain. The creature continued forward, accompanied by the screech of the injured man's hysteric calls joining with the on-comer's wheezing and rumbling in a cacophony of noise.

"Shoot it! Kill it! It'll get us! Kill it!"

"Last warning, big man!" The Arrow sighted carefully, though the shot was simple, to make sure that it would just go to muscle, not artery. Then he let loose.

The arrow went quickly across the short distance, piercing the thigh of the so very odd man...for yes, the hero had decided it was, indeed, a man, though one unlike anything he'd ever seen before. As the arrow entered, another was drawn and quickly notched.

A scream from the throat of the huge man-creature pierced the night, almost giving shivers to the Arrow. But the thing didn't stop.

Swiftly, the Arrow released his next shaft, piercing the Achilles tendon. The over-sized brute stumbled, fell, unable to stand. But he kept coming. With his one good leg and his arms he drew himself onward, toward the two men.

Reaching down, the Arrow grabbed the other off the pavement just as he lost consciousness. Swiftly he headed away from the giant down the alley.

And there, standing in front of them, were two more of the creatures.

***

The years passed swiftly, and Eddie learned much...how to swing, how to do some magic tricks, how to shout at the barkers. But to the crowds he was nothing but one of the clean-up crew that took care of the tents and the grounds. He couldn't perform for any but the circus crowd. And while they all loved him, they understood and kept to his uncle's wishes.

Slowly, Eddie started to understand the differences color made...the differences in the way that the people treated him when they came in for the show. Somehow, the way these people called him "boy" sounded different from when his uncles and the circus folk used the same word. And then there were the other words...

One day, a mysterious man came to join the troupe. His uncles treated him quite respectfully, and he began a sharp-shooting act that drew the crowds in well. His sense of showmanship was on a high level, and the strange black hood he wore added to the mystique of the Hooded Marksman. Though he shot guns, he knew something about the bow and arrow and was able to take what Eddie's uncle Long Bow had taught him and develop it into a fine art.

On the day the Hooded Marksman left, he spent some time with Eddie.

"Ah hope that shootin' ah helped yuh with will serve you good some day." The man smiled. His older face, about the same age as his uncles, crinkled into a smile.

"I hope so. I want to do something in the show eventually, but..."

The man nodded. "I know. The world hasn't treated your people well. My dad fought in the War to help free them." He sighed. "Ah barely knew him...muh uncle helped teach me right from wrong back in the day."

Eddie nodded back. Though there were few things about his past the man talked about, his slight drawl...something that when he talked to Eddie's uncles seemed to fade back...sounded Texan to him, though there was a slight trace of Northerner to it. "So we're both orphans?"

"'Fraid so. My dad died later than yours...I still remember him some. But it was rough." He sighed. "Ah have a son, back home, but..." He shrugged. "He's a bit of a no-account, ah don't know what's goin' to happen to him. Ah hope he amounts to sumthin' when he gets older." The man sighed, then, with a decisive look on his face, opened one of the bags he had packed. The cabby hadn't arrived yet, and the Marksman decided there was time.

"Ah got sumthin' for ya." He reached into the bag and pulled out a dark leather thing. He handed it over to Eddie.

It was his mask.

"Ah got that from my uncle. He made it when my dad died, and...well, never mind, that's not important. Here. It's yours."

Eddie gasped, taking the mask in his hands and running his fingers across the length of the face part. "You're sure? You might want this someday...maybe for your own boy?"

The Marksman shook his head. "Naah...and if I do, I have other masks. My uncle only wore this till he got the owl-hoot that killed off my dad. Then he hung it up, and eventually gave it to me. Now it's yours. Go ahead...try it on!"

Eddie put the mask on, and though it was still a bit loose, it was comfortable. The other man smiled.

"Now you look the part! Who knows...with that, maybe you can get a job in the circus without anyone getting' bugged 'bout your color!"

And with those words, the cab arrived, and the man drove off, headed toward the train station and the life his vacation had brought him from.

***

The Arrow shot off a few shafts, but the monsters were too close...they had reached the pair of them. Balling his fists, the masked man punched at them.

But it did no good. The things were too big, too strong, too resistant to pain.

Eventually, the creatures' blows took their toll and he lost consciousness.

When he awoke, he found himself in chains.

He looked around, and there were people around...most injured, screaming; some, the huge monster-types he'd seen earlier. But they all mostly seemed to be in bondage, except a select few that were keeping tabs on the others.

And then there was the man in the chair.

He was dapper, somewhat thin, but not unhealthy. He was reading a book when the Arrow awoke, but put it up as the masked man looked at him.

"Ah...you're awake! Good...I've been waiting for that. It works so much better than when you're unconscious. Something in the brain chemistry, I believe."

The Arrow shook his head, trying to clear it. And it was then that he realized that he wasn't wearing his mask.

The other man smiled. "Worried about your identity? Don't be...I really don't care who you were...only what you're about to become." He rose, and strode toward the Arrow.

"What do you mean?"

"I mean, Mr. Arrow, that you're about to become the latest in my line of experiments."

The Arrow struggled against the chains holding him, arms outstretched, several inches above the floor, but to no avail. The cuffs were tight...more tight than the bonds that escape artist had taught him how to slip off. He gave up quickly, conserving his strength.

"Who are you?"

"Oh, just call me the Professor. I like that." He grinned. "I have read Arthur Conan Doyle's works, you know."

"You're a madman! Like one of those mad scientists in the magazines and comic strips."

The Professor shook his head. "Oh, far from it. Indeed, my experiments may be what lead to the survival of humanity."

***

Shortly after the Masked Marksman's departure, the Circus was sold. His uncles, through the use of a well-paid front man, had arranged the sale, and now it was finished. They were in a hotel room in Florida, near the winter camping area that they and other circuses used. His uncles had bought a special bottle of wine and Ben was pouring it. He took two glasses over to Long Bow and Eddie, then lifted his own.

"We did it! We brought this enterprise up...despite all odds...and made it a going concern! Now we've ensured our future." He smiled.

"But what about Running Bear? How will he survive?" Long Bow frowned. "What he's learned won't serve him in good stead in this world." The man set his cup down, the Indian broken English he often used among the rubes nowhere apparent.

"Hell, he'll survive! He's a good kid, and he'll go far. Besides..." ...Ben shrugged... "...eventually, he'll inherit what we left behind. And with our investment in the stock market, he'll be well-heeled after that. We ain't no spring chickens no mo'!" He lifted his glass. "Here's a toast.

"To the future!"

And with that, all three clicked glasses, rose them on high, and drank the sparkling wine in the glasses.

It was Tuesday, October 29, 1929...a day that was soon to be known as Black Tuesday.

***

The Professor strode forward, examining the Arrow as he did. He reached forward and pinched the hero's arm. Immediately, the avenger raised his shackled feet and swung them, hitting the Professor hard enough to throw him off balance...but the mad scientist moved quickly backward, out of reach. The red-clad adventurer began swinging on the chains holding him, but to no avail.

"Naughty, naughty...there's no use trying to struggle. Despite your fitness of form...something my other subjects generally lack...you can't escape my bonds. And you'll be...perhaps...one of the saviors of the teeming masses of humanity."

"What do you mean?"

"I mean that the world's going to hell in a hand-basket. I'm sure you remember the stock market's crash." He stared into the Arrow's eyes, but the hero let no trace of his feelings shine through, his face a mask still despite the lack of the leather covering. Faced with silence, the Professor continued.

"That crash showed the weakness of humanity. We've come far since the days our species started. Darwin made it clear, you know." He sighed. "If only he'd had more sense."

"What does that have to do with anything?"

"Everything...and nothing. Do you remember hearing about those people plunging themselves out of buildings when they lost their stocks?"

The Arrow nodded, his face still stoic."

"Well, that just shows that humanity's evolution toward brain power has been incomplete...not fully productive." He smiled. "Despite my own genius, I recognize the problems that have happened over the last...well, since the few people migrated northeast of the cradle of our kind and began the mutations that would eventually lead a great deal of the world toward this."

"And what, exactly, does that mean."

"It means, my dear hero..." ...the man moved toward his throne-like chair... "...that I've been striving to return the physical fitness to the human race so that we can survive. Things won't go on like this forever. The population will increase, and the intelligent will compete with the brutes over the right to survive." He reached down toward the table beside the throne.

"So...what is it you plan to do?"

"Plan? Oh, no...it's what I am doing! Look around." He swung his arm, indicating the length and breadth of the chamber.

The Arrow looked, his eyes moving, scanning, taking in the details of the layout. There were a few of the giants there, in various states of disfigurement, standing, making their wheezing sound. And there were others, in various states of change, scattered around in cages, some locked in chains, others seemingly unable to move.

"These are my subjects. I've found, using certain herbal preparations that – well, never mind, I don't believe my research into double helixes will mean a thing to you." He reached down and took the Arrow's mask from the table, studying it for a moment. "You won't be needing this any longer." He tossed it aside.

"So...I'm going to become one of your 'monsters' now?" The Arrow stared the Professor straight in the eyes.

"Oh, no, my dear Arrow...these creatures are simply a phase of my research. But you..."

"Your people are closer to the original stock of humanity...ruder, tougher, with less of the brain mutations that are helping to ruin this world. And, as such...with your excellent physique, and the obvious skills you've had to use in your current position...you form the ideal subject for the next phase of my experimentation." He reached over and pushed a button. Immediately, the Arrow was hoisted up into the air by the chains attached to the manacles around his wrists. When he reached the height, the chains began moving...heading him toward some kind of bubbling, steaming vat full of glop.

He began struggling, writhing, trying to figure some way out of this.

"Say goodbye, Mr. Arrow...your days are gone. Look boldly at the new world!"

***

Eddie's uncles were dead within six months of the stock market crash. The Arrow's records, for that time and later, give no indication of exactly how they died. It is known, however, that he stood at their graves months later, sighing and giving what he thought would be his last respects to them. Then, his back toward the past, he began the next step in his life. Getting into the truck that was part of his inheritance, he drove off.

For several years he squatted in a little cabin in the woods, living off the land, and occasionally doing things with the Seminole, who lived nearby. His shooting became better, and he kept the few articles he'd saved from the circus days, carefully wrapped and packaged. Though he needed some of it, there was much that he had no use for, but couldn't bear to part with.

Eventually, someone showed up, claiming to be the owner of the property Eddie lived on. He came with officers with guns, and told Eddie he had only a short time to get out or they'd throw him out. Eddie spent the next 24 hours packing everything he had in the back of the now much used truck, and headed north...to New York City.

When he got there, he looked at the tall buildings, the crowded streets, the scent of things in the air and smiled. Somehow...he'd come home.

Though he didn't have much money, he did have a plan. He went to the Metropolitan Museum and spoke to the Curator, whom he'd contacted earlier.

"So...what is it you wished me to see?"

"These." Eddie unpacked several of the packages he'd brought in, and laid some items out on the display table that sat nearby. The Curator examined them, and nodded.

"I remember some of these...they were part of the exhibition that your uncles had put together. But..." ...the man frowned... "...I'm afraid I don't have any use for them here. I'm sorry, Edward...I wish you the best of luck."

330

Dejected, the young man packed his belongings and started heading toward the door.

"Just a minute."

Edward turned, a puzzled look on his face.

"Some of those items look pretty well kept. And though many had obviously been used...I know it's been a few years since your uncles died. How did they stay in such great repair. Some of those things are nearly a hundred years old."

The young man smiled. "I was taught how to do that by some of them in the company. And I've been doing it myself since then."

The Curator nodded. "Come with me." They walked down a long hallway, and ended up far from the man's office, in the back of the building where the display routes didn't lead. He opened a small door and waved Edward in.

"I've got something here to test your skills." He pointed toward a table on which several beat-up objects of historical interest were laid. "We just lost our chief restorer, and there's enough happening right now that his assistant can't keep up with the demand. We've been assisting other museums in this restoration work." He smiled, his arm sweeping to indicate the repair materials around the room. "Work on these awhile, and I'll check back in a few hours to see how you're doing."

And with that Edward got his job at the Metropolitan Museum.

***

The chains drew him onward, and soon he was above the bubbling cauldron, large enough to hold a man. It was deep; the steel walls lined with something about two feet thick...something the Arrow couldn't identify.

As he moved, the force of his efforts to free his hand scraped his wrists and blood started trickling down; flowing down the length of his arm. He stopped...no sense in that, he'd need his bow arm after he got out, he thought.

"I am looking forward to this." The Professor smiled. "Most of my subjects are screaming and yelling by now, some pleading for their release, others simply wailing at what they believe is their fate. But you..." ...the man threw out his arms in an expansive gesture... "...you strive to escape, to set your own course in the world, to avoid the destiny that now is yours." He chuckled, his finger pushing a button.

The chains turned around the pulley above, lengthening, decreasing the Arrow's height. As he approached the vat, he moved his legs up, delaying the plunge into the glop for as long as he could. His arms now valiantly struggled against the manacles, the injuries no longer a consideration in his mind.

But it was to no avail, the descent continued. And, with the pressing of a second button, the Arrow, every nerve in his body screaming with pain, plunged into the glop.

***

For a few years Edward lived life well. His museum job helped pay the bills, and nights, he took the sax one of the musicians in the show had given him and wailed it out at various places. Though it took a while, he soon earned his reputation. There are stories that he even played the *Cotton Club*.

And then came Tanya.

She was an artist in the Harlem Renaissance. Though her skills had made some paintings that went for a bit, her true skills and her heart – until Edward came along – was in photography. Though some of her living came from sales to various newspapers, it was in the exhibitions that the true value of her work became known. Investors, knowing the quality of her work, began purchasing some of her photographs.

The Arrow's journals don't cover the part of Edward meeting her for the first time...the pages for that time are ripped out. But there are some things about her in them.

She was prim and proper, always dressing elegantly. Her beauty was extraordinary. And she disdained the slang Edward had picked up in the jazz clubs, preferring good enunciation as the New York Intelligentsia practiced. So he began making sure to use his "telephone voice" he'd picked up from his uncles with her.

And, of course, she...wanted to wait until marriage.

Richard knew that's what he wanted to do. So, after a while, when they dated, he got up the courage to buy the engagement ring, and shortly proposed. She accepted.

It was an unusual day that June in 1938. There was a concert nearby, and they decided to go. The performers included Count Basie, the Andrews Sisters, Benny Goodman and many other noted performers from the day, whose songs were going out through the air waves across the country. Jazz, it seemed, was here to stay, and they enjoyed the festivities.

After a while, having recognized Edward in the crowd, one of the performers came to the mike.

"Friends, we have among us tonight one of the hottest sax men playing these days...and we want him to come on stage with us now for a jam.

"Ladies and Gentlemen, I ask you now to join in a round of applause for...Edward Bowyer!"

With an expression of surprise on his face, Edward looked around. There was a knowing smile on Tanya's face, and she waved him up there.

The improv set they played there was one of the classics. Though it was never recorded and wasn't broadcast, the tales of that day were passed down for several generations and written up in Langley's "The Jazz Greats" and other texts from those times. When the show ended, Edward came down, exhilarated, and rejoined his new fiancee.

And it was then that they headed to...that movie.

***

The Arrow writhed beneath the surface of the glop, his skin burning, his eyes watering; the bubbling around him growing stronger by the moment. He lost all track of the time, no idea how long he was down there. He knew that eventually he had to open his mouth and the glop went into him...into his lungs. But he could breathe it. Somehow, the substance was able to go in and out of him, and though his breathing was now labored, he didn't suffocate.

He kept struggling, unable to give it up, pitting his strength against the chains and manacles, but making no more difference than when he'd been hanging outside the vat.

Until one of the chains cracked.

The Arrow heard the popping noise as a line appeared on the surface of the chain. Surprised, he pulled harder. The gap opened, and began to separate. Soon the link was broken, and the Arrow's arm came plummeting down.

He did the same with the other, then grabbed one of the manacles with the other hand. The metal crumpled, no longer resistant to his strength. After undoing the other, he reached down and did the same to the manacles around his legs.

Now freed, the Arrow pushed upward and the strength in his legs sent him through the glop and his face broke the surface. He kicked, reached the edge of the cauldron, and held on, pulling himself up and out of the metal bucket. Then he looked around.

And saw carnage.

The cell doors were all open now, and though some were empty, most still had something in them. The bodies of the occupants lay within their cells, some appearing torn apart, as if by some strong wild beast; others, with their throats slit, the blood surrounding their fallen corpses. There were no signs of either the Professor or the creatures he'd created.

Then, he heard a noise.

Moving quickly, he donned his mask, grabbed his bow and arrow, and made it up the skylight over the room within a matter of minutes. Then the police entered as the door broke down. He looked down at them.

"Some mad scientist did this...him and his crew. I'll be following up on this." And with those words, he vanished through the skylight.

***

The movie starred Errol Flynn in *The Adventures of Robin Hood*. Tanya cuddled close to Edward, especially during the rescue scenes near the end. When it ended they headed out into the streets.

"He's just so...so dashing! The way he helped all those people...I especially liked how he escaped from the castle." She smiled, reaching over toward his chest.

He frowned and shrugged. "I don't know...seemed like a show-off to me."

"You don't understand...he was doing it all for the people. After all, not everyone can do what he did."

"I can!"

"Oh, Edward..."

He headed toward the street, jumping up, and pushing himself upward on top of a mailbox. "Just watch this, Tanya!" He hurtled outward, landing on the top of a taxi-cab, the driver of which started cussing him out.

"See?" He ignored the shouts of the balding driver.

"Edward Bowyer, you get off of that! I won't have the police taking you away the same day we get engaged!" She appeared to be angry, but Edward could see the hint of a smile in the corners of her mouth.

And then a gunshot resounded. They looked off in the direction it had come from. Around a corner came a car, filled with thugs, one hanging out the passenger window and firing at a pursuing cop car.

"Tanya! Get down!" Edward screamed, seeing where they were headed. But it was too late.

A single shot was all it took. It's uncertain where it hit her. Though Edward thought it was in her head, the account he left much later – when he'd discovered the hidden chambers beneath the Metropolitan Museum, where he could keep his private journal in secrecy – with one of the masked mystery men...the Clock, or one of the two people calling themselves that...is unclear.

"NO!" He screamed, rushing toward her. "Hold on love..." He looked up, screaming, "Help! Someone, help her! Please!"

She looked up at him, her blood flowing, and whispered, with almost no strength left, "Edward...remember me..." And with that, her eyes closed and she never spoke again.

Though Edward believed right then that she was dead, the ambulance that came thought differently. There were some signs of life, so they loaded her into the back of the hearse-like vehicle, and took the pair off.

But they passed the closest hospital.

"What are you doing?"

"We're taking her to Harlem Hospital for treatment."

"No...you just passed one. She needs to get to the closest one."

"We can't do that."

"She's dying! Take her there!"

"No can do, bub."

Angrily, Richard moved forward in the cramped confines of the vehicle, toward the driver. But the orderly stopped him, an angry expression on his face.

"Look, nigger, we got her, and we're taking her to the only place one of your kind might get help. Even if we did take her there, she wouldn't get treated. So it's Harlem or nowhere. Got it?"

Stunned, Edward sat, motionless, the weaving of the car throwing him around.

And Tanya died that day, nearly eighty years ago, for the simple reason that she was Black.

***

After her death, things moved quickly. Knowing that the police had little chance of finding the gunman, Edward donned the garb he'd inherited from the circus, including the mask, and for the first time, he went out as the Arrow. He captured the gang, but they got off in court...most likely because his testimony came from a Black man about a white man.

With the gunman's release, Edward continued his guise as the Arrow, and eventually caught the trio again, with the assistance of a young Japanese man whom Edward let have the original mask. He fought many street thugs, and brought many to justice, reserving the fatal black arrow he carried for those un-prosecutable that he knew for a fact were guilty.

***

Eventually, the Professor ran across his trail. And the Arrow, now possessing incredible strength, did trace him down to a mountain hideaway where the operation was shut down for good.

The Arrow's career after the bombing of Pearl Harbor is sketchy, as the records don't go beyond that. Though it covers some major items – his membership in the Fair Players' Club and the Centurions – his role in defeating the Eski-Mongolian Invasion after the first Wonder Villain group formation, his "retirement" in frustration when some tried to get him to use gimmicked arrows, and the assumption of the Arrow mantle by his government liaison, Ralph Payne, are all items on record.

Though largely forgotten by the world at large, the original Arrow has the distinction of differing from the masked mystery men that appeared before his debut, both the fictional ones and the ones that appear to have basis in the events of the time. Though there was a tale of a wonder-powered man in the comics of the time that was released shortly before Tanya's death, and the purple-clad African adventurers had become published by that time, the Arrow has the distinction of being the first of the new generation of Costumed Adventurers that arose in the years before World War II to help combat the Nazi menace.

And his death and final fate are, as far as anyone is aware, still unknown...

THE SUPERHERO'S FATTER COUSIN
Valerie Puissant

The scent of rotting flowers assaulted my sensitive nostrils. I looked up from the bonsai tree I was trying to trim and stared into the saddest, most wilted flower bouquet I had ever seen. Beyond the bouquet, I spied the slightly wall-eyed gaze of my best friend, Starkeisha Berry. "Didn't anybody ever teach you how to knock? What if I had been in here naked or, I don't know, doing important guy things?" I tried to sound irritated, but I'd known her since kindergarten and we both knew she never bothered to knock.

She rolled her slightly misaligned eyes, then wiggled the foul smelling arrangement in my face. "Well? Can you fix em? It's Momma's birthday today and I didn't have no money to get her nothing."

"Do I even want to know where you got this from? You haven't been grave robbing have you?"

She kicked me lightly in the shin. "Boy! What you think I am, some kind of criminal? A grave robber at that? First of all, that shit will get you sent straight to hell. Second, how Imma be a criminal when my best friend is a superhero?"

My name is Shacorey Watts. I am a B student at Washington High. I'm a short, fat, bookworm, and yes, technically speaking, I am also a superhero. My origin story is short and sweet. Super powers run in my family. I was born with a gift, but it is the lamest superpower known to man. The end.

"Hello! Earth to Corey! You need some hearing aids now to go with those Coke bottle glasses?" Starkeisha had her other hand on her slender hip. She tapped her foot impatiently.

"I'm still waiting to hear where you got these things. I'm not going to help you until I know."

Starkeisha rolled her eyes. "I got em from the dumpster behind the flower shop. Somebody threw they lunch on top of it so the wrapping paper is nasty. I can throw that part away though if you can make the flowers look nice again."

I've heard people joke about the superhero who can talk to fish. "That's the worst power in the world," they say. That's because they haven't met me.

My superpower is gardening. That's right, I have a Super Green Thumb. Needless to say, cool costumes and crime fighting are not in my future. Giving my friend's mom a happy birthday surprise was definitely doable. "Yeah, I think I can fix em. Let's go across the street to the empty lot. The weeds are getting pretty tall over there anyway."

We picked our way through the empty cans and broken bottles until we reached the middle of the lot and then I took the dying flowers from her. I stretched out my hand and felt the life force of the weeds surrounding us. Weeds get a bad rep. They are survivors and they thrive in the most unlikely places. They provide food and shelter for all kinds of wildlife. Some of them are actually quite pretty. I kind of hated to take their lives, especially here in an empty lot where they weren't doing anybody any harm, but I looked into the expectant eyes of my friend. I'd known her mom all my life and she was going through a rough time. I knew how much Mrs. Berry liked flowers, and I wanted to give her a good birthday. I pushed down my reservations and channeled the life energy from the weeds, through my body, and into the pretty, useless bouquet, bringing it back to life.

Starkeisha took the bundle from my hand and inhaled the fresh floral perfume. A wide grin parted her full, perfect lips and she leaned over and kissed me on the cheek. Her athletic body pressed against mine as she leaned in and I felt my face heat up. I was glad my skin was dark enough to hide the color I knew was rising in my cheeks. "Tell me again why you ain't using your power for something good like ending world hunger?"

I pointed to the wide circle of dead plant life surrounding us. "Because, I can't give life to one plant without taking it from another. I don't even want to think about what would have to die in order for me to give life to one acre of farmland. Face it, my power is practically useless."

She cradled the beautiful, multicolored bouquet in her arms. "My moms won't think your power is so useless. She loves flowers more than anything." I heard the break in her voice.

Starkeisha's mom was sick. Doctors were doing everything they could, but she didn't seem to be getting any better. "I hope they'll make her happy," I said, touching my friend's arm. The weeds would grow back because survival was in their nature and their temporary sacrifice would not be in vain.

We delivered the flowers together. Mrs. Berry smiled wide, despite the dark circles under her eyes. We made her tea because she said she wasn't really hungry for cake or anything else. I kissed her on the forehead and we left her to rest because the small celebration had worn her out. "She lookin' much better today, ain't she?" Starkeisha smiled weakly as she spoke.

"Yeah, she sure is." She wasn't looking better and we both knew it. I wished I could use my powers to give life to Mrs. Berry the way I had given it to the flowers, but I couldn't. My powers only worked on plants. I felt helpless and useless, knowing there was nothing I could do for the people I cared about the most.

Luckily I didn't have much time to dwell on it before a thickly muscled arm slammed into my soft, midsection and knocked the air out of my lungs. I was lifted off my feet and suddenly the world was moving by me in a blur. The only words I heard were "Dammit, Starkeisha! Let go of my cape! You're strangling me!" I didn't hear her respond, but I couldn't draw a breath so if she was along for the ride, I doubted she had the wind to respond either. We stopped just as I thought my lungs would explode. I dropped to my knees, coughing and spluttering and staring down at my own living room carpet. I finally caught my breath and looked up. Then I looked up some more, past a giant, spandex covered wall of muscle and into the masked face of this state's greatest superhero. He smiled down at me. "Hello, cousin." His voice was low and gravelly and completely unnatural. It was all I could do to stop myself from rolling my eyes at him.

"Cut the action hero speak, Kevin. You sound ridiculous."

In my generation, two of us inherited super powers. There's me and there's my older cousin. He got the super strength and super speed plus the rock hard body and chiseled good looks of a real superhero. The world knows him as Super Soartastic. I know him as the big cousin who always sat on my head and farted at family gatherings. Nowadays he fights for truth and justice. Back then he fought to get enough fiber in his diet. We're cool now, I guess. He's a few years older than me and living on his own, conquering evil in the big city. I'm still stuck in the burbs just trying to conquer eleventh grade.

"What in the hell is wrong with you??" Starkeisha punched him in the arm, hard enough to make my super cousin flinch. "How you gon' come up and grab somebody like that? Did you ever hear of asking? You don't gotta suffocate nobody, going super speed just to carry us three blocks. We coulda just walked like normal human beings."

Kevin looked around the room like he thought it might be bugged. "I didn't want anyone to see me in the neighborhood. I'm here on superhero business." He looked at her, rubbing his shoulder in the spot where she'd hit him. "Besides, I didn't even grab you. You took it upon yourself to latch onto my cape and come along for the ride. How did your reflexes get to be so quick?"

"Twelve years of mixed martial arts training, but that's beside the point. I saw something jump my friend. What you think I was gon' do in that situation?"

"Is that my baby Kevin, I mean, Mr. Super Soartastic I hear in there?" My mother's voice sounded from the kitchen just moments before she walked through the door. A wide grin split her face as soon as she saw him. "Aw! Don't you look handsome in your super suit! Come here and give your Auntie Rita a big hug!"

"Hey, Auntie Rita." He spoke using his natural voice and gave her a warm hug.

"Does your momma know you in town, baby? You want me to call her, tell her to come over?"

"Oh no, Auntie. I can't stay long. I just need to talk to Corey but I will call Momma later, I promise."

"Well, she will be so sorry that she missed you. But you two superheroes go on and have your talk." She turned and walked out of the room.

I knew the minute she left the room my mother would be on the phone to her sister. I'm sure Kevin knew it too. He was going to see his mother before he left and there would be baked goods involved. That was more than fine by me. My cousin grabbed me by the arm and looked into my eyes. "The mayor needs to talk to you. Where can we go for a private talk?"

"You've been in this family longer than I have, Kevin. You know there's no such thing as a private talk around here." No doors were ever locked in this house and anyone could barge in at any moment. He didn't respond, he just stood there staring down at me with those gray eyes, looking a bit desperate. I shrugged. "I guess my room is as good a place as any."

Starkeisha moved to follow us and he turned his masked face and fixed her with a stern look. "I said I needed a private conversation."

Starkeisha was one of those people who could speak volumes without ever saying a word. Her normally uneven gaze went straight and steady as she stared at my cousin. Her look won the argument he'd been gearing up to have before he could even draw breath to start making his case. He backed down and turned to follow me up the stairs. She brought up the rear. He pulled the blinds and then the curtains as soon as we were alone in my room. Then he pulled off the mask and rubbed his gloved hands over his face. It was the first time I noticed the dark circles under his eyes. He looked tired. Sometimes I forgot that he wasn't that much older than me. Most guys his age were still in college, getting drunk and posting embarrassing selfies on social media. "You alright, Cuz?"

He looked up at me as if he was surprised at the question. I'm guessing not many people ever stop to ask superheroes how they're feeling. "Yeah, I'm okay. I've just been," he paused as if searching for the words, "dealing with some things." He looked as if he wanted to say more, but a buzzing sound suddenly filled the silence in my room. He replaced his mask so fast I barely saw him move, then reached behind himself, underneath his cape and pulled out a cell phone, I didn't think I wanted to know from where. "Hello, Mr. Mayor. I have him here."

"Excellent, have you debriefed him?"

Starkeisha looked at me, wide-eyed. The voice on the other end of the line was the actual mayor of Onyx City! "No, sir. I haven't had the chance yet." My cousin's voice was deep and gravelly again.

"Well let me talk to him. This city needs him."

My mouth dropped open as my cousin beckoned me to sit beside him. My head barely reached his shoulder, so he had to hold the phone out at arm's length in order to fit us both in the frame. Surprise, followed by disappointment, registered on the mayor's face when he saw me. He cleared his throat and shuffled some papers while he regained his composure. "So, uh, I'm sorry, I didn't catch your name, son."

"Shacorey, sir. Shacorey Watts."

"I see, and you don't have a super alias or anything like that?"

I shrugged, feeling a bit embarrassed. "My friends call me Corey if that helps." I figured at least it sounded a bit less girly.

The mayor cleared his throat. "Right, well, Super uh Corey, this city needs your help."

"Me? What can I do?" I began imagining some sort of citywide shrubbery crisis.

"I'm sure you've been hearing about the latest drug craze on the news."

"Yeah, fungi are a hobby of mine, even though my mom won't let me grow them in the house." I snorted indignantly. "Like a couple of trays of compost in my bedroom closet could hurt anything. Honestly, you can hardly smell it." I pouted at the injustice of it.

Starkeisha gave me a firm "shut up Corey" pinch on my arm, which helped me get back to the point.

"They're calling it psychocybin or Psycho Silly. It's a type of mushroom, related to psilocybin or Magic Mushrooms, but it's way more dangerous. This was created in a lab through genetic engineering. They say it was an accident. Scientists were looking to create a more nutritious and pest resistant food source when they came up with this."

I paused and looked around. Over the years I've learned that not everyone is as fascinated by my hobbies as I am. I try to remember to monitor the interest level of my audience. No one looked ready to nod off, so I continued. "It can be eaten, snorted or smoked. It can even be absorbed through the skin. The mushroom itself is much too potent to consume in its purest form. It has to be cut and mixed with inert chemicals before it can be safely handled and distributed. I heard some people have OD'd just standing in the same room and breathing in the spores of the growing fungi. They say it produces the purest, most exquisite high imaginable."

Kevin grimaced. "That's all true. Unfortunately, I'm way more familiar with the effects of the stuff than I'd like."

The mayor interrupted before I could question my cousin. "This drug is destroying lives and killing our citizens at an alarming rate. New addicts seem to be cropping up every day. Crime is on the rise and our police force is quickly becoming overwhelmed. This menace must be stopped."

I nodded. "It makes me wonder where and how they're growing and packaging the stuff without killing their workforce and wiping out whole city blocks."

The mayor continued. "We have some intel on that. We don't know who controls the sale and distribution, but we do know where the mushrooms are being grown. There's a small island just off the coast with a large cave right in the center. We believe the people in charge have invented some sort of pill or vaccine that gives workers temporary immunity against the mushroom's effects. They work in short shifts throughout the day, but at night, the whole area around the caves is deserted. Sure, there are armed guards along the island coastlines, but no one further inland. No need to post guards since the mushrooms themselves will kill anyone who gets close.

"Not even I can get close and I've spent the last six months trying." Kevin's gravelly superhero voice had gotten quiet. "I tried special suits and helmets and gas masks and nothing filters out those spores. I can't get within more than fifty feet of the place before I'm on my knees, tripping balls." He sighed and shook his head. "The worst part is, lately all I can think about is going back there again and the last thing on my mind is fighting crime. That's why I can't go back to the cave. I might lose myself." I put a hand on his shoulder to comfort him. He was a jerk when we were younger, but he was still my family and I didn't like to see him hurting.

"Don't worry. As unlikely as it seems, this actually does sound like a job for me."

"Look, I don't mean to be rude, but what can this kid do that our strongest hero cannot." The mayor's voice dripped with skepticism.

His doubt was probably justified, but it still ticked me off. I gave him my steeliest gaze, then walked to my desk and got the bonsai tree I'd been working on earlier. I held it close to the phone's camera and put my hand over the branches. The leaves shriveled and browned as I drained the life energy from the tree, my eyes never leaving the mayor's face. "I can take care of your little mushroom problem, sir." He stared at the dead tree wide-eyed. I got up again and returned it to my desk, quickly pouring the life energy back into it. I'd worked too damn hard on that thing to just let it die.

"Forgive my skepticism, son. There are a lot of lives riding on this and I just wanted to be sure you had the right stuff." I nodded, my ego satisfied. The mayor continued. "Now, how do you plan to get close to the lair without feeling the effects of the drug?"

"Oh, I'm immune to all plant based poisons and drugs."

The mayor raised a skeptical eyebrow but Soartastic stepped in. "No, trust me, he is." We looked at each other but didn't elaborate. I'd first discovered my peculiar immunity at cousin Kevin's house. He was babysitting me and I found his stash of very special brownies while I was snooping around his bedroom. I ate three before he caught me. They had absolutely no effect on me, but I did get to keep his Playstation for a whole month for promising not to tell our moms about the incident. I'd done plenty of experiments since then and found absolutely no plant or fungus that could send me to heaven or hell.

"We'll just have to take your word for it." The mayor's face grew serious. "Super Corey, the plan is to strike tonight. The city's resources are at your disposal. We are counting on you to help us end this menace. I'll let Super Soartastic brief you on the layout of the lair." He hung up the phone and we sat in silence for a few moments.

Starkeisha's voice broke the spell. "I just gotta axe one thing. Is you crazy? Y'all both done lost yo damn minds right?" She got right up in my cousin's masked face and pointed in my direction. "He is a child! He ain't never even thrown a punch in his life and you want to send him after a drug lord with guards and guns and security cameras?"

"I'm pretty good with a knife." I had a lot of practice with a knife because I happen to be an excellent cook. I could julienne a carrot like a pro, but I wasn't sure the skill was transferrable.

She turned her glare on me. "You not chopping scallions! We're talking about fighting for your life with no training and no preparation."

Soartastic spoke quietly. "I was younger than him when I did my first mission."

Starkeisha snorted. "Yeah, and you also had super strength and super speed. He got a pocketful of daisies to protect hisself."

"He's also our only hope."

In movies, when someone tells the hero that he's the only hope, it fills him with resolve. The phrase just filled me with pants-crapping terror. Starkeisha was right. I was no hero. The only fighting I'd ever done was the video game variety. I didn't even like violence in real life and I was expected to take on an entire compound of evil henchmen in a few short hours. I started to feel genuinely ill. I sank heavily onto the side of my bed and put my head in my hands. Kevin knelt down in front of me and took my hands in his. "Look, man. I would never send you in there on a suicide mission. I've been to this place. I know it like the back of my hand. I will go with you as far as I can. I can take out the armed guards. The rest is up to you. You can do this."

I took a deep breath. "Okay, let's work out a plan."

"Yeah, and I'm going with him." Starkeisha looked determined. "He need someone by his side who knows how to throw a damn punch at least."

"Starkeisha, you just said yourself. This is dangerous and you are a child. You can't come along this time. You don't have any superpowers." My cousin was using his very best superhero voice, but he had never come up against a force with as much will as my friend Starkeisha.

"I was fast enough to catch your cape when you whizzed by earlier today and strong enough to hold on. I may not have any superpowers, but neither do those men on that island. I am just as qualified as him for this mission, probably more, since I have formal combat training. I will not let my friend go alone so get used to it. I will get as close as I can without killin' myself or becoming a junkie and you are wasting your time trying to argue with me."

"We don't have time for any plans or arguments right now, you two. I hear your mom pulling into the driveway now, Kevin."

A smile replaced the frown on his face. My mom had made the right call. Sometimes even superheroes needed to hug their mothers.

Four hours later, the three of us were on a ferry boat, crossing the bay towards the evil island of an unknown drug lord. As we sailed in silence, two things became apparent to me. The first was that Kevin's mom is an amazing cook and I had eaten way too much. As the boat pitched and rolled, I desperately hoped I wasn't about to give that mound of catfish I ate back to the sea. The second was that I was in way over my head. A squad of police officers in full riot gear sat riding in stoic silence to the left of me, and Kevin and Starkeisha stood apart to the right of me, watching the dark shape of the island loom up on the horizon. A lump rose in my throat and I couldn't stop the small whimper that escaped from between my dry lips.

Cousin Soartastic put a comforting arm around my shoulders. "Just do what we talked about. All the guards are right along the shore of the island. I've tried this run several times and I've never seen another soul anywhere inland. You won't see anyone else on the path and if you do, they will not be interested in fighting you." He paused and looked me up and down for a few moments. "Do you have everything you need?"

I patted the pockets of my tan cargo pants. I preferred cargo pants because they had lots of pockets which were handy for carrying gardening supplies. I felt the familiar lump of my pocket knife. There was a second lump in the pocket as well. Momma had insisted I take her pepper spray with me. The small canister was nearly as old as I was and it was just as likely to explode in my face as it was to blind my enemy. I had no intention of using it, but it made her feel better to give it to me, so I had it. I had my trowel and hand rake too, both excellent weapons in the right hands. Unfortunately, my hands were not the right hands. The other pockets were still filled with the seeds that I had planned to use in my own garden earlier in the day until the city called. I just hadn't bothered to empty my pockets before we left. "Yes, I think I'm ready."

He nodded. "Okay, have them lower the row boat. You two sit tight and wait for my signal."

Starkeisha had brought a polished wood stick with a handle. It looked like a police billy club. She pulled it out and swung it through a few very impressive martial arts moves, then she looked at Soartastic and nodded. "We'll be here waiting." I was suddenly very glad to have her with me.

The crew lowered the rowboat into the water and helped us climb in. We each sat next to a pair of oars and watched the shoreline. As soon as we were seated, my big cousin, the amazing Super Soartastic, waved to us both, then before our eyes could register him leaving, he leaped high into the air and spread his cape out behind him to glide through the air toward the island. The world grew silent then. The only sound we heard was water lapping against the sides of the boat. It seemed like an eternity before I saw the light on shore. We turned in our seats and started rowing.

I was winded and breathing heavy by the time we reached the shore. "Whew," I said breathlessly, "if I'm going to get into this superhero business, I need to get up off the couch once in awhile. I don't want to have a heart attack before I even get started."

I recovered quickly when I saw the dazed looking guards, tied up and sitting in the sand next to my cousin. "I did a sweep of the island perimeter. These were the only guards here. You should have a clear path to the caves now. Good luck, Super Corey." In my dragon t-shirt and khaki cargo pants, I didn't feel very super, but I nodded anyway. He pointed towards a light on a wooden post. "That's the beginning of the path to the caves. Follow that and stay in the light and you should be fine." He turned to my friend. "Starkeisha, you're only going to make it about halfway up that path. There are cones and flashing lights on the side of the path to mark the halfway point. You will know when it's time to turn back."

She nodded, then turned to me. "Imma have your back for as long as I can, Corey. It might not be any people out there, but who knows what kind of wild animals is in these trees." My stomach dropped. I hadn't even thought about wild animals. I swallowed hard and grabbed her free hand. She looked tough and ready for action and that made me feel a lot better.

The path was narrow but well lit. There may not have been any people on the island, but the place was far from silent. The air was filled with the screeches of night creatures, fighting for territory or mates or whatever animals chatter about when the sun goes down. When we started down the path, I had my hand in my pocket clutching my knife and Starkeisha held her truncheon at the ready, but with each step along the empty path, we relaxed a bit more. We really were alone. This really was going to be as easy as advertised. I had just turned to say as much to Starkeisha when the other shoe dropped. "Hey! What the hell are you kids doing here!"

A massive man appeared and blocked our way to the cave. He was as big as Soartastic and his voice rumbled out of his chest like pure menace when he spoke. "I asked you two a question. What the hell are you doing here?"

Terror paralyzed my tongue and I couldn't have spoken to save my life. Luckily, Starkeisha had no such trouble. She let out a high-pitched giggle. "We heard this is the place to get Psycho Silly. Please, Mister. We just need a little bit!"

He rolled his eyes. "Great, more fuckin' junkies. I spend half my nights dragging dead morons just like you back down this path because they didn't get the memo about pure uncut Psycho." He pulled out a very large gun. "It'll just be easier if I just walk you back to the beach and shoot you there. It'll save some wear and tear on my back."

"P-Please, sir. I swear to God and the GRASS you're standing on that we will leave now and we won't say nothing. We won't let any GRASS GROW under us!"

She was subtle as a hammer, but I knew what she wanted me to do. It was a little trick we used to trip bullies at school when they teased her about her eyes or me about, well, everything. Her words were exactly what I needed to unfreeze my terror locked mind. I reached out to the life energy in the trees surrounding us on the path and pushed that life into the grass at his feet. I guided the grass's growth so the lengthening blades wound themselves around his ankles and up his shins. He was so shocked, he nearly dropped his gun. We stepped back and he tried to take a step forward but the plants held his legs fast and he tripped and fell to the ground. I seized the opportunity and forced growth into the plants around his chest and his arms. He roared with fury and confusion, but he was unable to move. Starkeisha seized the opportunity and ran towards him, grabbing the gun and smashing her huge heavy stick into the base of his skull, knocking him out cold.

"Yes! Did you see that shit we just did there, Corey? We are a badass team!" She kicked the big man's side for good measure. "That's for pulling a gun on me, asshole!"

"Starkeisha, you have to go back to the beach and get Kevin." I was too keyed up to remember secret identities. "That guy isn't going to be unconscious long and this grass isn't going to hold forever.

She shook her head. "No way! What if there's more of them on the path?"

I looked at her. "I know how to handle them now, thanks to you," I smiled at her. "Go on, I'll be fine." For the first time since I agreed to do this mission, I actually believed what I was saying.

About twenty feet further up the path, I saw flashing warning lights and smelled a strange earthy and herbal aroma. I knew it was the spores from the cave because I could see its dark shape looming in the distance. The scent was very pleasant and I could definitely understand the appeal. I wasn't feeling high, my immunity held for designer drugs too it seemed. I was glad I'd sent Starkeisha back when I did because the smell became stronger with every step and she could easily have come too far.

After a further 50 feet, the light posts stopped. Luckily the moon was full and the path was still clear and easy to follow. I continued, praying there wouldn't be any wolves or bears or other beasts with a taste for my tender, well-marbled flesh. Luckily, nothing but bugs appeared.

It wasn't much further until I reached the mouth of the cave, but I was nearly on top of the opening before I spotted it because it was so dark. I reached into the very bottom pocket of my cargo pants and pulled out the flashlight I'd stashed in there for just such an occasion. It was a small light with a very bright beam but it was barely enough to cut the gloom in the pure darkness. A few bats flew over my head as they exited the cave and I did my best not to shame myself with high pitched toddler screams as I moved in deeper. The floor of the cave sloped down slightly as I went, but without any visual reference, it was hard to tell how deep or far it went. The tunnel made several twists and turn as it descended, but luckily the path was straightforward and easy to follow.

After about 20 minutes of slow walking, a faint blue glow appeared in front of me. I could hear a faint scraping sound in the relative silence. I turned off and pocketed my flashlight, then continued down the path, my body pressed up against the cave wall. Hugging the wall didn't make me invisible. Anyone who walked by would clearly see me in my bright red shirt, but they always stayed close to the wall in movies so it seemed like as good a plan as any for me. The blue light did not grow brighter as I got closer, but the size of the lighted area became clearer. The tunnel led to a chamber that was the size of a football field. I couldn't even see the top of the cavern, it rose so high into utter blackness. I quickly slipped into the entrance and stepped into a darkened crevice a few feet from the door. The cavern was filled with rows of ten-foot shelving units, each filled, from top to bottom, with trays of innocuous looking, pale green mushrooms.

The cavern was not unoccupied like Kevin had predicted. I could clearly see someone down at the far end of the aisle directly in front of me and I doubted he was here alone. He wore what looked like a bright yellow biohazard suit and he was picking mushrooms with his stiff, heavily gloved hands and placing them into a white canvas bag slung over his shoulder. He was intent on his work and still quite far from me in my dark corner so he hadn't seen me. I stood watching the man work, picking and choosing the mushrooms that were ready for harvest. For several minutes, he seemed unaffected by the chemicals in the air but then he swooned and had to grab the lip of the nearest shelf for support. He pushed a big red panic button on the chest of his suit and a loud siren began wailing, echoing off the stone walls.

"We need a shot on aisle 37!" The shouts rang out from somewhere to my left and several workers clad in blue hazard suits ran down the aisle towards the worker, who was now on his knees. One of the blue suits drew a vial and a clean syringe from the medical bag he carried. He drew some of the liquid from the vial into the syringe, then lifted up the flap of fabric draped over the downed man's shoulders and plunged the needle right into his jugular. Seconds later, they helped the worker to his feet and he retrieved his bag and went back to work. "We need to stay on top of this, people. The serum is wearing off faster lately. Let's get the shot to 23 and 42 now before they hit crisis point." Thankfully they moved off to the other side of the cavern.

I knew I couldn't stand in the shadows all night. I needed to act. It was time for me to save the day. I took in the size of the room and tried not the think of the enormity of the task ahead of me. I had never tried to channel this much energy, and though theoretically, it wouldn't be any different than removing the life energy from a patch of weeds, it was still a pretty daunting task. My powers depend on a transfer of energy. Taking the energy out of the mushrooms meant I'd have to put it into some other form of plant life and there wasn't much else growing in the cave. I reached out and found the thriving life energy of the mushrooms and I took it and channeled it into the moss and lichens on the cave walls until they looked like forests of ferns, but there was still so much more energy to channel and I was quickly running out of places to send it.

"What the hell?" The worker in the aisle in front of me looked up after the mushroom in his hand died and crumbled to inert dust. He turned in my direction and saw me for the first time. "Who the hell are you?"

I looked down at myself and saw that my bare skin was glowing with a faint light that was just enough to make me stand out in the gloom. He pushed the panic button on his chest once again and lumbered toward me. There was no plant growth at his feet, so I couldn't subdue him as I had the man on the path, and for a moment, I panicked. Then I remembered the seeds in the pockets of my cargo pants. I undid the snap on pocket number two and pulled out a handful of wisteria seed pods just as more men in hazard suits came running up the aisles and headed toward me. I scattered the seeds at the feet of the first five that approached me. I pulled hard on the life force of the mushrooms in the room, pouring the energy into the sprouting vines. The vines grew fast and thick and wound themselves around the legs and torsos of the work crew. I threw seed pods to the left and right of me to trap the workers emerging from other aisles. Soon I had the whole crew trapped and struggling and still there were more mushrooms to kill.

I pushed the energy up the tunnel leading out of the cave, sending it through all the moss along the way and out the entrance of the cave to a stand of tree seedlings which instantly added years of growth. The dying mushrooms began to release spores and I absorbed the nearly microscopic specks of life into me and felt the deadly cloud die along with the bodies of the fungi. So much life energy flowed through me, I could no longer tell where it landed. It was all I could do to make sure it was moving out of the mushrooms. I focused all my effort on making sure that every bit of fungal life in the cavern died.

The sun was just starting to lighten the horizon when I emerged from the cave. I'd been down there for hours, but I didn't feel tired. I felt strangely light and energized as I made my way back down the path. The walk back to the beach was slower going than the walk up to the cave had been. Branches and weeds had grown over the path and I had to push my way through the brush.

Starkeisha nearly bowled me over with the force of her embrace the minute I stepped onto the beach. "I was about two seconds from going back in there and dragging you out myself, then I seen how everything was growin' and I knew you had to be causin' it. I knew you was alright." She threw her arms around me again. "Don't you ever worry me like that again! You hear me?"

I hugged her back and spoke to my cousin over her shoulder. "It's time to radio the officers and tell them it's safe to come ashore. The wind is picking up so any stray spores that might be floating around in the air out here will probably be blown away soon and it will be safe to go up to the caves. All the Psychocybin is dead but there are workers tied up down there. They will need to be taken in for questioning. They were being injected with some sort of serum which gave them immunity. There should still be samples in the cave." I turned to Starkeisha. "I couldn't have done this without your cool head and fast thinking. We make a great team. Are you ready to go home now?"

Soartastic looked puzzled. "Go home? Cousin, you have just pulled off the largest drug bust in this state's history, possibly the biggest bust in the country. Every news outlet in the world is going to want to talk to you. You need to get ready to accept the praise of your adoring public. Welcome to the life of a real superhero."

"The only thing I need to get ready for is my calculus test on Monday. Right now, the only thing I want a welcome from is my own bed. I'll deal with everything else later. Right now, I'm going home."

Epilogue

Momma held up the bright green spandex body suit and looked at me hopefully. "What about this one?"

I sighed. "Momma, for the last time, no. I am not wearing spandex!"

"Oh, but Baby, all the other superheroes wear these and this green would bring out the color of your eyes so perfectly!"

In the week since I'd destroyed the city's supply of Psychocybin, life had mostly gone back to normal. I was still short, fat, unpopular and behind on my homework; but a few things had changed. The color of my eyes for one thing. They'd gone from swamp water brown to bright leaf green. No one could explain why. Starkeisha told me the color looked striking against my dark brown skin. That made me smile. I figure the color change must be some sort of superhero evolution thing because my powers had changed too. I still only had the one talent, but now it was a lot easier to use. I also had the feeling that my abilities might be growing, though I couldn't say why or how. I just decided not to worry about it until the next freaky thing happened.

"Look at me, Momma. We both know I'm not built for spandex. I would look ridiculous. Besides, I refuse to call myself Green Thumb. It's way too obvious for my taste."

"But your Auntie Floretta did this pretty emblem all in puffy paints just for you!" She pointed to the extended "thumb" emblem on the chest of the ridiculous bodysuit.

"Momma, it looks like a giant green toe. I am not wearing that thing on my chest."

Momma leaned in and whispered, "You know her eyes ain't what they used to be, but we don't want to hurt her feelings. She worked so hard!"

"We don't have to hurt her feelings. We'll just tell her I decided to go a different direction. I want to be called The Cultivator." I had looked it up on *Thesaurus.com* and thought it sounded pretty bad ass.

Momma raised one eyebrow. "Alright then, if you want to go around confusing people, go right ahead." I looked down at my new black cargo pants and the sturdy black combat boots that I'd bought at the army surplus, I was wearing a bright green t-shirt with a black ammo harness that I'd adapted to carry some of the supplies that I needed to dispense my special brand of justice. I looked cool, or at least as cool as a guy like me could look.

I pushed the picture of a large leafy plant inside a circle across the table to Momma. "Do you think your embroidery machine can stitch this onto my green t-shirts?" I wasn't going to wear a spandex body suit, but even I was savvy enough to know that branding was important. I had designed the emblem myself and used my allowance money to copyright it.

She took the picture, then smiled at me. "I guess that would look nicer than the toe and you do look handsome in your new slacks." She looked down at my design again. "I could do it in a real pretty dark green so it stands out."

"That sounds perfect, Momma!"

She was happy again as she took the stack of identical green shirts into her sewing room.

The screen door from the back porch slammed and Starkeisha stood before me. "Come on, Corey. It's time for your lesson." She slid out of a floor-length trench coat to reveal a red spandex bodysuit with a bright gold star emblazoned on the front. It looked great on her. She had appointed herself my sidekick and she'd taken the name, Superstar. I thought it fit her perfectly.

She had also taken it upon herself to teach me how to fight and she'd spent the last week kicking my ass all over our basement floor. "Now? Can't I get a break just for today?"

"You said it yourself, there's a dangerous drug lord still out there and supplies of Psycho Silly are already starting to seep back into Onyx city. We can't rest. We gotta keep fighting until this mess is gone for good! In order to do that, you gotta learn how to fight. Even though me and Super Soartastic got our shots to protect us against the drug side effects, we may not always be there to help you. You can't always depend on us to fight your battles. You need to learn how to fight for yourself. So on your feet, Cultivator and prepare for today's ass whoopin."

She reached out and grabbed my hands and pulled me to my feet, then led me down the stairs. I had no choice but to follow. A superhero's job is never done.

TALLY MARKS
Chris Wiltz

"Yo, what is that?"

"It's a cop uniform, right?"

"Man, cops don't come through here anymore. They stay downtown, protecting white folks. I ain't never seen a cop uniform like that. It look like some shit off Xbox."

I picked up the helmet and showed it to Jay. "Nah man, this is like military, I seen stuff like this on CNN."

"When you ever watch CNN?"

"All the time. I ain't a dumbass like you. I know what's up in the world."

"Please, you can't even *spell* C-N-N, talking about you know what's up with the world."

"Fuck you." Jay always gotta put you down. Just 'cause he can't even read, he act like everyone supposed to be stupid.

I shoulda cracked back on him, but he was pulling the rest of the pieces out from under all the trash.

A bunch of roaches popped up from under some bricks when he moved them. Jay didn't even flinch. "You scared of some roaches dog?"

"I hope you get AIDS digging around in all that shit."

***

Now we had all the pieces.

"See, it's body armor or something. Look at the bullet holes," Jay said. There was parts for your whole body and it all had holes in it. "And it's all scratched up."

I looked closer. "Those ain't scratches, it's tally marks. Dirty ass cops keeping track of how many niggas heads they cracked open."

"Well, then this dude cracked open every head in the damn area code."

I flipped over the helmet. It was shiny like a mirror on the outside but the inside was all dark like if you put it on you'd be blind. There was a bunch of circuits inside.

"What's it doing here? This stuff look like it cost more than the whole hood."

Jay started laughing after he picked up the piece that went around your nuts.

"Okay, okay I got it. Officer Tally Marks needs to take a piss, but see you gotta take all this shit off first."

"So he strips butt naked four blocks off of Woodward?

Jay didn't pay me no attention and kept going. "So, homeboy figures 'Damn I gotta hide this stuff so nobody sees it.' Then he goes off to cop a squat and gets dapped over his head by some goons. He probably lying face down in a empty field right now with shit halfway down his legs."

"Or he ain't back yet, and when he see you playing with his nut protector he gonna put a 12-gauge in your chest."

Jay dropped the nut protector and started looking all which ways.

"Damn. You probably right." He start picking up all the armor pieces. "C'mon man, help me get this shit up."

I picked up the belt and a gun fell out.

"Oh shit, is that loaded?" Jay was looking a little too excited.

I checked. "Nope."

I opened one of the little holders on the belt – three full clips for the gun.

"It ain't loaded. But it could be."

***

We went to three pawn shops, wouldn't nobody buy the gear off us. Crooked ass Arab Joey offered us a grip for it, but Jay and me ain't that stupid. We had the whole thing in a shopping cart, covered up, pushing it down the street – just two dudes hustling for empty cans. At least if somebody rolled up on us we had a gun.

I came out of the liquor store with two *Faygos* and Jay was trying to get one of the pieces on his arm. I had to run up and snatch it from this dude before anyone saw.

"You trying to get us jacked?"

"Yo, this is stupid. Ain't nobody gonna buy this. The cops probably got like tracking numbers and shit on it."

"So you wanna just dump it for the next fool to find?"

"Nah I got a better idea. Peep that."

As soon as Jay pointed to the house across the street I knew what he wanted to do. Crack houses look like other abandoned houses unless you know what gang graffiti looks like. Crescent moon means Vice Lords. You can get paid real quick knocking over a crack house. If you got the balls.

"You wanna roll up on that?"

"Hell yeah."Jay had that look on his face. Jay ain't never gave a fuck in general, but sometimes he *really* ain't give a fuck.

"Here..." He shoved a piece in my hand. "I can't fit in this shit, you gotta do it.

"Why I gotta put this on?"

"Cause you a skinny ass nigga."

"Man, them Vice Lords gonna shoot me in the head."

"Hell nah. Look at this shit. You gonna be like Robocop, just tell them you police and snatch they shit."

I picked up another arm piece and looked at it. Looked like it was blood stains on it. "Man I dunno Jay."

"You trying to get paid today or what, son?"

***

We was probably at it for a good hour trying to get the suit on. Jay stupid ass put the chest part on me backwards and we had to start over.

"Man, the crack-house is gonna be closed by the time we get all this on."

"Shut up, nigga."

The last leg piece clicked in place. "How's it feel?"

I moved around. "Feels light as hell; like I ain't got nothing on."

Jay pushed the helmet on me. It was pitch black inside it. "Just go!"

I could hear Jay's voice loud and clear though.

"I can't see shit."

But then all these crazy ass lights hit me. Like sitting real close to the TV. Then it was like the helmet wasn't there no more. I could see like I didn't have anything on my head.

"What'd you do, Jay?"

"Nothing. Can you see now?"

"Yeah."

"Good! Let's go get paid." Jay had loaded the gun already and put it in my hand. As soon as he did, a little green triangle target popped up in the air.

"Yo. Can you see that?"

"*I* ain't got the helmet on."

The triangle was following my eyes. It was zooming in when I looked at something hard enough.

"Yo this is some Modern Warfare shit right here, for real. Shit is tight."

Jay was all like "Whatever." I could tell he was hating 'cause I fit in the suit and he didn't. "March yo ass across the street and collect some bills, then."

"What do I say?"

"Tell them niggas you police and get they money. They ain't gone fuck wit' no cop."

I don't know why I knocked when I got to the door. I knew it was stupid while I was doing it. I turned around and shrugged at Jay. He was hiding behind a bombed out car across the street, looking at me like I was retarded.

He started motioning. I ain't understand. He swung his leg in the air and ducked back in his hiding place.

Right. I should kick the door in.

The cheap ass door collapsed around my foot when I kicked it.

There was human shit in the hallway. A bunch of half naked broads was laying out on the steps going upstairs. Some dude was at the end of the hall mumbling crazy shit to himself. There was babies crying from somewhere.

I took a step and stepped on a crack pipe. I looked down and a bunch of crazy shit popped up in the air – arrows and windows and numbers. Then it all went away and the words "CRIMINAL ACTIVITY DETECTED" flashed for a second. The triangle turned red.

Before I knew it, I was walking all the way into the back, right past the crazy dude and into the kitchen.

Four Vice Lords, dressed in all black, were playing spades at the table. There was a fat broad with her ass out, wearing nothing but an apron.

I shot all three of them niggas in like three seconds, right in the forehead. The broad got scared and spilled cocaine all over the floor. The helmet focused on the coke, then on her, then I shot her three times – two in the chest, one in the head after she already hit the floor.

I was already heading back out. Two more VL's came down the stairs, trying to climb over the passed-out crackheads. I shot another one at the top of the stairs in both knees. He fell down on the other two. They landed right at my feet and I put the heat in the back of all they heads.

It took me three steps to get upstairs. I found one VL smoking in the bathroom and shot him right in the heart and head. I caught another in the bedroom doggystyling some crack hoe. The hoe didn't notice his brains hit the wall in front of her. He kept at it for like a second after I shot him in the head, the hoe didn't realize what had happened until his body fell on her.

There was another bedroom, with like three kids and some crying babies in it. They were all huddled around a box of stale pizza that had some roaches crawling over it. The helmet flashed all around the room, then I just left.

The stash was in the second bedroom. The word CONTRABAND flashed in my face. Next thing I know, I was pouring the product into the bathtub and washing it down the drain.

I marched my ass back outside. Jay was pacing in the street.

"Holy shit, nigga, what the hell did…"

The helmet zoomed in on Jay, he was looking behind me.

I spun around. There was another Vice Lord coming out from around the back of the house – a fat, slow nigga with a shotty.

He raised the gun up. The triangle zoomed in on it and I fired. There was an explosion and next thing I know, fat nigga is on the ground screaming. His hands are missing a lot of pieces.

Before I could take it all in, the triangle was on fatty's forehead and a bullet sprayed his brain all over the overgrown lawn.

Jay gets up in my face. "The hell are you doing?"

I can't explain what just happened. I ain't do any of it. I mean I did, but at the same time, I didn't.

"The suit did it by itself," I said.

The triangle moved up to Jay's face…but it flashed and turned green again and settled.

I saw the words "ALL THREATS NEUTRALIZED" for a second, then they disappeared.

***

"What you mean, the suit did it? What'd you do? Did you get shot?"

The only blood I saw on me was the stains that had been there. "I was the only one shooting."

"You blasted all them fools?"

"The suit did."

Jay got all antsy, like he was gonna run up in the house.

"I looked. There ain't no money."

"SHIT!" Jay was having a fit. "We gotta bounce!"

Jay was way ahead already. I took off running after him.

My breath was funking up the inside of the helmet. I knew I should run. It don't matter if they think you a cop. You dead one Vice Lord, let alone like a dozen of them fools, and you better run.

Me and Jay kept running. There was another little window for a second in the corner of my eye – I ain't know what the words meant – ENDORPHINE STIMULATION.

I started feeling better. I wasn't breathing so heavy. I ain't never shot nobody before in real life. I felt like I'd just finished playing a video game.

I felt like I just had fun.

***

Damn, ain't hardly nowhere to put the tally marks no more.

Jay is over there on his Xbox trying to act like I ain't getting on his nerves with the noise. But the armor is tough as hell. You gotta really scrape the knife into this shit to get the marks on there.

"FUCK!" Jay yells. He probably just got killed by some 12-year-old in Korea or somewhere. Then he throws the controller at me. I catch it; no problem. The suit does everything.

"Damn nigga! You stink!"

362

I ain't tell Jay the suit is reading a "THREAT ASSESSMENT" on him and he outta calm his ass down.

"You need a bath. You can't take that shit off?"

I ain't seen no point in taking it off. I take the helmet off sometimes but I don't remember last time I did that. I ain't been sleeping much, so probably since last time I slept.

Jay talks a lot of shit, but he know I know he ain't left the house in like weeks. He scared the Vice Lords, or the Black Disciples, or just some random hood niggas is gonna run up on him. He don't like to talk about how that brand new Xbox and giant-ass TV came from dough that we took off them fools. It was all good when he was trickin' off strippers with the money we found in the stash spots, but now the streets is talkin' and he trying to be a hermit.

I don't remember why I started doing the tally marks. I can't tell which ones is mine anymore. I'm gonna have to start doing them on the inside of the suit soon.

"You gonna take it off or not?"

The triangle ain't turned red, but Jay is dancing on that line.

I'm at Jay like, "What you scared of? You don't want niggas finding us, maybe you shouldn't have that Camaro outside."

"Nigga, don't nobody know that's mine."

"How many of these broke ass niggas around here rollin' with the matte paint and turbo engine? You keep trying to please all them hoes and..."

"Tisha ain't no hoe, homie!"

Tisha is the newest hoe Jay been seeing. She got a big booty, but every dude around here know she ain't got all them fine ass clothes and that dope apartment downtown cause she work hard.

"Whatever, dog. Just don't be expecting me to be helping with child support when that broad trick you into having her seed."

"Man, fuck you!"

"I'm just sayin'...you ain't seen her in a minute right? She probably stealing some other dude's sperm right now and gonna show up in nine months talking about it's yours."

Jay swings on me, but I catch his hand. I want to let go, but the suit is squeezing and twisting. Jay's on his knees and I can hear his knuckles crunching.

I don't tell Jay about how much the suit can do. He knows something but not everything. Half the time, I don't even tell him where the money comes from. He too scared to come along anymore, so I don't say nothing.

Like I ain't tell him the reason he ain't seen Tisha in like two weeks is cause I went over to her spot downtown. She was in there with some other stripper broads and these lame looking niggas. After I got done shooting them I almost laughed. Turns out Tisha's place was a stash spot. I found a gang of cash inside the bathroom wall. Tisha was in shock or something, I think. I ain't wanna hurt her, but when she picked up one of them dudes' guns and came at me, the suit did the rest.

Shooting fools is like a virgin getting some ass for the first time. You just wanna keep doing it.

I manage to force my hand open and Jay is down on his knees. His hand look like crumpled paper. I ain't never seen a grown ass dude like Jay crying before.

I should tell him about Tisha, but I ain't feel like it. I ain't feel like a lot of stuff.

Like I ain't feel like telling him I told the VLs where they could find me. Right off Grand River, the yellow apartment building – the only one ain't been gutted for scrap yet – eighth floor, end of the hallway. They will probably be over here any minute. I ain't sure why I told them. It seemed like it would be fun.

The helmet picks up the sound of car engines. It says the sounds are half a mile away. It's a lot of car engines.

***

Jay is bleeding all over my shit. That's what I get for saving his heavy ass.

The first of them fools kicked the door right in. Jay even got a couple shots off with his pistol. I had the shotty we kept under the kitchen sink. Some more was climbing up the fire escape. One got through and Jay took a bullet in the back.

I shottied that nigga right in his face. Two more tried to come up but I grabbed them and threw they ass all eight floors back to the street.

The suit is telling me I'm low on ammo. It's flashing stuff about "TACTICAL WITHDRAWAL"

I take Jay's gun and clean out the hallway. Jay won't stop screaming and get his ass up, so I have to throw him over my shoulder. I catch two more dudes coming out the elevator and run for the stairs.

Jay is whining like a bitch, all, "I can't feel my legs, dog! I can't feel my shit!"

Instead of going all the way down, I get out the stairs on the second floor.

I'm running down the hallway fast as I can. A dude rounds a corner and I put two in him. I don't know if he was VL, but he was in all black, so fuck 'em.

I kick in the door to one of the other apartments. I'm glad it's empty.

I haul Jay across the living room to the fire escape window. The whole time he's all, "Damn! I can't feel my shit!" and "It hurts, nigga!"

I have to lug his fat ass out the window and jump off the fire escape. The suit helps me land.

Ain't nobody in the alley so I start running. I hear somebody yelling from upstairs. It's a dude sticking his head out of me and Jay's window. I plug him one in the head and he falls. I don't turn around, but I hear his body hit the ground – sounded like a water balloon.

I get out of the alley. There's cars parked all outside around the building – all black, engines running.

There's some dude inside a Challenger and we scare each other. Sometimes I forget I have the suit on. He goes for his piece, but I already got my hands through the window and around his throat. I drag him out and toss him head first into the Escalade next to us. He laying there like a broken toy now.

I set Jay down to get the door open. I don't remember when his bitching and moaning stopped.

"Jay!" I shake him. "Jay! Wake yo ass up!"

Jay ain't moving. The suit is telling me he ain't alive no more.

"Bitch nigga!" Voices come up behind me. I grab Jay, spin, and hold him up. He catches every last bullet. I ain't sure I can blame the suit for what I just did. But I got enough time now. There's three of them – three bullets in the head.

I hop in the Challenger and unload the rest of the clip into the Escalade's gas tank while I pull off.

The suit warns me I'm out of bullets. This Challenger got a loud ass engine, but I still hear the Escalade blow up. I ain't know where I'm going. Maybe the suit knows a safe place. Sometimes it knows better than me. Just like it knew how much fun this would be.

I ain't thinking about Jay. I'm trying to keep track of how many tally marks I gotta add later.

***

I turn off Jefferson and hit the bridge to Belle Isle. But the suit makes me hit the brakes.

There's a black helicopter in the air. Three dudes come down on ropes. They got suits just like mine.

One of them is holding a big ass *Call of Duty*-looking rifle at me.

"Exit the vehicle, now!"

I'm out the car without even realizing it. I'm standing there with my hands up. I want to shoot these dudes, but the suit won't move.

The triangle goes green and disappears.

The one with the big ass gun says something to the others I can't hear and they start walking up on me.

All I'm thinking about is the fun can't be over. It was so much fun. I'm thinking about all the good times me and Jay had the past few weeks. How them bitch ass VLs couldn't fuck with me. These dudes came to take the suit back. They want me to be just another skinny nigga again. These dudes ain't understand how the streets work. Once cats get word I ain't got the suit no more, they gonna come at me – and they gonna blast my ass.

NO!

The triangle appears again. One of the soldiers reaches at me, but I put my boot right in his chest.

"It's malfunctioning!" The leader raises his gun, but I dive and tackle that fool.

I'm up on my feet running with the big ass gun in my hand. Rocks are kicking up all over the bridge. The helicopter is shooting at my ass. The suit lets me clap some shots back at the helicopter but it don't seem to do nothing. The suit is recommending – EVASION.

I get to the edge of the bridge. The Detroit River is fast as hell. You always hear about niggas jumping in, trying to get away from cops, thinking they can swim to Canada or some shit. Them niggas all end up drowned.

But the suit got my back; I know it.

They still coming at me. But they ain't gonna get what I got. They can't have it. This feels too damn good. It's too much damn fun.

Look out below...

***

Journal of Biomechanics and Advanced Robotics

Research Report

Policing Themselves: Applications of Advanced Robotic Exosuit Technology in Urban Pacification

Xavier W. Yates: a, Gregory Fintch: a, Aisha Wentworth: b, Thanh Nguyen: a

a. Wayne State University, United States

b. University of Michigan, United States

Keywords:

Robotics

Exosuit

Artificial Intelligence

Urban Law Enforcement

Artificial Emotion Manipulation

ABSTRACT

Research has shown usage of robotic exosuits (REs) with AI-enhanced computer systems has multiple benefits for soldiers on the battlefield (Odom, et al, 2025) as well as cost savings for military institutions (Matthews, Williams, & Fisher, 2025).

With record rates of murder, as well as gang and drug-related crimes, as reported by the Department of Justice in designated Declined Urban Areas (DUAs) – most notably Detroit, Chicago, Cleveland, St. Louis, and Atlanta – REs have been proposed as a measure to increase law enforcement capacity and efficacy.

With zero funding allocated toward increasing law enforcement staff in these DUAs, we proposed a study to determine if a properly modified RE with upgraded AI capabilities could be used by a typical urban denizen in the absence of trained law enforcement personnel. Newly-developed RE units designated the D-810V5.0 (the "Smart Soldier") were strategically deployed to DUAs. Once found, they have been readily adopted by the local populace. The Smart Soldier is capable of recognizing violent and drug-related crime in progress and guiding the wearer to respond accordingly while delivering electrical stimulation to increase the wearer's endorphine levels as well as serotonin production – thus reducing the chance of psychological trauma.

Results have show an up to 25% decrease in violent crime in an area up to 23.5 square miles around each RE unit's deployment. These results suggest that automated REs worn by civilians of reasonable health and fitness are as effective as a police or militarized presence in high-crime urban areas.

Of the 58 D-810V5.0 units deployed, one was lost in the field and could not be retrieved.

ABOUT THE EDITOR

Balogun Ojetade is the author of the bestselling non-fiction books *Afrikan Martial Arts: Discovering the Warrior Within*, *The Afrikan Warriors Bible*, *Surviving the Urban Apocalypse*, *The Urban Self Defense Manual* and *The Young Afrikan Warriors' Guide to Defeating Bullies & Trolls*.

He is one of the leading authorities on Afroretroism – film, fashion or fiction that combines African and / or African American culture with a blend of "retro" styles and futuristic technology, in order to explore the themes of tension between past and future and between the alienating and empowering effects of technology. He writes about Afroretroism – Sword & Soul, Rococoa, Steamfunk and Dieselfunk at http://chroniclesofharriet.com/.

He is author of eleven novels: *MOSES: The Chronicles of Harriet Tubman (Books 1 & 2)*; *The Chronicles of Harriet Tubman: Freedonia*; *Redeemer*; *Once Upon A Time In Afrika*; *Fist of Afrika*; *A Single Link*; *Wrath of the Siafu*; *The Scythe*; *The Keys*; *Redeemer: The Cross Chronicles* and *Beneath the Shining Jewel*; Contributing co-editor of three anthologies: *Ki: Khanga: The Anthology*, *Steamfunk* and *Dieselfunk* and contributing editor of the *Rococoa* anthology and *Black Power: The Superhero Anthology*.

He is also the creator and author of the Afrofuturistic manga series, *Jagunjagun Lewa (Pretty Warrior)* and co-author of the *Ngolo* graphic novel.

Finally, he is co-author of the award winning screenplay, *Ngolo* and co-creator of *Ki Khanga: The Sword and Soul Role-Playing Game*, both with author Milton Davis.

Reach him on Facebook at www.facebook.com/Afrikan.Martial.Arts and on Twitter at https://twitter.com/Baba_Balogun.

Made in the USA
Las Vegas, NV
01 December 2020

11854355R00219